BELLES *of* BELFAST

Lucy McMullan

MMH PRESS

A catalogue record for this work is available from the National Library of Australia

National Library of Australia Catalogue-in-Publication data:
The Belles of Belfast/Lucy McMullan

Dedicated to every 'Belle' in Belfast and beyond.
Live your life without shame and full of self-love.

Craic, no craic.

Definition: Irish word for fun and/or enjoyment (but in this case... the opposite)

Men are fucking dickheads. At least during this period of my life.

"I swear all we do is hang out in pubs." Grace buried her head in her hands, avoiding sight of Olivia, who was on her third tequila shot.

"It's not as if we're alcoholics, we're just Irish!" Liv cringed as the tequila hit the back of her throat. She quickly placed a lime wedge between her teeth and sucked, willing the burning to disappear.

"I'm *Northern Irish*... but aye. Same - same." I joked.

Both girls rolled their eyes at me, avoiding a pointless conversation about politics or religion. None of us cared about which side of the wall we were from. This isn't that kind of 'Belfast' story.

Grace, with an Irish catholic mother and an Algerian father.

Olivia, born to an Irish mother and an unknown, supposedly North-ern -Irish father.

Me, raised by an English mother and Northern Irish father.

Whilst Olivia identified herself as a catholic, she claimed attending mass was out of the question due to her multitude of sins. Grace, on the other hand, was dragged to the local chapel by her mother every time she went home to Cork. As for me, beyond attending a funeral and a wedding, I'd never stepped into a church as my mum and dad were too busy working in Belfast City Hospital. My Sundays were reserved for trashy magazines, movies, and music, leading me to study Journalism and meet my two best friends.

"Sure, we have the best craic, don't we?" Liv winked, focusing partic-ularly on Grace, whose brown eyes rolled to the back of her head.

"Aye..."

"Plus, technically, we not in a bar, we're on the street..." She contin-ued. "Does tha' make you feel any better?"

The tunes of Van Morrison whistled in the background. I tapped my foot along to the music. Duke of York at 10.42pm on a Thursday night – now *that* was a vibe. It happened to be one of the finest spots in Belfast for a pint of Guinness, provided that's your libation of choice. Quality came at a cost, though. The popularity of the street and bars that littered the Cathedral Quarter only meant that the prices of pints kept going up.

I nestled a gin and sprite between my hands and sipped on it carefully, admiring the fairy lights glittering above and the antique signs about Belfast that adorned the brick walls. No-matter how many times I'd been to Duke of York, I always found something new and interesting to look at. On this night, however, it was hard to see much of anything amidst the vibrant street crowd. Somehow, we'd managed to snag a red wooden bench at the side of the street, sitting knee to knee, immersed in peo-ple-watching, conversation, and the clinking of glasses.

"How can you mix tequila and wine?" I giggled as 'Liv took a hearty sip.

She wiggled her eyebrows in response, "I'm trying to consume more fruit and – well – tequila comes with lime and wine is my favourite way to eat grapes."

Her cheeks flushed as she indulged on another sip of her white wine.

"Why don't we have a picture like that?" Grace interrupted and pointed towards a group of girls having their picture taken below the famous neon sign that illuminated the entire street.

On the glowing red sign, was a saying, 'There's only seven types of rain in Belfast... Monday, Tuesday, Wednesday..." which was unfortunately true. It rained almost every day of the week. The people however, provided sunshine.

"Because we're not basic." Olivia crossed her arms, shocked that Grace would even suggest such a thing.

"Says the woman who posts an Instagram story everywhere she fucking goes." I laughed, "Oh Anna, can you get a pic of me with my avocado toast? Oh Anna, can you snap a pic of me with my pint of Guinness?" I mimicked, my tone high and teasing.

Grace lightly shook her head, a smile stretched across her face. Olivia, meanwhile, tipped her head back laughing, unable to contain her smile.

"First of all, you're a bitch! Second of all, I don't like Guinness!" She spat, waving her hand in dismissal.

"Ahhhh...that's right. You just buy it for the photo! I guarantee there's about 5 posts on your Instagram holding a pint." I teased and placed my drink onto the cobblestones below and pulled out my phone, ready to source and present my evidence.

As I looked up from beneath my hair, I could see the anxiety etched above her eyebrows. She knew I was right. Grace also knew I was right...

"Oh, shut the fuck up you smart-ass!" She seized my phone and tossed it into her bag. "Men love it... and I love men. Sometimes we have to make sacrifices to get what we want..."

Grace held up her hand, halting the conversation, "Hold on a minute… are you confessing that you pretend to drink Guinness to attract men?"

A sly grin adorned her face, knowing the answer. "Oh honey, men are attracted to me, Guinness or not!" She exclaimed, "I have tits and I can talk… doesn't take much more than that."

"Oh Christ!" Grace lifted my gin from the cobblestones and took a sizeable gulp. Her lips tightened, nostrils flared, and a shiver coursed through her spine. She stuck out her tongue, "Good grief, how many shots are in that?" I couldn't help but stifle a snort in response.

"Just the one." I covered my mouth and bit my lip to avoid laughter. Grace really couldn't handle her alcohol.

"Speaking of pictures… wait until you see this!"

Before I could stop her, Olivia had thrust her phone in front of my face, proudly displaying a picture of an impressively sized … dick… by far, the largest I'd ever seen. My jaw dropped, and laughter bubbled up uncontrollably. Leaning my head on Grace's shoulder, tears welled in my eyes, rendering me speechless. I took in a deep breath of her sweet perfume.

"Whose… is that?!" Grace's eyes blinked rapidly, attempting to recover from the shock. She shielded Olivia's phone, desperately hoping that no one around us had caught a glimpse of the explicit image. Her mouth hung open as disbelief seized her. "Pretty sure he meant that for your eyes only!!"

"Jason." 'Liv shrugged. "His Instagram bio states he's from Armagh."

"And he just – he just sent you that? G'wan Armagh…"

"Yeah, like an hour ago…while you were ordering drinks and Anna was in the bathroom. He didn't even text me hello. What an opening message!" She stared at the picture, emotionless. Her lack of surprise made me wonder how often this kind of thing occurred.

4

"And what did you say?" I asked, curious.

"That I've seen bigger."

Grace's hand smacked against her lips as she burst into laughter. I joined in; the laughter so intense it turned soundless. "I'm gonna wee myself." She squeezed her legs together, shaking her head in an attempt to stifle her laughter.

"He hasn't replied since… I was only jokin' but don't think he's taken it well."

"P- p - poor man will never text you again!" Grace declared between bouts of laughter.

I clasped her hand in mine and gave it a reassuring squeeze as we giggled together. A smile crept onto Olivia's face, her 'oh so cool' façade crumbling.

"It's probably for the best… if you end up having sex with him, we'd probably need to cart you to A&E the next day." I added, finally able to string together a coherent sentence.

Olivia stared at me; eyebrows raised. "What are you talking about? I already have."

"Oh, for heaven's sake!" Grace's hand darted towards my glass, lifting it to her lips. She downed a drink of the strong bubbly liquid.

"I'm joking!" She defended.

"Right…" I rolled my eyes, not believing a word she said.

"Honestly… I'm joking!" She insisted. I still wasn't convinced.

***

By 11.30pm, a guitarist had stationed himself on the street, strumming sweet classic tunes. The crowd had started to sway, twirling each other with smiles adorning their faces. Grace, Olivia and I found ourselves dancing with strangers under the city lights until 1.30am. A typical Belfast night. As we stood in line, shivering in the cold for hot chips from the chippy van, my phone rang, disrupting our light-hearted, tipsy banter.

"I'll answer it! I'm the sober-est here!" Grace declared. I handed her my phone, acknowledging her point. I didn't trust myself. I wasn't confident in my own sobriety. It was likely my 'almost boyfriend' James wanting to know my whereabouts and who I was with. I wasn't in the mood for an interrogation or potential argument.

"Hellooooo?"

The street around us was filled with noisy, non-sober people, so as I pushed myself closer to try listen to the phone call, I was unsuccessful.

"Hi Paddy, it's Grace – Annas besttttt friend. Can I take a message?" She slurred, evidently influenced by the half-gin she'd consumed. *Lightweight.*

"Paddyyyyy!" I screamed, hoping he could hear me. A wave of relief washed over me. I was glad it was Paddy.

"Hello – can't hear you!" Grace bellowed into the phone. "Can ye hear me?"

Despite my genuine liking for James, he'd been toying with my emotions for far too long. He stood me up for lunch the day before, only to text an hour later claiming work commitments – a blatant lie, given that he'd previously told me he'd booked off both yesterday and today. Anyways… instead, he invited me to his flat, and we spent the night together. While I felt good in his arms, today didn't sit well with me. He hadn't texted me all day… which led to emergency comfort drinks with Liv and G.

Suddenly Grace's demeanour changed, halting my thoughts of James.

"Wait, what?" She mumbled, covering her ears with her hands, attempting to listen more closely. "Paddy I can't hear you… speak louder!"

Her expression shifted to a more serious tone, and when her gaze met mine, confusion and fear were evident in her eyes. I knew something was wrong.

"Hold on…hold on…Who's died?"

My stomach dropped. She handed me the phone.

7 DAYS LATER.

My freckles began to fade as I brushed foundation over my skin. I stared at my tired reflection. *God, what a week.* Glancing at my phone, it read 10.53am, indicating I still had an hour before I had to attend the funeral. The mere thought of going twisted my stomach, making it difficult to swallow. Nevertheless, it wasn't a choice; it was a requirement. I had to be there.

By 11.12am I had finished adding some colour to my dull complexion and was jiggling my way into some spanks. Sorry, struggling is probably a better word. *Sweating profusely and struggling.* Once all my imperfections were tucked away, I slipped my way into my tights and black dress. My reflection showed a simple, unremarkable girl; thankfully not exposing the chaos of my mind or the overwhelmingly depressive thoughts. I hoped the reflection wouldn't shatter as the day progressed.

I arrived 15 minutes early and joined the crowd of people waiting outside the cathedral. Derek was a well-known man; but I didn't think he was *this well-known.* Scanning the crowd, I spotted Paddy. I stared at him, not blinking, somehow hoping he'd get the sense that someone was watching him… but he stayed focused, deep in conversation with a short, bald man, who I didn't recognise. It was considerably cold for June and I began to wish I'd brought a coat and scarf.

A few minutes later, three black funeral cars pulled up. A woman, presumably Derek's wife, stepped out, tears streaming down her face. She was immediately embraced by someone unfamiliar. Although I didn't feel the same level of loss, my heart sank, empathising with their pain.

Glancing at my phone, I quickly checked for notifications, finding only one text.

GRACE

Hope today isn't too difficult. Call me any time x

My heart warmed. I quickly typed 'thank you G, should be fine xx' and pressed send.

I looked up from my phone and noticed my boss Mia, emerging from the third funeral car, exuding her usual 'Victoria Beckham-like' elegance. She never failed to impress me with her style and poise, clad in a sleek black pencil suit accompanied by a matching bag and sunglasses. I had no doubt she was donning a pair of red bottoms – Louboutin heels. Wrapped in a bubble of unassailable self-confidence, she was a presence to be reckoned with.

My eyes met hers and she smiled warmly, nodding her head to say hello. Following her, four men - Executives and Board Members from Spotlight Radio – stepped out of the car behind her. I recognised their faces but struggled with their names.

"What's the craic?" I was taken aback, turning to my left to find Paddy, wearing a sombre smile. His hair was slicked back, presenting a very polished appearance, a stark departure from his usual studio attire. The familiar baggy jeans, white t-shirt and denim jacket had given way to a rather uncharacteristic black suit jacket, trousers, shirt, and tie. It seemed unnatural to see him dressed so smartly.

"Hi..."

"This is weird, isn't it?" He mumbled, looking out over the crowd of people.

My stomach swelled, "God...yes."

"Attending a funeral... for a man we've never met..."

I rolled my eyes, "I know he was technically our boss, but I'd never spoken to him."

Paddy let out a low chuckle.

"Don't laugh. You'll make me laugh." I punched his arm.

"Just don't let the cameras see you laughing." He nodded. I followed his gaze and spotted a camera crew across the road with the 'Belfast Buzz' logo proudly printed across their van. *God*. They were filming the crowd, documenting Derek's funeral. As if I wasn't already worried enough about how to act or what to say, there was now a camera crew watching, waiting to catch something newsworthy.

As I glanced around to check for any additional hidden cameras, my eyes found Mia gracefully making her way through the crowd. She was heading towards us, so I definitely couldn't laugh; after all, there was nothing funny about a man dying.

"Paddy. Anna. Thank you for coming." We exchanged a brief hug. "It means a lot that you're both here."

"Of course." I felt an uncomfortable lump form in my throat. I picked at the chipped red nail polish on my fingers, regretting not having repainted them.

"So, do you know many of these people?" Paddy questioned.

Mia nodded, "Most. It seems a lot of people travelled over from New York."

"From Apex?" he added.

"Yep. Hopefully you can chat to a few people later."

Paddy looked around us, taking note of the different faces. I wondered if he knew many of the guests. He worked occasionally with our sister studio Apex and had been with Spotlight 6 years longer than I had.

The crowd began to disperse as people filtered into the cathedral. "We should probably go inside." Mia suggested.

I followed slowly behind them as they walked towards the entrance, engaged in hushed conversation. Mia's short black hair somehow stayed perfect as a gust of wind blew towards us. Glancing at the grey clouds above, it was definitely going to rain, and I was not prepared.

Paddy continued his questioning, "Is there anyone in particular that you want me to chat to?"

Was this a funeral or networking opportunity?

"Not really. Just anyone you come across. Make yourself known. Say good things about Belfast…great things." Mia sighed. I wondered how well she knew Derek. She didn't seem upset. But I suppose everyone copes with grief differently and who was I to judge? We approached the white marble stairs, moving closer to the imposing oak doors. Glancing over the crowd behind me, I searched for James, but was unsuccessful in locating him.

"Hey, you both go on in. I'll see you in a minute." I waved.

"Is he not here yet?" Paddy questioned and looked at his watch.

I shook my head, my throat tightening. *Of course he wasn't here.* Paddy's eyes asked me if I was okay. I nodded in reply.

"I'll try save you a seat." He said, assuming James wouldn't be showing up.

"I'll be sitting at the front." Mia pulled me into another brief hug. "But I'll catch up with you after, ok?"

As soon as they were both up the stairs and out of sight, I picked up my phone and dialled James' number. I was met immediately with his answering machine. *Was his phone off? Had he immediately declined my call? Had he blocked my number?* His Facebook stated he'd last been online 55 minutes ago… yet he hadn't replied to my text from 9am this morning asking if he would prefer to meet me at my apartment instead of the cathedral. I knew in my gut that he wasn't going to show up, but I still stupidly waited until the entire crowd had cleared inside… just in case he was hiding amongst the many faces.

The sound of an organ jolted me from my daze. *Shit. It was starting.* I jumped from stair to stair, mindful not to fall in my heels. As I stepped through the doors, I was handed a memorial service with a printed photo on the front. For the first time, a pang of sadness hit me as I saw Derek's photograph. Although I hadn't met or spoken to him, I felt a twinge of sorrow that he had passed away, leaving behind a loving family and undoubtably a legacy. The cathedral exuded warmth, likely from the multitude of people sharing the same air. Realising the pews were all occupied, I abandoned hope of finding Paddy and slipped into a back row.

I exchanged a thoughtful smile with the older lady beside me, before we both redirected our attention to the front. Over an hour passed with tributes, hymns and bible readings. It brought back memories of my grandmother's funeral, prompting me to dissociate even more. Something which Grace insisted was unhealthy... and that I probably needed therapy for. A sentiment my parents would most likely agree with.

Like all Irish and Northern Irish funerals, I anticipated some finger sandwiches and a cuppa tea or coffee. However, Derek's family had organised a singing and dancing celebration of his life in the fabulous Grand Central Hotel, the most impressive and tallest hotel in Belfast. It seemed fitting considering his legacy.

I stood by a table of prosecco, sipping on the remaining dribble in my glass whilst admiring the view of Belfast city centre from The Observatory. The entire city unfolded before me. A pianist played delicate tunes in the corner, which I could just about hear amidst the lively chatter of guests. The hotel seemed to host a larger crowd than the cathedral did.

Paddy appeared by my side. His cheeks rosy from the warmth in the air, "So he didn't show?"

My cheeks flushed, "Nope." I mumbled into my glass, embarrassed. *Bastard.*

"He's not worth your time. I've told you this before." He took my now- empty glass from my hand and exchanged it for a full one, the bubbles rising enticingly to the top, making my mouth thirst. I took a sip.

"He probably just got caught up with something... could have had a family emergency... he could have been in a car crash... could be dead for all I know."

I hoped he was dead. Very inappropriate to say at a funeral. I know.

Paddy chuckled, "Oh Anna... you need to stop making excuses for a man who smokes fifty fags a day and probably smells like... chip shop leftovers."

I choked, "He does not!" I took a rather large gulp of my prosecco, or maybe it was champagne... to stop myself from laughing. It tasted too good, unlike the usual cheap stuff I bought in Tesco... or Lidl. Whichever had an offer on.

"Anna?" he poked my side.

I wriggled, "what?"

"Are you listening to me?"

"Yes." I lied. I didn't want to hear all the ways that James was a bad person. He'd been good to me on many occasions over the past five months. Today was just a blip. Although there'd been a lot of blips over the last three months... I shook the thought from my mind. I couldn't crack. Not here. Not today. Today was about Derek and his life. Mine could wait.

"So, Derek..." I attempted to shift the conversation.

"Very wealthy man." Paddy mumbled.

I smiled. "Mhmm... what else do you know about him?"

He paused for a second to think. "Do you think this is the reason Mia has been stressed lately? She's been more... uptight. It's a bit unusual."

"Maybe, yeah."

Lately, she'd been more un-reachable. Her head was always glued to her computer screen or iPhone when she wasn't in meetings with 'The Board' aka 'the gods above.' Upon reflection, I hadn't seen her at all for the past week, apart from our meeting yesterday where she urged us to attend Derek's funeral. No other substantial explanation was offered, as she was visibly flustered and, in a rush, to go God knows where.

"Quite likely, actually." I added.

Paddy shrugged. "Have you met any Americans yet?"

I shook my head, "I think I've spoken to three people today. You, Mia and the man handing out the memorial service leaflet things. I did smile at a lovely old lady though."

Paddy rolled his eyes. He was well aware that conversing with strangers wasn't a hobby I wished to explore.

"Wellll…I spoke to the Head of Data Processing at Apex. He said he couldn't understand my Northern Irish accent and joked that I needed subtitles." He snorted into his drink. "It was an easy way for me to end the conversation."

I couldn't help but laugh. *Ah Americans.* I'd always wanted to go to America, and although mum and dad took me to many places growing up… The States wasn't one of them.

Waitresses and waiters walked around offering 'hors d oeuvres'… aka mini plates of food, a mix of Irish and American. Everything from Tayto crisp sandwiches to mini cheeseburgers.

My phone buzzed.

GRACE

Worried I haven't heard from you, are you ok? I saw the funeral press online x

I sat my mini plate with mini food down on an empty table.

ANNA

I'm fine. Belfast Buzz had cameras at the cathedral!! x

She responded a minute later.

GRACE

Ah. Still not a nice thing to attend. They've written a story about how he earned loads of money for Apex in America and left Spotlight Radio to die… eek.

13

Fuck. That wasn't ideal… even if I suspected some truth around it.

I placed my phone on the table and surveyed the room. The atmosphere was vibrant, filled with people enjoying drinks, engaging in conversations, and for the most part, wearing smiles. It truly felt like a celebration, far from the sombre tone of a typical funeral. A tall blonde woman delicately sipped on a cocktail, sharing a warm smile with a brown-haired man. The wedding band on his finger led me to assume it was her husband, and the admiration in his gaze as he looked down on her evoked a pang of envy within me. *Ah, to be in love and actually have somebody love you back.* I took another sip of my fancy bubbly, my gaze shifting hopelessly to my phone. Setting aside my self-respect, I decided to send a text to James and offer him an opportunity to explain himself.

ANNA
Are you ok babe? I'm worried you haven't replied. X

I continued to sip on my drink and hoped for a text back.

Once my glass was drained, I decided it was time to orchestrate my exit. I preferred to be depressed at home, rather than in a room full of mournful people. Stepping toward the door, I quickly scanned the room in search of Mia. She'd been eaten by the crowd and was conversing with a handful of men and women. Another swift glance revealed Paddy being preoccupied, so he couldn't stop me from leaving.

I slid out the door and walked down a short hallway until I found the elevator. It seemed to take an ungodly amount of time. I anxiously watched as it climbed from floor to floor. It stopped on Floor 11 and I stared at the exit door, praying that no-one would come out and obstruct me from leaving. Floor 14. *Oh, for Christ's sake.* Another stop on Floor 16. The party's ambient music and chatter spilled into the hallway as the door began to open. Frustrated, I bolted from the elevator and darted in the opposite direction.

"Anna?" I heard Paddy's voice call. *SHIT.*

There had to be stairs somewhere. Surely, there had to be stairs... I continued walking for about two minutes, navigating from one hallway to another.

Eventually I spotted a door with an 'emergency stairway' sign above. In mental preparation for my descent of approximately a million stairs down to the lobby, I took off my heels. I pushed on the door, which felt unusually stiff and heavy.

"Anna? Is that you?" Paddy called.

I huffed a frustrated breath and stepped back before shoving my entire body weight onto the door to force it open.

When it did, I was met with a view that made me squeal.

Holy fuck.

A half-naked woman peeked out from behind a man, who was passionately kissing down her neck and across her breasts. She let out a scream when she noticed me, and he immediately stopped.

"I'm so sorry! SORRY!" I turned to open the door and leave... only to find there was no door handle. A piece of paper with the words 'due to construction, nearest exit on floor 15' was stuck to the wood. AS IF!

"You can't go out that way!" She shouted. I refused to turn round.

"Ok... uh, which way can I go?" I asked. *This had to be one of the most awkward situations of my entire life.* I heard what sounded like shuffling of clothes being put back on. Every sound was magnified in the stairwell.

"Fuck... you'll have to go downstairs." A dark American accent commanded. My stomach trembled... a mixture of anxiety, shock and to be honest, I was a bit taken back by how delicious his voice was. *Sue me.* "That door doesn't open." He explained.

"I gathered that when I turned to open it and there was no bloody handle." I snapped and turned towards them, shielding my eyes with my free hand. My other hand was clutching my shoes.

Please lord, do not let me step on someone's underwear.

I kept my focus glued to the ground and manoeuvred my way around the clothing items on the floor. A white shirt, blue tie, *electric pink thong…* The woman started giggling, probably out of nervousness. I wasn't sure if I should laugh or cry. I continued down one flight of stairs and glanced into the centre of the staircase, fully acknowledging how many flights were below me.

"There's a door you can leave through on the 15th floor." The man spoke.

"Yeah, I read the sign. Thanks!" Without thinking, I looked up and waved at him. "Oh shit, sorry." I clasped my hand over my eyes once more. He chuckled at my reaction. Fuck, *the hot voice had a hot toned back covered in tats… Hello tall, dark and handsome…* I debated looking back to get a glance of his face. Quickly, I peeked through my hands just in time to witness him hastily pulling his shirt back on, catching a glimpse of what appeared to be a snake tattoo winding its way up his spine. An interesting choice that kind of gave me the ick.

As I descended the stairs, reaching floor 15, I paused momentarily to adjust my heels around my ankles and strained to listen for any sound from the mystery couple. I couldn't help but wonder if their rendezvous would persist or come to an end; however, the conspicuous silence suggested they had stopped.

The lift arrived with a jolt, and I wasted no time stepping inside, eager to leave the hotel behind. Despite its allure, I had no desire to linger another moment within its walls. As I walked through the streets of Belfast toward my apartment, I cursed at myself, glancing down at my blistered feet.

Grace and Olivia are going to love hearing about this… I mused to myself.

When I reached home, I threw off my shoes and double checked I'd locked the front door before stripping and jumping into a hot shower.

James still hadn't texted and I was absolutely fucking DONE WITH HIM.

Until the next morning...

Chapter One
Gobshite

Definition : A person that's very irritating and melts your brain.

F riday. After a brisk shower, I savoured a steaming cup of coffee and had three bites of a bagel. I threw on some clothes and headed to work, expecting another mundane day... minus my plans to fill Paddy in on the naked shagging strangers I'd walked in on the night before. He was sure to get a kick out of it.

Throughout the morning, a silent yearning lingered within me, hoping for the familiar ring of my phone, signalling James's call. Yet, the silence persisted, leaving me with an unwavering sense of disappointment. Unable to resist the impulse, I dialled his number, longing for the sound of his voice, only to be met with the unsurprising voicemail. It was only 8.49am so he was probably in bed... still my heart sank with disappointment.

In routine fashion, I strolled to the studio, a mere two-minute waddle from my apartment. Spotlight was nestled within River House, the most modern office block in Belfast. We'd only been working from there for a year and a half. A stark contrast to the musty walls and creaky floors of our previous office in West Belfast; the city centre location felt like a dream.

The Spotlight Radio LED sign twinkled as I exited the elevator and stepped into the office.

"Hi Dillon." I greeted, giving a wave as I passed his desk. Dillon, the head of content, would usually be eagerly waiting to pitch his 'next big idea' to anyone walking in… But today, he was strangely silent, staring fixedly at his computer screen. Jaw clenched.

In response to my greeting, he raised his hand without looking up and gave me a cold wave. It was a bit odd, and maybe I should've taken it as a warning sign, but I brushed it off and continued on my way, not dwelling too much on it.

In Northern Ireland, hangovers were a regular occurrence for most of the population. Thankfully I was feeling bright eyed and bushy tailed. Paddy, on the other hand, looked worse for wear. His eyes, red and glossy, were hanging from his head. He had reverted to his usual slightly dishevelled self. Baggy camel-coloured trousers, a graphic t-shirt, denim jacket and a grey beany hat covering his mop of curly brown hair.

"You hanging?" I snorted, dropping my bag onto my desk.

Hanging
Definition: 'To health' - a drinking toast when you cheers your glasses together.

He looked up, for a brief moment and then his attention went back to his computer screen. He responded by sticking up his middle finger.

"What time did you escape last night?" He mumbled. His voice was husky, like he'd just rolled out of bed. I had to stop myself from laughing.

"I don't know what you mean... I left after yo-"

"Wise up Anna." He rolled his eyes. "D'you not think I know you by now?"

"A solid ten minutes after we chatted. Twelve max." I shrugged, refusing to meet his eye. I unpacked my laptop, pen, and notepad, placing them in an organised fashion onto my desk. Paddy stayed silent. I couldn't predict his thoughts, but I could feel him squinting at me. "Stop staring." I muttered.

He laughed.

"I have a story for you!"

As I was about to divulge, Mia approached, stopping me in my tracks. *Classic Mia, always impeccable timing.*

"A juicy story perhaps?" Her lips were painted ruby red, and her eyes carried a bold, smoky allure. I couldn't help but regret my hasty application of just concealer and powder. I must've looked like Caspar the Ghost compared to her. It was as if she had a glam squad on standby every morning.

"Ah, it's nothing!" I blurted, feeling a sudden sense of panic. I hastily took a seat at my desk, opening my laptop with the desperate hope of feigning productivity and dodging her inquisitive gaze. *Perhaps this wasn't the kind of story meant for casual sharing with the boss.*

"Oh, but I insist you tell me..." Paddy's words dripped with teasing mischief. He had a knack for sensing my discomfort.

Inhaling deeply, I straightened up in my chair, feeling the weight of their expectant eyes on me. "So, yesterday, at the party... sorry — funeral... the funeral-party... as I was making my exit," I pinched at my skin, trying to set the scene just right. *Come on Anna, sell it! It's comedy gold.* I paused, taking a moment to collect myself before taking a deep breath.

"So, I felt shite yesterday. Pure shite." I looked at Mia, who seemed unfazed by my language - a green light to spill it all. "My boyfriend who isn't officially my boyfriend… but basically is my boyfriend… promised to come to the funeral. You know, you said we could bring a friend or family member if we wanted?" I looked towards Mia, who nodded in response.

"Well, he didn't show up! No text, no call to let me know he wouldn't be there, and I'm still in the dark. So, all day, I'm feeling like shit on a stick. And funerals, they're a bit traumatic for me. I see someone crying and immediately I have to hold back tears. So, here I am, feeling like shit and trying not to cry all day. Then… THEN there's a party with fancy champagne. Mix that with all my emotions, and let's just say, I wasn't exactly feeling fabulous."

"It was an open bar, to be fair." Paddy chimed in.

"I can tell by your appearance that you enjoyed it." Mia observed, nodding at him. He made a funny face at her in response. "Sorry, go on, Anna."

"Right, so I thought it might be a good idea to make my exit a bit early. Perhaps a tad too early – sorry Mia. But networking with people, especially at this kind of… event… was my idea of hell." A smirk crept across her face as I talked. I glanced at Paddy, who seemed to be holding in laughter. *Was he laughing with me or at me?*

"I'm just grateful that you showed your face at all." Mia said kindly, smiling. "Continue your story…"

"Okay. So, I go to the lift. It takes ages. Like, seriously… how long can a bloody lift take? Suddenly, the doors from the party start to open and I'm worried someone will stop me from leaving or take offence that I'm leaving… so I run. I ran down a hallway and then another hallway and then I spotted the stairwell."

"Did you take a detour down 23 flights of stairs just to avoid a conversation?" Paddy grinned.

"No - well…" I hesitated, "I prepared myself to. I even took off my heels and everything."

Mia giggled, probably picturing me awkwardly trying to unstrap my shoes while wobbling on one leg.

"Anyway, I opened the door and walked into the stairwell, only to stumble upon two lovers, half-naked and about to... well, you know." I recounted. "Shag."

Paddy exploded into fits of laughter; Mia followed suit.

Eyes widening, I continued, "Oh this isn't even the good part. Once I realised what was happening, I turned back... only to find there wasn't a damn door handle. I had no way out. I was trapped."

Mia started coughing involuntarily from laughing, tears forming in her eyes. "St-stop." She choked out, her face turning red.

"So, there I was, awkwardly shielding my eyes, descending the stairs until I finally found an exit door. Definitely not my finest day," I concluded my tale.

"My god, Anna. Only you," Paddy exclaimed, slapping his knee and still laughing.

I nodded in agreement. These kinds of situations were on par for the course in my life, keeping things interesting, I suppose.

"You know how to tell a story." Mia wiped tears from under her eyes, "If you ever have a story like that again, please come straight to my office."

"See you tomorrow probably."

"She's not joking. Anna is like my personal reality tv star. Next level entertainment." Paddy chimed in, his voice sounding worse than before, a hint of green in his complexion. Laughing seemed to drain all his remaining energy.

"Maybe you should be presenting your own radio show instead of running someone else's..." I took Mia's words with a pinch of salt. Speaking on air was out of my comfort zone and she knew it. Background work was what I was meant for.

"Anyway..." She exhaled, acknowledging my silence, "We have a team meeting at 3pm. I sent a calendar invite. Boardroom Two." With a wave, she strutted towards her office.

Paddy buried himself back into in his computer screen, sipping on a bottle of Lucozade, the ultimate sugary, hangover cure.

"Do you know what the meeting is about?"

"No, but I'd imagine it's to do with Derek…and what happens next."

I clicked my tongue against the roof of my mouth, my mind starting to wonder about the possibilities. Fortunately, I had a lot of tasks to distract myself with.

My to-do list glared at me…

1. Develop Conversation Topics for Weekend 'Breakfast Show'
2. Prepare any interesting News Stories and Features for tonight's news cast
3. Buy plant-food for Harry... (my desk cactus)
4. Gather insights from socials team on best performing shows this week and decipher why

I interrupted my work on the list with frequent trips to the break room for cups of coffee, a granola bar, apple, and water. *Must stay hydrated.*

2.55pm rolled around fast. Sipping on another coffee, not the best choice with my anxious, bubbling stomach, I walked towards the boardroom. The atmosphere was heavy; we all sensed something big was coming. Inside the boardroom, a bottle of water, glass and napkin sat in front of each chair. Perfectly placed. A sign that Lynda, with her OCD tendencies had probably set up the space. There were twelve chairs around the long, narrow table; half already occupied. I chose a stool by the window, leaving the remaining seats for employees who'd been at the company longer. A media screen had been set up and Charlie, our tech whiz, stood at the front fiddling with the tech. Paddy arrived at 3.02 and took up a seat at the table, smiling humorously as he spun around to look at me.

"You'll be at the big kids' table someday soon." He winked, trying to make a light-hearted joke to ease the uncertainty we both felt.

Mia walked in a few moments later, taking her place at the head of the table. Over 30 people had wedged into the room like sardines, either on stools or chairs they'd brought in themselves. I could already picture the fingerprints left on the floor-to-ceiling windows by those who decided to stand. In the meantime, Charlie had started a Zoom call, with another 20 or so people joining. This was a full company-wide affair.

Mia cleared her throat which halted any chatter, "So, first of all, thank you to everyone that attended yesterday. I'm sure you're all looking for an explanation as to why you were asked to do that and why we're having this meeting today." She presented calmly to the room. I looked around, sensing my colleagues were as clueless as I was.

"So, Derek laid the foundations for Spotlight many moons ago, and then he took a trip to America, where he met his wife. Together, they kicked off Apex – a radio station that blossomed into television and outpaced Spotlight's growth by leaps and bounds. At present, they boast a team of over 400 staff, producing radio shows and television news programs spanning the entire United States. They're also the brains behind advertising campaigns not only for Apex but for other stations as well," Mia explained. I had briefly researched Apex when applying for my job, but I hadn't grasped the company's scale. It was evidently in a constant state of growth.

"Here at Spotlight, our sponsorship fees are dwindling. The radio audience is shrinking by the day, so we have to evolve, or we risk being left behind," she continued.

As Mia spoke, my heart raced, my mouth felt gummy with excess saliva, and my legs began to tingle.

"There will be layoffs, much to my dismay. Budget cuts are on the horizon, and a lot of changes in store. Some shows will be dropped, new ones curated. We're shifting our focus significantly towards online media, aiming to broaden our digital footprint," Mia elaborated, clasping a hand around her neck as she stretched her strained muscles and cleared her throat once again. "Additionally, we'll be hosting a visitor over the next three months, Amir Daivari. He shared a close bond with Derek and before his passing, they had numerous conversations on how to enhance Spotlight. Amir has held various roles within Apex, and Derek believed he could bring valuable insights to us."

I didn't know whether to be worried or relieved.

"I will still be your managing director, however, Amir will be working alongside me on any decisions and how we progress as a company."

I wished I could see Paddy's face to try understand how he was feeling.

Mia continued, "Each of you will be having a performance review, in which we will evaluate your role and identify your strengths and your weaknesses. Some of you will be promoted. Some of you may be demoted and might have to take a step back and complete a training program for improvement. The next three months are incredibly important for the future of our station."

I glanced around the room, observing reactions. John, a production assistant for weekend evening shows looked angry, furious even. Abigail, our social media content manager was biting her lip, eyes wide with curiosity. She was probably safe, but her plate was about to become busier, with more work and more questions on what hashtags should we use or how long should a video be… etcetera. Maisy, head of commercial sponsorships, looked dull and withdrawn. Her shoulders slumped and she pouted her mouth. She looked exhausted and emotionally frozen.

"My assistant Archie will send everyone an email for when their reviews will take place."

John raised a hand, "Who will be taking the reviews?" His voice was sharp and lacked empathy.

"Senior leadership. Amir and I will also be present for as many reviews as we can fit into our schedules."

I felt slightly more optimistic knowing that Paddy would have some involvement in my future at Spotlight. I wondered if he was just learning about this now or if he knew before but couldn't tell me. At least his job was safe. After a few more questions, we were excused. Although I felt internally that I had bricks weighing my feet to the ground, I quickly speed-walked after Abigail. I needed to tick the last task from my to-do list and wanted to do so, before her to-do list would undoubtably explode with tasks from Mia and other members of staff. Thankfully I was able to steal 15 minutes of her time before her attention was pulled in another direction. Her wide-eyed expression told me she was apprehensive of the road ahead.

I was unfortunately unable to locate Paddy for the remainder of my shift. I left at 5.25pm with my to-do list complete and created another list for Monday, if I'd even be able to do it. I had no idea what was to come.

As I stepped out onto the street, I was reminded by the hustle of well dressed, smiley people that it was a Friday. The streets were buzzing. It was officially the weekend. I began strolling in the direction of my apartment, before having a realisation. Friday meant after work pints at The Harp Bar. That's why I hadn't spotted Paddy. He'd probably left just after 4pm.

You could just about hear the thumping music over the voices of customers and clinking of glasses. Merry people, drinks in hand, spilled out onto the tables lining the cobblestone streets of the Cathedral Quarter. It felt a bit European, street drinking in the sunshine. For once, not a rain cloud was to be seen.

I stood at the side of the street, glancing around, trying to spot a colleague or two. The only face I spotted was Mia, who was alone and searching, like I was. I pushed away the fluttery feeling in my stomach and approached my boss.

"Helloooo."

Why'd I say that so awkwardly? I could have just said 'hi Mia' or 'hey!'

She turned to me and a smile formed on her face.

"Anna! I can't find anyone, so unusual for Friday!" She exclaimed, motioning towards the bar.

I sighed, "Yeah, strange."

"Probably because of the meeting…" there was a sadness in her voice.

To be fair, I'd almost forgotten because of everything that was going on. I only rarely attended Friday drinks, but I was always aware it was happening.

I spotted a couple who were leaving, and suggested we ask for their table. Mia agreed and I quicky snatched the seats and began to people watch as she fetched us a drink. A few familiar faces from the offices nearby filled my tummy with a comforting Irish feeling of never being alone and always knowing someone, no-matter where you go. The neon lights of Duke of York animated the street, adding to the warm glow of sunshine.

Considering the circumstances, I felt at ease and comfortable. I don't know what about the Harp Bar made me feel this way… maybe it was the chairs. They were as old as the bar. Antique. Velvet. Red. Like a hug from a relative who you love but don't see that often; but every time you're with them you feel warm and nostalgic.

The sound of rustling crisp packets interrupted my reflective state. A packet of Tayto cheese and onion landed in front of me. My mouth watered. *Nostalgia, again.* Mia sat with a humorous smile plastered across her face.

"What?" I questioned.

She shook her head.

"Rory." She nodded her head towards the barman.

I smiled, knowingly. Rory was a flirt. Didn't matter what they looked like, where they were from or who they were. He always had a compliment to give.

By the time our drinks landed at the table a few moments later, I'd almost reached the bottom of my crisps and was feeling even more grateful for the taste of gin.

"I don't understand where everyone is..." she mumbled, looking around the bar and out onto the street again. I could feel her disappointment.

"Uh -I'll call Paddy!" I suggested, taking out my iPhone.

My phone screen lit up with notifications.

JAMES

Nausea flooded my senses. *James... oh my god... James!*

"Are you okay?" Mia questioned.

My eyes detached from my screen, heart still racing, "Oh – yes I'm fine. Sorry."

Her brows furrowed, as much as they could, considering she had a lot of botox. I could tell she didn't believe me. She knew something was wrong.

"Remember the boyfriend - who's not my boyfriend?" I splurged, "He's texted me..."

I looked towards my phone again and scrolled through my notifications.

"Eight times... and phoned me twice."

Mia looked at me, eyes alight.

"Open them!"

So, I did... *and I wished I hadn't.*

JAMES

Sorry

JAMES

Been super busy

JAMES

Work n stuff

JAMES

Tried calling u but

JAMES

This is too much for me. U need to not be so obsessed with me, we're not married u know yeh haha

JAMES

Honestly babe, I just don't think we're right for each other.

JAMES

Still not answering my phone call so I'm assuming u agree we aren't right 4 each other. Hope u find someone or if u ever want casual fwb call me x

I took a long sip from my gin to clear the ache that had built up at the back my throat. I re-read the messages in shock, unable to comprehend how he could just end things with such short shitty messages… after all this time. I didn't want to cry, but the rejection burned. It burned bad. I blinked a few times at the messages and then surfaced to look at Mia.

"Well…" I croaked, "My non relationship is officially over."

Until he gets bored and calls you at 2am and you uber to his flat. I pushed my inner thoughts away. Not this time. I wouldn't go back to him again. I couldn't.

Mia offered a deep sigh and thoughtful expression, lifting her hand across the table and squeezing mine. "It's probably for the best." She spoke softly. "He sounds like a gobshite."

I appreciated her empathy, but my ego was hurting.

"Thank you." All the emotions from my day felt like they were turning my body into goo and soon, I would slowly start to drip onto the ground. I'd turn to a puddle of mush.

I closed my eyes, taking a deep breath, hoping to re-energise my fatigued muscles and stop the trembling which was taking over my limbs. After a moment, I lifted my chin and plastered a smile on my face, hoping I could mask my emotions.

"Sorry…" I breathed, "I'll call Paddy now."

Mia's hand reached across the table, halting me, "No-no. It's fine. Take a breather first."

I sucked in another breath and sipped on my gin.

"Tell me about this – clearly idiotic – man…"

I snorted into my drink, "Well…"

Tears bubbled in my eyes as I began to think about some of our times together; for the first time reflecting… I felt stupid.

"I knew this was coming really, I've sensed it for a while. I just didn't want to believe it." I started. "When I first met him, I fell head over heels. I guess part of the problem with reading and watching so many romantic comedies is that you start to daydream about situations that just don't happen in reality… especially in Belfast… especially to me."

Mia gave me a knowing look and I felt comfortable continuing with an intuition she'd been through something similar in the past.

"We matched on Tinder, obviously. The modern-day cupid. *Strike one.*" I laughed, "Three days later I was hunting through my wardrobe for something to wear. I was meeting him for a casual lunchtime date, but I might as well have been attending the goddamn Baftas. Tensions were high. I was wondering 'What if he's the one? What if I'm about to meet the man I'll spend the rest of my life with?"

I watched as she smiled into her drink, and her throat bobbed, a sign she was holding back a laugh. "We've all been there."

"In hindsight, this was a bit ridiculous to think about a man who I'd never met *and* who I'd only been texting for a few days, but I couldn't help myself. I'm a romantic at heart. Or just stupid. Or both…"

Mia sighed, but before she could attempt to console me, I divulged. "We met for the first time in Nando's. *Strike Two*. Not exactly a romantic location, even though the food is great. It was at this moment that I realised he in fact *hadn't* planned anything for our date. He unfortunately got away with it as he was Christian Grey level of attractive and here I was, feeling like a B Tech Anastasia Steele."

"B Tech?" Mia giggled, but asked for an explanation.

"Like… lower grade. Less attractive. Not as good."

"Ah." She laughed, "Not true in the slightest by the way."

She didn't know James…

I smiled at her compliment and continued my story, "Anyways, I thought in the beginning that he only wanted me for… sex. His advances weren't subtle. However, this instantly felt like a challenge to me. I could picture the story in my head…

Beginning: Average looking woman matches with a gorgeous man on a dating app. Man just wants sex. Woman wants love.

Middle: Man and Woman meet. Man accidentally falls for woman. They spend every day together in love.

End: Man and Woman live happily ever after, have a big wedding and lots of babies."

"Don't forget a dog! You'd have to get a dog." Mia added, chuckling at my expense.

"Of course, how could I forget that? It's sad really… I remember sitting across from James as he passionately explained his love of Nando's hummus and flatbread. I mean, I liked hummus too, but I wasn't on his level of love. I remember thinking… maybe someday he'd love me as much as he loved the hummus."

"You compared yourself to hummus?"

God, I'm pathetic.

I shrugged, "Yep."

"Oh Anna." Mia facepalmed, shaking her head.

"The thing is…every date we went on I felt like he was falling for me. He'd chat about kids. He stopped one day and pointed at some expensive watches which were right beside engagement rings… so then he asked me 'oh which ring would you choose?' … then another day, he texted me a photo of his breakfast and said I make better pancakes in the morning. He remembered that I make amazing pancakes!" I began to feel the emotions sliding back in. "Just two weeks ago, he told me… he-he said he could see himself falling in love with me someday." I choked and looked at the sky. Clouds were beginning to form. *Fitting.*

"What changed?" Mia asked softly.

I shook my head and glanced at my phone, secretly hoping for a text that might shed some light on the situation. "I don't know. One minute it felt like he was all in and then the next minute I had to fight for his attention. I haven't seen him in… a few days."

As my mind raced, doubts crept in. *What if I had done or said something that day? What had gone wrong? Why did he leave?*

"Do you think he might have been love-bombing you?" Mia asked.

"What's that?"

She offered a sympathetic smile, "Showering you with promises for the future, public displays of affection, complimenting you excessively whenever you're upset with him…"

My stomach sank. He had done all those things. I nodded.

"Do you believe he's the love of your life?"

It was a heavy question. I stared into the liquid at the bottom of my glass, swirling the ice around with my straw. I wanted to say yes, but doubt churned in my stomach. "I don't know."

"How long have you known him?"

"Seven months." I exaggerated, feeling embarrassed. It had only been around five.

"Anna, you could live until you're ninety or one hundred years old. Don't stress about a man you've only known for seven months. That's such a small percentage of your life. I think he's a coward, and you're worth so much more than that." She shrugged and downed the remainder of her drink.

I nibbled on my lip, at a loss for words. My throat constricted, resisting the urge to let tears escape. He seemed to embody everything I'd longed for, everything I'd been missing. It was hard to fathom that his words were just hollow promises. I gazed at my phone once more, yearning for another notification, half-expecting him to return and recognise his errors.

"Another drink?" Mia questioned.

I nodded, "One more."

***

The peculiar charm of Belfast lies in this unspoken phenomenon: the more people have to drink, the wider their smiles seem to grow. No-one questions why they're smiling. Happiness is just a constant state of being. Everyone becomes instant friends, sharing camaraderie with strangers over drinks. Though inwardly, I wasn't feeling the joy, I managed to wear a small smile as we engaged in conversation with newfound acquaintances.

After spotting a few ominous rainclouds, Mia and I decided it was time to retreat indoors. I felt a bit wobblier on my feet than two hours before and my head was spinning a little. Perhaps it was the result of the countless antiques and memorabilia adorning the walls of Harp Bar... not the alcohol.

"I'll get the next round."

I made my way to the bar, greeted by Rory's radiant smile, and ordered two pints of Guinness.

"2 Guinness for two gorgeous girls!" He declared with a wink, warming my soul.

Ah, how I love Belfast.

As I savoured the frothy head of my Guinness, I pushed the heartache aside and compelled myself to sit upright, forcing a smile. I learned the family history of the couple beside us, laughed at stories from a group of men behind us, intentionally steering clear of thoughts about James and his callous dismissal of our 'relationship'.

A few more drinks had me feeling like I was floating. I relished in my new state of consciousness. It seemed much easier to ignore my emotions whilst drunk. Mia's eyes were glossy, and I could tell she was enjoying herself, although she regularly scanned the bar looking for staff members from Spotlight. Every time she looked around, pausing, searching different areas of the bar, my throat tightened, and I felt a small wave of nausea. *Was my company not enough? Was I saying the wrong things? Did Mia not like me?*

Huge anxiety ridden thoughts fuelled by a small, minor action.

"I'm going to try call Paddy." I shouted over the table and stood from my chair. Mia's eyes shot from the back corner of the bar back towards me. She nodded. "I'm just going to go outside. Better service! Less noise!"

I stepped through the crowd of people. The bar had gotten significantly busier since we'd arrived hours before. I could already feel the cold air as I approached the exit. A tall, bulky bouncer stood in the doorway. He was bald.

"I'm just making a wee call." I blabbed to him. He nodded and opened the red rope, allowing me to step outside. He then closed it again, stopping anyone getting back inside. The street was alive with seemingly sober but smiling faces. Many people waited, in hopes of being let inside the bar. Some waited patiently, some argued with the bouncer and some drunkenly tried to bribe him with the promise they'd bring him out a pint.

I dialled Paddy's number and shivered as I waited for him to pick up. It was fucking cold. The sky, a hue of black and dark blue, was filled with stars.

"Y'ellow." His voice echoed through my speaker.

"Wha's the craic?"

What's the craic
Definition: How are you? What's happening?

"You sound fucked. Where are you?" He laughed immediately.

"Harp. Where a'you?"

"Home."

I rolled my eyes and grumbled into the phone, "Aghhhhhh Paddy!! Get out. Come here! Mia is here too"

Silence.

"Ellooooo Paddy?"

"Who else is there?"

"Just us." I hiccupped.

"Hmmmm how mighty is the craic on a scale from 1 - 10?" he teased.

"Six. Needs a Paddy."

"Ok… and how uncomfortable are you on a scale from 1 – 10?"

"I am not uncomfortable but my anxiety is not exactly at ease being here with my boss and having lots of drinky dinks…" I mumbled. He knew me too well.

"Ah Christ, I'll be there in like twenty minutes."

That was much easier than I expected.

"YEOOO! Yes, yes. Legend. Love you." I tried to stop my words from slurring, however it seemed like an unachievable task.

The phone went dead. I found myself looking at the sky and praying, 'Dear Lord Jesus… Mary… and the wee donkey… please make Paddy come to the bar fast... amen."

After my straight-to-the-point prayer, I turned back towards the entrance and spotted the bald bouncer staring directly at me. *I hope he didn't see that.*

I walked over and smiled at him, as sober as possible. He flicked his tongue over his teeth and looked me dead in the eyes, deciding if I should be allowed back in OR if he should replace me with a sober person from the queue. Thankfully Jesus, Mary or the wee donkey must have been looking down on me as he opened the red rope and allowed me inside. "You go out again and you're not allowed back in." He warned.

I nodded, giving him my widest smile, and strutted through the bar and back to Mia.

She was staring at her phone as I approached the table, "Paddy's coming now!"

Her eyes shot up and a smile formed on her face, "Oh great!"

I smiled. I'd done something good. Mia was pleased with me.

"So…" I raced my mind for conversation topics. I loved Mia but I didn't know how far I could go or what I could ask without overstepping any boundaries, "Uh - did you know Derek well?"

She sucked in a deep breath, "I knew of him. He was never very present in the business however."

"Ah."

"Seemed like a lovely guy. But he had no clue about anything we were doing in Belfast. Apex and America was his North Star."

I nodded. It made sense that I'd never met or really heard of him.

"He was like this invisible figure." Mia giggled, and took a large sip of her drink, "He never complimented us when we did something good, only criticised when something bad happened."

"Bad things don't seem to happen that often-"

Mia laughed, "Tell you the truth…" she paused, looking down at her drink. She was battling with her thoughts.

"Hmm?" I encouraged gently.

"I believe Spotlight fell behind in Derek's priority list. None of his family in Belfast wanted to be part of it, so myself… and a few other original staff members have helped it grow and stand on its feet…" She bit her lip, unsure if she should continue. "Whilst we are one of the top performing studios in Northern Ireland, we're nowhere near on the same level as Apex."

Mia glanced around the bar, scanning once again. "This is confidential… b-but due to Derek's passing, his wife now owns the majority stock, a-and we have knowledge to believe that s-she would like to sell or d-dissolve the business." Mia's shoulders were back, and her lips were pinched together. I could tell by the glimmer in her eyes that she didn't want to and shouldn't be delivering this information, but it was probably eating her alive. Her admission was also probably fuelled by the alcohol that we were quickly downing.

"Hence the budget cuts and lay-offs?" I asked.

"Eh – it's more about budget re-allocation than cuts. I want to really move us into the future. We're very stuck on tradition and some people within the business seem hesitant or down right against change."

I instantly thought of the colleagues who I knew would resist. "Right…" I nodded.

We both sipped on our drinks, unsure what to say next. We trusted each other, but both knew we probably shouldn't be having this conversation. "Can I ask you something?"

"Sure."

"What can I do? I love my job but-"

My phone rang, interrupting our conversation.

PADDY

Mia nodded for me to answer.

"Hello?" I shouted, hoping he could hear me above the background noise. I pressed my free hand against my ear to try focus in on him.

"Where are you?" He was barely understandable.

"Harp."

"Aye but where?"

I looked around the bar, "front right near the stage-" and then I spotted him, walking inside. I stood up from my seat, waving. It took him a minute but eventually he spotted me.

That was fast... I thought he'd be 20 minutes. Maybe he'd been hiding in the office, working late.

Paddy, dressed in the same clothes from earlier in the day, glided through the crowd towards our table. "Packed! Isn't it?"

Mia nodded, "Mad."

"How'd you even get in?" I questioned, eyeing up the bald bouncer again.

"Mate – I'm a regular." He flipped some imaginary hair over his shoulders, "Basically own the place."

Of course. He was here most Fridays. The life of the party, our Paddy. If he wasn't working, he was out socialising.

"What are we drinking?" he looked at the table, spotting our almost empty drinks.

"Surprise me." I laughed. Mia rolled her eyes, "A G&T for me. Single, not double. I need to head home soon." She shot him a warning look, which he clearly ignored.

Paddy gasped, "I just got here. You aren't leaving anytime soon." He walked to the bar and was served almost immediately.

"God, I love him."

Mia raised her eyebrows, "Have you two ever- "

"Oh - no no no," my eyes basically bulged out of my head at her question, "I – no – he's like the brother I never had."

"Ah – okay." She looked towards him, "I just see how close you both are and if you ever wanted to, it's technically not breaking any employee guidelines, but I'd like to kno-"

"Mia, I can assure you... As much as I love him, the thought of loving him as anything other than a brother, makes me want to vomit."

"Why are you vomiting?" Our conversation was interrupted as he sat pints of some kind of beer onto our table. "One sec."

He walked back towards the bar, returning with not one, but two gin and tonics for Mia. My heart pounded. Paddy and I had never had this conversation. Although I didn't think he had feelings towards me, the tiny voice in my head wondered 'what if.' I immediately shut the voice up. *God no.*

"You said single... so I got you two drinks, both with single shots." He winked at Mia and pulled a seat to our table. "So – why are you vomiting?"

I looked towards Mia for help, but she abandoned me and began gulping at her drink. Gently, I touched Paddy's hand and inhaled deeply, "So I love you."

He cringed, turning his nose up, "right..."
Good response. That's what I wanted.

"And Mia asked if I – if we had ever –"

His face twisted, "Oh god, no!" I swore a shiver ran down his spine the same moment relief flooded through me.

I smiled at Mia, "see."

Paddy's face looked like he'd just smelled pure and utter shite. He looked ill.

"Hold on- why not? Am I not fit enough?" I teased, acting offended.

Fit

Definition : not in the athletic sense... but goodlooking / attractive...

"You're fit but I don't know. It's not that I don't think you're attractive, because you are… I- "

I held back a laugh as Paddy tried to defend his reaction.

"Like me, you… you and I. We just don't fit – that way…" he continued. "Right?"

"What way exactly?" Mia questioned, provoking him.

"The way that -…" he paused, trying to form his sentence, "Anna gets it. I love her but also hate her. She's can be really feckin' annoying."

"Oi!" I slapped his arm. "Don't be rude!"

"Okay maybe hate was a bit of a harsh word… You're too easy to take the piss out of."

Take the piss
Definition: Make fun of

I narrowed my eyes at him. Mia snorted a laugh.

"Look, look. Don't go taking offence!" Paddy raised his hands in defence, "I think you're amazing and you entertain me more than anyone I've ever met. Your stories and love life should be televised. It would make great reality TV!"

I bit my lip; he was probably right. *Definitely right, actually.* It was a total shit show and I'd yet to update him on James' texts tonight. He'd have something, probably comical but comforting to say about that.

"What about a podcast?" Mia interrupted my thoughts.

"What?" Paddy and I asked in unison.

"What if you had your own podcast… talking about this apparently humorous and captivating love life of yours…?"

She couldn't be serious. I didn't know how to respond to her suggestion. *Hosting a podcast? Dear god, no.*

"Genius…" Paddy whispered, "Feckin' hell, Anna… that would get some ratings!"

I shook my head, silent.

"You have so many stories! People would love it!" he gushed. "Could this be part of our digital transformation?" He turned to Mia, and I looked up, trying to judge her response.

"It's exactly the type of thing we need." Her eyes were alight, making me nervous.

"Anna?"

I looked back at Paddy. He was ready to jump from his chair with excitement. Meanwhile, I wanted the ground to swallow me up. Mia, on the other hand, seemed to be deep in contemplation. Her thoughtful gaze suggested she was weighing the potential impact of such a venture.

"Oh…I'm not sure." I replied.

Mia sighed, her fingers tapping rhythmically on the table. "I don't know, I just got this vision…"

Paddy's enthusiasm grew, but I remained sceptical. Mia continued, "Imagine the engagement, the conversations it could spark. People crave authenticity, and your stories have that… raw charm."

"I-I really don't know." I mumbled. *I didn't even want to consider the possibility.* "I plan on staying out of drama and as far away from men as possible."

Especially now that things were finished with James… kind of… he could still text me and apologise. We could start over…

"Understandable." Mia laughed, "But, I think opening yourself up to new experiences is the best way to get over a bad one…"

She kind of had a point.

As Paddy and Mia continued to discuss the potential of the podcast, my mind raced with doubts. I couldn't possibly share the chaotic mess of my love life with the world, could I? Mia's persuasive arguments, however, planted a seed of curiosity that lingered in my thoughts. The pressure built, crawling up the back of my spine as I wondered if my current job would be at risk if I turned down the offer.

"I guess…" I muttered. "I don't know. Can I think about it?"

Paddy clasped his hands together in a small celebration.

"I'm not offering you a show just yet…" Mia interrupted, "However, there's potential. If you're interested, come to me this week with a proposal. A name, a few episode concepts, and how often you would feel comfortable releasing."

Jesus Christ.

My stomach fluttered. Part of me wondered, if I was to have my own show, then I couldn't be fired from Spotlight in the near future? The other part of me was shuddering inside. How could I talk about the men I dated without their identities being revealed and relationships being ruined? I also felt nauseous at the thought of entering any more relationships or 'situationships' because, let's face it, men are fucking dickheads.

CHAPTER TWO
Hanging Like A Bat

Definition : extremely hungover after consuming a large amount of alcohol

Bang. Bang. Bang.

"ANNA!"

My eyes felt too heavy to open, but fucking hell...the noise of someone banging on a door was relentless. Very slowly, I opened one eye lid and then another to try to make sense of my surroundings. Thankfully, I was in my own apartment and fully dressed, in my clothes from the day before, shoes and all. Not ideal but still half an achievement.

The banging continued as I carefully stood up from my bed, feeling the blood rush from my head to my toes.

"I'm coming!" I attempted to yell, although my throat sounded and felt like sandpaper.

I already knew it was Grace before I opened the door.

"Hi," I grumbled.

She opened her mouth to speak, then paused, looking me up and down.

"What happened to you?" she asked, genuinely concerned. "And what's in your hair?" She picked out what looked like a chicken nugget crumb.

When did I have nuggets? I'm meant to be vegetarian. "I wish I had an answer, but I don't remember much," I replied. "Come in."

Grace stepped inside, visibly relieved. Her eyes softened with genuine concern. "Did you just get home?" she asked, eyeing me up and down.

I shrugged off my shoes. "I don't think so. Drunk me just doesn't like pyjamas, apparently."

I took note of her appearance. Glowing, goddess-like as usual. A stark contrast from the crumbs in my hair. I admired how hers was so silky smooth.

"Coffee?" I asked.

She nodded and immediately went to the kitchen. "Go sort yourself out; I'll make it."

I headed for the bathroom and began washing my face, hoping the cold water would wake me up and relieve the headache I could feel building.

"I was worried about you. I tried calling you twice last night and three times this morning," she shouted over the sound of the kettle.

"Sorry! I was avoiding my phone!" I screamed down the hallway.

"Why?"

I cleared my throat and splashed some more cold water over my skin. "James."

It hurt to say his name. It wasn't as easy to discard my feelings while sober, even worse while hungover. Grace's reflection appeared a moment later. She stood behind me as I washed my face.

"What happened this time?" Her bushy eyebrows furrowed, heavy with concern.

"He actually ended things," I sighed, wiping oatmeal cleanser from my cheek. "Texted me last night. I should have told you, but I was out with my boss and I didn't want to let him get to me. So, I immediately tried to ignore it…"

She lifted a clean towel from the hook on my bathroom wall and handed it to me, so I could dry my face. "Are you okay?"

I shrugged nonchalantly. "Eh…I guess."

My pillowcases told a different story. Black mascara stains covered them from when I'd drunkenly crawled into bed and cried myself to sleep.

"Throw on something comfy, and we can chat about it in the kitchen." She squeezed my shoulder and disappeared to give me the space I needed to organise my thoughts. I wiped my face once again and brushed a comb through my tangled hair, automatically improving my appearance. I could hear Grace in the kitchen; she'd turned on some light music and was no doubt preparing something for me to eat, as well as coffee for us to sip on. My stomach grumbled with hunger. I needed a hangover feast.

I peeled off my clothes from the night before, feeling relieved to be rid of the smell of Guinness and cigarette smoke. I didn't want to leave her alone for too long, so I quickly wiped my body with some baby wipes instead of taking a shower. I pulled on an oversized green jumper, which I'd owned for far too long, and a pair of black comfy leggings.

The smell of toast drew my stomach towards the kitchen. Grace sat at the table, chewing on a piece while reading a fashion magazine that she'd left at my apartment a few days prior.

"See – this is why I love you." I drooled, sitting at the table. She had placed every condiment I owned in front of my toast. I decided to lather one piece with Nutella and another with butter and marmalade.

She lifted her half-eaten triangle and smiled at me, her mouth full.

"Mmmmhmm." I moaned, biting.

"We've to meet 'Liv in-" she looked at her watch, "23 minutes."

I sank deeper into my chair and took another bite. "K. But I'm going like this."

She stifled a laugh. "Fine by me."

Olivia would be dressed to the gods. She was practically Belfast's version of Carrie Bradshaw.

"So, James…" She breached the subject gently, but I still wasn't ready to talk.

"Could you call my phone? I'm not sure where I put it…"

She clicked her tongue against the roof of her mouth but said nothing. I stood up, chasing the sound of it ringing. Thank god it was still charged.

"Try again," I said as it stopped.

I followed the sound to my coat closet, where I not only found my phone (which was in my handbag… obviously) but also a bright orange traffic cone. I had no idea where it came from and refused to entertain the hazy memories of me believing it would be hilarious to bring it home while I was highly intoxicated. I picked up my phone and closed the door on the mystery cone. That was another problem for another time.

"Did you get it?" Grace asked.

"Yeah." I stood at the doorway, sickened as I read through my texts and call log.

"I called James twice last night and texted him." I hid my embarrassment, burying my face in the sleeves of my jumper.

"Well, you know what they say!"

"What?"

"If you don't drink, how else will your ex know you love him at 2 am?" Grace laughed. She was doing her best to lighten the mood.

I laughed, feeling a little bit of a sting. We continued talking until our coffees went cold, and Olivia called, of course, asking where the fuck we were.

As expected, she stood at the doorway to Established Coffee in knee high boots, a sparkly skirt and booby blouse. She had tits that made every girl jealous and every guy drool.

"I'm bloody frozen!" was the first thing she said. "Why do you look like you're going through a divorce?" was the second.

I stifled a laugh. Whilst her comment was mildly offensive, there was some truth to it. At least I didn't look as rough as I felt inside.

"Olivia!" Grace scolded.

She rolled her eyes in response, "All I'm saying is that Saturday brunch is a very instagrammable occasion…"

I couldn't hold back my laugh this time. "Fuck sake."

Her hair was curled to perfection. It almost looked like she'd been for a bouncy blow-dry…

We waited another ten minutes before being seated. Usually, I'd have suggested we go elsewhere instead of waiting, but this morning… or should I say afternoon, I was grateful for the fresh crisp air.

Inside we were met by the usual crowd. Hipsters with their heads in either a MacBook or a hardcover book… also occasionally an iPad but only if they had an apple pencil to go with it. An elderly couple sat in the corner, a contrast from the younger crowd but not out of place. Established was a friendly spot. The inviting twelve-seater table at the heart of the space encouraged connections, coaxing smiles and conversations from customers. As the rich aroma of coffee enveloped us, a gentleman at the communal table winced slightly after sipping his robust brew. A quick follow-up with a sip of water revealed the love-hate relationship he shared with the potent beverage. Established Coffee blends were loved by many overcaffeinated coffee connoisseurs, and personally, I was all about it, particularly when served iced with a touch of honey added for natural sweetness. At Established, there was no room for sugary syrups; they were too trendy and organic for such conventional additives. Nevertheless, it remained one of the best spots in Belfast.

My mouth watered as I ordered brioche French toast with blackberry compote and maple syrup. Even though I'd just eaten two slices of toast, I desperately wanted more carbs and sugar. Olivia went for the house-made granola and yogurt, whilst Grace opted for the wholesome honey coconut porridge. The healthy alternatives that I, with my post-hangover disregard for calorie counting, blissfully ignored.

We took our seats after ordering at the till and shortly after, our trio of matcha lattes arrived at the table. As I lifted the cup to my lips, the frothy warmth enveloped my senses, creating a moment of pure contentment. I couldn't help but hum in satisfaction, grateful I had chosen to venture out of my apartment. Otherwise, I'd have lay half asleep on the sofa all day binge-ing Netflix and reading… and re-reading James' texts. I shook the thought of him from my brain.

"How was last night 'Liv?" Grace asked.

She inhaled deeply and her eyes rolled to the back of her head, "Orgasmic!!"

Lord. She had zero shame. Zero.

I choked on my latte and began to laugh. I admired Olivia massively for her confidence, but sometimes I wished she'd be a little quieter so people around us wouldn't stare in horror at her outbursts.

Grace shushed her, "someone will hear you!"

To our right, a moppy brown-haired man sat with headphones covering his head as he wrote in some kind of journal. Two espresso cups sat on the table in front of him. One empty. One barely touched. I prayed his music was loud. Knowing Olivia, we were about to hear another one of her fascinating 'sexcapades'.

She cocked her head to the side, a smirk appearing on her face. "Three orgasms."

Grace looked mortified. Talking about sex in public was her idea of hell. Christ, even talking about it in private made her squirm.

"Three? Wow." I was genuinely impressed. I'd never had a man give me an orgasm before. James tried but… *STOP THINKING ABOUT*

HIM.

"Honestly, she was – ahhhhmazing."

What?

"She?" Grace questioned, equally as confused as I, "What about that guy Callum you were dating? Who… she?" Her tone alight with surprise.

"She…" Olivia's eyes were hazy as she probably replayed her antics from the night before.

"You slept with a girl?" I asked. That was a first… and 'Liv didn't have many firsts left to experience. She'd been there done that with most things.

She nodded, sharing a playful grin.

"Ahhh…that explains the three o's?" I could easily give myself three orgasms if I wanted to, but a man couldn't even gift me one. But a woman… she knew where the clit was for sure.

"I'm obviously not judging – at all by the way." Grace lifted her hands in defence, interrupting, "I love that for you… but Cal-"

"Callum is – eugh. Boring! Old news." Olivia scoffed and began sipping on her matcha.

I admired how she could discard unwanted relationships so easily, but it also scared the shit out of me. Before we could continue our conversation, our food arrived. As hard as I tried to focus on the chatter, I was practically drooling as the smell of sugar engulfed my senses.

"Just wasn't doing it for me anymore…" I snapped back to reality, catching the end of Olivia's sentence.

"So you just ended it? How?" Grace asked.

"I called him up and said that I really wanted a relationship and he basically ended it for me." She laughed and took a spoonful of granola. "Men – our age – don't want a relationship. They want fun! Offering commitment to a fuckboy is the easiest way to get rid of him."

"Christ." I mumbled.

"What's wrong with being committed at 23?" Grace asked.

"24. You're 24." I replied. "Liv and I are 23."

Grace swatted me with her napkin. "I'm 20 inside."

"So anyways… last night…" As Olivia informed us of how she met her lady friend, my mind wandered to the main dilemma which had been bubbling in my mind.

Not James…

Mia wanted me to pitch an idea for my own podcast and as Olivia spoke, I couldn't help but think she'd make a much better host. I appreciated how fearless she was with her sexuality. There was no reason for her not to be… I just struggled with my own. If my show was to feature around relationships and include sex talk, I'd have to make her a 'character.'

Grace too. She was timid but self-confident. She adapted a 'no bullshit' attitude when it came to men. One flicker of a red flag and she was out. I on the other hand didn't mind a red flag. I could often squint, and they'd turn pink… and pink was one of my favourite colours.

"Do you think you'll see her again?" Grace asked.

"No. I've had a taste and I'm satisfied." She took a deep breath, as if she was savouring the memory.

"So, are you dating girls now?" I asked. It was new and I felt surprised at her sudden interest in dating women, but if she was happy, then that was obviously all that mattered.

She shrugged, "I'll date anyone. I'm seeing Aiden tonight."

"Who's Aiden?" Grace asked. I was as clueless as her.

"I matched with him on Bumble last week. Anyways, enough about me, how's James?"

My stomach twisted. *I knew this was coming.*

So, I filled them in, watching their expressions change from curious to furious. As I read out his texts… I avoided reading my heated, drunken replies. I felt embarrassed at how I could be so stupid.

1.43am - ANNA
I'm really hurt by this

1.50am – ANNA
It just feels so unfair after the time we've spent together. I thought we had something special…

1.51am – ANNA
You said you could see yourself falling in love with me…

1.54am – ANNA
What changed? Can you at least give me that?

James hadn't replied, but he'd read every message. My desperation made me feel sick.

"He's a coward!" Grace scowled.

"Honestly, he's just a man." Olivia shrugged, "They're all afraid of commitment, like I said earlier."

"I disagree. I don't think all men are. Just this one, and a handful of others. We shouldn't generalise!" Grace interrupted. "We all have our own trauma and-"

I unintentionally interrupted, "I don't know what to do now. Do I just forget it ever happened or do I text hi-"

"NO!" they both shouted at the same time.

I filled my mouth with another forkful of French toast, knowing I wouldn't be allowed to suggest anything else. I swallowed, hoping to subdue the pit of nausea that was bubbling deep in my stomach.

"Do you really want to know how to get over him?" Olivia questioned.

I nodded and dabbed leftover sticky syrup from the corner of my mouth.

"You get under someone else." She announced.

In response to that, Grace choked and spat matcha all over the table and Olivia's booby blouse… and that's how brunch ended.

***

On Monday morning, I found myself buoyed by a new wave of energy. Determined to shed the loungewear I had embraced the day before, I opted for confidence in my attire. I chose a cute black dress, accentuated with a chunky belt and stylish boots. Adding a touch of flair, I adorned a pair of patterned tights from Primark, purchased just a few days earlier. In my mind, they bore a striking resemblance to the outrageous £300 Gucci ones that adorned my 'Someday I will own these Wish List.'

As I strolled to work, I immersed myself in the divine melodies of our Lord and Saviour, Harry Styles, tuning out the world around me. I forced myself to believe that today would be a good day, despite the growing pit of nerves in my stomach. Two songs later, I took a deep breath and painted a smile on my face, removing my headphones as I entered the building.

"What's the craic?" I yawned.

Paddy occupied his desk, sporting a grey beanie and glasses that shielded his eyes. He stared intently at his computer screen, likely engrossed in the realm of listener analytics. That task was usually his first and most challenging of the day—determining the exact moment our listeners dropped off, followed by the inevitable request for me to decipher the reasons behind their disengagement.

"Have you sorted a proposal for your podcast yet?" he inquired.

"Ah – I'm doing great, Paddy, thanks for asking! Had a horrific hangover at the weekend. Texted my ex. Went for brunch. Read half of a gorgeously romantic novel. Only had one existential crisis and cried myself to sleep… wondering, will I always be single? What is wrong with me? Should I cut and dye my hair?" Sarcasm laced my words as I skilfully sidestepped his question.

I had a tentative concept for my podcast, but the show lacked a name, and the thought of executing it made me want to pee my pants.

Paddy forced a laugh and then immediately narrowed his eyes, squinting at me. "Wise up."

Wise Up

Definition: Another way of telling someone to stop making jokes / be sensible/stop being silly, etc.

"Coffee?" I asked, walking away towards the break room.

To my despair, he followed.

"Anna..."

I turned in my tracks and sucked in a long breath. "Okay! I—I don't know yet. I'm apprehensive. This is all a bit much for a Monday morning."

"What's scaring you?"

"I dunno... what will my parents think? What will—" I looked around the office, "Dillon! Jill... I don't know if I want my co-workers knowing the inside and out of my...sex life." I whispered.

Paddy laughed, "What they think about you or say about you is a reflection on them. As for outside the studio, you could be anonymous. Have a secret identity."

I paused. I hadn't considered that possibility. "How would that even work?"

"Well... legal could produce an NDA for everyone inside Spotlight to sign, pretty standard practice," he added. "We could record the show on... like... a Friday night... when most people aren't in the office."

God, he had an answer for everything. The weight of the decision lingered, but Paddy's practical suggestions eased the anxiety, though only slightly.

"Maybe you should host it since you've figured all of this out." I attempted to mask my insecurity with humour.

"Anna." He scowled. "You're being handed the reins to an opportunity that most people dream of."

"I know! That's what scares me!" I hissed, being careful that no one was within ear-range and could overhear us, "How do I know if I'm good enough?"

"You don't know. No one knows. But feel the fear and do it anyways!" He had a point.

"Ok, Mr. Inspirational Quotes. You should do a TED Talk."

He glared at me. "Anna…can you be serious for one moment? A lot of people are about to be made redundant, meanwhile you could be promoted!"

My muscles seized. I needed this job. This job was all I knew. I glanced around the office, my heart warming at the familiar friendly faces. I couldn't say goodbye to any of this.

"Okay, okay!" I sighed, finally admitting my feelings. "I want to do it. But I have no idea where to start." The realisation hit me like a ton of bricks, and the apprehension transformed into a moment of clarity. There was no turning back; I had to embrace this opportunity, uncertainty, and all.

"Well let's sit down and brainstorm so you can give Mia your concept this afternoon." Paddy walked back towards his desk, a smile plastered across his face. I dragged my heels, wondering what the hell I was getting myself into.

The weekend had been dominated by contemplation of my potential podcast and he who shall not be named (not Voldemort… but James)… a name I'd prefer to erase from memory. Though a semblance of a vision had formed, the mere idea of divulging it tightened my chest. A swarm of sceptical questions prowled my mind, casting shadows over any potential for clarity.

Paddy hummed a tune, exuding a sense of tranquillity and creative readiness. His foot danced with anticipation… waiting on the thoughts I was struggling to share.

I sighed, appreciative of his unwavering support, whilst he opened a blank document poised to craft a plan.

"Right!" He swivelled toward me, theatrically waving his hand in front of my face.

I leaned back in my chair, parting my lips to speak. Hesitation crept in, and I closed my mouth, bewildered by the unexpected spectacle. He maintained his stare, eyebrows raised, completely unphased.

"What the fuck was that?" I chuckled.

"I just cleansed your aura. Saw it on TV last night," he shrugged. His upper lip twitched, attempting to restrain a smile.

My laughter persisted.

"It means that all of your bad energy is gone. From now on, it's nothing but good vibes and confidence."

"Ah. Okay." I giggled, "That's a new one."

He redirected his attention to the computer screen, "So… now that that's sorted, what kind of show would you like to have?"

I pursed my lips. The question that had lingered in my mind for days still seeking a satisfactory answer.

"I suppose I could play the role of an agony aunt, offering advice to local women dealing with their… issues," I sighed, battling against the waves of insecurity threatening to overwhelm me. It felt ironic – I struggled to heed my own counsel, yet there I was contemplating doling it out to others.

Sensing my shifting energy, he once again waved his hands in front of my face. "Snap out of it. Whatever insecure thoughts you're entertaining, toss them out the fucking window."

"It's a habit!" I defended. *One that I needed to break.*

Paddy raised an eyebrow, contemplating. "Well, you've given me solid dating advice before."

"I'll share stories about the men I encounter…" I paused, a mischievous grin forming, "But I'll have to give them nicknames to dodge any potential… lawsuits."

I chuckled at the notion. Despite my desire to expose James and caution every unsuspecting girl, the fear of him discovering my identity as host and potentially murdering me in my sleep… loomed large. After all, he knew the pin of my apartment building. It would also ruin any chances of us getting back together…

"Easy."

"James could go by…" I mentally scanned for suitable ideas.

"Dr Dickhead." Paddy suggested, a hint of distain in his voice.

"Hmmm…no…" I mused. Yes, he was a dickhead often, but we did share *some* nice moments.

"Mr Playa! Casanova. Dr Lurvvvvve." Paddy's Belfast accent attempted a cringe-worthy American imitation.

"I feel sick." I shivered, feeling an instant ick for Paddy's attempt, "Absolutely not."

"Then what?"

"Can I swear?"

He met my gaze with a deadpan expression. "Yes. It's a podcast. Not 8am school-breakfast radio."

"Fuckboy." I said, swallowing the lump in my throat. The discomfort and unconventional nature of the conversation was palpable.

"Mr Fuckboy." Paddy affirmed, "SEE? Perfect! Breaking all traditional boundaries. Now, let's plan the flow of the first episode…"

"This is ridiculous." I admitted, my mind racing with the surrealness of it all.

"You've got the best stories, this part will be a breeze!"

Unlocking the part of my brain labelled 'exes and emotional traumas' made me uneasy. It felt like unravelling a black book that I wanted to bury. The past is the past… right?

Then, a lightbulb moment. "What if I use the show as a journal?" I suggested.

"Explain?"

"Every week, I'll talk about what I've experienced… I'll document the NOW." *And conveniently sidestep the past.*

"Are your weeks interesting enough for that?" Paddy smirked, well aware that my weeks usually revolved around work, Netflix, and coffee or drinks with Olivia and Grace.

"Well… I guess I'll just have to spice things up. Meet more men. Experience more. Live a more zestful life."

Who knows? Maybe I'll even have my first orgasm. The last part remained unspoken…

"How would you do that?" Paddy asked, a mix of curiosity and doubt.

"Olivia loves any excuse to leave her apartment, so I've already got a partner in crime."

"Right…" Paddy looked unconvinced. "What could go wrong?"

"Lots of things probably. But Grace will be there to help us out of jail."

A few hours of brainstorming pursued and by the time lunch rolled around, I felt excited by my new potential career shift… however, my meeting with Mia loomed heavy on my shoulders. She could absolutely hate the concept. Then what? Would I still have a job?

I left the office for some fresh air and dandered down to Established to pick up a quick bite for lunch. As I nibbled on a toasted cheese croissant, my insecurities about the podcast began to take over. I pulled out my phone and began typing into my notes app.

Reasons WHY NOT

1. Only had sex… 9 times? All with the same man.
2. Never had an orgasm from 'penetrative' sex… or a partner. Only

from myself.

3. Only given a handful of blowjobs. All were amazing (so he said). 4. Probably because I'd read every Cosmo article on the internet AND listened to 'Call Her Daddy' podcast. Thank you, Alex Cooper.

5. No clue how the male brain works. Does anyone though?

6. Severely lacking in confidence. Can't look at my naked body without cringing at my hip dips, stretch marks, and thighs.

7. Need to lose a few kilos... at least the podcast isn't filmed... just audio and anonymous. Doesn't help with dating though...

8. Going through the emotions of a break up with a man I was never really dating. Pathetic.

9. Easily intimidated by other women. Embarrassing.

10. I don't have a lot of friends. I've never been popular. I don't like many people.

11. I don't know who I am or what I want in life. Never mind a partner.

The thought of letting Mia down made bile rise to the back of my throat. I couldn't.

As I read over my list, I began to think... Do other people share these experiences? Yes, I hadn't a clue about men and dating... but maybe this would give me the opportunity to learn? I'd never had a one-night stand. I could count the people I'd kissed on my hands. I hadn't a clue where my G Spot was, and neither had James obviously. I was actually worried that I didn't have one at all. Confidence was an issue I'd struggled with forever, but maybe this was my chance to overcome my insecurities? A reinvention... I could craft a brand-new identity.

Without giving myself any more time to overthink, I walked through the streets of Belfast ready to launch myself into the unexpected.

This is where the Belle of Belfast was born. *Kind of.*

CHAPTER THREE
Up To High Doh

Definition : To be in a very nervous or excited state

Note to self: *Purchase new nail polish ASAP. My nails have reached a point of disgrace.*

I found myself staring at the chipped polish, unable to resist picking it off while waiting for Mia to return from a meeting. It was crucial I spoke to her before I talked myself out of my decision.

"Ready?" she appeared moments later, almost magically, in front of my desk.

I instantly stood, "Ye-yes. Ready!"

She looked as elegant as always, donning a black jumpsuit and her classic Louboutin heels. Her hair was styled into a slick bun, and her winged eyeliner was on point, as usual. Mia had a way of commanding attention when she entered a room. Just being around her boosted my confidence.

Following her Louboutin's with my clunky black boots from New

Look, I entered her office. Though I had stepped inside a few times before, it had always been brief. The room exuded an air of professionalism, with its plain walls adorned by framed pictures of esteemed company leaders, shelves displaying awards, and polished plaques commemorating significant achievements. The ambiance suggested a history of success and dedication which was quite the contrast to the current state of the station…with budget cuts, lack of sponsors and layoffs. History indeed.

Mia's large oak desk, positioned at the heart of the office, drew attention. An iMac sat prominently upon it, a sleek and modern contrast to the traditional richness of the desk. The surface was immaculately organised, conveying a sense of order and purpose.

As Mia maneuvered the Nespresso machine, an awkward silence settled over the room. The aroma of brewing coffee permeated the air, adding a layer of comfort to the professional setting. The hushed ambience allowed the details of the office to come into focus—the subtle hum of the technology, the sunlight filtering through the partially drawn blinds, and the meticulously arranged items on shelves.

"How are you feeling?" she asked, her question breaking through the quietude. Despite the immense power and responsibilities she held, Mia's presence continued to exert a calming influence on me.

"I'm unsure," I admitted, glancing around the office, "I probably shouldn't be saying that, but I'd be lying if I said I felt totally confident in the opportunity. I'd only be digging myself into a hole."

She turned, her lips pursed, and eyebrows drawn together, "Take a seat."

The chair was large and uncomfortable, seemingly designed for those averse to prolonged sitting. I wondered if Mia had deliberately chosen it, hoping that people's bums would hurt, so they'd have to leave and then her meetings would be kept short. Hers, on the other hand, appeared plush and inviting.

She handed me an americano in a matte black Spotlight mug,

prompting thoughts about updating our branding—it seemed rather dull.

"I'm just anxious that I don't have the experience." I admitted.

"Oh, you can learn it. There are plenty of people to help with recording each episode, handling the tech, and distribution-"

"No, that stuff I'm fine with. I mean… life experience to share on a show."

Mia's mouth formed an 'oh.'

"I have plenty of horror dating stories, but that's as far as it goes."

"What's holding you back from experiencing more? You're at the prime age to date, meet people, expose yourself to different scenarios…" She smiled, "You know, as women, we often carry the weight of expectations and judgments of starting something new. But your voice is powerful. And this show is not just about the experiences you've had, it's about your authenticity, your resilience…."

Her words made my stomach flutter with hope. "I want to. I do. I can try put myself out there more, as uncomfortable as it may be to begin with."

I chuckled into my coffee; apprehension built in my stomach. I had no idea what those situations were—maybe a new sex position? Sex toys? Did this all have to revolve around sex? Lord. To me, sex meant two partners in a relationship, and I was very much single and alone.

"I'd be lying if I said this industry was easy, especially for women. So, we have to have each other's back. I want you to do this. I want to help you do this. You have the opportunity to maybe break barriers and empower not just yourself, but countless others. And this show has the potential to do something amazing for the station."

I nodded; my cheeks flushed.

"I spoke with Paddy. He wouldn't shut up about the concept. Want to tell me more?" she encouraged.

As I filled Mia in on my idea of sex, dating, relationships, life lessons, and shared a few comical stories from my dating history, I didn't notice the time passing.

Over an hour later, a knock on the door interrupted us.

"Come in," she hollered.

"Sorry for interrupting," Craig, a sponsorships coordinator, popped his head around the door, "Mia, you have a meeting in Holywood in 25 minutes, do I need to reschedule? Or we can head on without you?"

"No, I'll be out in a minute," she sighed, "Is the car waiting?"

He nodded.

"Ok, be right out."

He closed the door behind him. I guessed our meeting was coming to an end.

"Sorry for taking up so much of your time," I blabbed and stood up without thinking. "I'll wash our cups." I reached over the table and lifted her coffee cup and mine.

"Anna?" she stopped me as I reached the door.

I turned on my heels, "Yep?"

"I want you to speak to your friends, see if they'd be comfortable sharing their opinions on the show too. You could also interview women across the country…"

"Belles of Belfast." I hummed.

"What?"

I shook my head and balanced both cups on one hand as I used the other to open the door. "Nothing, it was stupid."

"No – no – what was it?"

I paused and inhaled a large, much-needed breath. "Do you like the name 'Belles of Belfast' … like it means 'girls of Belfast'… like that song…"

Mia's eyebrows raised. "Great song…hmm…"

I nodded.

"Interesting. I really do think you should do this…" She encouraged.

While I was uncertain, afraid, anxious, I nodded in agreement. Less than 24 hours later, I was staring at my future – typed in black ink, and nothing felt real.

Belles of Belfast - A Proposal.

Hosted by Anna Mulholland *(Anonymous to listeners)*

Running Time : 30 – 45 minutes

Frequency : one show every seven days

Start Date : Friday 2nd July (TBC)

Preferred Time Slot : Podcast to premiere on Spotlight radio every Friday evening (between the hours of 10pm and 11pm) and will be available ON DEMAND on podcast hosting platforms after live stream. One episode per week.

Show Description : 30 minute weekly update / storytelling session on the romantic / life status of our main 'Belle' aka Anna. Thoughts and opinions from other anonymous 'Belles.' Followed by optional 10-15 minutes of Agony Aunt style Q&A, with appropriately themed music in between.

Target Audience : Gen Z and Millennial – primarily women but not limited to a female audience.

I turned to page two and read through the contract. Then at the bottom…

If you agree to the terms of this employment offer, please sign, and return a copy of this document.

Sincerely,

Mia Robinson

Spotlight Radio // Station Director

I stared at the pages in complete disbelief, feeling a whirlwind of excitement, anxiety, and dread. My palms felt sweaty as I clutched my pen, my fingers tingling in anticipation of a decision.

The idea that my personal experiences could potentially help others resonated with me, even if I hadn't amassed a wealth of life stories just yet. At least I had Olivia, with her multitude of tales, sure to provide an entertaining character, and Grace, offering heart-warming advice despite her avoidance of men like the plague.

I gazed back at the contract. My name was in big bold letters. Miss Anna Mulholland. They wanted me. Clearly, they believed I was capable of the job.

Without giving myself any more time to overthink, I took my pen, signed the contract, and marched to Mia's office.

I knocked on the door and, after a brief moment, was met with a calm 'come in.'

"Signed." I spoke confidently and placed the contract onto the desk in front of her.

Mia's face lit up with genuine joy, a sparkle in her eyes. "Anna, this is so exciting! I knew you had it in you. This podcast is going to be something special; I can feel it."

Her enthusiasm was contagious, and as she expressed her delight, the weight on my shoulders lifted. Mia seemed genuinely thrilled about the prospect.

She informed me that Paddy would be my program coordinator, and the news made her smile even wider. "He's as excited as I am."

I left her office with a newfound sense of confidence, her infectious happiness echoing in my ears. The pressure was still there, but Mia's support made it feel like a challenge worth embracing. I walked home that evening feeling not just bubbly, but genuinely excited about the journey ahead. I couldn't wait to share the news with the girls and embark on this new chapter of my career.

By 7.30 pm, I was ready for a casual night out—just dinner and a couple of drinks. Grace arrived first, on time as usual. Olivia, fashionably late, followed 25 minutes later. She was looking a bit too glamourous for a Monday night out in Belfast, but I didn't expect anything less.

"Oh, you both just look so cute," she gushed as she walked in.

"Thanks, Liv. So do you," Grace replied.

"I love that top," she said, nodding towards my 'corset like' top. It was quite booby, a bit tight. I'd had it for a while, but never had the confidence to wear it. However, tonight marked a new beginning. A night for celebrating a new job, and ... a new me

"What's the plan then?" Grace asked.

"I was thinking of Bootleggers?" I suggested.

Bootleggers was a cool spot with great bar-type food, good vibes, and occasionally, some good-looking men

Baltic

Definition: a low temperature; cold weather; a cold environment.

We sat outside at a funky looking picnic table and snacked on a few food platters. It was baltic, as Belfast often was, but thankfully the outdoor heaters were doing a decent job at keeping us warm... until a gust of wind blew every so often.

Each time Grace complained that we were going to get a foundering and needed to sit inside. But Olivia claimed that the good-looking men only sat outside, so we needed to suck it up. Usually, I'd be on Grace's side, but tonight I was a new woman, who needed to be surrounded by an abundance of men.

A Foundering

Definition: When you're in the cold for an extended period of time and end up sick.

I was extremely excited to share my news with them, surprised I had lasted until after our food.

"So, I need to tell you both something..." I couldn't conceal my excitement, feeling like I was ready to explode.

"Go on then..." Olivia encouraged.

As I filled them in on the details of the show, I watched as they both had mixed expressions.

Olivia, seemingly elated, was smiling wide. "This is incredible. I mean, about time you got your ass on the market."

"But… you've only just split from James…like two…or three days ago?"

I felt a sting hearing Grace say his name. He treated me so badly, and yet… I allowed it. I was so weak. I wasn't good enough. I gulped, feeling anxious even thinking about him.

"Anna, are you sure? This seems like a lot of personal information to be sharing publicly." Grace's brows were pulled together, concerned.

I nodded. "I get what you're saying… but it's going to be anonymous. So, no one will know my identity."

I started to feel doubtful again. *If I wasn't good enough for James, who would I be good enough for? What man would actually want me? How could I have something meaningful to share with an audience each week?*

"This is madness!" Olivia screamed, clapping her hands together. "I'm so excited! Like I said, best way to get over someone… is to get under someone else!"

I kept looking at Grace, waiting for her to speak again. "I just don't know how much getting 'under' someone will help you right now. I think the show is a good concept, and great that your identity is protected… I just want to see you do well."

"I know, I'm not rushing to sleep with someone else. I mean, yes, I'd like to experience more, and I'm open to those … experiences… but -"

"But you should – it's great fun!" Liv cheered.

"You need to keep your self-respect." Grace interrupted.

"Yeah, what's left of it." I took another sip of my drink, my thoughts drifting to the wounds James had left.

"Stop that. You're an amazing person, and your boss obviously thinks highly of you to put you in this position. Hold yourself with the same level of respect. Don't create drama in your life, just to entertain an audience." Grace reached out and squeezed my hand.

"Thank you." I smiled, really appreciating her words.

"I think this is class. It will give you a chance to experiment more and find what you like." Olivia added.

"Plus, many women probably go through what I'm currently going through." I responded. "Right?"

I still felt hesitant. Anxiety still bubbled.

"Okay… okay… To new opportunities and experiences." Grace lifted her glass, signalling for a toast.

"To the Belle of Belfast!" Olivia giggled.

Our glasses clinked together, creating a sound of relief. We all smiled. I was grateful for sharing the news in person, appreciating Grace's advice, and glad to have Olivia's support in navigating this new journey.

Yet, deep down a lingering embarrassment whispered through me. Despite James hurting me, I couldn't deny the craving, the shame of still wanting him. It was a secret I held close, one I knew I shouldn't confess, even to my closest friends.

"Three shots of Tequila." The waiter interrupted and began to set drinks on our table.

"Sorry we didn't order these." Grace explained.

"It's fine, though. Uh, I'll pay for them." I smiled, scrambling through my purse for my bank card. I hated confrontation and worried about the hassle he would get if he returned with the drinks.

"They're already paid for." He smiled and left without saying a word.

Oh. We all looked at each other.

"I wonder who sent these?" Grace sniffed the Tequila and cringed.

"Told you sitting outside was a good idea." Olivia laughed. We all began looking around, hoping to spot a group of men who had obviously sent the drinks to our table.

Unfortunately, none. I kept looking around and caught the eye of a blonde-haired muscular man. He looked like the rugby player type. Aka… my type. Liv's type. Not really Grace's type.

"So don't look round, but there's a group of guys. I just made eye contact with one of them, blonde hair, looks like a rugby boy."

Both girls instantly looked round.

"Oh, for fuck's sake, what part of 'don't look round' do you not understand?" I giggled.

We all laughed and downed our tequila shots. Grace gagged, threatening to throw up.

Mr. Rugby player kept making glances. I pushed my usual feeling of discomfort down and decided to let my new alter ego come out to play. *I could do this. I wanted to do this.* I just needed to soak up some of Olivia's confidence.

"I'm gonna go over to them." Olivia stood up from the table, pulling at her dress.

"What? No, you are not." Grace winced. "Wise up! Let them come to you-"

"Watch me." She jumped up and walked to their table, oozing with confidence.

"She's on the pull…" I snickered.

On The Pull

Definition: To be out (usually drinking) with the aim of finding a partner to bring home.

She stuck out her hand towards a brown-haired man, for a handshake. Some words were exchanged, and then she walked back over to our table.

Within a quick minute of her sitting down, the three guys stood up and began walking over towards us.

"What's happening?" Grace asked, avoiding turning her head to look.

"They're c-coming over." I panicked. Her eyes widened.

"What's the craic, ladies? Can you spare some room?" Mr. Rugby player asked.

I gracefully slid further down the bench, creating space for him to squeeze in beside me. His friend joined, pushing me even closer to the edge. The brown-haired man, who Olivia had spoken to, nestled himself between her and Grace.

Mr. Rugby player placed his palm on my lower back as he sat down. Though I didn't entirely appreciate his touch, I remained silent. He seemed harmless?

"Excuse me, mate." The brown-haired man hailed the waiter. "Yeah, could we get three Corona and - ladies?"

"Three vodka tonics." Olivia confidently replied.

Despite sticking to Gin throughout, with the exception of one Tequila shot, I didn't want to mix my drinks. Yet, the decision was made for me. *Perhaps it would help me loosen up a bit.*

"Cheers, mate." The brown-haired man nodded at the waiter as he noted down our order.

I found the waiter more attractive than any of the men at our table. Slightly curly brown hair and piercing green eyes – he had a magnetic charm.

I discovered that Mr. Rugby player's name was Darren, hailing from Holywood. I could sense his high-class aura from his sharp haircut, Veja trainers, and Polo Ralph Lauren jacket.

"You're gorgeous," he said, looking down at me. "How many drinks have you had? I think you need another."

"Thank you." I smiled politely. "I'm good, still sipping on this one. Thanks, though."

"And what about me?" He flashed a set of perfect white teeth.

"Would you like another drink?"

"No, am I attractive?"

"Oh, uh, you're very handsome." I awkwardly responded, giving him

69

the validation, he was craving.

His hand lingered on my lower back, rubbing his thumb up and down, and he winked at me – instantly giving me the ick. I didn't like him. Sure, he was attractive, but he exuded a 'fuckboy' vibe, reminding me of James.

The other two, Leo and Henry, both studied Sports Psychology at Ulster University. Leo had Olivia charmed as soon as he accepted her handshake. The two flirted back and forth, even doing a shot of Fireball together. Grace, on the other hand, wasn't interested in Henry. She steered the conversation toward his studies and five-year plan, disregarding any advances or flirtation on his part.

I let Mr. Rugby Player, or rather Darren, continue his attempts at charming me. I smiled along but skilfully avoided reciprocating his flirtatious advances. When his hand moved lower, feeling under the lining of my jeans, I promptly jumped up and asked Grace to accompany me to the bathroom.

CHAPTER FOUR
A Ride

Definition: Sex. It means sex.

The bathroom smelled of piss. After ten-minutes in the queue, we finally got in. With dim lighting, flickering neon signs, and a mirror adorned with smudged lipstick marks reflecting the camaraderie of the night, it offered a moment of respite.

"I'm no weather woman, but I'm forecasting a fucking incident tonight," I said, blotting my makeup with toilet paper.

"What?" Grace giggled. "You're not interested?"

"No, he won't keep his hands off me though," I laughed. "I wanna go home."

She shook her head and bit her lips to hide a smile. "Liv's enjoying herself."

"Are we surprised?"

"No. I just... didn't she just go out with that guy Aiden from... what was it... Bumble or Hinge? What happened to him?"

Unfortunately, this was a recurring pattern with Olivia. She'd grow bored of her current conquest and swiftly move on to a new one. Meanwhile, I struggled to even attract and keep one man.

"What do we do?" I asked, already anticipating the response.

"I don't think there's much we can do." Grace sighed, popping her lipstick back into her purse.

Returning to our table, we noticed both Mr. Rugby Player and Henry were gone. Leo chatted with our waiter in the corner while smoking a cigarette.

"Where'd they go?" I asked.

"Oh, they're off to Ollie's!" Olivia exclaimed, already on her feet and smoothing out her dress with a touch of anticipation. Ollie's, nestled in the basement of the Merchant Hotel, was more than just a nightclub. it exuded a unique and effortlessly cool vibe, having once served as a bank vault. It gave Soho House energy, with loyal members who attended each week to socialise; especially on Monopollie Mondays – where drinks were on offer and the line was down the street. The allure of Ollie's extended beyond its ideal location; it was a convergence point for a diverse crowd. University students, trendsetting influencers, and footballers, who loved buying bottles just so they could flex on their Instagram stories. The air also buzzed with the energy of rich older couples and their friends, appearing fashionably late at 1am after the Merchant Cocktail Bar closed, eager to extend the night's festivities… because, why let the party end?

Now, Ollie's nightclub was Olivia's turf, a top pick in her weekly playbook. I already had a hunch she'd be heading there, but I couldn't help but tease her. "And where are you going?"

"Hell most likely." She downed the remainder of her drink. "See ya! Love ya!"

She started to walk away, before Grace grabbed her by the arm.

"Liv!! What about Aiden?" Grace asked.

"Nah… he's not for me. I want to have fun tonight. I want to go with

Leo." She pouted her lip. "Plus, a few girls from work have a table in Ollie's already!"

She tried to be funny, fluttering her eyelashes, but it landed more on the annoying side. I had witnessed this scenario one too many times, and as predicted, she sauntered off in the direction of the nightclub, arm in arm with Leo, whom she'd known for less than an hour. I wondered if that was the key: taking a chance and not getting to know someone too much… jumping in before they see your flaws or icks.

Grace and I sank back into our seats, sharing a mutual sense of relief. "Thank goodness for that." Grace giggled. "I don't think I had any questions left to ask yer man."

"Your bill, ladies." The waiter placed our bill on the table.

I opened it and observed in pure horror.

"Oh you have to be joking!" I screamed. "They left us with their bill!"

"Nah, hold on a minute!" Grace grasped the bill from me in horror.

There was easily £100 worth of drinks on their tab, and two portions of chicken wings. I held my head in my hands.

"I'll try to call Olivia to get them to come back. This is not on." Grace said, getting up.

This is not on
Definition : This is not acceptable

She held her phone up to her ear and walked to a quieter spot.

"Is everything okay?" The waiter asked.

"Well, honestly no. Those guys that sent us the tequila, we don't know them and they've just left us with the full bill." I responded.

"Oh. I asked them, and they said you were handling it." He looked puzzled.

"Fucking hell." I breathed. "We'll get it sorted. I'm so sorry for this."

I could see Grace shouting down the phone, with one hand over her ear so she could hear properly.

"Bit shit of them to do that." The waiter cringed. "Also, they didn't send you the tequila."

I looked at him, puzzled. *If they didn't, who did? And why was Mr. Rugby Player staring at me?*

"What? Who did?" I asked.

"I did. You looked like you had a reason for celebration." He smiled.

I was genuinely taken aback. I hoped he hadn't overheard our conversation, but his unexpected generosity left me grateful.

"Wow, thank you. Won't you get in trouble?" I inquired, genuinely concerned.

Before he could respond, Grace returned. "Okay, so I'm going to run down to Ollies and get some cash off them. I'll be right back."

She left, moving quickly in the direction of the club, which fortunately was only a five-minute walk away.

"I'm so sorry about this," I apologised to the waiter.

"It happens. Rarely, but it happens," he reassured me, running a hand through his hair.

"That tequila was a nice touch. You really didn't have to do that," I expressed my gratitude.

"Nah – honestly, I see you guys here multiple times a month. It's just a little token of appreciation," he replied, flashing a genuine smile.

Taking a moment to observe him, I was surprised that I hadn't noticed him on previous visits. He seemed…nice. However, my attention had been consumed by a book titled 'JAMES,' and I hadn't looked up to consider other possibilities… until now.

"Let me return the favour. Can I buy you a drink?" I surprised myself with the confidence to offer such a thing.

His face flushed. "Ah, I'd like that, but I don't finish until 10.30," he responded, glancing at his watch.

I hesitated, contemplating whether this was my chance to break free from routine and meet someone new. It felt a little too coincidental to ignore. Inspired by Olivia's bold approach to men, I decided. "I - I can wait," I smiled.

Before our flirtatious conversation could continue, he was called to another table. Grace returned ten minutes later with the cash and a stern look on her face. We settled the rest of the bill.

"Well, let's go then," she said, obviously flustered from the money chase. I didn't blame her. On the contrary, I felt elated. I was genuinely looking forward to getting to know the waiter.

"Actually... I want to... stay." I checked the time on my phone.

10.08 PM

"What? Don't you have work tomorrow?" She questioned, eyeing me curiously.

I felt my cheeks warm. "Yes, but I also have to buy the… waiter… a drink at ten thirty." I admitted with a giggle.

"Oh my goodness." Grace chuckled. "Who are you, and what have you done with Anna?"

"I'm not sure. But I'm trying to be spontaneous." I defended.

"He's not bad looking…seems nice." Grace observed.

"Yeah, he seems it." I replied, catching a glimpse of him engrossed in conversation with another customer.

Grace interrupted my gaze. "Do you want me to head? You can call me at any time."

"Yeah, you can head. Thank you for tonight. I can always rely on you." I said, embracing her in a tight squeeze.

"Of course. I'm really excited for you and the show. Just don't do anything you don't want to do, just for the sake of pleasing others." She reminded me.

A very long twenty minutes later, I received a shoulder squeeze. I lifted my head from my phone to see the waiter, now in a different t-shirt. "Oh hi."

"Hi." he breathed. "Uhm- do you mind - if we go somewhere else? Just don't want my co-workers watching over us." He shifted awkwardly on his heels, his eyes darting around the beer garden.

"Oh yeah... No worries!" I gathered my handbag and stood up.

As we strolled in the direction of the Cathedral Quarter, I couldn't help but break the ice. "So, what's your name then?" I chuckled, feeling a bit embarrassed.

"Oh, uh, Darragh. Yours?" He awkwardly swung his hands back and forth as he walked.

"Anna." I said, relishing in the realisation that I might have made him a bit nervous for a change. Typically, I was the one feeling jittery.

We continued our casual walk, and he broke the silence saying, "So, you enjoyed the tequila?"

"Oh, yes, very much. Thank you!" I felt a bit awkward at his question, obviously I enjoyed the tequila, I'd said so already. "Did you happen to overhear our conversation?" I inquired.

'Oh, no! N-no, no, I just... I saw you all smiling and seemed like you were celebrating." He shrugged, his awkwardness adding a touch of endearment.

"I'm sure a lot of people were celebrating," I responded.

He turned to look at me, a hint of a smile playing on his lips. "But none were quite as polite and beautiful as you."

His compliment caught me off guard, kind of making me uncomfortable, and impulsively, I reached out and gently grabbed his arm, halting our walk.

"Can I be honest with you?" I questioned.

"Yeah, of course."

"So, I've just split from my boyfriend. I'm not looking for anything serious. So… just to make it clear. I don't want to date or have a relationship with anyone. It's not you, by the way. You seem great. I just don't want to be awkward but I – "

Before I could finish, he silenced me by pressing his lips to mine. Surprisingly, I found myself kissing him back, my body momentarily frozen with shock. There we stood at the side of the road; our lips locked. One hand pressed against my back, and the other delicately held my chin. I was kissing a stranger. A STRANGER! I had never kissed a total stranger before!

"I'm really craving a glass of wine," he said as he pulled away. I nodded and followed him into a bar just up the street.

The wine was going down smooth, but the conversation was dry. I desired him, kind of, in a physical sense. But mentally, he wasn't very stimulating.

He was 26, studying game development at Queens University but debating dropping out. He worked part-time in Bootleggers and part-time in Urban Outfitters. He had a little sister and still lived at home. His favourite food was Subway.

With each passing minute, my disappointment grew. I'd willingly thrust myself into an uncomfortable situation, asking a man I didn't know for a drink. Was it all for nothing?

"Last orders!" someone behind the bar echoed. The only other couple in the bar exited, leaving us as the last customers. I felt a twinge of guilt.

Darragh leaned in, whispering in my ear, "Should we find another spot? Or…" then kissed my cheek… and turned my face towards him attaching his lips to mine. I supposed I could kiss him again. He wasn't James, but then again, James didn't want me…Darragh did.

I had two options. End things there and then with disappointing drinks or take another chance.

"My apartment is a two-minute walk. We can have a drink there?" I suggested.

He raised his eyebrows and nodded, before pecking my lips.

We didn't speak inside the lift on our way up to the 6th floor, or as I fumbled with my keys to unlock the door to my apartment. The silence was heavy and awkward. I pushed away the shame and uncomfortable thoughts in my mind at how ridiculous this scenario was. *Really fucking ridiculous.*

It was as if our lips would now only work for kissing, not talking. As soon as I managed to open the door, it appeared my theory was correct.

We shared a passionate kiss from the hallway, making our way to my bedroom, shoes kicked off along the route. As he skilfully peeled my top off, I couldn't help but wonder if he sensed the rapid rhythm of my heartbeat. Uncertain about what to do, my body felt strangely heavy. My arms remained at my side as he pulled me against him, exploring every inch. Amid the intensity, I was focused on reciprocating the kiss. Thoughts consumed me – *was I a good kisser? Was I doing it right?*

His lips moving down my neck, he gently pushed me onto the bed. Semi-naked, clad only in my embarrassingly plain black bra, I watched him remove his t-shirt and unbutton his trousers. A deep breath escaped me as I noticed his arousal straining against navy boxers. Somehow, I had turned him on. *How had I achieved that?*

I momentarily wondered what I looked like from his perspective. Shaking off the uncomfortable thought, he approached me and smoothly slid my jeans down to my ankles.

We had average sex. I knew within the first 45 seconds that I wasn't going to be able to orgasm. Despite that fact, I decided to put on the performance of a lifetime. I rhythmically contracted my belly, moaned, breathed with intensity, and shook my legs, culminating in a passionate "Yes! Yes!" as I pulled at his hair. I even clenched my legs around his waist for added effect.

A minute later, as we lay beside each other, I pretended to catch my breath.

"Good?" he asked.

I nodded silently.

***

I lay wide awake, fixated on the ceiling, while he lightly snored beside me. A peculiar smile adorned my face, a mix of nervousness, disbelief, discomfort, and mixed feelings.

Oddly, I felt pride that this man found me attractive enough to fuck… and I'd let him do so. Yet, a lingering sense of cheapness unsettled me. He hadn't really 'earned' it by gifting tequila shots and an unenjoyable glass of red wine. I wondered if Olivia ever felt this way.

As my mind wrestled with emotions, I couldn't escape the realisation that, despite Darragh lying beside me, James lingered in my thoughts. He represented familiarity, shared comfort, and an intimacy that time had cultivated. A man who I'd just met couldn't erase the history and emotional investment I had with him. It was only a momentary distraction. One that I'd hoped would last longer and make me feel better… but it didn't.

CHAPTER FIVE
Scundered

Definition: Feeling embarrassed and/or uncomfortable.

My alarm blared at 6.45am. I felt like I'd barely slept... which was pretty true. Throughout the night, I had lost count of how many times I had jolted awake, fearing I might be snoring, talking in my sleep, or unwittingly monopolising the blanket from Darragh. I even found myself checking my phone twice during the night, anxiously wondering if it was nearly time to wake up.

He began pulling his clothing back on, as I sat in bed checking through my iPhone notifications and emails.

"Mind if I use your loo before I head?" he asked. "Dying for a piss." *These were the first words we'd spoken since...*

"Yeah, it's just through that door there." I pointed.

While he was away, I threw on some sweats and a vest top, feeling a bit grim. The room was uncomfortably warm, prompting me to head for the window in search of some fresh air. As I pulled open the curtains, I was greeted by an unexpected hailstorm, the clouds hanging ominously black and heavy.

"I'm going to need an umbrella." He remarked, appearing by my side, and speaking over my shoulder. A sudden chill ran down my spine.

"Uh, you can grab one from my closet. It's the door beside my bedroom." I pointed. Strangely, I now felt uneasy with him being so close, despite the fact he had quite literally been inside me the night before.

He scampered off in search.

"Oi! You know you have a traffic cone in here?" He shouted down the corridor.

Oh shit. I'd forgotten about the cone.

"Oh… yeah."

"Sick." He was too chirpy for this time of the morning.

"You can have it if you want." I jokingly suggested, crawling back into bed. I needed warmth. I needed comfort.

"Really?" He stood in the doorway, glancing between me and the closet.

"Uh, yeah."

Surely he wasn't serious? Or maybe he was… He looked like an excited child. I began to wonder why I'd found him so attractive the night before?

"Class! It'll be my souvenir." He winked and leaned down to kiss me. I let him.

He unfortunately hadn't the sense to steal some of my toothpaste while he was in the bathroom, so I was greeted by his morning breath.

Darragh left, traffic cone awkwardly in one arm, umbrella in the other. I hoped and prayed I could leave our encounter in the past, and that he wouldn't hunt me down and call me.

First one night stand? Completed it… but not without a bucketful of shame the morning after.

***

I dedicated extra time to my appearance for work, carefully curling my hair and perfecting my Mia-inspired winged eyeliner. Despite the struggle of squeezing into a slightly too tight red blouse and wearing heels that I knew would cause later regret, I felt a boost of confidence. I admit, finding a coat *without* a traffic cone in my closet was much easier, so at least Darragh was good for that?

Walking through rain-soaked cobblestone streets in uncomfortable heels was far from enjoyable, but reaching my desk brought relief. Surprisingly, a black leather journal awaited me, a luxury I'd admired but never bought. Opening it, I discovered a thoughtful note.

Anna,
For documenting the experiences you undertake
and the emotions you feel. Hopefully this will
help you plan your episodes!
Mia

The thick, expensive-feeling pages fuelled my inspiration for writing as I headed to the break room for a much-needed coffee.

Thoughts were flying through my brain. My first episode... *What should I include?* James was a definite, unavoidable must, delving into how he wooed me into a 'situationship' where he hinted at commitment, but never followed through, eventually leaving me high and dry without any explanation. Yeah. That would do. The more I ruminated on the situation, the angrier I felt. Not just anger towards him for how he treated me, but at myself for allowing it to happen.

The kettle hummed in the background as I scooped a teaspoon of coffee into my mug, completely lost in my own thoughts. Unbeknownst to me, someone else had entered the break room. I jumped in surprise as a hand suddenly popped into my field of vision, placing a coffee mug beside mine.

"Coffee?" I inquired without lifting my head. No response. "Tea, then?" I chuckled, still met with silence.

I turned on my heels to address the mysterious mug-bringer, but no words came out when I saw him. *Now, I know I've talked about attractive men before, but seriously, the man standing in front of me was on another level.* He defied all standards of attractiveness, making previous contenders seem mundane. If he were to grace a show like Love Island or The Bachelorette, the other contestants wouldn't stand a chance. He embodied the epitome of a tall, dark, and strikingly handsome love interest straight out of a blockbuster romance. Mr. Grey would envy him, Clark Kent would take notes, and Mr. Big would feel upstaged. My mind raced, and I had to close my mouth to prevent drooling.

As he raised his gaze, meeting mine, I silently hoped he hadn't caught the small gasp that escaped me. His eyes, a mesmerising shade of green with ample pupils and lengthy lashes, made it feel unjust for a man to possess such arresting features.

His face was a masterpiece – a flawlessly clean-shaven visage, a chiselled jawline, and striking cheekbones. Check, check, check. I had never been rendered speechless just by looking at someone's face, but this guy had effortlessly won the genetic lottery. I could picture him being well-acquainted with the abrupt silences that fell upon people, the distracted stares, and the discreet attempts to conceal a smile when they saw him.

Suddenly he motioned to his lips as if to say, 'be quiet,' and then to the AirPods in his ears. He was listening to music. *A bit rude.*

My facial expression must have mirrored the confusion in my mind because he then lifted his phone to show a Zoom call that was currently in process.

"Oh. No problem." I whispered, turning my back to him. My cheeks heated, embarrassed I'd even bothered him in the first place.

Yet, the uncertainty lingered. *Did he want coffee or tea?* Awkwardly tapping my foot, I waited for the kettle to boil, which seemed to be taking an unusually long time. Turning back around, I held a tea bag in one hand and the coffee container in the other. I lifted them towards him and hoped my facial expression conveyed 'Which one do you want?'

He took a second of reflection which frustrated me a little…wasn't it a straightforward choice? Maybe it was just the pressure I felt while under his gaze that was stressing me out. He pursed his lips. It felt like he was taking his time on purpose, just to make me feel uncomfortable. He eventually pointed towards the tea bag, and I dropped it into his mug.

As I watched steam rise from the kettle, I could feel his eyes beating into my back. *Why was he still staring at me?* The kettle finished. I poured the water into his mug and then my own. I stirred his tea and then realised my next issue. Did he want milk or sugar? I could have just walked away at this moment, but that would mean I might lose the opportunity to ask him his name. *Maybe his call was about to finish…* I decided to stir his tea for a few seconds longer, before stirring my own coffee.

Under his watchful eye, I walked over to the fridge to find some milk. I admit, I sucked my stomach in as I walked, and tried to be as graceful as possible when opening the fridge door, which usually always needed a good tug.

I turned to him and held the milk up. He nodded. His face was otherwise expressionless. I removed the tea bag and poured a dribble of milk into his tea, looking over at him as I poured. He nodded again and held his hand up, as if to say, "That's enough."

I felt like I was back taking my GCSE exams again, uncomfortably making eye contact with the adjudicator as they walked up and down the exam hall. I hated how he was making me feel. This was a BREAK ROOM. Not a 'take zoom calls and make people feel uncomfortable' room.

I snapped, fully turning towards him. "D'you want sugar?" I asked, slightly louder than expected.

He shook his head and walked towards me. His body ever so lightly nudged mine as he picked up his mug. He then exited the room, without so much as a "thank you" or a glance backwards.

I let out a breath I didn't know I was holding. I didn't know his name; I didn't know what department he was from. I didn't know what his bloody voice sounded like and it made me furious. He was so rude.

One of my colleagues, Laura, walked into the break room. "He's quite something." She wiggled her eyebrows.

"H-how do you show biceps in a suit jacket?" I asked, gazing at him as strutted through the office. He walked with such power, drawing eyes towards him with every stride.

"He had biceps? I was too busy looking at his arse." She responded.

I hoped no-one overheard our highly inappropriate remarks.

"Is he new?"

"Not sure… maybe he's being interviewed on this morning's economic breakdown. He looks like the smart and serious type."

I hummed, unsure.

"You might want to fix your blouse by the way." She pointed at my top, interrupting my pondering.

I looked down to see my button had popped open… proudly showcasing my black lace bra. Typical. Just typical. Not only had I rudely interrupted his zoom call, but I'd also flashed my tits at him.

The mystery man was nowhere to be seen as I walked to my desk. I was hoping it was just a once off encounter as I couldn't deal with that amount of distraction around the office.

I had a job to do.

I tried pushing any feelings of imposter syndrome away as I spent my afternoon sketching and planning ideas for my first episode of 'Belles of Belfast'. My debut was going to be in one week and four days' time. It was *very* soon…which made me *very* anxious.

I've realised that on this podcast, I can't use actual names… so we'll be diving into the tales of Mr. THIS and Mr. THAT, each bearing a title based on the wreckage they've left in my life.

Now, let's unpack the saga of Mr. Fuckboy.

Urban Dictionary paints a vivid picture of a fuckboy as a deceptive character, misleading you into believing they're special. They'll paint a picture of a perfect future, only to vanish or sever ties abruptly when things get a little too serious. Mr. Fuckboy, in my narrative, expertly played this role.

He lured me in, creating an illusion of uniqueness with non-romantic dates that left me feeling the need to work harder for his attention. This made me want him more. Scratch that. In reflection, I'm not sure I ever wanted HIM. What I wanted was for him to want me. I craved his attention. I craved his touch and how he would call me 'sexy' or 'hot' or 'gorgeous.' All these things I never really fully believed, but I wanted to hear. This craving stemmed from an intimidation factor—he was a few years older, undeniably good-looking, and I felt the need to measure up.

Reflecting on his looks, I compared him to the mystery man in the breakroom. He was hot but not mystery man level of hot.

I remember walking past a couple of girls, seeing one of them nudge another in the ribs to say, 'look at him'. I felt so satisfied as they all looked over to admire him as he was holding my hand. I would have done anything to please him, foolishly envisioning a happily-ever-after scenario.

Mr. Fuckboy took me to the stage of being 'his' without being 'mine.' He claimed my virginity in less-than-ideal circumstances, under Captain America bedsheets in his parents' house, creating a stark contrast to romantic movie expectations. The aftermath led to self-doubt, self-analysis, and a heightened sensitivity to my own flaws.

Afterwards, I endured an agonising wait for his text, questioning every aspect of myself. His nonchalant return seemed oblivious to the emotional turmoil it caused. The cycle continued—sex, a week of silence, a coffee date, and repeat.

But one day, it abruptly stopped.

Regretfully, Mr. Fuckboy consumed too much of my life. While I don't regret losing my virginity, I regret it was with him. Driven by a decision made under the influence, I sought solace in someone new—enter Mr. Barman, a choice I question upon reflection.

My pen slipped from my grasp, and a surge of sickness washed over me, leaving me momentarily paralysed. Leaning back in my chair, I felt a heaviness in my chest, my eyes clouded with a mix of anxiety and vulnerability, rendering me unable to continue. As I tentatively reviewed my work, the weight of the emotions hit me—I felt incredibly nervous. This act of pouring out my true feelings onto paper was a novel experience, and the mere thought of sharing it aloud stirred a tornado of emotions within me. A lump formed in my throat, threatening to choke me, and a nauseous feeling intensified. It screamed desperation, but, in the midst of it all, I found comfort in the fact that I was, at the very least, staying true to myself.

I was abruptly pulled from my thoughts by the jarring sound of a door slamming shut. Paddy was storming towards me, and for the first time, fear gripped me. His eyes were ice-cold, bulging with anger that seemed to radiate off him.

"Give me one reason why I shouldn't quit this fucking job!" he roared, forcefully dropping a stack of paperwork onto his desk, scattering individual sheets across the floor.

"Whoa, what's happening?" I stammered, taken aback.

Paddy, typically the jovial giant, seemed transformed by rage. His usually smiling face was now contorted with fury.

"That mother fucking American!" he growled, slumping onto a chair beside me.

Mia, in her own state of agitation, approached my desk and directed stern words at Paddy. "You should NOT have stormed out."

Silence hung in the air as I hesitated to intervene, clueless about the unfolding drama. Mia, visibly drained, ran her hands through her hair and took a deep breath. Even beneath the Botox, her creased brows conveyed frustration, and her tired eyes revealed the toll of the situation.

"He's a pretentious ass," Paddy huffed, his frustration palpable.

I was bewildered by the sudden change in Paddy's demeanour, especially in how he addressed Mia.

"He doesn't know anything about Belfast. Yet he's acting like he's our fucking saviour!" Paddy declared, punctuating his statement with a fist on my desk, causing a bit of freshly poured coffee to spill over the edge of my mug.

"I'm sorry, but what's going on?" I finally mustered the courage to inquire, glancing between the two of them.

"I'll tell you what's going on! That American jackass is -"

Mia swiftly interrupted, "Amir has arrived. He and Paddy aren't seeing eye to eye."

"I'll give him a black eye," Paddy huffed, practically bouncing on his feet. In my imagination, he transformed into a cartoon, bright red with smoke billowing from his ears. "This place is swarming with Americans! I swear to fuck… if one more person calls me 'dude' or says 'hey man… how's it going man?' I'm going to walk out of here."

Unable to contain myself, I snorted and quickly covered my mouth to stifle a laugh. Paddy shot me a narrowed glance. "What?" he snapped.

"I've just never seen you angry before," I admitted, struggling to hold back my laughter. Paddy's demeanour seemed a bit like a petulant child, and I apologised, "Sorry, I don't know why I'm laughing."

My nervous laughter seemed contagious as Mia's frustrated frown twisted into an attempt to hide a smile. Paddy prodded, "Are you finding this funny?"

"Yeah, yeah, g-guess I am… sorry… dude," I confessed, now unable to suppress my laughter. Mia joined in, and soon, the two of us were cackling. Despite knowing that we shouldn't be laughing, it only fuelled it more.

"Can you both please shut up? I can't hear myself losing the will to live."

Our laughter persisted, acknowledging the absurdity of the situation. Even after a moment of quiet, as we caught our breath, eye contact triggered another round of hysterics. The reason for our laughter became a blur, but the release felt incredibly cathartic.

"Ahem," a voice interrupted.

My head shot up, hastily clearing the tears that had started to cascade down my cheeks.

It was the mysterious breakroom man.

Mia turned to face him, trying to recover the situation. "Ah. Sorry… Anna was just informing us… of her plans, uh, for her pilot episode next Friday!"

She shot me a wink, and I wiped away a few tears of laughter, looking up. My heart skipped.

"So, you're the famous Belle of Belfast," he remarked, towering above me, his intense eyes locking onto mine.

Lord. Those fecking eyes. They could see through my soul.

CHAPTER SIX
A Melter

Definition: How you would describe someone who is annoying and/or rude.

The office felt oppressively hot, and suddenly, I became acutely aware of my own heartbeat.

"Sorry?" I responded, slightly puzzled. *Belle?*

"You're the Belle of Belfast?" he clarified, "I've heard some things."

His thick American accent presented a stark contrast to the Norn' Irish tones I was accustomed to. The timbre of his voice sent a shiver down my spine—it was both confident and alluring. "I'm looking forward to listening to your show," he added.

"Oh, are you?" I cursed silently as I felt my face flush. "I'm surprised you've heard about it..." My eyes flicked towards Mia, "I thought I was going to be anonymous."

Mia's eyes widened as she chuckled, "It will be, but obviously employees will know... NDA's essential, of course."

"Of course," he nodded, his voice maintaining a magnetic quality that had an unspoken effect on me.

So, he was an employee. Christ. Talk about distraction in the work-place.

I could have sworn his eyes briefly darted to my chest and back, perhaps checking that my blouse was properly buttoned this time. I glanced down, relieved to see that it was. However, the red blouse I had chosen seemed to offer him an ample view of my breasts as he towered above me. As I stood to offer a handshake, I found myself awkwardly frozen, realising he was much taller and overall larger—easily 6ft4. My eyes darted uncomfortably around the room, regretting my choice of attire.

"Anna is very excited about the new show. Aren't you?" Mia gracefully interrupted my awkward silence. "I think it will be a huge hit with our female audience."

I nodded along, exchanging glances between Mia and the Mystery Man. While Mia seemed enthusiastic, he appeared less so.

"Digital Transformation," I blurted out.

"Sorry?" he asked, brows creased.

My breath shook as I spoke, "I – I think a podcast will be great for our digital transformation."

Hold yourself together, Anna, Jesus Christ!

"I'm really looking forward to recording the first episode. I've been preparing all day today." I tapped my notebook. Mia glanced at it and back to me, a small smile forming on her face. I returned a smile quickly but couldn't draw my eyes from him for too long.

"It sounds like it will be quite engaging," he teased, a smirk playing on his face. He continued to stare directly at me, ignoring Mia and Paddy. *Cocky.* He spoke like he knew everything. I didn't like that.

"You'll have to listen and let me know," I snapped, smiling cheekily at him.

He raised his eyebrow, doubting me undeservedly, considering he didn't know me.

"Actually, Amir will be heavily involved in the review process of your first few episodes," Mia spoke hesitantly. "I don't think that you have been formally introduced… Anna, this is Amir Davairi, from APEX."

Blood stopped flowing through my veins. Any colour on my face had instantly drained. *You've got to be kidding me… How did I not piece it together?* Holy fuck.

"Oh, we actually met earlier today. Right Belle?" He smirked.

My name is Anna, jackass. "Yes," I said, teeth gritted. I then plastered a fake, over-enthusiastic grin on my face.

I hoped he wasn't about to go into details about our first encounter. It wasn't the best first impression. Our eyes locked, a silent war waging between us, an unspoken challenge simmering beneath the surface.

"You know… she makes a great cup of tea," Amir said to Mia.

I quickly interjected, eager to steer the conversation away. "I was actually going to ask if we could grab a cuppa? To go through my notes for the first episode?" I directed the question to Mia, eager to escape his irritating gaze.

"Awesome," Amir interrupted, clapping his hands together. "Paddy and I have to go through some paperwork anyways… right man?" He reached over and squeezed Paddy's shoulder. I couldn't help but notice the black nail polish on his fingernails, a bit chipped on his index finger. Maybe he was a nail-biter; it seemed plausible. I found it kind of hot, as much as I hated to admit it.

Paddy cleared his throat. "Yeah, no bother," he said, breathing deeply through his nose, trying to rein in his frustration. I could relate; I was feeling the same way.

"I'll see you for our meeting at 4.30pm, Mia. Nice to meet you… Belle," Amir said as he walked away. Screw him.

Paddy hastily gathered the paperwork he had dropped moments earlier and scurried after.

I was tempted to stand up and shout after him, "MY NAME IS

ANNA, YOU AMERICAN MELTER," but instead, I closed my eyes, took a deep breath, and turned to face Mia. She seemed to be doing the same, her eyes closed.

"I think I might need to spike our coffees," I blurted out.

Mia snorted. "If I drink, I won't be able to stop myself."

Two steaming cups of coffee (unfortunately not spiked) and four bis-coff biscuits later, Mia and I finally settled down to discuss my upcoming show. Anxious anticipation gripped me as I opened my journal, preparing myself for her evaluation.

Would she find me uninteresting? (Possibly)

Would she think it was too much? (Likely)

Had I overshared? (Probably)

Would she be disappointed in my lack of a sex life? (Not exactly the entertaining material she might have expected)

Was I too inexperienced? (Most definitely)

These were all bizarre questions to ponder, especially in the presence of my boss, but I pushed aside the discomfort. This was about crafting a successful show. As Mia perused the journal, her expression remained inscrutable, fuelling my anxiety.

What if she decides I'm not cut out for the show?

What if she has to tell Mr. American Melter that the show is cancelled?

What will he think of me? He already seemed to look down on me. Wanker.

My thoughts on the journal, Mia, and the show dissolved as I grew increasingly frustrated with Amir. I felt a growing need to prove to him (and myself) that I was worthy of hosting my own show and capable of making it a success. What irked me most about him was that, without a doubt, he was the most handsome man I'd ever seen. If he weren't such a pompous ass, I might have let him ruin me... anytime... anywhere—

"Wow," Mia breathed, interrupting my inner monologue.

Shit. Did I just say that out loud?

"Anna, this exceeds all my expectations," Mia continued, her smile radiant and affectionate.

Oh, thank god. She was referring to the journal.

"I can feel every emotion. I've been through exactly what you've written here, and I know many other women who have as well. You articulate it so perfectly, I don't know how to describe it, but it's just right. It's exactly right," she said.

"Thank you so much," I sighed in relief. "I was so worried—"

"You need to have faith. This is going to be great."

Mia's eyes remained fixed on my notes as her fingers glided over the pages, analysing, and anticipating the audience's reaction. I pinched my skin, admitting, "I just worry about what people will think about me, even though it's anonymous."

"And I would too. However, you need to set that aside. This show is for the people who need it. This show is for your listeners, who may be or have been going through the same issues as you," Mia said, smiling. "This show is for the Belles of Belfast."

Her words struck a chord within me. This wasn't just about sharing my experiences, it was about empowering women to be honest with themselves, to look inward at their actions, and to strive to change how they view themselves and their relationships. My show had the potential to be a platform for real change... and hopefully in the process, I could try change myself...

We continued discussing show logistics for a few more minutes, but I could tell Mia was needed elsewhere. Before leaving, she assured me she'd be reachable by email or phone, though I probably wouldn't see much of her around the office for the next week. She also encouraged me to work outside of the office. Technically socialising was show 'research' after all. This worked in my favour as avoiding Mr American Melter would have to be a top priority, in order for me to stay focused.

Unfortunately, I couldn't avoid him in my dreams. Fuck. That.

ONE WEEK LATER

Head's in the clouds

Definition: When you spend an excessive amount of time dreaming or daydreaming.

I walk into the break room, fill the kettle, and tip a teaspoon of instant coffee into my mug. I'm awakened suddenly by the sound of the door closing behind me. The energy in the room shifts and I don't have to turn round to know who's standing behind me. I can feel it.

"Belle," he whispers, his voice a tantalising murmur that sends shivers down my spine. I tilt my head towards him, curiosity mingling with anticipation.

Running a hand through his tousled dark hair, he scans me with an intensity that sets my pulse racing. "I've been looking for you," he confesses, his voice rough and breathless.

My heart leaps into my throat, a rush of heat flooding my senses. "You have?" I respond, hanging on his every word.

Amir doesn't hesitate. He strides towards me, animalistic in nature, as if I'm the prey he's been hunting and he's desperate to devour his long-awaited meal. His hands claw at my thighs as he throws me up onto the counter and spreads my legs. Ravenous. Heat burns through me as I feel provoked by every touch, every breath, every second that passes. It's like nothing I've ever felt. A moan escapes my mouth and vibrates against his lips as his hands grip my waist, pulling me closer and closer into him; but not close enough. Wet kisses electrify my skin...from my ear, down to my collar bone. His right hand forcefully grips my throat and I take a deep, struggled breath before he crashes his divine lips into mine. He tastes wonderful. Minty. Fresh. I crave being even closer so without hesitation I lock my legs around him, pulling his hips towards me. Our kiss is rushed as if we can't get enough of each other and never want this pursuit to end. His fingers slide from my throat and end up tangled in my hair. He pulls, yanking my head backward making me moan against his lips involuntarily. His tongue fights mine and it's the most delicious game of tug of war I've ever played. My hands find themselves pulling at the buttons of his white cotton shirt, begging to see the skin underneath, dying to feel him closer. I jolt as he bites my bottom lip and pulls it thirstily towards him.

'Fuck, you are so sexy,' he mumbles against my mouth. His deep, dirty accent strips my senses. I'm totally and completely lost in him. 'Where have you been hiding?'

He breaks our kiss, his intense gaze locking with mine. We're both breathless, caught in a charged moment. He steadies himself by holding onto my thighs with such pressure I suspect and hope I'll have bruises afterwards. I struggle to breath as I stare into the darkness beneath his pupils, pleading silently for him to take all of me. Own me. Consume me.

With one fierce pull, he frees my breasts from the confines of my red blouse, his lips descending hungrily upon them in a flurry of wet kisses. I grasp at his hair, grateful for the barrier of my black lace bralette yet yearning to feel his touch against my bare skin. As his left hand trails up my thigh, pushing my skirt higher, and his right hand remains entangled in my hair, I let out a moan, consumed by the desire for all of him. My breath hitches, the words catching in my throat, desperate to spill forth. He could take me, right here, right now.

You... you... you..." he mumbles.

'What?' I moan against his lips. 'I what?'

He plays with my bottom lip, sucking it fervently, making me wonder if it might burst under his intensity. His fingers trace teasingly slow along my thigh, drawing nearer and nearer until...

The kettle's whistle breaks the moment, and he abruptly withdraws, stepping aside with an emotionless demeanour.

"What?" I demand, confusion and frustration bubbling up.

He clears his throat, adjusting his shirt, his eyes avoiding mine completely.

I ache to delve into the depths of his gaze once more, but he denies me that opportunity.

"I what?!" I repeat, my voice tinged with frustration.

He ignores my question, nonchalantly dropping a tea bag into a cup and filling it with hot water from the kettle.

*I stare at him, feeling bile rise in my throat and goosebumps prickling my skin. I close my legs, speechless. Without a glance in my direction, he promptly exits the break room, leaving me not only needy but **absolutely fucking furious**.*

I screamed and jumped up into consciousness. My morning alarm blared beside me, but I remained paralysed. I'd only met him twice, for less than ten minutes in total. What the hell was that dream about? And more importantly, how was I supposed to shake it off and face him at work? I slammed the snooze button and sunk back into my bed sheets… maybe if I closed my eyes, I could change the ending.

***

"You look… worse than you do hungover." Grace's concerned gaze met mine as she took in my dishevelled appearance in sweats and a hoodie at Established on Wednesday afternoon. Clearly, I stood out amidst the well-dressed hipster crowd, but fatigue outweighed any concern for fitting in. "Are you alright?" she asked.

"I didn't sleep well," I sighed, taking a sip of my matcha. "But other than that, I'm fine."

"I can't believe you went home with the waiter the other night," Olivia interjected.

"Me neither. Did you end up heading home with…?" I struggled to recall the name of the rugby boy she had been flirting with.

"Yeah, it wasn't the best though. Wouldn't do it again."

"Cheers to that," I said, raising my drink for emphasis before taking another long sip. The frothy milk provided a comforting warmth. "I can't believe my first one-night stand ended up so humiliating. I didn't even get an orgasm out of it," I whispered, cautious of our neighbouring table.

"Humiliating for who? You or him?" Grace's question brought me back to the conversation.

I rolled my eyes. "Me, obviously. I can't believe I allowed myself to do that. I'm so embarrassed."

"Hun, if he didn't make you cum, he should feel more embarrassed than you should," Olivia remarked before munching on her blueberry muffin.

Glancing at the couple beside us, who thankfully remained engrossed in their own discussion, Grace replied, "Olivia, shhh... Anna, you shouldn't feel humiliated for having sex," she chided gently. "It's natural to feel sensitive, but you shouldn't feel embarrassed in the slightest."

"Thank you for that. And to be fair to Darragh, he probably doesn't even know that I didn't... finish," I admitted. "I faked it."

"You fucking faked it?" Olivia was taken aback. "For what reason?"

Grace pinched her nose, clearly stressed by Olivia's volume. I chose to give up... if anyone overheard our conversation then so be it.

"To make it end," I chuckled.

Both girls chuckled in solidarity, having experienced similar situations in their pasts. "I will never... ever... fake another orgasm again, and neither should you," Olivia admonished, wagging her finger at me. "I don't want to hear any excuses. Next time, you show him how to make you."

"Show him? I can't do that!" I blurted out, cheeks flushing. I grabbed her muffin and stuffed my mouth with it.

"Yes, you can. Guide him through exactly how to do it," she insisted, as if discussing a strategy game.

"I agree," Grace chimed in, surprising me. She never spoke about sex. She rarely spoke about her own relationships...Not that she was in one.

"You what? Why haven't you told me this before?" I was shocked. "And how do I guide him through it?" I pulled out the black notebook Mia had given me along with a pen. "One second." I unlocked my phone and opened the voice memos app, ready to press record. Both girls laughed. "What?" I asked. "This is perfect material for the podcast. Mind if I record and make some notes?"

***

Wednesday saw me bypassing the office entirely. Instead, I devoted half of my day to quality time with the girls before retreating to my apartment, immersing myself in writing and refining the inaugural episode of the podcast. Around 3 pm, Mia checked in via text, and we arranged a review meeting for Thursday morning. Despite my nerves being in turmoil, I reminded myself of the purpose behind the podcast, which offered some solace amidst the uncertainty.

At approximately 6:30 pm, I glanced at my phone, intending to message Paddy to see if he was still working at Spotlight or if Amir had driven him to quit his job. I was halted however, seeing a missed call from *James*.

Time seemed to stand still as I dialled him back.

"Finally!" James exhaled audibly through the speakerphone, catching me off guard.

"Hi, James?" I rose from the sofa, absentmindedly running a hand through my unkempt hair—today was a no-brush day.

"I think I left my phone charger at yours last night, and I'm desperate for it. My battery's down to eight percent," he explained impatiently.

My stomach churned with a sickening sensation, bile threatening to rise in my throat.

"But you weren't here—" I began, my voice trembling.

"I'm literally outside your apartment. Can you just let me in?" His tone was tinged with frustration. "Please?"

Without a second thought, I made my way to the intercom. "Yes, of course. Dial the number, and I'll buzz you in."

Silence greeted my attempts. Panic pulsed through my veins.

"Hello?" I ventured, my voice barely a whisper. "Are you there?"

"Steph?"

Tears welled in my eyes as realisation dawned. Without another word, I ended the call, refusing to hear any further explanation from him. Determinedly, I slipped into my trainers and hurried into the hallway, fingers pressing the lift button in vain hope of catching a glimpse of him, of seeking closure. But obviously he wasn't there.

The chill of the evening air greeted me as I wandered to my quiet spot by the River Lagan. Settling onto a weathered wooden bench, I gazed at the shimmering city lights dancing on the water's surface, contemplating the illusion of the relationship I thought I had with James. I would no longer allow myself to feel things for a man who clearly had no feelings for me to begin with. He wasn't worth getting upset over anymore. I was worth more than how he'd ever treated me. *I was worth more than how I allowed myself to be treated.*

With resolve, I opened his contact on my phone and tapped "BLOCK," ending a chapter that should never have been written.

CHAPTER SEVEN
Feck it!

Definition: Fuck it!

One day remained until I had to record my first episode, and I found myself needing a nervous pee every five minutes. Seated at my desk, I discreetly applied stick-on fake nails to conceal the fact that I'd chewed my real ones off with nerves. My meeting with Mia, Paddy, and Amir was scheduled for 11:15, and with the current time at 10:55, I knew I needed to make myself more presentable. Despite feeling edgy inside, I had to show up confident and sure of myself.

I had typed up the notes from my 'little black book' onto my computer and had prepared snippets of recordings from my conversation with Grace and Olivia about faking orgasms. Part of me was excited to see Amir's reaction to that. Spotlight had interviewed sex therapists, relationship coaches, and even a man who claimed to be 'intimate with a ghost' once, but nothing quite as raw and honest as what I had planned. Part of me wondered if I'd gone too far.

Coffee was the last thing my churning stomach needed, but I smiled as Paddy kindly placed a large latte onto my desk before settling into the chair beside me.

"Ready?" he asked.

"Almost..." I replied, sticking on my last nail.

He glanced at his smartwatch, checking the time. "Knowing Amir, he'll probably show up late anyway. Too busy flirting or firing someone..."

"Flirting?" I asked.

Paddy rolled his eyes, "It's like all the women in the office are on heat."

"What?"

"Like dogs on heat." He clarified.

"Oh... right. How are you finding him now?" I inquired. "You still hate him?"

"I don't completely hate him... I understand he has a lot of pressure on his shoulders to turn things around here, but he could be nicer about it."

Before we could delve further into our conversation, I noticed Mia entering the boardroom from the corner of my eye. "We should go," I said, pulling myself up from my chair and grabbing my laptop and coffee before following suit.

Inside the boardroom, Mia was wiping down the whiteboard, which still had notes from a previous meeting. "Hello!" she greeted excitedly as we entered.

"Americano." Paddy placed a coffee onto the table for her, and she smiled graciously.

"My saviour. So, where do we start?" She held a blue marker in her hand, poised and ready.

Glancing toward the door, Paddy checked his watch again. "Um... aren't we waiting on Amir?"

"Oh, you'll be pleased to know that he couldn't come!" Mia announced with a grin.

I wasn't pleased. I had spent all morning mentally preparing myself to face him. However, I feigned relief and opened my laptop, ready to share what I had planned.

It felt strangely surreal to divulge such personal accounts of my life to my boss. I had no reservations about sharing this information with Paddy; he probably knew most of it already. As I read aloud, Mia diligently made notes on the whiteboard, aiming to highlight the value that listeners could derive from my episode.

Her favourite part was the voice recordings of Grace and Olivia, using character names:

Olivia – Miss Sensuality.

Grace – Miss Sensibility.

In these recordings, they debated whether to be explicit or subtle about expressing preferences in bed and how to communicate these desires to a partner. Liv described her approach, initiating actions herself and instructing her partner to observe and replicate. Grace, visibly mortified, shared her method of softly whispering in her partner's ear and gently guiding him if he didn't get it right the first time. Olivia argued that Grace was too focused on the male ego and not enough on her own pleasure.

Meanwhile I'd never focused on my own pleasure. In contrast, my experiences centred more on concerns about my appearance, my partner's feelings, and the constant internal dialogue about where to place my hand or how I should moan... or maybe I should dig my nails into his back? (I read about that once in a fanfiction). My 'encounter' with Mr. Barman wasn't overly enjoyable, but I craved the validation that he found me physically attractive. He didn't cringe at the sight of me naked, and he seemed to genuinely enjoy having sex with me. Meanwhile, I found myself awaiting an Oscar for my performance in faking orgasms.

But more importantly than that – I had the realisation that I hadn't even been truly happy when I was dating James. I'd spent the whole time trying to make him happy and didn't once think about myself.

"God, I've been through all of this. Brilliant!" Mia exclaimed as she read through the notes.

Paddy, meanwhile, looked like he'd just been on a ghost train. His face paled as he seemed deep in thought.

"What do you think, P?" I asked, snapping him out of his reverie.

"I'm just wondering if every girl I've ever been with has faked it." His eyes remained distant as he most likely revisited every sexual experience he'd had with a woman.

I couldn't help but giggle, "Well, you'll just have to tune into next week's episode where we'll teach you how to please a woman, so she never has to fake an orgasm again…"

Mia squealed like an excited teen, "BRILLIANT! Brilliant! Brilliant! Tapping into the male audience! I love it."

Paddy shook his head, a smile finally breaking across his face, "To be fair, every guy I know would listen to that. They'd deny it… but they'd listen."

FRIDAY

I felt like I'd been dragged through a hedge backwards. Sleep had been elusive, leaving me feeling as restless as a child on Christmas Eve. Amir had once again invaded my dreams, his presence lingering in my subconscious like an unwelcome guest. It was baffling how someone I'd only encountered for ten minutes was sticking so much to my subconscious. Perhaps it was just hormones wreaking havoc, or maybe it was because he resembled a Greek god incarnate. Whatever the reason, I knew I needed to get a grip on myself. It was fucking ridiculous.

My agenda for the day was a few hours at the office, followed by an afternoon spent at home before returning to record my show at 9 pm. Opting for minimal makeup, hair pulled back into a ponytail, and dressed in a black jumpsuit paired with a faded, well-loved striped jumper and black boots, I felt sufficiently put together. The jumper, a faithful companion for the past six years, had seen better days, but its comfort and familiarity provided a sense of grounding.

Taking a slight detour on my walk to work, I indulged in two more Harry Styles songs and treated myself to a Vanilla Latte from Starbucks. As I rubbed my tired eyes, I reviewed my episode plan and rehearsed lines at my desk. While I intended to freestyle it for the most part, there were important points I needed to convey, and I wanted to ensure I came across effectively.

"Hello, hello," Amir greeted, strolling towards me, and casually perching himself on the edge of my desk, his hands gripping the wood. Instinctively, I pushed my chair back, creating a bit of distance between us. The mere sight of him was enough to stir up frustration. He had already been a thorn in my side since our first encounter. As if plaguing my dreams wasn't enough, he had to intrude into my reality as well.

"How's Belle getting on with her... stuff?" Amir inquired, gesturing towards my cluttered desk adorned with sticky-notes, variously coloured pens, my Starbucks coffee, and laptop where I diligently typed my episode notes.

He loomed over me; his eyebrows raised in curiosity.

Stuff? I retorted internally. It wasn't just stuff. Tonight was my first show, a pivotal moment for the station. If he had bothered to show up to our meeting yesterday, he would know exactly what I had planned. Clearly, it wasn't a priority for him.

"Fine. Thanks," I snapped, my irritation palpable. "I have to feed my plant." I grabbed the plant food from my desk drawer and headed towards the window, eager to evade further conversation.

"Fine? You seem rather...avoidant," he observed, his gaze burning into my back. I refused to acknowledge him, unwilling to reveal any hint of vulnerability. "You know your plant is dead, right?"

I paused, examining the yellowing leaves. He wasn't dead yet. He just needed some TLC. "I just moved him to the window last Tuesday. He'll be fine with more sunlight."

"Your plant is a… he?" Amir raised an eyebrow, a hint of amusement in his tone.

Ignoring his jest, I sprayed some water onto the plant's leaves. He sidled closer, leaning against the windowsill.

"So, as I was saying…" he began.

When I finally glanced up, his attention had shifted to the street outside. A pang of disappointment swept over me that he wasn't fixated on me.

"I would have liked to have seen more from you this week," he continued, his voice pulling me back to the conversation.

You got a pretty great view of my tits in the break room on our first day, I thought wryly.

Clearing my throat and pushing aside my dirty thoughts, I asked, "What do you want to see? I thought we were going to review my notes in person yesterday."

Amir diverted his gaze, fiddling with his cufflinks unnecessarily. "Something else needed my attention. With that being said, I'd like to see your plan for the first episode - if you could email it across?"

The idea of him hearing me talk about orgasms and my insecurities made me feel slightly sick. Hosting this show was starting to feel like a crazy idea. But I pushed the imposter syndrome aside, determined not to let him see any weakness in me.

Squinting playfully, I teased, "Do you not have faith in me?"

"Why should I?" he retorted coolly.

"Why should you not?" I countered, crossing my arms defensively. "You don't know me, so why assume that I'm useless or won't meet your expectations?"

He clicked his tongue thoughtfully, and I fought to suppress the inappropriate thoughts threatening to surface about his tongue and mouth.

"Fair enough. But for the record – I never said you're useless," he clarified, fixing me with a steely glare. "But I'll be listening. Don't be too intimidated by that."

"Intimidated?" I giggled nervously. "I'm not intimidated."

Of course, I was. The thought of him listening while I shared my tumultuous relationship status on air made my stomach churn. I dreaded his judgement.

"Won't you be nervous?" Amir prodded, his gaze piercing as he bit the inside of his lip. It felt like he was testing me, searching for any crack in my composure.

Nervous? Why? Because you have the power to shut my show down, fire me, and ruin my career? Or is it because of the intense attraction...but also the hatred I simultaneously feel towards you?

Keeping my cool, I replied firmly, "No, I'm pretty good to go." With a nonchalant air, I lifted the plant food and sprinkled a handful into the soil. "Actually, I'm looking forward to it."

"Hmm..." He observed me with a hint of scepticism in his gaze. "I'd be a lot more nervous if I were you. It's a big deal."

I shrugged, masking any trace of vulnerability. "Well, it's a good thing you're not me then, otherwise we'd have a problem."

His mouth opened slightly in surprise at my cheeky response. I knew I probably shouldn't have said that, but I couldn't help myself. This wasn't my usual demeanour.

"Touché," he nodded, acknowledging my retort. "I have to admit, I think this show is a terrible idea."

Just as I was about to apologise for my cheeky remarks, he hit me with another negative comment.

"I just think that a risky show like this one isn't a good idea... Especially with the current state of the radio station." He continued.

My heart sank. "I don't really know what you want me to say?" I replied, feeling deflated.

He shrugged, crossing his arms in a self-assured manner. "Just a lot of pressure on your shoulders to make sure it succeeds." His mouth twisted into a self-satisfied smirk, and I realised he had no faith in me.

"I can handle it." I snapped, turning my back to him. I walked back towards my desk, feeling fed up with his irritating comments. Taking a much-needed, long sip from my coffee, I exhaled deeply through my nose. *If he speaks any more negativity, I will cover his designer suit with this vanilla latte...*I thought.

Fed Up
Definition: Annoyed and/or bored, especially by something you've experienced for too long.

Amir disappeared without saying another word, leaving me feeling relieved but also infuriated AGAIN. Was it that hard to say 'goodbye'? I know I was snappy, but Jesus Christ! His disappearing act really pissed me off.

Leaving the office midday as planned, I indulged in an afternoon nap to ease my sleep deprivation and the growing pit of anxiety in my stomach. Sitting on my sofa afterward, I listened to soft music in the background and tried this 'manifestation' technique I saw on Instagram.

My 'manifestation' was really just a cover-up for procrastination. Procrastination of what exactly? Well… Olivia had informed me that I had to dress my best, as after my first show, we would be celebrating like Belfast girls do best.

I struggled to fit into a pair of tight black leather trousers that I had stored away for a 'special occasion.' The thought of having to sit or bend in them made me want to cry, so they probably weren't the best idea for sitting while recording on the radio… My stomach slightly flopped over the top of the waistband, so I decided to wear an oversized white blouse to try to cover that up. I paired the outfit with some heeled leather boots and stared at myself in the mirror. I felt… sexy. For the first time in a while, as I looked at myself, I actually felt sexy. When things ended with James, I couldn't even look at myself for a week. I would poke at every bit of fat on my body, wondering if that grossed him out. Was that why he didn't like me? I wondered every day… Am I not attractive enough?

Today, however, as I observed myself in the mirror, I couldn't give a crap what James thought. He could go screw himself for all I cared. Tonight, was my night. Tonight, was going to be a life-changing, career-shaking night.

I may have had a shot of tequila before I left my apartment. I brushed my teeth twice before leaving… just in case I bumped into anyone else at the office. However, not many people worked at night, especially on a Friday night.

As I walked to the office, I checked my email for the thirtieth time. Amir had finally replied to the email containing my show notes with one, single, intimidating line.

amir.davairi@apex.com
Let's review after the show airs.

***

"Yeoooo. Look at you!" Paddy exclaimed, giving me a playful whistle as I walked into the studio.

I laughed. "Oh, shut up. I'm only dressed because I'm going for drinks after."

"Aye, cheers for the invite." He teased.

"You can come if you want. I'd love for you to come." I countered.

He waved his hand, dismissively, "Nah, I've been stuck in this office since the crack of dawn. Another time, sure."

Jesus. Wasn't it illegal to work that many hours? Labour laws and all…

As I settled in, untangling my studio headphones, and opening my laptop to have my notes handy, I couldn't help but feel a twinge of nerves. I'd condensed my journal scribbles into bullet points to keep me on track during the podcast.

"So, the intro song's all set, and you're familiar with leading into the ads between segments. We'll give the live podcast a shot this week, but if it's too much pressure or doesn't pan out, we can switch to pre-recorded episodes from next week," Paddy briefed.

"We've been through this a couple of times now," I teased back, noticing Paddy's flustered demeanour. His hair was tousled, like he'd been running his hands through it in stress, and his eyes were tired, with dark circles underneath.

"I know, I know. Can't be too prepared," he muttered, trying to regain composure.

I idly rearranged the items on my desk, realising we had a good chunk of time before showtime. Paddy sat across from me, glued to his phone, occasionally taking sips from a can of Red Bull. We lapsed into a comfortable silence, both of us mindlessly scrolling through social media until a knock on the door interrupted our quietude.

"Are you joking me?" Mia chuckled as she entered the studio.

"What?" I asked.

"IT'S YOUR FIRST SHOW!" She exclaimed, pulling a bottle of prosecco out of her handbag, along with three plastic glasses. "You should be celebrating with a sip of this stuff, not sitting in silence. Let's loosen the nerves!"

Paddy eagerly grabbed a glass and held it out, waiting for Mia to open the bottle. "Go on then."

We all clinked glasses, toasting to my debut show, perhaps breaking a few rules along the way, including…

"Don't drink in the studio," I mused, noting Paddy had already broken this with his Red Bull.

"Don't consume alcohol in the workplace," Mia added, though it was a rule often overlooked, especially on Fridays or any other days ending with a 'Y'.

"How are you feeling?" Mia asked, her eyes full of encouragement.

"Honestly, I feel great. I'm genuinely excited to get started," I replied, taking a deep breath.

This was mostly true.

"You're going to be amazing," Mia assured me with a warm smile.

We spent the next twenty minutes going over the show, Paddy reminding me (again) of the mechanics while I reassured him (again) of my confidence. He jokingly gave me the middle finger, but I knew he meant well. He wanted me to succeed almost as much as I did.

A few minutes before the show, I dashed to the bathroom, feeling goosebumps prickling my arms. Staring into the mirror, I gave myself a pep talk. *You can do this. You are good enough. You are worthy of this opportunity.*

Returning to the studio, I settled into my chair, placing my headphones over my head, and watching the 60-second countdown on my screen. Mia sat outside, listening in, while Paddy sat across from me, ready to tackle any tech emergencies.

My stomach churned with nerves as the beat of "Tell Me Ma" by Sham Rock filled the studio, followed by the pre-recorded voice-over: *"Coming up next, your new favourite show... Belles of Belfast... swiping, texting, sexting... an insight into modern dating."*

3.. 2..1

"Hello and welcome to the first ever episode of 'Belles of Belfast'"

And so I spoke.

Introducing Mr. Fuckboy... the man I tried to get over by getting under... Mr. Barman. And then was left feeling less than disappointed by the lack of connection, passion, and... orgasm. Enter Miss Sensuality and Miss Sensibility, who shared their tips. My first episode was one of realisation.

Embarrassment only has power over us if we give it permission.

Shame only thrives if we allow it to.

If we don't speak up, how will he know what he's doing is wrong?

Self-love is fundamentally a choice. It's time for me to prioritise choosing myself before others, especially men.

But also, all this talk about sex has made me really horny. But horny for a man who will know how to make me cum... *respectfully.*

***

"I can't believe my voice was on the radio!" Olivia screamed, clapping her hands together.

After wrapping up my inaugural episode, I met the girls at Muriel's Bar. A touch boujee compared to the usual hangout spots, it exuded an upscale charm that set it apart. The ambience, a delightful fusion of dim and moody, provided a cosy retreat that beckoned us to relax and enjoy. While the drinks may have stretched the budget a bit, the friendly staff elevated the entire experience.

The interior was adorned with an intriguing choice of decor — an assortment of lacy bras and underwear adorned every inch of the ceiling. The unconventional choice left me with a lingering curiosity, a silent pondering on the rationale behind it.

Why underwear? What was the story? Despite my curiosity, I had always found myself too reserved to ask. I just hoped they were all freshly dry-cleaned or never worn.

"I'm just glad you can now openly talk about sex without cringing!" Olivia exclaimed. "SEX is not something to be ashamed about!"

We had chosen a table tucked away at the back, where the lighting was dim. It was as bustling as ever on a Friday night, with people jostling at the bar and seizing any available seat as soon as it became vacant.

Grace wore a pained expression, likely embarrassed by how loudly Olivia was exclaiming the word 'sex.' She silently sipped on a pint of water she'd ordered alongside her gin and tonic. Her routine involved alternating between sips of water and sips of alcohol. While Liv's statement about shame resonated with both of us, we weren't quite on her level of confidence.

"Thanks Liv. I think it'll get easier the more episodes I record. I'm actually already looking forward to my next one."

"It takes a lot of courage to be *that honest.*" Grace nodded. "I thought the voice notes from Olivia, and I were a nice touch. You could interview more people each week. Show the diversity across Belfast… you know?"

It was like we shared the same mind.

"As long as I get a weekly cameo!" Olivia winked.

I laughed along. "As long as it's appropriate."

"*Oh honey*, I am never appropriate… I thought you knew that by now?"

"At least you're entertaining." Grace sipped on her water. I couldn't agree more.

"I wonder if anyone's talking about me online? … the mystery attractive voice…" Olivia mused, pulling out her phone and opening Twitter, her eyes brimming with hope for a taste of fame.

I hadn't even considered social media yet. Our shows typically garnered the occasional message or tweet, nothing major. I didn't have high expectations for my debut episode, but as Olivia's face lit up and a smile crept across her lips, my heart began to race with anticipation.

"What's going on?" I asked, curious.

She shook her head, a proud grin spreading across her features. Taking out my phone, I opened Twitter, and the three of us scrolled through the tweets about the show. Surprisingly, there were quite a few, more than I had anticipated.

@emmacroryxo tweeted
I have met many Mr. Fuckboys. To the host of the Belles of Belfast (whoever you are) - I promise it gets better.

@oonareily posted
omg I put on @spotlight_belfast tonight to listen to some music while getting ready to go out and I found the Belles of Belfast podcast... I can see this being a new Friday night ritual! Can't wait for next week!

@sineadb99 wrote
Love the new Belles of Belfast podcast @spotlight_belfast I'm already listening to it again!

Grace had the widest grin on her face as she scrolled through Facebook, eagerly sharing every positive comment she found. Meanwhile, Olivia sat quietly scrolling through her phone.

@carol82quinn posted
lol @spolight_belfast another shit show with an insecure immature host. Seriously?

@jason_movenna commented
Belles of Belfast? Really @spotlight_belfast? Load of shite!

I had expected some potential negative feedback from certain quarters, but it still stung. I'd rather not see it.

The one person I was actually anticipating feedback from was Amir. I began to wonder what he was up to. I had hoped for a text or an email from him after listening to the episode. Instead, all I received was silence. Complete and utter silence.

"Oh, look at this one!" Grace exclaimed, shoving her phone in my face. "They said you're like a modern-day Hannah Montana. You know... because no one knows your identity!"

"Sounds like I need a wig," I joked. "Just in case..."

"No one has mentioned my bit," Olivia huffed, her smile fading into an overdramatic frown. "I'll have to try harder for next week. You will have me on next week, right?"

"I'm sure someone will mention you," Grace reassured her, placing a hand on her shoulder. "It only went live about an hour ago."

"Well... If I'm not going to get any fame from it, you can tell your boss to at least pay me!" Olivia laughed, though I could sense a hint of seriousness behind her words.

Grace looked at me with sympathy in her eyes. I sighed, biting my tongue.

"So, have you heard any more from Aiden?" Grace changed the subject.

Olivia shook her head.

"What about... the Holywood rugby boy?"

She sighed. "I had to block him on Instagram. He kept responding to every story I uploaded with the fire or eggplant emoji."

"And the girl—?"

"Yeah, she's been lovely, but I let her know it wasn't going to work out. I think I might start speed dating on my lunch breaks... it'll make my workday more entertaining."

A brief silence fell between us as I lifted my drink and took a sip. Olivia was fully single tonight, which could be a dangerous scenario. She had no ties to anyone for the first time in a while...

"What about you, G?" I asked, already knowing her response.

Grace, as usual, had no boy drama. "Not really interested right now... I'm too busy. I'm working on a new TV pilot for work. Just research at the moment, but I think it'll get made. I feel hopeful about it."

I admired how hardworking she was. Grace regularly travelled all over the UK and Ireland, finding locations and developing concepts for a major local production company. It was a creative job, but I knew how exhausting it could be for her. While it looked glamorous online, the reality was that when she wasn't working, she was often sleeping.

"Are you still on a man-ban?" Olivia asked, making air quotes with her fingers. She didn't believe in all that.

"Yep," she confirmed proudly.

To Grace, a man-ban essentially meant 'I'm banning myself from dating any men until I have my career sorted.' I had often considered imposing my own 'man-ban' before the show. As I glanced around the bar, the thought crossed my mind: *Should I try to meet someone tonight? How would I even go about approaching a man?* I'd never properly initiated a conversation with someone I was interested in before. I didn't know any good pickup lines. Maybe I could do a Joey from FRIENDS impression... *'How youuu doin?'* No, absolutely not. Scrap that idea.

"Olivia, do you have any good chat-up lines?" I blurted out, curious.

"Chat-up lines?" She snickered. "Nope."

"Then what do you do?" Grace asked, intrigued. Truth be told, men usually approached Olivia. She didn't need to put in much effort. Her Instagram following mainly comprised of men who had liked and super-liked her on Tinder... but she hadn't responded to them yet. I had witnessed her meet many men whom she'd picked up from her Instagram DMs.

"Pick a name," she challenged us. "Any name."

"What? A name? Like... John?" Grace replied, innocently.

I had a bad feeling.

With a mischievous smirk on her face, Olivia cleared her throat and then shouted, "JOHN!"

The few tables around us looked around in shock. The bar was loud, but not THAT LOUD. Grace buried her face in her hands, utterly mortified by the situation. I had to cover my mouth to stifle my laughter.

"JOHN?" She repeated.

A moment later, two boys walked by our table.

"Uh, did you shout for John? I'm John," one of them said. He was short with blonde hair, looking about 18. Cute, but essentially a child, none the less.

"No. Sorry." Olivia replied, smiling sweetly. "I was looking for my friend Joe."

"Oh, sorry, uh..." John awkwardly hit his friend in the ribs as they walked off. "You're such a wanker," I overheard him mutter to his friend.

I burst into hysterical laughter, tears streaming down my face. Grace joined me, gasping, "That-that's not f-fair!"

Olivia didn't laugh, not even a peep. She just sat there proudly smiling. "It works every time."

"I'd prefer not to make such a scene," I giggled nervously. "And ideally, I'd like a man over 25."

"So, how about him?" Olivia pointed behind me.

My head shot around. "What? Who?"

"He could be your conquest of the night," she teased, wiggling her eyebrows. I turned to see a tall redhead standing alone at the side of the bar, proudly sporting a pint of Guinness, and sipping thoughtfully while people watching.

"I don't want a conquest," I replied firmly.

"You can't just use men as a 'conquest' anyway," Grace interjected. "That's just wrong. Imagine if the roles were reversed."

I pointed at Grace in agreement, nodding as she spoke.

"I'm just saying, you need content for the next episode," Olivia teased, trying to lighten the mood.

She had a point. I glanced around the room, my eyes searching for a potential special someone, but I just wasn't feeling it. I couldn't meet someone just for the sake of it. I had tried that with Mr. Barman, but low-value, casual one-night stands weren't how I wanted to live my life.

Sleeping with him only left me feeling emptier than before.

"There's no one attractive here," I shrugged, not entirely truthful. There were definitely a few good-looking faces, but none that particularly caught my eye.

"That can't be true. What's your type?" Olivia asked, leaning in with curiosity.

Before I could answer, Grace jumped in, launching into her ideal description. "My dream guy reads a lot, listens to podcasts, attends interesting events, has great family morals. Maybe he's a writer or a singer. Thoughtful, calm, with green eyes, brown moppy hair, both feminine and masculine, with a great fashion sense—"

"Harry Styles. Grace, your type is Harry Styles," I interjected, grateful for the diversion before Olivia could press me further. "I wholeheartedly agree with you. Completely. Entirely. Thoroughly. Now… Olivia, let me guess… your type… he …""

"He has a pulse," Grace quipped.

I nearly doubled over from laughter, surprised by her witty retort. It wasn't like her to make such a dig.

"No! No! He also needs to be at least 6ft2," Olivia defended herself.

"Lord have mercy," I muttered, pinching the bridge of my nose. "You've introduced us to approximately twelve men under 6ft2 in just the past year,"

"TWELVE!" Grace chimed in. She took a long sip from her G&T, then followed it with an even longer sip from her water.

"Look, I'm not embarrassed about the quantity of men I've slept with… but I am sometimes embarrassed at the quality. I have new standards now. No need to bring up the past." Olivia raised her hands in defence.

I felt a twinge of curiosity about her new standards. Did she have a checklist like Grace?

"Good to know," I smiled, trying to hold back a giggle.

"So, Anna - what's your bloody type then?" Olivia questioned again, wiggling her eyebrows.

I paused for a moment, contemplating. "I don't know. I either do or don't find him attractive. There's no set quality or thing I look for. It's just a connection. It's either there - or - it's not."

She stared at me as if I had three heads. "I don't get it."

"Very romantic. You should write a novel," Grace chimed in, smiling thoughtfully.

"I know it's kind of shallow, but I just need that instant attraction... I think," I explained, feeling a bit foolish trying to articulate my thoughts. "But I have no idea what actually makes a man attractive." I buried my face in my hands, feeling a bit embarrassed. "It's an energy thing."

"Ok then..." Olivia downed the remainder of her drink, clearly not interested in my deep uncovering. I wondered if she'd even been listening to begin with. "Shall we get another drink?"

"Nah - I think we should call it," I suggested, checking the time on my phone. It was nearly 1am.

"I agree," Grace added, stifling a yawn.

We all left the bar unaccompanied that night. Olivia's new 'six foot two' standard narrowed down her search for a partner, so she also left alone, which was quite frankly unheard of.

As I lay in bed, the room felt unusually cold despite the warmth of the covers. My pillow seemed to leech the heat from my cheek, sending a chill down my spine as I pulled the blankets tighter around me, shivering involuntarily.

My mind was consumed by thoughts of Amir. I couldn't shake the feeling of unease that gnawed at me. Why hadn't he emailed? What was he doing at this very moment? The uncertainty weighed heavily on my chest, a constant companion in the silent hours of the night, keeping me awake when all I wanted was to sleep.

Despite the nagging doubts, I couldn't resist the urge to reach out. I refreshed my emails twice, once using WiFi and then once using 4G, just in case one was down. Silence greeted me, amplifying my anxiety.

Ignoring the voice in my head screaming 'NO, DON'T DO IT,' I began typing.

Would love to know your thoughts on my first episode. The reaction online has been positive so far.
Kind Regards,
Anna.

SEND.

CHAPTER EIGHT

Costa Del Portrush

Definition: a trip to Portrush (the North Coast of Northern Ireland)

The next day, Saturday afternoon, I met the girls for brunch at Maggie May's cafe. On the days when we felt too exhausted and anti-hipster for Established, we'd always end up here. It was our comfort spot, a haven of familiarity in the midst of trendy cafes. There was nothing particularly remarkable about the dated décor, which had remained unchanged for years. But Maggie's exuded warmth, a special feeling that can't be described.

Maggie's was primarily a student spot, and it was obvious. Names and doodles adorned the wooden tables, with the occasional phallic drawing peeking through, despite the staff's attempts to cover them up. Yet, the main selling point of Maggie's however, lay in its magical milkshakes, the kind that people would queue down the street for on warm summer days.

Unbeatable. A proper Belfast gem.

Today, Olivia and I were nursing mild hangovers, while Grace, unsurprisingly, looked fresh as a daisy. She claimed her secret was a mixture of vitamin B, milk thistle (wtf is milk thistle?) and magnesium… washed down with a pint of water and some dry toast before bed. That sounded like way too much effort for me. I could barely manage to take off my makeup, and I was extremely lucky if I changed into pyjamas… never mind vitamins.

Olivia sat across from me, her hair pulled back into a ponytail (coated in dry shampoo) and a full face of makeup. She looked good, unlike me. I had thrown on a pair of black jeans and a hoodie. I'd kind of wiped off my makeup from the night before and applied some concealer under my eyes… But that was about it. My hair was combed, but you probably couldn't tell.

Olivia started our morning with a bang, as she began to cry about her lack of a sex life, "It's just so unfair… to me… to my vibrator… God, we're both going to die alone!"

As usual, Grace's face resembled a tomato.

"It hasn't been that long Liv." I soothed. "Is this because you didn't meet someone last night?"

She lifted her head, eyes glaring at me, "It's been like ten days Anna! TEN FULL DAYS!"

I couldn't help but snort into my cup of tea. "You've survived worse. Also – it's been less than ten?" I began to question if Liv could be a sex addict… or maybe she was just feeling lonely.

"You're probably just hormonal." Grace whispered across the table.

"Or you've most likely just got the hangover horn," I shrugged. Olivia buried her head in her hands.

"I almost texted an ex last night! AN EX!" she exclaimed. "I've never texted an ex before! They always text me!"

Three milkshakes were sat onto the table in front of us. I'd chosen a

Kinder Bueno flavoured shake. The perfect cure for a hangover alongside a greasy Ulster Fry.

"Probably a good thing, love," Aileen, our waitress, chimed into our conversation with a warm smile.

We had gotten to know Aileen quite well during our time at school. We'd often ditch our Monday morning class and head to Maggie May's for breakfast. She'd give us a playful slap on the wrist, always threatening to call our teachers, but I think she enjoyed our company too much as she never once made a call. During quiet moments in the cafe, she'd slide into our booth, listen to the gossip, and often offer some sage advice. With the brightest smile and widest eyes you've ever seen, she was like a ray of sunshine.

"You should never text an ex," she scolded Olivia.

"Don't be telling me that!" Olivia exclaimed. "Tell Anna!"

I gasped in horror, knowing she was referring to my past tendency to text James... too many times... but...

"Hey, hey, hey. We aren't talking about me here," I laughed, trying to deflect. "This is about you... and your lack of a sex life."

Aileen chuckled. "I think you'll need some Baileys for your milkshake, Olivia."

Olivia let her head fall onto the table. "Oh no. No alcohol. I'm never drinking again."

"Aileen, I have a question," Grace hummed. "What's your type?"

Not this conversation again...

"What?" Aileen replied, looking curious.

"So last night, we were chatting about 'types.' Like, what do you look for in a man?" Grace asked.

Aileen looked puzzled. "Well, I've never really thought about that. Sam and I have been dating since... well, I was fourteen."

"And you're what age now?" Olivia chimed in.

Aileen playfully slapped her. "Twenty-one. Drink your milkshake!"

I suspected she was in her mid-60s, maybe even 70s, but her spirit was that of a 21-year-old.

"So, what made you so attracted to Sam?" I asked.

"Well... I don't know. We just clicked. I never really had the chance to date around. From the moment I met him, he was always in the back of my mind," she explained with a fond smile.

"That's so wonderful," Grace gushed.

Olivia scoffed. "So cheesy."

"Did I not tell you to drink your milkshake?" Aileen teased.

Olivia grinned and went back to sucking on her straw.

"I just don't know what makes a man attractive. Like it just clicks. Or it doesn't." I explained.

Aileen was called over by another waitress. "One second," she waved. "Anna, in that case, my best advice is for you to date a variety of men. See what sticks."

She winked at me before rushing off to another table.

See what sticks? What does that even mean?

"It's all well and good Aileen saying that, but there isn't exactly an abundance of men I'd like to date in Belfast," I complained.

Olivia's eyes widened with excitement. *Oh no.* Her lips curved into a mischievous smile. She had an idea.

"Oh my god. Oh my god. Come with me tomorrow to the North Coast!" She hit her hand off the table in excitement. "I've got to go for work, to document The Open! My co-worker Rachel was meant to attend with me, but I just found out this morning that she has food poisoning... to be honest, I think she's lying, and her weird boyfriend won't let her go but... still!"

Grace sighed. I laughed. *How convenient.*

"I have an all-access press pass for the entire week. I can get us into every party," Olivia added. "There's so many parties. So many men!"

"Party?" Grace asked. "Aren't you meant to document the golf?"

Olivia worked for 'Northern Magic' magazine as a celebrity journalist, mainly covering sporting events. She lived the life of a socialite, networking her way into high-class events and then documenting every drama that took place.

"I—well—yes, but the parties too," she replied. "It's extremely high security. The fact we even have access is insane. You have to come with me!"

"Well, thank you for the invite, but I have plans tomorrow," I added, feeling hesitant. I didn't have plans, but I imagined the golf event would involve lots of drinking and trailing after Olivia. Plus, I knew less than nothing about golf. "And I don't think I can get the time off..."

"Do your plans include re-watching episodes of Bridgerton on Netflix from your sofa?" Grace asked, interrupting my daydream, and effectively dismantling my excuses. I narrowed my eyes at her. Fuck. Sake.

"You're going," Olivia declared.

"Going where?" Aileen questioned as she set hot plates filled with greasy Ulster fry's in front of us.

"Anna is joining me on a trip to Costa Del Portrush. She's going to meet a sexy golfer."

"Well, if I can't have the Duke of Hastings, I suppose a sexy golfer will have to do," I quipped, mustering a smile as I reluctantly accepted my fate.

***

I perched myself on the kitchen countertop, waiting impatiently for the kettle to boil. When Amir walked in, his eyes glued to his phone, I couldn't help but sit up straighter and suck in my stomach.

"Morning," I greeted with a smile.

He lifted his head, nodding in acknowledgment but not returning the smile. Then, he went back to his phone.

Well, fuck you too.

I tried to refocus on making my cup of tea, dropping a tea bag into my mug, and still waiting for the boiling water. I couldn't leave the room even after the kettle finished boiling; I liked my tea strong, like 'Builder's tea'. It would take a few minutes to brew. Glancing at the clock in the corner, I cursed leaving my phone on my desk. I had nothing to distract myself with.

Amir leaned against the cabinets, facing me, and finally pocketed his phone into his blazer. "I listened to your podcast," he said, instantly stirring the butterflies that had been dormant in my stomach since our last encounter.

"Oh?" I couldn't hide the anticipation in my voice. I'd been anxiously awaiting his feedback, checking my email countless times as my disappointment grew. Mia, Paddy, and even my mum had texted me glowing reviews. Spotlights' social media was buzzing more than usual... but I couldn't shake this nagging need to know what he thought, to ensure his approval, and safeguard my job.

His gaze locked onto mine, and I found it impossible to look away.

"Mhmmm," he hummed, clicking his tongue against the roof of his mouth. "Honestly?" He stepped closer, his presence suddenly all-consuming.

I nodded eagerly, my breath hitching in anticipation as his presence overwhelmed my senses. I couldn't resist the urge to pull him closer, craving the electric connection between our bodies. As his hands roamed over my body, sending shivers of pleasure coursing through me, I melted against him. With each caress, the heat between us intensified, driving me to the edge of reason.

"You want to know what I think?" he murmured, his voice sending waves of desire crashing over me. I nodded eagerly, unable to form words as he kissed down my neck and across my chest. His fingers gripped at my thighs, setting my senses ablaze with longing. "I said... do you want to know what I think?" He repeated.

"Yes..." I moaned as his hands clawed at the skirt I was wearing, forcing it up my thighs.

His lips met mine in a passionate kiss, igniting a fire that spread rapidly through my veins. With a hunger born of desire, he explored every inch of my mouth, leaving me breathless and wanting more. "I don't think I'd need instructions on how to..." His words trailed off, replaced by a low growl of pleasure as he teased the fabric of my skirt, sending sparks of electricity dancing along my spine. "Fuck you." In that moment, all thoughts melted away.

Suddenly, the kettle's shrill whistle pierced the air, jolting me awake from my fevered dream. Panting and flushed with arousal, I cursed my subconscious. That was the worst one yet.

With a frustrated sigh, I swung my legs over the edge of the bed, the cool air of the room a stark contrast to the warmth of my fantasies. As I stood under the biting spray of the shower, I let the icy water cascade over me, hoping it would wash away the lingering sensations. Never again, I vowed to myself.

"Date a variety of men. See what sticks." As the water ran down my spine, the words echoed in my mind, a reminder of Aileen's sage advice. Perhaps she was right.

I needed to date someone, kiss someone, maybe even sleep with someone... because I needed to get Amir out of my mind. He was sticking – but not in a comfortable way. Like he was slime, and I was a fluffy carpet. It would take a lot to scrub him out.

***

Unfortunately, my day wasn't going to improve. Two hours later, I found myself in the passenger seat of Olivia's car, en route to the golf. Surprisingly, Mia was excited for me when I asked to work at the North Coast for a few days.

"That should provide great content!" She cheered over the phone. Her reaction had me feeling slightly more positive. Only slightly. I hoped it would be more engaging than the golf I'd seen on TV. It looked extremely boring, and I'd never been into sports.

Liv hummed along to some music, while I attempted to catch some sleep with my head pressed against her car window. I had a dreaded feeling we would be up late, so I needed all the ZZZs I could get.

An hour later, we found ourselves stuck in standstill traffic on our way into Portrush. I rubbed my tired eyes and checked my emails again to see if there was anything from Amir. To my disappointment, I still hadn't heard from him. I opened Google and typed in 'Apex NYC.'

"What are you looking at?" Olivia questioned.

"Oh, just, uh, there's a new guy from NYC in the office. He's from our sister station… Apex."

"Ah yeah, I've heard of Apex," she mumbled. I knew she hadn't heard of them, but Olivia never liked to admit that she didn't know something.

"I'm basically just trying to find out more info about the company, and the… new guy."

"Oh." Olivia turned the music up in the car, perhaps hinting that she wasn't interested in the conversation. I found myself wanting to talk about Amir, even though I knew very little about him.

"His name is Amir." I blurted.

"Don't hear that name often in Northern Ireland. Very… different."

"I like it." I shrugged, feigning nonchalance as I scrolled through Apex's Instagram account. They had a lot of content to sift through.

I could feel Olivia staring at me. "You like it?" she chuckled. I looked at her, noticing the smirk plastered on her face.

"Yeah… it's a… unique name."

Silence fell upon us as Olivia turned down the music.

"A unique name?" She raised her eyebrows, her expression curious.

"Yeah, it's a… strong name… I guess. Why are you looking at me like that?"

"This isn't about the name. You like him!" She exclaimed, her voice tinged with excitement. "Oh my god… You like him. You like someone that isn't that wanker James!"

I lowered the car window, allowing some fresh air to circulate inside. "Olivia! I don't like him. I - I hate him!"

"No, you don't! You're blushing. You like this Amir guy!"

I hesitated, debating whether to reveal my embarrassing infatuation and the steamy dreams I'd been having. But this weekend was supposed to be about finding someone to distract me. I'd already fucked up.

"Okay, so I think he's attractive," I admitted, the words escaping reluctantly.

"Oh my god," Olivia gasped. "What's he like?"

"Absolutely infuriating, arrogant, cocky… a total melter!" *All true statements.*

"Oh, for fuck's sake, Anna!" Olivia slammed her hands against the steering wheel. "What's he look like?"

"Tanned, jet black hair, he dresses well, seems very muscular…" I paused, savouring the words as they tumbled from my lips, "Um… he has those kind of eyes that seem to change colour depending on the light… and his lips - ugh Liv, honestly." I described, unable to hide the effect his features had on me.

Olivia raised an eyebrow. "Dreamy?"

"Yeah, dreamy until he opens his mouth and you realise he's a walking contradiction," I retorted, attempting to shake off the lingering attraction. "He's so arrogant. It's maddening to work with him."

"Sounds like a handful."

"More like a handful of heartache," I muttered under my breath. "I kinda want to jump his bones but also punch him in the face."

"That's a kink for some people. He might be into that. BDSM and all."

"Oh god." I facepalmed, "I am *not* into that."

As traffic began to move again, my mind wandered back to Amir and what he might actually be into. He had consumed my thoughts, infiltrating even my dreams with his enigmatic presence. Yet, every time we got close to having hot, steamy dream sex… he walked away or just disappeared. As I imagined multiple scenarios, time passed quickly, and soon Olivia and I arrived in Portrush. The salty sea air filled my lungs as I rolled down the car window, welcoming the refreshing breeze that swept through the town. Our progress was sluggish as we navigated through the bustling streets, thronged with people. Banners adorned the lampposts, proudly displaying advertisements for the golf event and its illustrious players.

Finally, we reached the gates of our accommodation—a block of gated waterside apartments. Despite the slow journey, I felt relieved knowing we were just a stone's throw away from the golf club. The sky stretched out above us in a serene shade of blue, and the temperature hovered at a comfortable 16°C. It wasn't exactly warm, but it wasn't chilly either. At least the picturesque seaside and lush green cliffs promised to provide the tranquil atmosphere I desperately sought.

***

Golf is mind-numbingly dull. Despite spending four excruciating hours at the event, I remained utterly clueless about the sport. Olivia, on the other hand, had dedicated 95% of her afternoon to 'networking' in the VIP marquee. I made a brief appearance there myself, lured in by the promise of free tapas and cocktails, but my stay was short-lived.

As I downed my bellini, I couldn't help but notice a wild-looking man making his way towards me. He had short, tousled blonde hair that seemed to defy gravity, and his outfit was a riot of colours: a vibrant blue polo shirt clashed with hot pink shorts, making him stand out like a neon sign in a sea of muted tones. Feeling utterly out of place, I swiftly made my exit.

At around 4.30 PM, we returned to our apartment for a much-needed afternoon nap. One of the good things about watching golf all afternoon was how numb my brain felt, so sleep came easily.

Later in the evening, we had plans to attend a dinner party at Basalt, located somewhere near Portrush Harbour. Ever the meticulous planner,

I had already Googled the menu in advance. Needless to say, it looked absolutely incredible.

We got ready while playing some tunes and sipping prosecco on the balcony. The sea-view transported me to a place that felt more like sunny Spain than Norn' Iron. According to Google Maps, the restaurant was just an 8-minute walk away, so we opted for that.

As we strolled towards the venue, two things overwhelmed me.

Firstly, the sheer number of people bustling through the town centre.

Secondly, my own stupidity in choosing to wear my tallest high heels. How on earth would I manage to navigate my way home in these towering shoes after a few drinks?

The harbour at Portrush was teeming with activity, its waters alive with the gentle bobbing of row boats and illuminated by the twinkling lights of the restaurants lining its shores. I relished in the cool embrace of the sea air, grateful for the chance to cool down after our brisk journey from the apartment.

I thought reading the menu beforehand would offer some insight into what awaited us at Basalt, but I couldn't have been more mistaken. The restaurant occupied the top floor of a sprawling white brick building complex, its warm yellow lights casting a soft glow over the surrounding streets and water below. Photographers stationed outside clamoured to capture shots of the esteemed guests arriving for the event.

Glancing down at my outfit—a simple black slip dress—I felt a wave of panic wash over me. The entire complex had been cordoned off from the public, with police officers stationed at every corner to ensure that only authorised guests gained entry. As we approached, we presented our IDs and VIP passes, even submitting to a body scanner before being granted access. I half-expected someone to call out, 'SHE'S NOT MEANT TO BE HERE!' but thankfully we were ushered inside without incident. The scene that greeted us was nothing short of breath-taking. A long table stretched down the centre of the restaurant, adorned with flickering candles and vibrant bouquets of flowers. To the left, a bustling margarita bar beckoned.

Classic Margarita

Pineapple and Ginger Margarita

Strawberry Margarita Spritzer

Watermelon Margarita

Hibiscus Mint Margarita

Spicy Cucumber Margarita

Honey Thyme Margarita

My mouth watered.

"Wow," Olivia gasped beside me, equally taken aback. "This is madness."

"I know, I never knew there were so many flavours of Margaritas," I replied, watching as a woman behind the bar expertly mixed ingredients.

"No," Olivia nudged me, "I meant the guitarist."

To our right, a musician strummed his guitar and sang softly.

A sharply dressed man, clad in black jeans and a crisp blue shirt, guided us to our seats at the end of the long table. Once settled, he offered to fetch us drinks. I opted for the classic Margarita, though I secretly planned to sample each and every flavour on offer. *What? They were free—don't judge me.*

Olivia ordered a glass of red wine. "Large?" he asked, flashing her a smile.

"Of course," she giggled in response.

As I sipped on my delicious drink, my anxiety began to dissipate. By the time dinner was served, I felt completely at ease. Is it possible to fall in love with a dish? Because if so, I was ready to propose to the Atlantic smoked salmon starter. After indulging in a pineapple margarita followed by a refreshing watermelon one, I finally felt brave enough to mingle with some of the "golf folks."

"So, do you know many of these people? Are there actual players here?" I leaned in to ask Olivia.

She paused, momentarily caught off guard by my question, before whispering, "Anna, we are surrounded by some of the top golf talent in the world. There are two practice days left before the competition starts, so everyone's quite tense..."

I scanned the table, observing the lively interactions and relaxed demeanour of the guests. They didn't seem tense at all.

"I don't know anything about this world. I feel so out of my depth," I confessed, taking another sip of my drink. "Why do they have practice days?"

"To familiarise themselves with the course, adjust to conditions... Honestly, some of them have won so many times that I wonder why they keep playing," Olivia explained.

I nodded, absorbing the information.

"Driven by money I suppose. Like me..." She elaborated and nudged me, a playful smile on her face.

I chuckled, "Do they earn a lot?"

"See the guy on the very end of the table? That's Michael Bradworth. He was named PGA's Player to Watch at this year's Open. He earned around 24 million pounds last year."

TWENTY FOUR MILLION from golf? I was astounded. Glancing at Michael, he seemed like an ordinary guy enjoying a pint of beer. His scruffy hair and simple white shirt gave no indication of his immense success.

"Across from him is Jacob Harrods. He won the Dubai Duty Free Irish Open last year, gaining him a 1.1-million-dollar pay check. He's sponsored by Nike, BMW, loads of huge brands," Olivia continued, her tone casual but filled with insider knowledge.

I tried not to be too obvious with my glances at Jacob. He was deep in conversation with the lady beside him.

"See the bald guy down there with the big nose?"

I nodded, intrigued.

"He's probably the most successful man in this room. He's retired now but has earned something mad like over a billion dollars in endorsements, appearance fees, competition winnings. He's even designed a few courses in Florida."

"How do you know all of this?"

"I have to know who I'm talking to," Olivia explained, a hint of mischief in her eyes. "Also, golf courses are a great place to find a sugar daddy."

I burst into laughter as she nonchalantly sipped her wine.

"Ah, I see your motives now." I giggled.

Our dinner continued with a main course of roast monkfish with caramelised cauliflower, sautéed baby potatoes, pancetta, roasted shallots, and the most amazing mystery sauce.

"Oh my god," Olivia gasped suddenly.

"I know, it's just divine," I said, my mouth full of food.

She slapped me across the arm. "No, not the food, Anna. Oscar Lamoré just walked in."

"Who?"

"Holy shit, Sebastian Reynolds is with him."

I lifted my drink and took another long sip, wondering how I'd gotten into this situation. The two men were dressed impeccably, sporting black jeans, crisp white shirts, and what I assumed were expensive watches. They were both handed drinks as they mingled their way through the room.

"Which one's which?" I queried; curiosity piqued.

"Oscar is French, he's the one with dark hair. Sebastian is Australian I think, blonde hair," Olivia informed me, her eyes darting back and forth between the two men. "I'd take either."

Feeling utterly ignorant, I made a mental note: Research famous golfers. *At least attempt to fit in.*

My pondering was interrupted by the sound of someone tapping their knife on their glass. The big-nosed, bald man, whose name I didn't know, stood up to make a toast.

"Thank you all for coming to this evening's event," he began, his thick American accent cutting through the room, distinct but not as smooth as Amir's. "I am so grateful to be surrounded by such rich talent. I have watched each of you practice today, on wow, one of the most gorgeous golf courses in the world. It's going to be a tough competition this year. I want to raise a glass to all of you, your talent, and your dedication."

"Here, here!" Sebastian shouted, prompting everyone to lift their glasses in cheers.

"Ah, Sebastian. Make sure you don't drink too much. Your putting is already patchy when sober," a voice chimed in, eliciting laughter from the crowd. I joined in, even though I wasn't entirely sure what the joke meant.

After enjoying the heavenly dessert, our table was cleared, and we were ushered to another area, clearly set up for more networking and revelry. The live guitarist had been replaced by a DJ, spinning upbeat tunes that transformed the dinner atmosphere into a lively party. People began to dance, and some even started doing shots of expensive tequila at the bar.

As we moved around, Olivia continued to fill me in on the most important people in the room, her excitement palpable. She was as happy as a pig in shite.

Happy as a pig in shite
Definition: extremely happy / having a really great time

"I really want to try to speak with Oscar," Olivia whispered excitedly.

"The French guy?" I confirmed.

She nodded eagerly. "Come with me. We'll just stand by him, and then I'll try to chime in on his conversation."

Wine glasses in hand (I'd grown tired of the Marg's), we both glided closer.

"Laugh," Olivia instructed in a hushed tone.

"What?" I whispered back.

"Laugh," she repeated urgently.

I let out a forced chuckle and took a sip of my wine.

"They're looking," Olivia whispered, her eyes darting between me and the group.

"Should I laugh again?" I asked, ready to play my part in her scheme.

"No, oh, the couple they're talking to is leaving." She strutted away from me and walked directly up to Oscar. I admired her overwhelming confidence, although it scared the shit out of me. I followed suit like a lost puppy.

"Oscar, Sebastian!" She exclaimed excitedly as if it wasn't her first time meeting them, "This is Anna, she works at -"

I panicked, "Northern Magic Magazine, I'm a sports journalist. Here to document the week's activities!" I shook my hands awkwardly, kind of like jazz hands. It was a fucking strange move.

Olivia shot me a look that screamed, 'What the actual fuck?'

But it was her fault for introducing me to two strangers. *What kind of opening line was that?*

"Great to meet you." Oscar pulled me in for a kiss on each cheek, confirming his French origins. His cologne was strong, with a scent of sandalwood that lingered in the air. I held my breath, trying not to choke on the overpowering aroma.

"Olivia and I have been working together for many years," I quickly added, pinching her side to prompt her to play along.

"Yes, yes we have," she chimed in, recovering from the unexpected introduction.

I was too afraid of her accidentally blabbing about my new show and exposing my identity. If that happened, surely no man would want to speak to me.

"That's great. Oscar and I have been working against each other for many years," Sebastian joked, lifting his pint and taking a sip. I wondered how he could drink and why he wasn't resting up, with the golf tournament starting in just a few days. But maybe he didn't care about winning… or the prize money.

We chatted with the men for around 20 minutes before Oscar announced he wanted to head outside for a smoke, and Olivia said she would join him.

I awkwardly tried to make small talk with Sebastian, asking him if he'd tried Bushmills Whiskey and if he'd seen the Giant's Causeway.

"I haven't explored much here," he admitted.

"It's such a gorgeous country. So much to see! So much to do," I commented.

He smiled, took a sip of his drink, and said, "You'll have to show me."

I paused, feeling a knot form in my stomach. Was he flirting with me? Surely not.

"Me?" I asked, trying to maintain my composure.

"Yeah, if you'd like." He winked. "There's a lot I've yet to experience."

Holy shit. He was flirting with me.

"I don't know anything about golf," I blurted out, immediately cursing myself. *Why the hell did I just say that?* I'm meant to be a bloody sports journalist!

Sebastian laughed. "Well, I guess we could both benefit each other."

He grazed his hand against the side of my arm and pushed my hair off my shoulder. "What are you doing after this? I could teach you… a few things," he smirked, eyes weighing heavily into mine, "About golf, obviously."

I felt a wave of discomfort wash over me at his suggestive tone.

"I - uh - I'm not sure, I actually really need to find Olivia," I stammered, backing away, and making a beeline for the balcony. "It was nice to meet you though." I smiled.

He laughed and shouted, "Oh, I'll just go fuck myself then, will I?"

His crude remark sent a shiver down my spine. I ignored him and continued walking.

As I stepped onto the balcony, a rush of cold air enveloped me, causing me to shiver involuntarily. Despite the chill, the atmosphere was electric outside, with the faint strains of music mixed with mingling and the crashing waves from the water below.

I leaned against the railing for a second, taking in the scene before me, feeling a sense of calm wash over me amidst the chaos of the evening. The view was breath-taking, the moon casting a soft glow over the water.

As I approached Olivia and Oscar, I couldn't help but notice the way her eyes lingered on him, a glint of desire hidden beneath her playful demeanour. She leaned in closer to him, laughing at his jokes with a touch more enthusiasm than necessary. It was evident that she was drawn to him, her body language betraying her attraction.

"Hey, sorry to interrupt," I interjected, sensing the magnetic pull between them. "I think I'm going to head back to the apartment."

Olivia's attention briefly shifted to me, her smile faltering for a moment before she regained her composure. "Oh, alright. No problem. Eh… I'm going to stay a bit longer," she replied, her gaze darting back to Oscar.

I gave her a swift hug. "Text me when you're home." She said, squeezing me.

"I will." I smiled, "Lovely to meet you, Oscar."

"You too. I look forward to reading your articles," he said with a charming smile.

Ah, shit.

I nodded, feeling the awkwardness creeping in. "They'll be… full of golf!" I blurted out, cringing inwardly at my own words. "Okay – eh

– enjoy your night. Bye," I added hastily before making my exit.

As I made my way through the restaurant, I spotted Sebastian engaged in conversation with a slim lady with long, shiny black hair, who seemed much more appealing than me.

Instead of heading directly to the exit as I'd planned, I maneuvered my way through the crowd, eager to eavesdrop on their conversation.

"I hear the Giant's Causeway is meant to be amazing," Sebastian was saying to the woman.

"Oh yeah, it's class!" She replied with a strong Northern Irish accent. *Derry maybe?*

"You'll have to show me."

I couldn't help but find it amusing, almost ironic, as I watched him touch her arm, the same way he had done to me only a few minutes prior.

"Have a good night." I spoke, surprising him. His eyes widened as he wondered what to say next. I didn't give him time to speak. With a wry smile, I downed the remainder of my wine and strutted out of the restaurant.

I awoke at 2:28 am to the sound of Olivia's unmistakable moans echoing through the thin walls, accompanied by a French accent exclaiming, "Oui! Tu es une fille sale!"

CHAPTER NINE
Eejit

Definition: A stupid person

"It was just so... passionate," Olivia exclaimed, her eyes lighting up as she lifted a Bloody Mary off a passing tray. "He knew exactly, and I mean exactly, what to do."

"Oh, I know. You were very vocal," I remarked, a smile tugging at the corners of my lips as I picked up a ham and cheese-filled mini croissant and placed it onto my plate.

"Sorry! I promise I'll be quieter tonight!" she giggled, her laughter infectious.

"Tonight? You're seeing him tonight?"

"Oh! Yes! He invited me to a dinner party at someone's house," she said excitedly, taking a bite of wheaten bread topped with smoked salmon.

"Ah," I sighed, a pang of loneliness hitting me.

"Well, you're coming too, obviously!" she mumbled between bites.

I placed some fruit, a little yogurt parfait looking thing and a cinnamon apple muffin onto my plate, deciding to send Paddy a photo. A minute later, he responded with a photo of himself holding a coffee in one hand and giving me the middle finger with the other, a playful smirk on his face.

PADDY
Get fucked. Looks like you're having a horrible time

Get fucked
Definition: fuck you! (but slightly more sarcastic than serious)

I giggled to myself. Little did he know, the food was the only thing I was actually enjoying… and I was kind of having a horrible time.

ANNA
Don't think golfers are my type. It's all rather boring.

PADDY
At least you aren't me. Single. Alone. Followed by the devil.

ANNA
Wtf are you talking about?

PADDY
Amir. I'm due to have lunch with him today. Wish me luck.

I nearly choked on my coffee. I'd actually managed to forget about Amir for a little while, and thankfully he hadn't tortured me in my dreams the night before.

After a breakfast bite in the marquee, Olivia and I walked towards our seats for the morning practice. Along the way, to my dismay, I was spotted by Sebastian. In a moment of panic, I grabbed Olivia by the arm, my eyes wide, silently pleading for her to pick up on the urgency to move along. Instead, she looked behind me, spotted him, and enthusiastically screamed, "Oh, hi Sebastian!"

I clenched my jaw, fighting the urge to roll my eyes or let out an exasperated sigh.

"Hello, ladies!" He approached us with a smirk, his eyes lingering on me for a moment longer than necessary.

Dressed sharply and looking remarkably fresh for the early hour, he made some comment about my sudden disappearance at the party and how he 'missed me.'

The flash of a camera distracted me as Olivia began to flatter him, "I'm so excited to see you play!" She gushed, clearly oblivious to my discomfort.

"And you, uh…" Sebastian paused, racking his brain for my name.

"Anna," I supplied tersely, shooting Olivia a pointed look.

"Anna! Yes! Are you looking forward to a day of golf?" he asked, though his attention seemed to be more on me than the game.

"Yep." I replied curtly, my discomfort growing with each passing moment.

"It's okay. If you don't understand something about the game…" He paused, taking a beat, "I can uh… fill you in later." He winked.

His innuendo made me feel sick, but he seemed to relish in my obvious discomfort.

I chuckled, "No thanks."

As I tried to make a quick escape, two photographers suddenly appeared, their lenses trained on us. Olivia jumped, fixing her hair.

"Mmmm. I reckon you need some private lessons? No?" He continued, "Have you ever played before?" The smile on his face widened as he spoke.

I tried tugging Olivia's arm, but she wouldn't budge. "No, I'm not really interested," I replied.

"You sure? I could show you how to hold the club?" He laughed. "You any good with balls?"

I shook my head, shocked at his persistence.

"I reckon you're brilliant," he said shamelessly. "Those tiny hands…"

"Okay," I said, shaking my head, exasperated. "I know what you're insinuating, but truthfully, I'd rather throw up in my mouth and swallow it," I smiled, overly enthusiastic, letting the cameras grab their shots of him. "We should probably get going and find our seats," I said hurriedly, attempting to break away. But before I could take more than a couple of steps, Sebastian's hand closed around my arm like a vice, yanking me back with a force that left me stunned and off balance. His grip tightened around my waist, pulling me closer, and before I could even comprehend what was happening, his lips were on mine, crushing, invasive. The flash of cameras seemed to freeze the moment in time, capturing his overbearing dominance and my shock and disbelief.

Instinctively, I lashed out, stomping down hard on his foot with all the force I could muster, a surge of anger and defiance coursing through me. His grip slackened instantly, the surprise evident in his eyes as I broke free from his hold, staggering away from him with a mixture of shock and revulsion.

"Um, our seats…" Olivia mumbled, her voice barely audible, as we speed-walked away from the scene.

My stomach churned with a mix of shock and revulsion.

"I can't believe he kissed you…" Olivia spoke, her words tinged with disbelief. "You didn't tell me something was going on between you two? Did this happen last night?" Her voice trailed off, a mischievous smile forming on her lips, "when I went to the balcony with Oscar? Good choice…."

I shook my head vehemently, feeling a surge of frustration. "What?

143

No. He's revolting!"

She snorted, her tone teasing, "He's hardly revolting. He's hot, has an accent AND he's rich."

I couldn't believe her obliviousness. "Did you not just witness our entire interaction?"

She looked genuinely clueless, "Which part? The flirting or the snogging?"

"I was not flirting and I DID NOT want to kiss him!" I exclaimed, frustration boiling inside me.

"Then there's something wrong with you. He's Sebastian Reynolds," she retorted, dismissing my feelings.

"Right..." I sighed, feeling a sense of defeat wash over me, "I'm going to head back to the apartment for a bit. It's going to be a long day, and I want to try to get some work done."

As I walked away, I heard her shout after me, but I didn't turn back.

When I arrived at the apartment, I practically tore off my jacket, desperate to escape the memory of Sebastian's unwanted advances. The sensation of his lips on mine lingered like a stain, and I couldn't shake off the feeling of disgust that consumed me.

I splashed my face with water, trying to wash away the lingering sense of violation. Glancing at my outfit in the mirror, I felt a surge of anger. My attire—a simple pair of denim jeans, heels, and a black satin top—was far from provocative. I hadn't dressed for attention, yet he had made his move without a second thought.

And to make matters worse, I had verbally rejected his advances. I had made it clear that I wasn't interested, yet he had ignored my words, forcing himself upon me in a blatant display of entitlement.

Anxiety, embarrassment, and fury churned in my gut. It wasn't just a kiss—it was an assault on my boundaries.

I had a shower, made fresh coffee, and spent an hour lying on the sofa, mindlessly scrolling through social media. Outside my window, I watched the foamy waves crash against the shore, their rhythmic motion a stark contrast to the chaos brewing within me. Time seemed to crawl at a snail's pace, much like the tedious hours spent watching golf.

Deciding to steer clear of the golf course for the remainder of the day, I needed a break from the atmosphere. I did my best to push thoughts of Sebastian to the back of my mind, refusing to dwell on the unsettling encounter.

At 5:15 pm, Olivia arrived, drenched from the sudden rainstorm that had caught her off guard during her walk home. She didn't pry into why I had avoided the golf course, a silent understanding passing between us for which I was grateful. While she got dressed, I nibbled on toast and sipped tea, hoping to muster some semblance of energy for the evening ahead.

"Do you want me to help you with your eye makeup?" Olivia offered as I sat at the kitchen island.

"That would be great," I replied, grateful for the distraction.

As she worked her magic, expertly applying eye shadow and liner, I couldn't help but notice the transformation in the mirror. Thanks to her skilful hands, my makeup looked flawless, and my eyes were smoky and alluring. I ran my hands down the smooth fabric of the blue silk dress I'd chosen for the evening, but instead of feeling confident, a sickening sensation crept up my spine.

"Will Sebastian be there?" I asked cautiously, hoping my appearance wouldn't send him any mixed signals. Not that it should matter what I was wearing. He should still ask for consent.

Olivia shrugged indifferently, her nonchalant attitude grating against my nerves. "Maybe..." she trailed off, a mischievous glint dancing in her eyes, "Why, are you hoping for another kiss?"

Her teasing smirk grated on my nerves. *Surely, she wasn't serious?*

Stepping back, I couldn't contain my shock. "No, quite the opposite actually. What happened earlier was so wrong, I've felt awful all day."

Olivia regarded me with an incredulous expression, as if my reaction was exaggerated. "Oh, come on. It was just a kiss."

I was speechless, unable to articulate the violation I felt. As she grabbed her purse and made her way to the kitchen, leaving me alone in the room, I couldn't shake the unsettling feeling that lingered.

It was a kiss that I didn't ask for.

***

Around 7 p.m. we found ourselves traversing what initially appeared to be a quaint country road, only to realise it was the driveway leading to the largest estate I'd ever laid eyes on in Northern Ireland. The stones beneath our tires were rugged, and towering oak trees framed the driveway, casting long shadows in the fading light.

"Where the hell are we?" I exclaimed; my eyes wide with awe.

Olivia eagerly snapped photos on her phone as we approached the imposing home. Its red door stood out vividly against the facade, and I craned my neck to take in the sight of the three-story structure.

With each step closer, I marvelled at the sheer scale of the building. I imagined sprawling halls, grand staircases, and luxurious rooms decorated with gorgeous furniture and expensive art on all the walls.

I followed Olivia up the grand steps to the front entrance, my excitement mounting with each stride. As the massive door swung open effortlessly before us, I braced myself.

The air was alive with laughter and music; the tinkling notes of a piano drifted from one room, while the soulful strains of a guitarist and singer serenaded from another. The melodic hum of conversation, punctuated by a myriad of accents—Irish, German, Italian, French, Australian, American, and more—echoed throughout the space.

But, I couldn't help but feel a pang of disappointment. The grandeur of the exterior didn't seem to extend to the interior. The hallway, though spacious, felt strangely empty, lacking the warmth and cosiness I had expected.

Navigating through the hallway towards the dining area, I couldn't shake the nagging feeling of unease. It was as though the house held secrets beneath its polished exterior, leaving me unsettled and wary. Everything felt off-kilter. No picture frames, no ornaments, nothing. I wondered if the decor had been taken away to make more room for the party.

"There he is," Olivia whispered, pointing towards Oscar, who stood by the patio doors.

He waved at her to join him, and I followed reluctantly.

"Hello, gorgeous," Oscar greeted Olivia with a kiss on the cheek. Then, turning to me, he smiled, "Hello, Miss Anna."

I was pleasantly surprised that he remembered my name, unlike Sebastian. I smirked, suddenly thinking of a new name for him... Mr. Player sounded about right. I stifled a laugh, but it seemed my thoughts had summoned his presence. And Mr. Player, I mean, Sebastian, certainly made his presence known with a loud "Woohooo, my lucky charm!"

"Olivia, fancy a drink?" I snapped, refusing to entertain him. Despite my inner turmoil, I maintained a facade of composure, hiding the trembling nerves coursing through me.

Sebastian's touch on my waist felt invasive, and the stench of alcohol on his breath made my stomach churn. "I knew the Irish were lucky!" he declared with an irritating grin.

Swiftly, I removed his arm, taking a step back to create some distance.

"I assume you've been celebrating that birdie from this afternoon!" Oscar interjected, sensing the tension.

Sebastian gloated about his success, adding yet again, "She's my lucky Irish charm," he squeezed my arm in a display of ownership.

Oscar's amused expression only added to my frustration.

Beside me, Olivia remained frozen, unsure of how to intervene. I shot her a pleading look, silently urging her to speak up. *Say something.*

Literally anything.

"I don't believe in luck," I stated firmly, my irritation evident in my tone.

Sebastian's laughter grated on my nerves as he attempted to encroach on my personal space once again. I pushed him away, refusing to tolerate his inappropriate behaviour.

"Meeting me was *very* lucky," he teased, his arrogance infuriating me further.

Rolling my eyes at his audacity, I couldn't contain my exasperation. *More like, very unlucky.*

But before I could confront him further, Sebastian's unwelcome gesture crossed another line. "Oh come on, it's only a bit of fun," he insisted, pinching at my bum.

The sharp pain elicited a cry of protest from me, my anger boiling over. "You asshole! How dare you-" I began, but Olivia's timely interjection offered me an escape from the uncomfortable situation.

"Anna, drinks?!" she interrupted, her voice a welcome relief.

"Yes, yes, bring me back a beer." He shouted. I only managed two steps before he tried pulling me back, probably wanting a kiss. *Not again.* I used all my strength to shove him off me.

"What the fuck! Why are you getting on like that?" Olivia snapped as we walked away.

My eyes were blurry with tears as I marched off. She called after me, "The bar is this way…"

"I'll just be a minute." I snapped. I needed space… which seemed impossible. I waved through the hoard of people that lined the dining space, trying to keep my calm.

Anxiety surged through my veins as I struggled to contain my angry tears. Desperate for a moment of solitude, I scanned the room and spotted a closed door tucked away to the side of the bustling dining area.

Without hesitation, I made my way toward it, my heart pounding in my chest with each step. I swung the door open, finding an empty utility room. It was filled with cardboard beer boxes, empty Tesco bags and a pile of laundry in the corner. *Someone had to live in the house if there was laundry.*

I leaned against the counter, next to the sink cluttered with empty champagne and wine bottles. Absently, I lifted a few, hoping for a remnant of liquid inside, but they were all dry. Frustration welled up, mingling with the anxiety tightening my chest. It had been years since I'd felt this way, but here it was again, overwhelming and suffocating.

Focusing on my breath, I tried to regain control, though tears streamed down my cheeks unabated. Desperate for distraction, I resorted to pinching my skin and wiggling my fingers and toes, anything to divert my mind from the panic.

Was I being dramatic? Or was he a complete and utter asshole?

The sudden sound of a door opening and slamming shut made me jump, nearly knocking over a bottle. My gaze shot up to find a well-dressed man standing there, eyes closed, breathing heavily. He seemed as startled as I was when he opened his eyes and noticed me perched on the counter.

"Sorry, I didn't realise anyone was here," he stammered, his Northern Irish accent bringing a sense of familiarity and comfort.

I hopped down from the counter, hastily wiping away my tears, unable to meet his gaze. "No, it's my fault," I murmured, my voice barely above a whisper.

"Are you alright?" he asked, genuine concern lacing his words.

"Yes, yes. Sorry," I mumbled, gesturing towards the door, but he halted me with a firm grip.

"DON'T touch me!" I exclaimed, pushing his hands away, my voice raw with emotion.

He recoiled, his eyes widening in surprise. "I'm sorry, I wasn't... I mean, you don't look alright," he stammered, taking a step back.

My lip quivered, and I couldn't hold back the tears, feeling utterly embarrassed by my outburst.

With my face buried in my hands, I heard him rummaging through a cabinet. He emerged with a roll of kitchen paper, offering it to me. "Sorry, there are no tissues," he said softly.

I nodded, taking the roll, and delicately wiping my eyes, hoping my mascara hadn't smudged too badly.

"I'm sorry. I didn't mean to lash out at you," I managed to choke out, swallowing hard. "This is all just... overwhelming. I came in here for some sort of escape."

"I totally understand. If it makes you feel any better, I came in here for an escape too," he admitted, running a hand through his hair.

His flushed complexion hinted at his own inner turmoil, though he wasn't drunk. I glanced awkwardly at the scattered empty bottles on the ground.

"You seem really upset. Can I get you anything? Do you want me to call someone?" he offered; genuine concern evident in his voice.

"No, no. I'll be fine," I reassured him, taking a deep breath to steady myself. "Just being dramatic. This man wouldn't leave me alone but maybe he just wasn't getting the hint…"

He nodded and started rummaging through a cabinet. The silence was awkward.

"Whoever owns this house uses this room as a dumping ground," I remarked, attempting to lighten the heavy atmosphere.

The man glanced at me, a puzzled expression crossing his face. His green eyes squinted as if trying to decipher me. I offered a small smile.

"Ah, yes. They must do," he replied, nudging a few boxes with his feet.

"It's not a very welcoming house anyway," I continued with a sigh. "I imagine it's rather empty and dull when it's not filled with people."

"Why's that?" he inquired.

"There are no decorations, no signs of life... well, apart from that pile of laundry," I pointed out. "I haven't seen a single photo frame. I imagine a very lonely old man lives here."

"You're probably right," he agreed quietly.

He moved past me and picked up an empty wine bottle from the sink, inspecting it closely as I had done just minutes before.

"I tried that. They're all empty," I informed him.

"Damn," he whispered, disappointment evident in his voice. "Well, I fancy a drink... do you think we can handle the party together?" he asked with a half-smile, attempting to inject some levity into the situation.

I inhaled deeply, calming myself. "Yeah, I need to find my friend too. She's probably worried."

As I followed him back through the party, his presence was unmistakable. I assumed he was famous in the golf world, but I didn't feel inclined to ask.

As he pushed his way through the crowd to reach the front of the bar, I couldn't help but feel a pang of embarrassment, offering apologies to the few people I made eye contact with. However, as he approached, one of the bartenders tended to him immediately. I couldn't help but be impressed.

"Two glasses of Moët please," he ordered confidently.

Within 30 seconds, a glass was in my hand. "Do we have to pay for this?" I asked, feeling a twinge of uncertainty.

He looked at me, pausing for a moment, probably trying to gauge if I was serious or joking. Then, he burst out laughing. "Nah, it's free," he reassured me.

I nodded, feeling my cheeks flush with embarrassment, and took a sip of my glass.

"So, what's your name then?" he shouted over the lively crowd.

"Anna!" I yelled back, trying to be heard above the booming music and the enthusiastic rendition of 'Money, Money' by ABBA—a fitting soundtrack.

"Anna who?" he screamed back.

As I glanced around, taking in the scene of people singing and dancing, I spotted a few golfers from the previous night who looked utterly plastered. I couldn't fathom how they'd manage to play golf the next morning.

"Anna Mulholland. What's your name?" I replied, raising my voice to be heard over the music and chatter.

He jerked his head back slightly, raising his eyebrows as if testing me. I gathered he was surprised I didn't recognise him, but frankly, I didn't really care how much of a hotshot golfer he was—my experience with golf had been abysmal so far.

"Tom Beckham," he answered, a tentative smile forming on his lips.

"Related to David?" I quipped, trying to lighten the mood.

"Haha, no, unfortunately not," he chuckled, taking another sip of his champagne. It struck me as unusual for a guy to choose champagne, especially in Northern Ireland. But I supposed this was a high-class event, with high-class people, and high-class refreshments to match.

Suddenly, a young man shouted, "Beckhammmmm!" and pulled Tom into a manly hug. Tom rolled his eyes in my direction, and I couldn't help but laugh at the scene.

Deciding to give them some space, I pointed towards the quieter side of the room and made my way out of the bustling crowd. Standing at the periphery, I sipped on my champagne, observing Tom's interaction with the other man. He seemed affable, his smile genuine, and wrinkles appeared around his eyes as he laughed. From his appearance, I guessed he was in his late thirties or early forties, with a few strands of grey peeking out amidst his mop of black hair. Overall, he struck me as a nice man. I took out my phone and attempted to call Olivia, but it went straight to answering machine. I assumed she was probably off learning French somewhere.

A dreaded voice interrupted my thoughts. "You're lookin' chirpier than earlier!" Sebastian slurred his words, wobbling unsteadily on his feet. He held a beer bottle in his hand, taking a sip as he spoke. His shirt hung messily out of his trousers, and he looked absolutely paralytic.

Paralytic

Definition : Someone who is extremely drunk

I turned back to the crowd, where Tom was still engrossed in conversation. I silently hoped he'd notice me and make his way over, but luck wasn't on my side.

"Whatcha drinkin'?" Sebastian's voice intruded again, breaking my concentration.

I didn't answer him, hoping he'd take the hint and leave me be.

"Oooooo champagne… fancy. Wanna get some shots? I owe you a drink anyways," he persisted, his words slurred.

"The drink is free," I reiterated, hoping he'd get the message and leave me alone, but he continued to pester me, undeterred.

"That's even more of a reason!" Sebastian exclaimed, his words slurred as he leaned in closer.

I turned towards Sebastian, frustration evident in my voice. "I don't know how many times I have to ask you to leave me alone!" I sighed, hoping to convey my exasperation.

My rejection seemed to only excite him further, as if I were some kind of delicious challenge for him to win over. His eyes lit up with anticipation.

"Whaaaaat? But babe, it's just a drink!" he protested, taking another step closer to me. Instinctively, I moved two steps away from him, trying to put some distance between us.

"Or maybe… maybe you want a line?" he suggested, his voice lowering as he eyed me suggestively.

Refusing to dignify his offer with a response, I turned my attention back to the crowd, silently praying that Tom would notice me. Just as I made eye contact with him, Sebastian startled me by grabbing my arm. I recoiled, shaking him off violently and stepping further away, my heart racing with discomfort.

"Come on. I need to get my lucky charm another drink!" Sebastian exclaimed, taking another step closer to me. "Your glass is almost empty!"

I glanced down at the remaining Moët in my glass and briefly considered throwing it over him. But better not...

"Don't make me beg!" Sebastian laughed; his tone laced with a hint of desperation. "I don't like games!"

I turned to face him squarely, my patience wearing thin. "This isn't a game. Will you just leave me alone? I'm not interested."

"Hey Anna," a voice interrupted, causing the tension in my body to automatically release. "Is everything okay?"

I turned to face Tom, relief flooding through me as he intervened. "Hey," I murmured, grateful for his timely interruption.

Tom glanced down at me, his expression softening as he caught the panic in my eyes. Without a word, I conveyed my distress, nodding subtly towards Sebastian. There was a silent understanding between us.

With practiced ease, Tom threw his arm over my shoulder, drawing me close to him. I leaned into him, letting my head rest against his chest. "Sebastian, how are you?" Tom greeted him with a confident smirk, his voice calm and collected as he addressed the intruding presence. He gently squeezed my shoulder, a subtle gesture of reassurance.

Sebastian froze, his muscles rigid as he processed the scene unfolding before him. "Wait... Are you two...?" he trailed off, pointing between us, his eyes widening in surprise.

"Yes," Tom replied casually, confirming the unspoken question hanging in the air.

I looked up, grateful that this stranger I'd just met was going along with the charade. Sebastian's reaction was palpable; he nodded slowly, inhaling a deep breath as if trying to process the situation. He appeared a bit speechless, which only served to reaffirm Tom's authority in the room. It felt oddly empowering to be on his arm, yet simultaneously disappointing that Sebastian only respected me as Tom's territory.

"Oh shit! Oh shiiiiiit! I'm sorry, dude!" Sebastian exclaimed, holding his hands up in a gesture of surrender, his voice filled with disbelief.

Tom simply nodded in response, pulling me in closer to him, his protective stance unmistakable.

"I'm just - I'm gonna grab a beer," Sebastian muttered, his restlessness evident as he avoided making eye contact. "Do you? I mean, can I get you one?"

Before Tom could even answer, Sebastian had already slipped away into the crowd of bodies, leaving behind a sense of peace and relief.

"Thank you so so so much," I exclaimed, releasing a sigh of relief.

"You looked like you needed saving," Tom chuckled. "That Sebastian guy is a hallion."

Hallion

Definition : A messer. Someone who's a bit wild, loud-mouthed and annoying.

I snorted in agreement. "Ever wish you could meet someone again and walk straight past them?"

Tom erupted into a loud belly laugh, his body vibrating against mine. "Yes, I know exactly what you mean. I'm not his biggest fan. He should have retired a while ago. So, what was that all about?"

I briefly filled him in on the encounter with Sebastian, not wanting to dwell on the unpleasantness.

We then spent the next 20 minutes engaged in conversation about the party, the people, and even the golf, although I tried to steer clear of that topic as much as possible. I found myself growing even fonder of Tom as we chatted. He spoke smoothly, pausing every so often to carefully consider his words before speaking. Maybe it was just an older person thing? I imagined him to be about ten years older than me, exuding a maturity and respectability that I rarely found in men my own age.

"So, what do you do for work?" Tom inquired, his curiosity evident in his expression.

I paused, unsure of how to answer. "Oh, I'm a sports journalist for Northern Magic Magazine," I replied, hoping my fabricated answer sounded convincing.

"Oh really?" His smirk hinted that he didn't quite buy my explanation.

"Mhm," I replied with a smile, inwardly cursing myself for not being better at lying or coming up with a more believable cover story.

"I work with my friend Olivia, who is actually here tonight… we should find her. I'd love to introduce you!" I said hastily, grasping his arm and pulling him through the crowded house, hoping to change the conversation. He followed along, laughing softly to himself. I couldn't tell if he found my urgency amusing or if he was chuckling at my 'I'm a sports journalist' lie.

"This is an awfully big house!" I groaned as we navigated through the sea of people, grateful for the distraction from any further work-related questions.

"You said that already," He teased with a grin.

"Imagine the cost of heating this place!" I exclaimed, throwing my hands in the air.

"I'm sure whoever owns it can manage," He shouted over the noise of the crowd.

"I'm sure whoever owns it is a bit of a dickhead… no one needs this much space, especially being so empty," I joked, shaking my head. "It's just a bit over the top. You could have fifty people living here and it would still feel too big."

"Miss Anna!" a familiar voice yelled from across the room. I spun around, trying to locate the source of the voice amidst the maze of hallways and people.

"Oscar, hi!" I called out, finally spotting him waving from yet another hallway. My head was spinning from the sheer number of rooms and doors, not to mention the throngs of people.

"Oscar, this is Tom. Tom, this is Oscar," I introduced them.

"We've met." They said in unison.

Oscar, like many of the people at the party, looked absolutely piss drunk.

"Where's Olivia?" I questioned, my concern growing. I had assumed she would be by his side for the rest of the night.

"She's in the bathroom," he slurred, pointing unsteadily to a large brown door. "In there."

Something about the way he spoke raised alarm bells for me.

"I should—I'll go check on her. Be back in just a moment," I said, scanning the room for a place to set down my empty champagne glass, but there were no tables or benches in sight. "Why does this house have no fucking furniture!" I vented in frustration before storming towards the bathroom.

I knocked on the door gently. "Liv, it's me."

"Not good Anna, not good..." I heard her mumble from behind the door. Concern gnawed at my stomach as I tried the door handle, only to find it locked.

"Are you sick?" I asked, though I already had a sinking feeling that I knew the answer.

She unlocked the door, and I slid inside, immediately greeted by the sight of her hunched over the toilet.

"Oh shit, Liv," I murmured, gathering her hair back from her face. "How long have you been in here?"

"I dunno like..." she slurred, barely coherent. "Ten or fifty."

"Fifty or fifteen?" I asked, trying to make sense of her drunken rambling. "How did you get so drunk?"

Before she could respond, she was interrupted by another bout of vomiting into the toilet bowl. Holding Olivia's hair back was something I'd done countless times over the years, but it never got any easier. I hated vomit, and Olivia knew it. In fact, she'd earned the nickname 'Boke-ahontis' from me due to how many times we'd found ourselves in this exact scenario. Unfortunately, she wore the badge with pride and found it comical—though usually only a few days after the vomiting had occurred. She never seemed to learn her lesson.

When Olivia paused from being sick, I turned to the sink, washed my champagne glass, and filled it with cold water. "Rinse your mouth," I instructed, handing her the glass. "Did you... take any drugs?"

She nodded her head, then shook it in denial and took a small sip, then spat into the toilet. I flushed it afterward, hoping to rid the room of the stench.

"What did you take?"

She shook her head again and began to gag.

As I held her head back, there was a knock at the door. "It's Tom. Everything alright in there?" he called out.

Olivia nodded weakly. "I'm fineeee," she managed to reply, her voice strained.

I wedged the door open to allow Tom to pop his head in. His nose wrinkled and he visibly cringed at the sight and smell.

"She's just, very sick," I mumbled, feeling embarrassed by the situation.

Tom nodded understandingly and covered his mouth as he spoke. "Do you need anything?"

"I think we'll just have to head home," I sighed, feeling the weight of disappointment settle in.

His expression mirrored my sentiment. "I'll call you a taxi," he offered, his voice sympathetic.

Olivia moaned something incoherent as she mopped her mouth with toilet paper. Eight uneasy minutes later, Tom and Oscar were helping me guide her into a black taxi. The taxi man anxiously over-looked as we slid her into the back seat. He was probably already preparing himself for the journey and imagining how much he could charge us if she was to vomit in his car. I glanced up at the starry night sky and prayed 'God, Jesus, Mary… the donkey… if you're there…please do not let her vomit in the car. Amen.'

"Do you want me to accompany you home?" Oscar questioned, interrupting me from my oh so godly prayer. He looked genuinely concerned, however I felt more comfortable taking care of her on my own.

I shook my head, "No, no. We'll be fine. Thank you though."

"Great to meet you." He said, opening the passenger side door for me.

"Thanks." I smiled solemnly. "You too."

Tom quickly embraced me in a hug. "Get home safe."

As we drove off, I stole a glance at Olivia, who was almost totally unconscious and sprawled across the back seats, held in place by two seat buckles to prevent her from rolling onto the car's floor. In the rear-view mirror, I could see Tom standing outside the front door, his hands tucked into his pockets as he watched us drive away.

A sense of sadness washed over me, mingled with relief. It was a strange combination, but I couldn't shake the feeling that I'd have liked more time with him. Pushing the thought aside, I turned my gaze to the passing scenery outside the window, allowing myself to drift into a state of mindless contemplation for the remainder of the journey home.

I was woken up twice during the night, holding Olivia's hair back and fetching her water.

"Don't take drugs." She shivered over the toilet bowl. "Not even a little bit."

"Who gave you drugs? What kind?" I asked, rubbing her back.

She shook her head and heaved once more. "Ket. I think." After a moment, she stood and turned on the shower. "Doesn't matter. Go back to sleep, I'm fine now. Promise."

"But-"

"Anna go to bed." She demanded.

By morning, I felt dizzy with tiredness. Despite there still being many days of golf left, I decided I had had enough for a lifetime. I packed up my bag and explained that I had to go back to work. Thankfully, after a quick phone call, it worked out that Olivia wouldn't be alone. Her colleague Rachel had miraculously recovered from food poisoning—although 'Liv reckoned her endless posts on social media made the event look 'too good to resist', and Rachel obviously couldn't deal with the FOMO.

***

The journey was a blur. I dozed off for a stretch, my head awkwardly propped against the window. Raindrops, as expected, began their descent around Bangor, and by the time I returned to Belfast city centre, the heavens had fully unleashed their fury. From the shelter of the train station, I observed people darting across the road, their frantic movements matched by the downpour. Mia expected me back in the office by 1pm; it was now 12:40. Cursing my luck as Uber showed no available cars due to the rain-induced surge in demand, I reluctantly used my bag as makeshift protection while sprinting towards the taxi rank. Naturally, the last black taxi departed just as I arrived, fuelling my frustration to boiling point. I let out a scream, feeling utterly defeated.

Contemplating whether to retreat to the station or brave the elements to get to work, I realised I was already thoroughly drenched, rendering the six-minute walk to the office inconsequential. Or so I thought. The sky unleashed a barrage of hailstones, its grumbling serving as a fitting accompaniment to my misery. Shivering as cold rain seeped through my clothes, I cursed Northern Ireland's infuriatingly unpredictable weather. When I departed Portrush, the sun had been shining!

By the time I stumbled into the studio, my hair was plastered to my face and my clothes clung uncomfortably to my skin. I had never felt more miserable. Storming through the entrance, I swiped my pass without a glance at Aoife, the receptionist, though I couldn't miss her audible gasp and muttered exclamation of "oh my god" as I passed by.

Leaving a trail of water behind me as I stepped out of the lift onto my floor, my boots squelched with each soggy step.

Paddy's eyes widened as he glanced up from his desk. "Jesus... what happened to you?"

I gave him the middle finger.

"Looks like you got caught in a monsoon out there. No life raft?" he jested.

I shot him a wry smile, my mood not quite up for banter. "Where's Mia?" I asked, my tone more clipped than I intended.

"In her office," Paddy replied, his expression sobering as he noticed my demeanour.

Without further ado, I headed straight for her office and knocked on the door.

"Come in," Her voice called out.

Pushing open the door, I found her inside... and to my astonishment, Amir was there too. The realisation hit me like a splash of cold water. I had completely forgotten about him in the whirlwind of the last 24 hours.

"You look... stunning," he remarked, his signature smirk on display, "You're quite the sight."

Mia's eyes widened in realisation. "What on earth happened to you?"

Drenched

Definition: Soaking wet

"Didn't you see the rain? I got caught right in the middle of it," I explained, feeling uneasy under Amir's scrutinising gaze as he looked me up and down. Up and down. Up… and… down.

"Anyways, I just wanted to let you know that I'm back. I can change in the bathroom. I think I have some clothes here from the weekend," I said, holding up my bag. Water droplets cascaded from the bag onto the floor as I did so. "They might still be dry."

"Good to see you back. I suppose you have lots of content for the next episode," Mia said, wiggling her eyebrows suggestively at me.

I cringed at the thought of my next episode. My weekend had been a complete flop. I hadn't flirted with anyone, slept with a man, or learned any new sex positions. Instead, I spent my nights alone in bed, listening to Olivia try out various activities. I still hadn't managed to achieve a single orgasm… Truth be told, I hadn't accomplished anything noteworthy or scandalous. I hadn't even mustered the courage to exchange phone numbers with anyone intriguing, so any potential developments in the golf department were out of the question. But also, I'd blocked James, so he couldn't contact me even if he wanted to. There were no 'Mr. Fuckboy' updates. And as for 'Mr. Barman'… I'd tried to wipe him from my memory – not that he was all that memorable to begin with.

"Anna?" Amir's voice broke through my thoughts.

"Hmmph?" I grunted in response.

"Aren't you going to get changed?" he prompted.

I snapped out of my daydream, nodding hastily. "Yes, yes. I'll ehm… get to planning my episode." I muttered, quickly exiting the office.

I nearly screamed when I caught sight of my reflection in the bathroom mirror. *Dear god, why hadn't I checked my appearance sooner?* I knew it would be bad, but the level of disarray staring back at me was beyond belief. Absolutely horrendous.

Mascara streaked down my cheeks, my hair a frizzy mess sticking to my damp face. My once-white blouse clung to me, fully revealing the lace bra underneath. I cursed under my breath. Just great… Now Amir had basically seen my tits twice without my intention. It was a miracle I still had a job after such inappropriate flashing.

Glancing out the window, I sighed as I saw the rain still pouring down relentlessly. Though I lived just a few minutes away, walking home in this weather was out of the question. Mr. Barman had also swiped my only umbrella, so returning home to change meant getting soaked all over again. I emptied the contents of my bag onto the bathroom floor in frustration.

I had a cream t-shirt and jeans with trainers.

Or… a black dress and lace-up heels.

Usually, the decision would be a no-brainer – opt for casual and comfortable. But as Amir's voice replayed in my mind, taunting me with 'You look stunning'… Arrogant ass… A risky idea formed in my mind.

It took me a painstaking twenty-five minutes. I found myself awkwardly squatting under the hand dryer, attempting to tame my unruly hair. Every thirty seconds, I gave up, sinking back onto the floor to massage my burning thighs. *Mental note: hit the gym more often. Do more squats.*

After wiping off my makeup and applying a fresh layer of concealer, foundation, and mascara, I swiftly changed into the black dress, its hem grazing just above my knees. With the black lace stockings still in their unopened cardboard packet, I carefully slid them up my thighs. There was no way I'd allow him the satisfaction of catching a glimpse beneath my dress, but the confidence these stockings bestowed upon me was worth it in itself.

Perched on the toilet seat, I awkwardly laced up the black heels around my ankles, my heart pounding against my ribcage. This outfit was a far cry from my usual office attire; I had never dared to wear something like this before. Running my hands through my hair, I focused on my breathing, inhaling and exhaling slowly as I took in my reflection. I may not fit the conventional definition of stunning, but in my own way, I was attractive, whether he recognised it or not.

As I approached my desk, I caught Paddy's double-take. "Hold on a minute... you looked like you'd been through a hurricane the last time I saw you!"

I chuckled, settling my bag under the desk. "And now?"

"Better," he quipped with a grin.

I shot him a teasing glare. "Are you trying to flirt with me?"

The colour drained from his face, a mix of shock and amusement. I laughed, knowing Paddy would never. "Relax, I'm just messing with you. So, fill me in, what have I missed? How was your date with the devil?"

"Coffee – was fine. He was actually dead on, you know." Paddy hummed in contemplation.

Dead on

Definition : often used to affirm that something is accurate / okay / fine
('spot on')

"He just wanted to know my thoughts on where I could see Spotlight in a year from now. Didn't debate with me. Just listened." He shrugged, "However, I'm beginning to wonder if he's bipolar. Today he's been fucking ruthless Anna – honestly. He fired Quinn - gave her 30 day's notice but she was too upset to come back after the meeting."

A wave of frustration washed over me at the injustice of it all. Quinn was one of our good producers. She didn't deserve that.

"And it doesn't stop there," Paddy added, nodding towards the boardroom. "11 staff have been made redundant so far. He's probably going to fire Andrew next." Amir emerged from Mia's office, his laptop in hand, and walked straight into the boardroom. Andrew, wearing a shirt and tie (which he never wore), followed behind with a ghostly pale face.

"God..." I sighed, at a loss for words.

"Soulless American Bastard," Paddy muttered under his breath.

I absentmindedly twirled a pen between my fingers, trying to calm my racing thoughts. "I should probably get some work done before he decides to fire me too."

"Yeah, just be careful. You seem to get under his skin a lot..." Paddy raised an eyebrow at me.

I was taken aback. "What? Did he tell you that? I barely speak to him."

My heart began to race at the thought of him discussing me. I stood there, replaying all of our interactions. Yeah, I'd kind of tried to get under his skin, but only in response to how he made me feel.

"Anna?" Paddy interrupted my daydream. "Work?"

I shook myself out of my reverie and headed back to my desk. Sitting down, I chewed on the end of my pen, my mind swirling with thoughts. "Did he actually talk to you about me? What did he say?" I shouted to Paddy, making sure no one was around to overhear.

"Don't you have an episode to write?" he deflected, before leaving his desk and heading into the break room.

I sighed, feeling a mixture of frustration and curiosity gnawing at me. Pushing aside my concerns for the moment, I focused on the task at hand, though my mind kept drifting back to the unsettling possibility of Amir discussing me.

I shook my head and decided to drown out my thoughts with some music. Placing headphones over my ears, I let the familiar melodies wash over me, attempting to find solace in the rhythm

Golf. What happened at the golf that I could use for my episode?

Olivia and Oscar... her latest romantic interest. I contemplated reaching out to her for some juicy details on whether French men lived up to their reputation. But the idea felt empty, devoid of meaning. Plus, if their escapades were as intense as I'd overheard, it could inadvertently encourage a mass exodus of Belfast girls to France – a potential blow to my viewership.

Then there was Tom…Beckham? While he appeared to be the epitome of a gentleman, there was little substance to write about. That is, until my thoughts drifted to Sebastian.

Sebastian, the antithesis of a gentleman.

A man who disregarded my boundaries, showing a blatant disregard for consent. He revelled in my dislike for him, viewing it as a challenge rather than a deterrent. The mere thought of him made my blood boil, stirring up a mixture of anger and unease that I struggled to push aside.

MR PLAYER (Sebastian)

During a girls' brunch, I vented about my frustrations regarding the lack of desirable men to date in Belfast. In a flash, my friend, dubbed 'Miss Sensuality,' convinced me to attend a high-profile sporting event teeming with local and potentially dateable international men. Now, there's a stereotype about sports stars being womanisers. This past weekend, I encountered a man who not only plays sports but also plays women.

Enter Mr. Player.

So, what defines a player?

A player is typically someone seeking nothing more than a good time—a casual hook-up. They're not interested in genuine connections and often disregard any emotional attachment. Now, there's nothing wrong with this if everyone is on the same page… But a player will have you believing they want more than they actually do. They're often masters of emotional manipulation. They'll do anything, say anything, and act a certain way to get what they want, leading you to believe that eventually, you'll get what you want too.

Women are merely pawns in their game.

In my case, I had no interest in participating in his game. I didn't find him appealing, and I made it clear that his flirtatious advances were unwelcome. Yet, my disinterest seemed to fuel his desire to play even more.

Abruptly, my productivity was pierced by the unwelcome intrusion of an email alert. Startled, I witnessed my pen slipping from my grasp, its clatter against the desk jolting me from my concentration. With a resigned sigh, I reluctantly shifted my focus to the glowing screen of my phone, where the subject line of the message flashed ominously:

INBOX (1) amir.daivari@apex.com
Are you free for a moment? Need to talk asap.

CHAPTER TEN

Fucking fuming

Definition: Extremely angry

REPLY anna.m@spotlightbelfast.com
Yes. Free anytime. Let me know when suits.
What did he need to talk about? Why was he being so vague?

INBOX (1) amir.daivari@apex.com
1.30pm – you arrived late so shouldn't mind meeting me during lunch?

I exhaled a long sigh, brewed a cup of coffee, and scribbled aimlessly in my notebook as my mind refused to cooperate. Time seemed to crawl as I stared at the clock. Suddenly, at 1:12 PM, Andrew burst out of the boardroom, his expression stormy, and jabbed the down button for the elevator. It was evident: he'd likely been given the axe... and I was likely next in line.

By 1:20 PM, the office had emptied out for lunch. Paddy began gathering his belongings, swivelling his chair to face me. "Ready to head out?"

I chewed nervously on my lip. "Unfortunately, no. I've got a date with the devil."

"Oh?" He swallowed hard. "Well, let me know how you get on," he said, then departed, leaving me alone, bracing myself for what was to come.

***

At 1:28 PM, I rapped lightly on the boardroom door. As I took a seat, Amir's gaze lingered on my altered appearance. "You look... different," he remarked, his tone devoid of humour. His face remained impassive, but I detected a slight twitch in his eye, a subtle indication of... what? *Disapproval? Surprise?* It was hard to tell. His observation made me break out into a slight sweat, suddenly self-conscious of every detail.

He had shed his suit jacket, and his muscles were prominently defined beneath his crisp white shirt. Anticipating a discussion, I waited for him to join me at the table. Instead, he strolled over to a side table and poured himself a cup of tea.

"Care for some tea?" he offered.

"No, thank you," I declined.

The atmosphere weighed heavily upon me. I squirmed uncomfortably in my chair.

"Where were you?" he inquired.

"I was at the Irish Open," I replied, though I knew he was likely already aware, courtesy of Mia's updates. His questioning threw me off guard. *What was his angle?*

"I didn't peg you as a golf enthusiast," he remarked, as he dropped a sugar cube into his tea. A memory of our first encounter in the break room flashed through my mind. Didn't he prefer his tea without sugar?

He flexed his back muscles, sending a shiver down my spine. God, even his back was hot. Thoughts I shouldn't be having raced through my mind. I forcefully pushed them aside.

"It was research for my show. You never let me know your thoughts on the first episode," I reminded him, feeling the warmth intensify as he turned to face me.

"What does the Golf Open have to do with your show?" Amir's voice was measured, his tone indicating a disregard for my previous inquiry about his feedback. I bit my tongue, resisting the urge to challenge his lack of response.

"Well, I wanted to immerse myself in different social circles," I replied, smoothing over the truth, attempting to maintain composure despite the frantic beating of my heart.

"So, you're telling me that all day yesterday... you were essentially paid to flirt?" His question felt like a verbal jab, and I struggled to maintain my composure.

"No, I was paid to... I spent my time researching and meeting new people. I was trying to... find something... valuable to talk about on my show." I retorted, trying to keep my tone steady despite the rising tension.

"But your research involved flirting?" Amir's lips curved into a restrained smile, his eyes dancing with amusement. His words stirred an unsettling flutter in my stomach, leaving me feeling unnerved. It was as if he was testing me, probing for something beyond the surface conversation.

I hesitated, unsure of how to respond. "Well, I wasn't exactly doing much of that. But yes, my show is centred around relationships, so—"

He chuckled softly and approached me, towering over my seated form. I instinctively squeezed my legs together.

"I see," he murmured, taking a sip of his tea. "You can go."

"Go?" I echoed, confusion clouding my thoughts. *Was that all he wanted to discuss?*

"Yeah. I'm sure you have plenty to keep you occupied after indulging in a full day of leisure," He remarked with a smug undertone.

His words hit me like a punch to the gut. *Fucker...* I seethed internally.

"Or should I say... pleasure?" His insinuation ignited a fire in my stomach, leaving me momentarily breathless. "Anyways, I'm sure you've lots to write about?"

"I'd prefer if you refrained from speaking to me like that," I managed to breathe out, my voice tight with frustration. With newfound confidence fuelled by indignation, I rose from my seat, locking eyes with him. "My pleasure is my business unless I choose otherwise. It's entirely inappropriate for you to suggest or insinuate such matters in the workplace."

Amir visibly gulped, clearly taken aback by my sudden outburst. It seemed he wasn't accustomed to being challenged.

"If we're discussing appropriateness," he began, his eyes sweeping over me, "perhaps you should reconsider the attire you choose to wear to work."

I felt mortified. I couldn't find the words to respond, paralysed by a mixture of humiliation and anger. The fear of saying something irreversibly damaging hung heavy in the air.

Without another word, I turned on my heels and briskly exited the boardroom. I heard him growl my name as he followed me, but I refused to look back.

I ignored him, striding purposefully toward my desk. Paddy's return caught my attention, and I called out to him, "Paddy! Coffee?"

He glanced up at me with a smile, but his expression quickly shifted to one of apprehension as his gaze darted past me. "Not in the mood. Sorry," he muttered, avoiding further eye contact as he settled at his desk, immersing himself in his work.

Not in the mood? Since when was he not in the mood for coffee?!

"Belle, we need to continue this conversation," Amir's voice cut through the air from behind me.

"No—I think we've covered everything. And my name is Anna?" I retorted, my frustration boiling over as I stormed past him toward the break room. I pretended not to notice him trailing behind me, his presence like a shadow.

As I filled the kettle with water, I could feel his eyes boring into my back. The urge to whirl around and tell him to "fuck off" surged within me, but I resisted, keeping my composure.

"Come on..." Amir sighed, his tone softer now, almost pleading.

"You know what? I would have appreciated a genuine conversation, but all I seem to get from you are interrogations," I snapped, frustration evident in my voice. "You haven't once spoken to me about the show. You haven't given me any feedback on the first episode. All I get from you is... well... shit."

He closed the breakroom door behind him, and I scolded my subconscious for even considering comparing this situation to any of the erotic dreams I'd had about Amir in the breakroom in the past. I detested him. There would be no more dreams. He was a dick.

He moved closer, retrieving two mugs from the cupboard, and I instinctively retreated to the opposite side of the cramped kitchen, putting distance between us. "I haven't had the opportunity to," he explained, his words sounding hollow to my ears.

I let out a scoffing laugh. "That's a lie, and you know it."

He hesitated before responding, his demeanour shifting. "Well..."

"From the moment we met, you've been putting ridiculous pressure on me regarding the show and haven't offered any opinions except negative ones," I accused, my frustration bubbling to the surface.

Amir sighed, seeming to weigh his words carefully. "Okay, well... I thought it was good. Authentic. Slightly refreshing... but it's bound to cause controversy, which isn't ideal for the station, especially given its current state. You have to understand where The Board is coming from."

My heart pounded in my chest. "In my opinion, if the show gets people talking, then it's worth continuing. No?"

"I get what you're saying." He replied evenly, but I could sense the underlying disagreement in his tone.

He may have claimed to understand, but he didn't truly agree. I narrowed my eyes, trying to decipher his thoughts, searching for any hint of what lay beneath his composed facade.

"I've only recorded one episode, and it feels like you just don't want to give me a chance to succeed. You already have me pegged for failure," I expressed, frustration evident in my voice.

Amir sighed, his demeanour softening slightly. "That's not true," he insisted.

"It certainly feels like it," I countered, my tone tinged with bitterness.

"You have to understand that I have people above me, dictating what they want and don't want," he explained, a hint of weariness in his voice. His dark eyes, usually sharp and piercing, now held a hint of vulnerability, as if pleading for understanding beneath their steely exterior. "The Board has a multitude of opinions about Spotlight in general. It's too complicated to delve into, but just know that I don't want to be your enemy. I'm not trying to be the bad guy."

His words caught me off guard, momentarily silencing my anger. I could sense the weight of his position, the pressure he faced from higher-ups. Despite my frustration, I couldn't deny a flicker of empathy toward him.

"Well, you aren't doing a very good job at that," I muttered, absently picking at my nail polish, deliberately avoiding his eyes.

"It wasn't my intention to upset you," he responded, his tone softer now, tinged with regret.

Silence enveloped us, broken only by the faint sound of the kettle boiling in the background.

"You didn't upset me," I lied, finally lifting my eyes to meet his. "You just... you aggravated me."

His dark eyes bore into mine, seeming to see through the facade I desperately tried to maintain. I swallowed nervously, feeling uncomfortably exposed under his unwavering stare.

"Well... you've also done a great job at... aggravating me," he admitted, his tone a mixture of frustration and something I couldn't quite decipher.

As he spoke, a tumult of conflicting emotions churned within me. The word "aggravating" suddenly took on a whole new meaning, conjuring memories of my forbidden desires and the forbidden dreams of Amir that had haunted my nights.

God, those fecking dreams though...

"I didn't mean to," I murmured, breaking the tension that hung heavily in the air.

"It's okay," he replied softly, though the words felt hollow, laden with unspoken truths and unresolved tensions. "Chamomile?" He questioned.

I rolled my eyes. "Regular tea please."

The kettle finally finished boiling, offering a welcome distraction from the intensity of our exchange. Amir turned away from me, his movements fluid as he stretched his muscles and poured water into our mugs.

"When Derek died, I didn't expect all of this to happen or to be put in this position," Amir began, stirring his tea with a contemplative air. As he lifted the spoon and tapped the metal against his lips, I sternly reminded myself not to get distracted. "When I got the call, I immediately booked a flight to Belfast, knowing he wanted to be buried here."

I furrowed my brow, trying to decipher where he was going with this unexpected revelation.

"Now the funeral... it taught me immediately how much people from here love to party and—"

"You were at the funeral?" I interjected; surprise evident in my voice.

"Yes, of course," he replied, raising an eyebrow before turning his back to me once again. "Shit, there's no sugar." He stared down at the empty cannister. I pointed to the top shelf.

The abrupt shift in conversation left me feeling unsettled, but as Amir stretched his arm up to the top shelf to grab the bag of sugar, my mind suddenly raced back in time...

"As I was saying—it taught me how much..." his voice trailed off, blending into the background as my thoughts spiralled uncontrollably.

The funeral.

The stairway.

The American man with the hot voice... and the hot tattooed back.

"Oh my god," I gasped, instinctively covering my mouth in shock.

Amir froze, the bag of sugar forgotten in his hand as he turned to face me, confusion etched into his features. "Are you listening?" he prodded, his tone tinged with impatience.

But I couldn't hear him. I couldn't see anything but the vivid memories flooding my mind. A sudden realisation struck me like a bolt of lightning, electrifying every nerve in my body.

"Oh—my—god," I repeated, my voice trembling with disbelief.

"What?" Amir's brow furrowed, his eyes narrowing with concern as he took a step closer.

"Take off your shirt," the words spilled from my lips before I could stop them, my voice barely above a whisper.

He blinked in surprise, a nervous laugh bubbling up from deep within him. "What?" he stammered, clearly taken aback by my sudden demand.

But I couldn't hold back. My hand reached out, fingers trembling as they grazed the fabric of his shirt. "Take it off," I urged, my voice trembling with urgency, my eyes pleading with him to confirm what I already knew.

His expression shifted from confusion to shock, his eyes widening with realisation as he finally comprehended the situation.

"You have a snake tattoo... up your spine...?" I whispered; the words barely audible as the truth hung heavy in the air between us.

He stood frozen, his breath caught in his throat, as the world seemed to tilt on its axis. He nodded, confused.

"You—you were the man in the stairway!" I accused, my finger pointing directly at him, my voice trembling with a mixture of anger and disbelief. "With that girl!"

Amir's expression remained unreadable, but a flicker of recognition flashed in his eyes before he quickly masked it with confusion. "W-what are you talking about?" he responded, his voice unsteady, but I could see through the façade.

"It was you! I walked in on you!" I insisted, my heart pounding in my chest as I confronted him with the truth.

A tense silence settled between us, broken only by the sound of our ragged breaths. I could feel his gaze burning into me, his mind racing for an excuse, a way out of the situation.

His eyes widened imperceptibly, a tell-tale sign of guilt, as the weight of my accusation sank in. But still, he maintained his charade.

"I can't believe this. You were... fucking someone at your boss' funeral?" I spat; my voice laced with disgust.

"I..." he began, but his voice faltered, betraying his deception.

I held his gaze, refusing to back down. The truth was written all over his face, despite his attempts to deny it. His eyes darted around the room, avoiding mine, as he searched for an escape route. But I stood my ground, my determination unwavering.

"I don't even know what to say to you right now. You act like you're Mr. Perfect, Spotlight's saviour... but you're no saint!" I seethed, my voice laced with frustration and indignation.

Amir took a seat at the table, running a hand through his hair in a gesture of distress. His shoulders slumped, and his eyes fell to the floor, unable to meet mine as he struggled to find the right words. His usual air of confidence seemed to evaporate, replaced by an unmistakable sense of shame that hung heavily around him like a suffocating shroud. "I don't— that was you?!" he exclaimed; his tone filled with disbelief.

I had never seen him so visibly stressed before, and I couldn't help but revel in it. For once, I stood tall, towering over him, my gaze unwavering as I met his eyes.

"Yes, it was me," I confirmed.

"Holy shit…" he cursed under his breath; his expression pained. "I… I can explain this."

"Go for it," I urged, my voice dripping with scepticism.

His Adam's apple bobbed nervously as he struggled to find the right words. "Okay, so there's no valid explanation. But I was extremely drunk and had a very weak… moment— and I was locked out of my hotel room."

"So… you decided the best option was to fuck her in an emergency stairwell?" I retorted, unable to hide my incredulity.

"Christ! Will you lower your voice?" he hissed, his eyes darting around anxiously, afraid someone would burst in through the door at any moment. "I didn't actually do… anything… in the stairway."

"Because I interrupted you," I pointed out, a smirk playing at the corners of my lips.

He pinched the bridge of his nose, a sign of frustration, while closing his eyes in an attempt to compose himself. "I wouldn't have," he insisted, his voice strained.

"You're not a very believable liar. At least look me in the eyes when you speak instead of closing them," I remarked, unable to suppress the smirk that threatened to overtake my face. "Probably a good thing you didn't. I'd imagine there's cameras."

"No. I checked that. No cameras because of the.. uh… construction." He sighed loudly and reluctantly opened his eyes to meet mine.

"Of course you did." I chuckled. "Christ. You are unbelievable…"

He pursed his lips together and rose to his feet, once again towering over me with an air of authority. "Can you stop? This cannot go anywhere. Have you told anyone about that... moment?"

"Yes, both Mia and Paddy know," I replied, pushing myself back against the counter, a subconscious attempt to put some physical distance between us. "Well—they know about that moment... but obviously not that you played a part in it."

A furrow appeared between his brows as he processed my words. "Don't tell them," he implored, his tone edged with a hint of desperation. "Please Anna."

I cocked my head to the side, considering his request. "Okay. But don't fire me."

"Why do you think I'd fire you?" he asked, genuine curiosity colouring his voice.

"Well—it's clear as day that you don't like me. You've fired people who've worked here longer than me... You don't seem to think my show is a good thi—"

"Chill out—I have no intention of firing you. Also, if you're talking about me firing Andrew... he takes a sick day for every three days he works. It's ridiculous." he interrupted, his tone softening slightly as he sought to diffuse the tension between us. "Can we just forget this whole thing ever happened? I can't even explain how much I regret it. God, this is actually crazy that that was you."

I hesitated, searching his face for any trace of sincerity. Despite my reservations, a part of me yearned for resolution, for the chance to move past this uncomfortable encounter. With a reluctant nod, I agreed, "Publicly- I'll never mention it. Privately, I might tease you every so often."

He rolled his eyes, "For the record, I wasn't planning on doing anything with her in the stairway... we planned on taking the stairs to her room and got stuck... like you did," he explained, his tone tinged with defensiveness.

"But you told me the way out? What did you do? ... go to her room, grab condoms and go back to the stairs? Christ. Take some acting lessons," I retorted, unable to hide the scepticism in my voice.

"No, actually. There was a sign on the wall about construction and said the next available exit would be on whatever floor it was..." he attempted to justify, his words trailing off weakly. "We were planning on leaving."

I couldn't help but laugh incredulously. "Right, of course. But a quicky beforehand made sense..."

"Of course it didn't make sense but—"

I cut him off with a dismissive wave of my hand, turning on my heel and leaving the breakroom, feeling the power I now held in the wake of our confrontation.

He didn't follow me.

CHAPTER ELEVEN
Acting The Maggot

Definition: To behave comically / immaturely

I left the office early, seeking solace in the embrace of a hot shower before slipping into my pyjamas. Despite the early hour, my agenda consisted solely of indulging in a Gossip Girl marathon on the sofa. As I prepared some pesto pasta for dinner, my phone chimed with Olivia's call. Feeling overwhelmed from the weekend, I opted to ignore it. Less than ten seconds later, her persistence manifested in another call, which I again ignored, assuming she wanted to regale me with details of her latest sex-capades, a conversation I had little desire to entertain.

Lounging on the sofa, cocooned in a blanket with my bowl of pasta resting on my chest, I eschewed the effort of sitting upright. With each spoonful, my annoyance mounted along with the incessant ringing of my phone. *What on earth did she want?*

Finally succumbing to curiosity, I lifted the phone to my ear.

"Jesus Christ, Anna, took you long enough!"

""I-m eafffting!" I mumbled, my words slightly muffled by a mouthful of pasta. Not exactly the epitome of grace, I admit.

"Well, you better swallow before you choke on what I'm about to tell you!!"

With a gulp, I sat up, ready for whatever bombshell she was about to drop. "What's happened?"

"Tom Beckham was looking for you!" Her voice echoed through the phone, a mix of shock and excitement.

A surge of flattery washed over me, accompanied by a grin. "Ah, yeah, we crossed paths at the party."

"Hold on, why didn't you tell me this?!" As Olivia's excitement reverberated, I felt goosebumps prickling my skin.

"I didn't think I had to…" I chuckled, recalling the scene vividly. "He helped haul you out to the car at the end of the night. In fact, if I remember correctly, you kept asking him to come with."

There was a moment of stunned silence on Olivia's end, likely as she revisited the memories of her drunken escapades.

"Liv?"

"Yes, yes, sorry. It's just clicking now how he recognised me… Oh god, Anna, I'm never drinking again! Ever!"

"Are you drinking right now?" I couldn't resist teasing, already envisioning her with a cocktail in hand.

Her voice dropped to a whisper. "Yes, but it's a Bellini, so that doesn't count. It's got Vitamin C, and I'd wither away without my daily dose of Vitamin C."

"You could just eat an oran-"

"ANYWAYS - Tom Beckham! What the hell, Anna!" She shouted.

"I - yeah. Is he like a big deal? I didn't chat to him for too long."

"Aye, right." Olivia scoffed. "As if you don't know."

"I don't," I mumbled, feeling a pang of unease. "You know that I have no clue about golf."

"Anna... it was Tom's house that we were at last night. He hosted the party. He's a retired world-famous golfer..." Her voice grew with enthusiasm, "and now he's like COO or something of the tourism boa-"

I nearly threw up my dinner. "You're joking."

"No, why would I joke?" she questioned genuinely.

"Oh, fuck. Oh, fuck. Oh, FUCK," I screamed, panic rising within me. I set my pasta bowl aside and stood up.

"What? What is it?"

"Olivia, I made so many comments about his house and I - FUCK!" I paced around my living room coffee table, my mind racing.

"What do you mean you made comments about his house?"

"I - I just said about how big and empty it was, and Lord... I was a real bitch about it! Like a good 30% of our conversation involved me slating that big-ass house!" I glanced at the bottle of gin on my bar cart, debating whether to drown my embarrassment.

"Well, you apparently didn't offend him as he asked me about you like ten minutes ago!" She exclaimed. "We're at Ocho Tapas for a private dinner. He's seated at the other end of my table."

I sank into my chair, burying my face in my hands. Guilt washed over me for the things I'd said, but a part of me was starting to find the situation ridiculously amusing.

"This would only happen to me. He never told me he owned the house, and he had many opportunities to!"

Olivia laughed. "I have to go back inside. It's so cold here tonight and I feel like my nips are literally about to fall off. But I had to call and let you know!"

I sighed heavily. "Thanks... if you speak to Tom again, tell him how sorry I am."

"Will do!"

"And also, Liv, I told him I work as a sp-"

She hung up the phone before I could finish my sentence.

I retraced every insult I'd hurled at the house in my mind. The remarks about the decor—or lack thereof—the ridiculously high ceilings, the emptiness... My stomach churned. I'd even gone as far as to suggest that whoever lived there was probably a dickhead. It was completely uncalled for and just totally stupid. *Why did I say that?!*

***

The next few days at work were uneventful. I gathered audience feedback and questions for my show, Paddy taught me how to use a new mixer console, and Amir was nowhere to be seen. The highlight of my day was catching up with my mum on Facetime. I filled her in on my time at the golf event and my unexciting love life, along with the saga of Sebastian.

"You should have drenched him in your champagne!" She gasped, then quickly added, "Actually, I take that back. Champagne is too good to be wasted on someone like him."

"I wholeheartedly agree," I giggled.

"Are you going to talk about it on your show?"

"Yeah, I'm recording tomorrow night."

"I'll be listening…" She smiled into the camera. "Seems like you could actually make a career out of this whole thing, huh?"

I nodded, feeling a sense of hope wash over me. "Hope so. It's only my second episode. It's difficult, a challenge for sure to be so open and honest."

"Well, the toughest challenges often pave the way for the greatest rewards." She replied.

My heart swelled at the sight of my mum's hopeful expression. It was a rare moment; usually, she seemed disappointed in my career choices. Neither of my parents had been overly pleased when their only child pursued a creative path instead of becoming the master scientist or mathematician they had hoped for. Understandably, their expectations were high, given their own academic and professional successes as doctors.

"Your dad hasn't listened yet… and I'm thinking maybe it should stay that way?" She wiggled her eyebrows mischievously, giggling. "Any information is too much information for him. He's very protective of his little girl."

I cringed at the thought.

***

At 6:15 PM on Friday night, I scoured my kitchen for sustenance and a little liquid courage. My gaze fell upon a bottle of Bushmills whiskey tucked away in the cupboard. *Should I do a shot for good luck before my show? Do people even take shots of whiskey?* I hesitated, then decided to give it a try. I lifted the bottle down and cringed as I took a sniff. I had been gifted it by my uncle as a secret Santa (not so secret) present at Christmas past. Tentatively, I raised the bottle to my lips, but as I attempted to take a swig, I gagged before it could even touch the back of my throat. *Note to self: don't drink whiskey straight from the bottle.* I let the remaining liquid dribble out of my mouth as I leaned over the sink, then rinsed with water from the tap. I just needed something to calm my nerves. If this was any indication of how my show would go, I was in trouble.

I sped into the studio, arriving in record time. I was particularly on edge, more so than during my first show. Now, I had expectations to live up to.

"Paddy is off tonight, so I've decided to step in and assist," Mia's voice cut through my thoughts as I scrambled to organise my tech desk.

"Oh…Is he okay?"

"Yes, he just has the night off. I told him to head home early. He's basically lived here for the past three weeks, and as it's only your second show, I thought you might be more comfortable with me in the booth than someone else."

I looked at her with wide eyes, feeling a mix of gratitude and nervousness coursing through me. "Well, yes. That means a lot, thank you."

She gave me a reassuring smile before turning back to her own tasks. I fidgeted with the cables on my desk, trying to steady my trembling hands as I attempted to focus.

Arranging my desk, I sat with my headphones over my ears, but my mind was racing. The tracks I'd prepared earlier seemed to blur together as my thoughts circled back to the upcoming show.

"We'll start with a listener question – are you okay talking about James?" Mia's voice broke through my anxious haze.

"Ah, yes. I can try. Is there a particular question?"

"I don't want to give you the exact question now; I want it to be organic," Mia responded. "I'll pop in and narrate with you, then ask it when you're ready."

I forced a nod, attempting to appear composed despite the knot of nerves tightening in my stomach. "Okay."

"You're on in just over two minutes," Mia signalled, her voice steady and reassuring.

I took deep breaths in and out, attempting to calm the storm of nerves swirling within me. Would this ever get easier? I could hear my heartbeat pounding loudly in my ears, feel the blood rushing through my veins.

"Twenty seconds," Mia's voice broke through my thoughts. I looked at her, my expression strained, and sucked in a deep breath. She noticed my anxiety and offered a thoughtful smile. "You will be fine. You've got this."

Three, Two, One.

"Welcome back to Belles of Belfast, the podcast where I embarrassingly admit all the secrets of my love life in the hopes that someone out there might be impacted or inspired in some kind of way…"

As my intro song played, my pained and anxious expression melted away, replaced by pure excitement and adrenaline. I could do this.

"Hello, listeners. You're probably wondering whose voice this is and are confused as to where your Belle of Belfast has disappeared to. Well, we'll be starting off this episode by asking her some listener questions. Social media has been buzzing, and there's one big question on everyone's mind…" Mia's voice filled the studio.

"Go on then…" I spoke into my mic, practically on the edge of my seat.

"It's a big question. A hard question…"

"Oh, I'm intrigued…"

"'@megnoland' among many others want to know: how do you get over an ex? She says she's struggling and needs some guidance. So can you share what you are doing to get over yours?"

I paused, feeling like I'd had the wind knocked out of me. I wasn't expecting that. Mia continued to talk, her voice soothing, "Now, I know that's a difficult question, so we'll be back after this first song of the night for the answer. Have to give our host some time to think."

Mia pressed the switch board; triggering a song to start playing.

"You good?" She asked.

"Yeah." I nodded. *I didn't feel good.*

My brain felt like it couldn't comprehend anything she was saying. Had I gotten over James? I don't know…

As the song closed, I took deep breaths, trying to compose myself.

I cleared my throat and moved closer to the mic, my heart pounding in my chest. "With my current situation, I have made myself too busy to even think about him… I've thrown myself into my career, spending time with my friends, and meeting new people. When I do have a quiet moment to myself, I reflect on my relationship, and I'm starting to see the truths that I blinded myself from. It makes me feel sad, but as the days go on, I'm more accepting of it." I paused, feeling heavy with emotion. I'd been thinking about everything I spoke of for weeks but saying it out loud was a different ball game.

"He didn't treat me right; there were signs he wasn't loyal yet I chose to brush them off at the time… Do I miss him? That's the question I still don't know how to answer. I guess I miss the person I thought he was, the things we did together, the experiences he opened me up to. I miss the feeling of connection, but I don't want to be connected to HIM anymore. I don't know if I'm 'over him,' but I don't really know what that means. Does being over someone mean that I have no desire to be with him? If that's the case, I think I'm over him. Or does it mean... I've stopped thinking about him? I don't know. I've learned what my boundaries are. I wouldn't accept the same treatment again, and I think that's powerful in itself."

I took a huge breath in, feeling the weight of my words settle around me. I hadn't meant to ramble on for so long. "Sorry, I didn't expect to go off on one there!"

Mia turned on her mic, her voice filled with admiration. "Well... if that isn't powerful, I don't know what is."

"I've very much closed his chapter in my life. In fact, I even went to the North Coast this past week with the hopes of meeting someone new..."

I shifted gears, going into autopilot as I recounted the events of the past week, filling my listeners in on my trip to the golf event in the hopes of finding better men than there are in Belfast. But beneath the surface, my heart rumbled and my stomach twisted. It was time to get serious and talk about the topic I'd been dreading.

"I want to delve into a profoundly important topic tonight: *consent*. It's crucial that we all grasp the true meaning of consent, which is 'permission for something to happen or agreement to do something.' 'Mr. Player' disregarded my boundaries and kissed me after only a few uncomfortable moments of conversation... moments in which I clearly expressed my lack of interest. I left feeling violated and disrespected. Some may dismiss it as 'just a kiss,' but it's not about the physical act; it's about the principle. Consent. Respect for me and my boundaries.

Encountering him again at a party, he once more asserted his dominance over me, gripping me possessively. Despite my attempts to break free, he only relinquished his hold when another man... a taller, stronger, more influential man came towards me. I've spent days questioning if I could have done more to stop him. Maybe I should have been louder. Maybe I should have been more forceful. But this isn't my fault; it's not about what I could or should have done. No one should ever feel pressured to fend off unwanted advances.

Dressing attractively isn't consent.

Silence isn't consent.

The absence of a 'no' isn't consent.

Even being in a relationship isn't consent.

Consent isn't a one-time pass for everything. Agreeing to one thing, like a drink or a kiss, doesn't imply consent to anything else.

True consent is enthusiastic. It's hearing a clear 'yes' from someone's lips. It arises from open communication, and it's important to know that it can be revoked at any moment.

It wasn't 'just a kiss' or 'just a touch' or 'just a hand on my back' – it was a violation of my boundaries that left me uncomfortable. In the future, I'll assert myself more confidently; but ideally, I won't need to."

And so, episode two concludes: A revelation of resilience.

Moving on from a relationship requires time.

Yet, as time passes, the tinted glasses gradually lose their hue.

You begin to perceive it for what it truly was.

You comprehend why it failed.

You establish fresh standards and boundaries.

And you steer clear of any man who crosses them.

As for any man who fails to grasp the concept of consent... they can go to hell."

***

Monday kicked off with an impromptu boardroom meeting that brought together all our morning, daytime, and evening radio presenters and producers. Alongside, we had twelve weekly entertainment show segments spanning from 'Daily Mindfulness and Meditation' to 'What's The Craic Belfast? - your go-to for local news,' and, naturally, 'Belles of Belfast.'

The boardroom felt uncomfortably crowded as about forty of us squeezed in, occupying all the chairs, and standing along the walls. The air buzzed with anticipation and nervous energy, amplified by the muted hum of conversations and the occasional shuffle of papers. A projector screen loomed large, displaying approximately twelve others who were participating via Zoom, their faces flickering in and out of focus as the connection stuttered.

Mia, our anchor amidst the sea of faces, appeared visibly anxious, her restless movements betraying her nerves. She bounced back and forth on her feet, a picture of tension as she stood at the front of the room, her eyes flitting between her phone and the expectant audience.

"We'll just begin in a moment," she mumbled, her voice barely audible over the murmurs of the gathered crowd.

A few minutes later, the heavy glass door opened, and Amir made a dramatic entrance. It was a rare sight to see him dressed so casually. He sauntered in, exuding an effortless confidence, clad in sleek black jeans and stylish black sneakers. His signature white shirt, usually crisp and immaculate, had been replaced by a more relaxed version made from a light cotton fabric. The top buttons were undone, revealing a slight glimpse of his chest, while his sleeves were casually rolled up, exposing more intricate tattoos that danced along his skin. He looked... magnetic, his presence commanding attention as he effortlessly stole the spotlight.

"Hello everyone," Amir greeted, his demeanour unusually jumpy and excited. "You're probably wondering why you've all been squeezed in here."

No shit Sherlock. The room collectively shot him disdainful glares.

"Since arriving here, I've noticed a lack of morale or community," he continued, undeterred. "Except when alcohol is involved. I don't know, is that an Irish thing?"

Many of us nodded in begrudging agreement, but no one spoke up.

Amir's smile widened. "Well, I've spoken with the lovely Mia here, and we've decided to do something to change that."

Why was he so smiley? Why was he being so overly nice today? Mia stood silently beside him, her discomfort palpable, making me feel like none of this was her idea.

"We're having a group bonding day!" he announced enthusiastically.

A chorus of groans and sarcastic remarks filled the room.

"Oh, that's a wonderful idea!" Ellen exclaimed, pushing her platinum blonde hair over her shoulder and gazing at Amir as if he were a deity. Everyone else in the room exchanged incredulous glances. Ellen had been the number one breakfast show presenter for the past three years running. Though she often teased about leaving Spotlight someday soon because her face was 'too good to be hidden on the radio,' she was undeniably pretty.

Amir smiled back at her. "Thank you, Ellen."

She blushed profusely and let out a slight giggle. I bit my tongue, trying to stifle my amusement.

"I think— we think," Amir said, motioning to Mia, "We think it would be a great idea to bring everyone together and get out of the office. We have some options for activities, and today you're going to vote on where we go."

"Can I go home?" George, an audio tech, mumbled.

"So here are the options," Mia said, ignoring George. "We have Game of Thrones inspired Archery and an Escape room."

"Or we can do a Dragon Boat Race," Amir added.

Suppressing a laugh, I glanced around the room, observing the 'wtf' expressions plastered on many faces. This had to be a joke.

"Or an indoor go-karting and virtual reality experience," Mia mumbled unenthusiastically.

"Lastly, indoor trampolining and a ninja master course," Amir concluded.

Dillon interrupted, "What if— and hear me out— what if I'm already a ninja master? Can I be excluded?" His expression was completely serious, yet everyone knew he was joking and trying to rile up Amir.

I burst out laughing, joined by most of the room. As I caught Amir's eye, however, my laughter tapered off. He had a sullen look in his eyes, silently pleading for help. My amusement turned to concern, and I gulped, realising he was feeling deflated by our reactions.

"I - Uh, is the trampolining and…" I cringed as I spoke, "The um ninja course at We Are Vertigo?" I asked, breaking the awkward silence that had settled over the room.

Eyes burned into me, and the laughter died down.

"Yes, it is," Mia replied, her tone neutral.

"I've heard it's a great centre," I murmured, trying to diffuse the tension. "It would be a good laugh…" Amir smiled graciously at me, and despite my embarrassment, his approval made it feel somewhat worth it. God, I was as weak as Ellen.

We Are Vertigo was Northern Ireland's premier entertainment complex, offering indoor skydiving among many other attractions. I felt grateful that Amir had suggested trampolining and whatever the 'ninja' course was, and NOT skydiving. Jesus, no.

"I suppose I could use some extra ninja training," Dillon joked. "But don't hold it against me if I show off my moves inside the office." He threw his hands up and chopped at the air, making me cringe inwardly.

"If you all can email your preferred choice by the end of today, then we'll organise it for a few week's time," Amir announced with a satisfied grin on his face.

Most of the room nodded, resigned to the fact that this was happening whether they liked it or not. "That's everything," Mia smiled. "The team day will take place during work hours, and you will all be paid for the day. We'll break you into groups so regular programming won't be interrupted."

As everyone filtered out of the room, Amir motioned for me to come towards him. "Thank you," he nodded as I approached.

I smiled back, feeling a bit awkward, unsure of what else to say.

"It could have gone worse," Mia laughed as she packed up her belongings into her bag.

Amir looked at her with wide eyes, "Worse? That was awful!"

"I have to agree with Mia. We're not exactly the team bonding type. Maybe if you had started by telling everyone they'd still be paid for it…"

"I don't understand it," he mumbled, running his hands through his hair.

"You'll learn," Mia laughed, clearly relishing his lack of understanding. Frankly, I was enjoying it too. It was rare that Amir didn't exude an 'I know everything and I'm better than everyone' aura.

"I have to go jump on a call. See you both later." Mia announced, leaving us alone in the boardroom.

I awkwardly started cleaning up the coffee cups that had been left behind, feeling the weight of Amir's stare bearing down on me. His gaze felt intense, like it was probing into my thoughts.

After what felt like an eternity, he broke the silence. "Are we… Are we good?"

"Yeah, of course," I replied, forcing a smile. The tension in the room was palpable, thick enough to cut with a knife. I couldn't shake the feeling of unease that hung in the air between us.

He continued to watch me intently as I dropped an empty coffee cup into the bin. When I looked up, our eyes locked, and I found myself momentarily frozen in place.

"I appreciate that you've kept our little secret," he said, his voice low and smooth. "I half expected you to go straight to Paddy and spill the beans. He didn't seem to know anything on Friday night, which surprised me…"

"Wait—Friday night?" I interjected.

"Yeah, I ran into him and ended up having drinks with him and his friends," Amir explained casually, but there was a hint of something in his tone—a flicker of uncertainty, perhaps.

I didn't quite believe him. Paddy hadn't mentioned anything to me, "Oh, really?"

"Yeah, just a few, nothing crazy," he replied, his eyes never leaving mine.

"Ah, well, yeah. I didn't—I didn't tell him," I stuttered, trying to mask the turmoil brewing within me.

"Thank you," Amir said softly, his gaze intensifying. "You look good today."

I shifted uncomfortably under his gaze, feeling a flush rise to my cheeks. The tension crackled between us, thick and charged with unspoken words.

"So, you approve of this outfit?" I teased. "It's not too inappropriate for the workplace?" I teased.

He rolled his eyes. "Just take the compliment."

"You look ok too." I managed to reply, my voice barely above a whisper. He smiled, his lips curving into a knowing grin.

"I was wondering…" He paused, his words hanging in the air, laden with uncertainty.

My heart skipped a beat. "You were wondering…?"

"Never mind," he muttered, retreating to the opposite end of the table and picking up a stray pen.

"What?" I pressed, curiosity gnawing at me.

"It's nothing…" He trailed off, absently pressing the pen against his lips as he pondered.

"Don't do that," I mumbled, unable to tear my gaze away from his lips.

"Do what?" he asked innocently, rolling the pen between his fingers.

"That," I replied, a flush creeping up my neck.

He raised an eyebrow in confusion.

"You don't know where that pen's been…" I pointed out, trying to suppress the fluttering sensation in my stomach. *And also, you're making me wish I was a pen.*

"Oh," he said, finally realising, and promptly discarded the pen into the bin. "You're probably right…"

"That doesn't mean bin it!" I protested, pacing across to try recover it… however as I looked inside the bin, it had been dropped amongst an indistinguishable liquid.

He shook his head, a small smile playing on his lips, and stretched his arm behind him, his movements fluid and graceful. God, why did he have to be so attractive?

"You're making me nervous. What were you wondering? Can you spit it out?"

"I make you nervous?" He tilted his head, his gaze intense yet veiled. His eyes flickered briefly towards the door behind me, confirming that we were alone.

My cheeks warmed at his question. *Did I seriously just admit that?*

"Sometimes," I admitted softly, shifting my gaze away from his penetrating eyes. My attention shifted downward, finding solace in the mundane sight of my shoes.

"In a bad way?" His voice held a hint of concern as he took a small step back, his demeanour cautious.

"Not necessarily," I replied, my cheeks burning with embarrassment.

With a subtle movement, he reached out, his touch feather-light as he lifted my chin, coaxing me to meet his eyes. I felt a rush of warmth at his touch, but I tried to conceal my reaction. It was like a gentle breeze, stirring something within me, yet I dared not let it show.

"What are you doing?" I whispered, cautious that people could potentially see through the glass.

His eyes lit up with a hint of worry as he dropped his hand. "Sorry. I just wanted you to look at me. Sorry, I don't know why I—"

"It's okay. Forget it."

His hand lightly brushed against my elbow, sending a tingle down my spine, but I kept my composure, refusing to betray the tumultuous emotions swirling within me. His own nervousness seemed evident.

My cheeks flushed, and my pulse quickened as his presence seemed to envelop me. I couldn't help but wonder what lay beneath his enigmatic exterior, yet I dared not explore those thoughts further.

Mr Mysterious.

"So, I know this is a bit... strange, but I was wondering if—"

"Amir, can I have a word?" a chirpy voice interrupted, slicing through the charged atmosphere like a sudden gust of wind. With a quick nod, he took a slight step back, the subtle gesture going unnoticed by Ellen.

I turned to see her standing at the door and gulped, feeling rather flustered. She stared between Amir and me, her mouth opening slightly, acknowledging she'd potentially interrupted something.

"I have to - I'm just going to go..." I stammered, feeling the need to escape the awkward tension.

"Belle, wait," he shouted after me, but I kept walking. I needed some fresh air.

CHAPTER TWELVE
Wise Up

*Definition: A saying which means to act more wisely /
have more sense.*

I bolted out of the office, gasping for fresh air. I needed to clear my mind, to free myself from the intense moment with Amir. I couldn't afford to get involved with a colleague, no matter how tempting it was. But his actions left me questioning. Did he really want me, or was he merely testing, teasing, aggravating me?

I opted to spend my afternoon working from Established and texted Paddy to inform him I'd be back in time for lunch and that we needed to chat later. As I settled in, the barista served me a large, iced latte with a drizzle of organic honey for sweetness, alongside an oversized cinnamon bun. Comfort food, a necessary indulgence to fuel my creativity as I felt inspired to start planning Episode Three.

There's a man I'm itching to talk about...

I paused, grappling with the delicate dance of describing Amir without revealing his identity. Maybe I could assign him a completely random alias...

There are some things in life that we desire but know we shouldn't pursue. There are individuals we encounter whom we should only admire from afar—

No, too conspicuous?

So, there's this man. He's the epitome of forbidden fruit—maddeningly alluring, infuriatingly out of reach.

My feelings for Amir poured onto the paper in front of me. I'd pushed them down, but finally admitted to myself how much I wanted him. It was BAD.

I HATE the attraction I have to him.

This man has been haunting my conscious AND unconscious mind. He is now the new main character in my dreams, completely replacing Mr Fuckboy. I think I'm finally over Mr Fuckboy, I haven't felt any impulse to contact him. I've barely even thought of him. I just keep reminding myself that I'm worth more and that MORE is out there. I didn't expect to move on so fast, however I've been distracted, and I've also spent quite a lot of my time trying to understand this new man. I can't figure him out yet. So, I guess we'll call him... Mr Mysterious.

I furiously crossed out the notes, feeling a pang of embarrassment. It was too blatant, too transparent. Besides, entertaining the idea was pointless. Dating him was out of the question. I set down my pen with a sigh of resignation. Attempting to articulate my thoughts about him felt futile.

GRACE

Hey hey, how's your day going? Have you recovered from the golf yet?

x

I smiled down at my phone.

ANNA

Hi babe, just about recovered haha. I'm struggling to write my episode for this week though! How's work?

GRACE

At least you have Galway to look forward to next week. I can't wait! I'm dying for a break. Everything feels so stressful. Must be something going on with the moon... is mercury in retrograde?

My texting session was abruptly halted by the creak of a chair against the hardwood floor. Startled, I glanced up, my mouth falling open in surprise. In walked Amir, his face flushed and his hand gripping the wooden chair with a tightness that bordered on white-knuckled.

"Hi…Can I sit?" he asked, his voice slightly strained.

I nodded, trying to compose myself as I hastily tidied up the table. Placing my coffee cup on a coaster, I crumpled the napkin and tossed it into my bag along with my notebook and pen.

"Do you come here often?" I asked, trying to mask my nervousness. This was my spot, and I'd never seen him here before. "Did you follow me?"

"Uh, yeah, often enough. I mean – I didn't follow you, but I come here often enough…" he replied, his eyes flitting around the room. He seemed uneasy, a stark contrast to his usual composed demeanour.

"Okay." I giggled, unable to hide my amusement.

He opened his mouth to respond, then let out a small snicker.

"What?" I prodded, a smile tugging at my lips. There was something intriguing about seeing him out of his element.

"Every time I come here, you're sitting in the corner on your laptop or with a book in your hands," he said, his hands fidgeting with the rings adorning his fingers.

"So, you not only follow me, but you also watch me from afar?" I teased, feeling a rush of excitement at the playful banter between us. "That sounds quite stalkerish."

He rolled his eyes in response to my teasing.

"I'm sorry, but did you just roll your eyes at me? That's rather impolite—"

"Oh, shut up. I don't watch you. But I always end up turning around so I don't interrupt you," he retorted, a playful glint in his eyes.

I couldn't help but laugh. "Yet here we are, in Established together. Your efforts to avoid me have failed."

"Funny," he chuckled. "But on a serious note, we should talk—properly talk— without arguing for once."

Before we could delve into conversation, his phone rang. He lifted it from his blazer pocket and gave me an apologetic look. "I have to take this."

"Be my guest. After your call, we can talk—properly talk—without..."

He rolled his eyes once more and diverted his attention to the call. "Hello?"

I shifted my paper straw around, kicking the ice from side to side. Amir sat opposite me, engrossed in a conversation on his phone. His eyebrows furrowed in concentration, but I wasn't listening to a word he was saying. My mind was racing with questions. Could I date Amir? Were there rules against workplace relationships? Did we even have rules? What would it be like to date him? What would it be like to have sex with him? The thought sent a shiver down my spine, and I squeezed my thighs together, feeling a tightness in my stomach.

As he ended his phone call and his eyes darted back to me, I realised I had been lost in my thoughts, and I quickly snapped back to reality.

"Is everything okay?" he asked, concern evident in his voice.

I shook my head, trying to clear the haze of my thoughts. "Sorry, no. I mean, yes. Yes, I'm great," I stuttered, attempting to regain my composure. "Are you okay? You looked stressed on the phone."

"Yeah, just lots going on in New York. I have to return sooner than planned." He played awkwardly with the rings that covered his fingers.

Of course he had to leave eventually, but I'd kind of ignored that thought. He looked at me expectantly, but I wasn't sure what to say next.

"I thought I had another ten weeks, but now I only have around six at most..."

"Oh."

"Surely you should be relieved?" He chuckled.

"I hated you at first, you know. Really, really hated you."

"I know." He grinned, nodding. "What about now though?"

I shifted my gaze from his overbearing eyes to the remaining ice inside my glass. "I don't completely hate you," I mumbled.

His smile widened. "You don't hate me?"

I shook my head.

He squinted his eyes, trying to read my expression. I felt nauseous, wishing I hadn't drunk such a milky coffee. He continued to prod, "So if you don't hate me... Do you, I mean, have you, no..." I found myself clinging onto every word. *Just ask me. Ask me if I like you.*

"Okay, be honest with me-" He began, but his words were cut off by an unexpected interruption.

"Amir? What are you doing here?!" A stunning woman with long, glossy brown hair entered the cafe. She was dressed in a tight white dress that accentuated her curves perfectly.

Two interruptions in one day. The universe was sending me signs, surely?

He stood up and embraced the woman in a hug. "Kate! How are you?"

"Good! Just meetings... lots of meetings," Kate said, placing her hand on Amir's arm. Her nails were painted a gorgeous shade of red, a stark contrast to my short, nude nails. She kept her hand on his arm, and I felt awkward just watching their embrace.

"Good to be busy," Amir replied, turning back towards me. I shifted uncomfortably, feeling the weight of the situation. "This is Anna. Anna, this is Kate. Kate is the MD of Entertain Ireland."

So she's successful and beautiful.

I stood up immediately, though I fell a few inches shorter than her. She had to be almost 6ft… *God, why do I sound so shallow?*

"Hi, it's lovely to meet you," I said, shaking her hand.

Amir shifted backward, his hand lingering a centimetre away from touching my back. I melted into him, allowing him to touch me.

"Lovely to meet you too," Kate replied, her eyes darting from me to Amir. "This is a great spot," she remarked, looking around the coffee shop. It was quieter than usual.

"It's Anna's favourite!" Amir interjected with a smile.

I pushed myself even closer to him, relishing in the warmth as his fingers pressed into my skin. "They make great coffee… everything actually… have you tried their pies?"

She shook her head. "No, but I'll make sure to."

I balanced from foot to foot, hoping the awkward exchange would soon be over.

"When do you go back to Dublin?" he asked.

How did he know so much about her? I tried suppressing my anxious thoughts.

"Tomorrow," she responded, "but I'll be back in two weeks. Let's catch up then?"

My eyes shifted to the door. *Maybe I should leave.* The small wiggle of Amir's thumb gracing my back erased the thought from my mind. I inhaled.

"For sure," he nodded.

"Well, I should head on. It was great to see you again."

"You too."

"Lovely to meet you, Anna," she said with an overly friendly smile directed at me.

I watched as she turned and walked out the door, coffee in hand. She was probably a sophisticated black coffee drinker. No dairy. Occasionally, she would have oat milk, but only once in a blue moon. I bet she was also afraid to drink caffeine after 3pm in the afternoon. She wouldn't get her beauty sleep otherwise. I wanted to be her. I bet she had her life together. Meanwhile, I occasionally... okay... often, drank coffee at 10pm at night and regretted it when I couldn't get to sleep until 4am and woke up the next morning feeling like I'd just blinked, not slept. I looked up at Amir, expecting him to be watching Kate as she left, but he was staring at me.

He brushed his hand on my back again, "We should probably get going. What do you think?"

I jumped slightly but turned to face him. His eyes. I couldn't help but gawk at his eyes. I wondered; did he have feelings for her? Or... was there a chance... that he had feelings for me?

"How do you know her?" I asked.

"Ah, I had coffee with her on my first week here."

"Like coffee-coffee or just coffee?"

His eyebrows furrowed, "What does that mean?"

"You know – is she like a 'stairway girl'?" I teased.

He took a step back from me, mouth aghast, "A stairway girl?"

I held back my smile, "Like a girl you'd have fun with in a stairw-"

"I understood what you meant," he laughed, "And no – she is definitely not a stairway girl. I'm working on a partnership between Entertain Ireland and Spotlight..."

I tipped my head to the side and squinted at him, trying to decide if he was telling the truth. Amidst the chatter of Established, his eyes held mine, a silent invitation lingering in the air between us. I glanced down to his lips. Everything inside me wanted to kiss him.

For a moment, my daydreams overcame reality. I imagined him pulling me tight, his fingers burning into my back, one hand tangled in my hair. And then… his lips crashed into mine, granting me the closeness I'd been craving. Our lips melted together like butter. His tongue graced mine delicately yet so passionately.

But as quickly as the fantasy had appeared, reality crashed back in, reminding me of the impossibility of such a moment. We were co-workers, bound by professional boundaries that couldn't be crossed. With a heavy sigh, I tore my gaze away from his lips, suppressing the longing that threatened to consume me.

FUCK.

"Anna?" he breathed, breaking through the haze of my daydream.

I shook myself from the reverie, blinking rapidly to refocus. "Yes, sorry. Let's head back to the office," I replied, trying to regain my composure.

As I moved to grab my coat, his hands reached out to assist me. "Here, let me help you," he offered.

I hesitated, feeling the heat rising in my cheeks. "Oh, I don't think I can wear it right now. It's a bit hot," I stammered.

Really hot.

As we stepped outside, like some kind of movie magic, the sky opened up, unleashing a deluge that drenched everything in sight. It was as if the heavens themselves had decided to join in the drama of our encounter. For once, I was grateful for the weather's timing. Hastily, we pulled our coats over our heads, shielding ourselves from the downpour as we dashed through the streets.

I stole a glance at Amir as we ran, and to my surprise, he wore a wide, almost childlike grin on his face, clearly enjoying the chaos. It was comical, but undeniably endearing, reminiscent of a young child gazing at a birthday cake adorned with glistening candles.

"Are you enjoying this?" I shouted over the drumming of the rain.

"It's amazing!" he exclaimed, his voice barely audible over the downpour. Raindrops cascaded down his face, blurring his vision, but he seemed utterly undeterred. I couldn't help but laugh as we splashed through the puddles on the pavement, the water soaking through my shoes and drenching my feet.

As if embracing the chaos of the storm, he dropped his coat and tied it around his waist, exposing himself to the elements even more. I couldn't contain my amusement at his carefree attitude.

"What the hell are you doing?" I called out, laughter bubbling up inside me. It was a sight to behold, watching him revel in the rain without a care in the world.

"Oh, come on! It's only a bit of rain!" he exclaimed, his laughter echoing in the storm.

I squealed as I ran, the chilly water splashing around my feet. "Y-you're crazy!" I managed to gasp between breaths, my voice trembling with exhilaration.

His arms wrapped around my waist, pulling me close as he snatched my coat away, leaving me fully exposed to the icy rain. "OH. MY. GOD," I shrieked, the cold seeping into my bones.

He threw his head back in laughter, the sound filling the air around us. Tears brimmed in his eyes, mirroring my own laughter. Despite the freezing rain, there was an undeniable warmth between us.

"You're crazy." I giggled. His grip on me tightened, his laughter growing louder.

As a roll of thunder rumbled overhead, a surge of panic gripped me, feeling the electricity of the storm crackling in the air. Our bodies pressed together, and I pushed against his forearms, attempting to break free, but it was as if we were bound by an invisible force, unwilling to let go.

"Will you just stand still!" he chuckled, the raindrops glistening on his lips. Despite the chill in the air, his warmth enveloped me as he held me close.

I nodded, trying to steady my breath as his hand pressed against my back, drawing me nearer. Our gazes locked, the intensity between us palpable with every heartbeat. "Just, stand still," he murmured softly.

I blinked away the raindrops clouding my vision, feeling his touch as he wiped the rain from my cheek, his thumb lingering on my lips. A surge of anticipation coursed through me, urging him closer. I leaned into his touch.

His fingers tangled in my wet hair, "This might be crazy… but can I…" His voice trailed off, his gaze lingering on my lips, his heart thundering against mine.

"Please do," I whispered, my voice barely audible over the drumming of the rain.

With a silent understanding, his lips met mine in a tender, electric kiss. Slowly. Gracefully. With one hand buried in my hair and another wrapped around my waist, he pulled me closer and closer; drawing me in more with each second that passed. He kissed me with an agonising passion. Despite the cold rain, the air shared between us became stifling as his lips fervently drew at mine, attempting to pull every inch of desire towards him. It felt as though I were water, and he had been stranded for months in a dry desert, desperately seeking relief. I gasped as he nipped at my lower lip, and feverishly forced his tongue into my mouth, turning the kiss from slow and delicate to hot and forceful; our bodies melting into each other and the rain. The sound of thunder faded into the background, all I could focus on was the taste and smell of Amir.

I breathed him in deeply, allowing him to explore my mouth for a moment more before I pulled away. I needed to breathe for a moment but fully intended on diving back in once the air had returned to my lungs and my feet had returned to the ground.

I could just about see through my rain-soaked eyelashes as I stared at him, overcome from what had just happened. How could one chaotic kiss make me feel so calm?

He let his head fall back, his face upturned to the rain-filled sky. As he breathed in deeply, his chest rose, then fell with a heavy sigh as he turned his gaze back to me. The weight of his silence hung between us, unsettling in its intensity.

"Are you okay?" I asked, my voice tinged with concern. Something felt off, a palpable shift in the atmosphere.

His eyes flickered to my lips again, a momentary pause before he closed them, withdrawing his hand from my face. My heart sank at the sudden disconnection. "I shouldn't have done that. I don't know what came over me," he admitted, his voice strained with regret.

"What?" The word caught in my throat, disbelief washing over me.

"I shouldn't have," he repeated, barely audible. Without another word, he turned on his heel and hurried away, his steps quickening as he disappeared into the misty streets, leaving me standing alone in the rain, bewildered and unsure.

"Amir! Where are you—what do you mean?!" I chased after him, the taste of his lips still lingering on mine, the memory of his touch haunting me.

"AMIR!" I reached out, grabbing his arm in desperation.

"We shouldn't be doing this!" His voice was strained, his fingers running through his wet hair as he avoided meeting my gaze.

"Because we work together? Do you even care about that? Because right now... after that... kiss... I couldn't care less," I choked on the words, my throat constricting with emotion.

A heavy silence enveloped us, thick with unspoken tension. I waited for him to reveal his feelings, but he remained silent, his eyes darting everywhere except to me. Frustration bubbled within me, boiling over as I demanded answers.

"What's with you?" I snapped, my patience wearing thin.

"What's with me?" His words hung in the air, loaded with withheld emotion. His gaze finally met mine, but his eyes were dark. Then, in a moment of raw honesty, he uttered words that cut through me like a knife. "Maybe… maybe I—I don't want to be just another storyline for your podcast," he confessed bitterly, kicking at a puddle of water.

The traffic lights changed, casting a red glow over the street, halting the flow of cars, and giving us a moment of stillness. He glanced at the lights, then back at me, the weight of his words hanging heavily in the air.

"Just go," I whispered, my voice barely audible amidst the sounds of the city.

And with that, he turned and walked away, leaving me standing alone in the rain, the echoes of his words reverberating in my mind.

I texted Paddy letting him know I'd be working at home for the rest of the day. He hadn't replied.

When I arrived back at my apartment after our rainstorm make out session, I stood under the showerhead and tears began to flow. But after the shower, I was fine. Okay, that's also a lie. I wasn't fine, I was hurting badly.

It hurt. *Fuck, did it hurt…* But if he didn't want me, then I wasn't planning on wasting any more time crying over him. I wasn't going to try to convince him to want me. I'd done that too many times in the past.

Instead of soaking my pillow with tears, I forced myself into a routine of self-care and rebuilding. My plan consisted of a facemask, hair mask and some light fake tan. Along with plucking every stray eyebrow hair on my face and even attempting to pluck two (short, but present) nose hairs. I think that almost hurt more than his words. *Almost.*

The urge to drown my sorrows in wine, to lose myself in the comfort of a mindless rom com, was strong. But I resisted. Even though my heart was sore, and ego bruised, I somehow felt stronger by resisting the vices I usually gravitated towards. Instead, I turned to my writing, planning my next episode - a chance to vent, to release the turmoil bubbling within me.

MR MYSTERIOUS

I jotted down the headline and debated how I could talk about Amir, without anyone realising it was him. I'd have to fabricate the truth… just a little bit. Enough to disguise his identity so even he won't realise. He said he didn't want to be talked about, but if I took his characteristics and stuck them on an imaginary man… no one would know.

Mr. Mysterious is a local man. (Well, this was kind of true. He was living nearby, though I left out the part stating that he hails from New York)

Recently, he's become a perplexing presence in my life.

He's a rollercoaster of emotions, swinging between hot and cold. One moment, he's acting like a complete dick, and the next, he's quite sweet. He keeps me on my toes, and I can't deny that he's ridiculously attractive. But there's something about him that intrigues me, something mysterious that draws me in.

It's like being caught in a never-ending game, each interaction feeling like a scene from a bizarre reality TV show that I never signed up for.

Why can't dating be simple? You meet someone you click with, and that's it — boyfriend to husband to happily ever after. Is that too much to ask?

Right now, my life feels like it's drowning in mixed signals. And honestly, I'm not sure how much longer I can keep playing this game.

CHAPTER THIRTEEN

Shell Shocked

Definition: extremely shocked and surprised.

It wasn't until 11pm that I finally heard from Paddy.

PADDY

Are you okay??

I pondered how to reply.

ANNA

Yes, why?

Less than a minute after sending the text, my phone rang. I sat up from the sofa, taking a deep breath to brace myself for a potentially uncomfortable conversation.

"So, were you going to tell me or?" he asked.

I sighed, "I'm guessing you already know. Why do you know? Does anyone else know?"

My heart began to race. *There's no way Amir would say anything… or would he?*

"No. He just told me, don't worry. What the fuck happened?" He sounded hoarse, like he'd been talking for a while. I couldn't help but wonder what Amir had told him and why. The idea of them being all 'buddy-buddy' made me feel more anxious than I'd like to admit.

"Paddy… I'm asking myself the same question. I have no idea." I mumbled, "Why did he tell you? When?"

"I thought you hated him?" He questioned, confusion lacing his words, ignoring my other questions.

"I do," I lied.

"Clearly not."

Silence enveloped us as I attempted to gather my thoughts.

"I don't know how I feel. It's all so confusing. There's an attraction there, but it's irrelevant. He's not interested, and I'm not going to try convince him to be."

A burst of laughter interrupted me.

"What?" I asked.

"That's a first." He poked.

A gulp formed in my throat, "Look he's just too complicated, and getting involved would only add unnecessary drama to my life. Besides, he's made it clear- he literally doesn't want me. It was just a kiss, nothing more. I can guarantee you it won't evolve into anything meaningful."

The line fell silent.

"Paddy?" I prompted, making sure he was still there.

He cleared his throat. "I can't believe I didn't see this coming."

I rolled my eyes. *How could he have figured it out when I hadn't?*

"I have a bone to pick with you, by the way. Since when do you have drinks with Amir?" I asked.

"Since when do you kiss Amir?" He retorted.

"Stoppp. I don't want to talk about it."

He chuckled. "He's not a bad guy, I've decided. I was out with some mates last Friday night, and he was just having a drink on his own, so I invited him to join us. I was just being friendly, you know, kind of felt obliged because he was at the table right next to us, but he turned out to be great company. We ended up at a house party and didn't head home until like 3am."

"Right." I reclined back on the sofa, hoping to calm my spinning head. The softness of the pillow behind me provided some solace in this chaotic situation.

"So, what are you going to do?" he inquired.

"Nothing," I sighed, shutting my eyes.

"Nothing?"

"Why would I do anything?"

Paddy huffed, exhaling a long breath. "Right, okay."

"Seriously. I don't know what he told you but he's a bit of a dick. That's all I'm saying." A sense of panic began to flutter within me. "So don't go playing matchmaker, please. It won't work."

***

"So how are you doing?" Mia asked, avoiding eye contact as she fidgeted with her phone.

Perched in her office guest chair, I felt my tights cling uncomfortably to the leather, the heat making me sweat. "Um, I'm good," I replied tentatively, unsure of how to navigate the conversation.

Her phone buzzed, but she ignored it, placing it face down on her desk. "Go on," she prompted, her tone serious.

"What?" I asked, feeling a sense of unease settle in the pit of my stomach.

"How are you really? How are you coping with the show?" She

inquired, her gaze finally meeting mine.

"Um, I'm honestly doing okay, I think. What's your opinion though?" I replied, trying to gauge her reaction.

She nodded, seemingly satisfied with my response, before turning her attention to the papers scattered across her cluttered desk. Something about her demeanour seemed off, but I didn't dare question it. "What's your plan for this week?" she asked, her voice sounding slightly strained.

Swallowing the lump in my throat, I replied, "I don't exactly have any exciting love-life updates to share."

"The show doesn't have to revolve around your love life." She stated.

"It kind of does though, no? That's what will keep people engaged."

She shook her head, "It doesn't have to be all steamy and sexy. The love you have with yourself comes first. You know that, right? You can relax a bit and - ."

A knock on the door interrupted our conversation. Amir, looking a tad dishevelled his head through. "Ready?" He asked Mia. "Oh, sorry, I didn't realise you were busy."

Our eyes met and panic brewed beneath.

Had he told Mia?

Is that why she was being kind of weird?

The earth began to shake beneath me. The door closed before she could respond.

"Must be my lucky day! That's the first time he's ever been mildly polite and not bossed his way in here." She laughed, throwing some papers into her bag. "I have to head out, but can you send me your draft plan for this week's episode to read at some point today?"

I nodded, feeling a sense of relief that our conversation was coming to an end. "Is everything okay?"

Picking up on my internal panic, Mia's expression softened. "Anna, don't panic. I'm just making sure you're feeling good about things. I know it can be overwhelming starting your own show, especially one that's so personal," she reassured me. "You're doing great."

I smoothed out my dress and hurried towards the door, a small part of me wishing Amir would still be waiting outside. However, as I stepped into the hallway, he was nowhere to be seen. Throughout the remainder of the morning, I kept an eye out for him, but he seemed to have vanished. As the afternoon wore on, I found myself completely occupied with planning, the earlier encounter with Amir temporarily pushed to the back of my mind.

***

Friday had arrived, and as I sat facing my microphone, a wave of nerves washed over me. Paddy, my trusty companion for these recordings, was engrossed in his phone until my sudden declaration broke his concentration.

"Right, so, I'm just going to get this out of the way," I announced, catching Paddy off guard.

"What?" he responded, looking up from his screen.

"You're the only person who can know," I stressed, my tone serious. "I mean it. You can't tell anyone. At all."

Confusion flickered across his face as he listened intently. "Alright..." he replied cautiously.

"My episode tonight is about Amir," I confessed.

He let out an exasperated sigh. "Oh, for fuck sake, Anna."

"What?" I groaned defensively. "I won't mention his name, obviously, and..."

"What's his 'code name' then?" Paddy interrupted, leaning forward onto his desk with a visible display of stress.

"Mr. Mysterious," I muttered, feeling a blush creeping up my cheeks.

He sighed once more, his frustration palpable. "We're about to go live in... six minutes... and you tell me this now? Let me read your notes! If he realizes this... if anyone realises..."

"Mia already read them and she had no clue," I interjected defensively.
"I'm not worried about Mia, I'm worried about Amir – I mean, Mr..."
"Mysterious..." I clarified.
"Christ," Paddy muttered, shaking his head in exasperation.

***

With a few minor note changes from Paddy, I was ready to roll. After Mr. Mysterious's first introduction, I decided to dive into a conversation on...

"Mixed signals – we've all experienced them at some point in our lives. It's that confusing cocktail of words and actions that leaves us scratching our heads, wondering what the other person really wants. Whether it's in friendships, romantic relationships, or even professional settings, decoding mixed signals can be like trying to solve a puzzle without all the pieces. Why do people send mixed signals? I've yet to figure that out. But when it happens – it makes me feel more insecure than ever.

I can't help but question my own worthiness. Am I too flawed for someone to actually love me? Like FULLY love me? Not just want me sometimes – but all the time. Would losing weight, being more polite, talking less, or having fewer opinions make me more appealing?

But then again, if I were to change myself entirely to fit someone else's mold, would I still be me? Would I recognise the person staring back at me in the mirror?

I feel like relationships are a relentless cycle of hope and disappointment, a carousel of anticipation and let-downs. Each time, I hope that maybe this time it will be different, that maybe this time I'll find someone who sees my worth, I'm only met with yet another disappointment.

Something needs to change. Maybe I need to change the type of men I choose to date. I'm craving someone mature, in control of his emotions, adventurous and not confusing. Some days I dream about moving abroad and starting a whole new life. Maybe my dream man is living in

Italy trying to manifest me as much as I am him.

Actually... maybe I need to change my entire outlook on dating.

I suppose dating doesn't have to lead me to my soulmate, but discovery instead. What do I like in my partner? What do I like about myself? How can I improve the choices I make? How can I change how I feel and deal with my emotions? I'm hoping that going forward, I can be more relaxed and focus much more on if I like the person that I'm on a date with... instead of worrying and wondering 'do they like me?'

I hate that most days I feel incomplete without a partner. I want to feel empowered to meet someone. I don't want to feel like it's essential.

What will it take to complete myself?

My episode this week isn't one of empowerment, but of questioning. Maybe you, a listener, can give me some advice this week? How do you deal with mysterious men who have you questioning their intentions? How do you set boundaries? How do you decide who to date?"

***

Monday started with a jolt as my phone rang loudly in the break room. It was barely 9:05, and I was already greeted by Olivia's frantic voice on the other end, her words punctuated by screams.

"What's going on?" I shouted, attempting to make sense of her hysteria.

She sounded like she was on the verge of hyperventilating. "Oh- oh- oh my god!"

"Olivia! Please, what's happening?!" I urged, growing increasingly concerned.

"I'll tell you, NO - I'll SHOW YOU. I need to see you! Where are you?!" she exclaimed urgently.

My plans for the day had been relatively mundane - reviewing the latest show, checking online comments and statistics, and brainstorming topics for the next episode. Olivia's urgency threw a wrench into that plan.

"Come to my office, but you can't stay for long. I have work to do," I replied, trying to maintain a sense of calm despite the chaos unfolding.

"I'll be right there!" She shouted, her voice crackling with urgency before abruptly hanging up the phone.

What on earth was that about? I made my usual morning coffee and strolled over to my desk, attempting to shake off the unsettling feeling gnawing at my gut. Ten minutes later, an email from the receptionist flashed on my screen, notifying me that Olivia had arrived and was en route to my office. Lost in the sea of emails flooding my inbox, I barely noticed Paddy's muttered exclamation to my left.

"Oh my god."

Curiosity piqued, I glanced up from my screen, only to be met with the sight of the most extravagant bouquet of flowers I'd ever laid eyes on. Purples, pinks, reds, and whites intertwined in a dazzling display of floral opulence. Olivia struggled under the weight of the blooms, teetering precariously as she made her way toward me. Without a second thought, I sprang from my seat and rushed to her side, offering my support.

"What in the world?" I gasped.

We carefully set the oversized bouquet down beside my desk, realising there simply wasn't enough space for it on top. Despite the overwhelming size, I couldn't help but admire the impeccable presentation of the flowers. Paddy stood up, his eyes wide as he gawked at the extravagant arrangement.

"So... TOM... Tom Beckham!!" Olivia exclaimed, bent over, and struggling to catch her breath. "He sent flowers... to my work... for YOU!"

My heart skipped a beat. Tom Beckham? For me?

"Oh, good god," I muttered, a mixture of disbelief and amusement bubbling up within me. I turned back to the flowers, trying to wrap my head around the unexpected gesture.

"Olivia…" I began, struggling to contain a laugh. "Are you sure?"

She looked up at me, her face alight with a mischievous grin. "Positive!"

Paddy's laughter filled the room as he struggled to contain himself.

"Is this a joke?" I asked, looking back and forth between the two of them, my mind still reeling from the unexpected turn of events.

"I have nothing to do with it! But I'm quite enjoying it," he managed to choke out between laughs.

"Honestly, just read the card!" Olivia insisted, pointing towards the bouquet.

Hidden amidst a sea of roses and hydrangeas was a small note card. I might have overlooked it if she hadn't pointed it out. Carefully, I lifted it, being mindful not to damage any of the precious petals. The paper felt expensive, the texture smooth beneath my fingertips. Written in elegant gold pen were the words:

Anna,
Would love to see you again and maybe get some interior design tips? ;)
Tom x

A surge of warmth flooded through me as I read the message. On the other side of the card was his phone number. I couldn't suppress the smile that spread across my face. I hadn't even considered the possibility of seeing him again. After my endless bank of insults about his mansion of a home, I was certain he'd want nothing to do with me.

"Right, do you want to fill me in on what's going on or do I have to rip the card from your hand?" Paddy chuckled; his amusement evident. I glanced up at him, feeling a flush of embarrassment wash over me.

"Anna has an admirer!!" Olivia declared gleefully, snatching the card from my hands and passing it to Paddy.

"She has a what?" My head shot up at the sound of Amir's rich

American voice. His sudden appearance sent a jolt of surprise through me.

He wore a stern expression, his features etched with seriousness that immediately made me feel tense. Instinctively, I shifted, positioning myself in front of the bouquet of flowers, as if to shield them from his scrutiny.

"It's nothi-"

"Well, apparently we'll be hearing about a new love interest on next week's show," Paddy interjected, his laughter punctuating the sentence as he wiggled his eyebrows mischievously.

"Not new!" Olivia blurted out, her words escaping before she could stop them, her eyes widening in realisation.

Amir's gaze shifted from my face to the flowers I was trying to hide… but let's be honest, nothing could hide them. They were ginormous.

"Right," he said, his expression unreadable, a blank mask that irked me more than I cared to admit. Even though I had made a firm declaration to myself not to feel anything for him and to let go of any lingering desire, I found myself still so affected by his every gesture or expression. It was frustrating how I couldn't seem to help it, how his mere presence could stir up emotions I thought I had buried deep within me.

"Aren't they magnificent!" Olivia exclaimed, her excitement palpable as she turned to me and subtly nodded her head towards Amir. She seemed practically entranced, devouring him with her eyes. I half expected drool to start dripping from her mouth.

Amir, however, seemed unimpressed. "They're a bit much… don't you think?" he questioned, his tone tinged with something that resembled jealousy. My heart skipped a beat at the possibility.

"I think they're wonderful," I replied, standing up straight with a proud smile fixed on my face. It was a lie, of course. I couldn't stand how ostentatious and over-the-top they were. But I couldn't deny the thrill of the thought that Tom had bought them for me, so I wasn't entirely lying.

Amir's straight face transformed into a smirk as he raised an eyebrow. "Oh really?" he remarked, his tone teasing.

I glanced towards the extravagant flowers and then back to him, maintaining my composure. "Yes," I affirmed, trying to match his playful demeanour.

He bit his lip, clearly suppressing a laugh, and I couldn't help but feel a flutter of attraction. I quickly shook the thought out of my head, refusing to indulge in such dangerous territory. I hated how he found the situation amusing. *Was he laughing at the idea of someone buying me flowers? Was I truly so unlovable that receiving flowers was a novelty?* Anxious thoughts raced through my mind as his eyes locked with mine, intensifying the moment.

"They are soooooo fab!" Olivia interrupted our staring contest with her usual exuberance. "Like I would DIE if someone bought these for me!" she exclaimed dramatically, throwing her arms into the air for emphasis. As she leaned towards Amir, touching his arm on the way down. "They had to have cost a fortune!" I felt a surge of irritation as she pushed her hair over her shoulder and adjusted her top, seemingly trying to garner more attention from Amir. Thankfully, his gaze remained fixed on me.

"Well, thank you for dropping them off! I have sooo much work to do today otherwise I'd grab you a coffee, Liv!" I interjected, eager to divert the focus away from her antics.

"Yeah, no problem," she replied, her eyes still lingering on Amir.

I noticed Amir's eyes darting between me and Olivia, a flicker of amusement dancing in them. He ran his tongue over the top of his teeth slowly, a subtle gesture that sent a shiver down my spine. Then, he glanced back at me, lifting an eyebrow in a silent question.

"It's okay Anna… I'll walk you out -" he began but was interrupted by Olivia extending her hand for a handshake.

"Olivia," she introduced herself with a smile, to which Amir courteously accepted.

"Olivia, I can show you out," he offered, eyes darting back to mine.

I bit my tongue, restraining the urge to voice my frustration.

As Olivia quickly pulled me into a hug before leaving, she whispered in my ear, "Jesus Christ! How do I get a job here?!"

As the elevator doors closed, Amir cast a lingering gaze in my direction, a silent provocation that sent a shiver down my spine.

"I don't like her. Or those flowers," Paddy's voice broke through my reverie. I sighed, sinking into my chair, and forced myself to focus on work.

I slipped one headphone into my ear and scrolled through Spotify, hoping to find a playlist that could help lift my mood.

Paddy's voice cut through my thoughts. "You okay?"

My lips trembled involuntarily, and I let out a sigh, squinting my eyes shut. "Yeah, I'll be fine. Do you think he was acting weird?"

"Define weird?"

"Doesn't matter…" I mumbled. "He definitely doesn't know that he's…" My voice turned to a whisper, "Mr Mysterious? Does he?"

Paddy snorted, "Definitely not. If he did, he'd have called straight after the episode aired. No doubt."

***

Later that night, I mustered up the courage to text Tom.

ANNA
Thank you so much for the lovely flowers. I definitely didn't deserve them based on our first interaction, but they were very much appreciated x

Surprisingly, he got back to me right away, asking if I wanted to go on a date the next week after he got back from a golf trip. Despite my apprehension, he seemed genuinely nice. Sure, he was older than any guy I'd ever been out with, but maybe that was a good thing.

If I changed the type of men I usually dated, maybe it would change the outcome?

***

Maggie Mays buzzed with activity, a stark contrast to the usual calm of a Tuesday afternoon. Grace and Olivia sat at the table, waiting for me as I entered. I had summoned them because I knew discussing the recent kiss in our WhatsApp group wouldn't suffice.

"Heyyyy…" I greeted, slipping into the booth.

Both girls stared at me, a heavy silence lingering in the air.

"What?" I asked, feeling the weight of their scrutiny.

"What's wrong with you? Did you get fired?" Grace's concern was palpable.

"Whatever it is, I can make it better. Here!" Olivia interjected, thrusting two purple gift bags onto the table—one for me and one for Grace.

Grateful for the momentary distraction, I accepted the bag with a weak smile.

"Open them! But… carefully," Olivia instructed, a mischievous grin playing on her lips.

Carefully? That word alone sent a ripple of apprehension through me as I gingerly peeled back the sellotape sealing the bag. With cautious fingers, I sifted through the tissue paper until my hand brushed against a rectangular box nestled at the bottom.

"OLIVIA!" Grace's gasp of surprise echoed in the air.

My eyes widened in shock as I hastily shoved the box back beneath the paper. Olivia's laughter bubbled up, and I tentatively peeled back another layer of tissue to confirm my suspicions. Inside the box lay what appeared to be a sleek, bright purple sex toy. I had never owned anything quite so… sophisticated. Back in college, I'd settled for a £10 bullet vibrator, but this one seemed light-years ahead in terms of technology and, undoubtedly, price.

"I take it we both got the same thing?" I asked, trying to keep my voice light despite the awkwardness of the situation. Grace nodded, her eyes wide, her face pale.

"Oh, will you both shush! They were PR gifts. Seriously, my work was sent like FIFTY of them… I just maneuvered them out of the office and into your hands. I hope you both make good use of them!" Olivia chimed in, attempting to diffuse the tension with her characteristic nonchalance.

I peered back into the bag, feeling a mixture of curiosity and excitement stirring within me. But Grace seemed utterly mortified.

"I'm not accepting this! I wouldn't even know how to use it!" She whisper-yelled, her cheeks flushing crimson.

Olivia rolled her eyes and reached into the bag, pulling out the box. Grace panicked and attempted to snatch it back.

"Grace, more women in this world own a vibrator than a dishwasher!" Olivia exclaimed, undeterred by Grace's embarrassment. "Plus, there are so many options." She pointed at the picture on the front of the box, eagerly demonstrating its functions. "This is a sucker; it goes on your clit. Feels very realisti-"

"Shhhhh!"

"Oh, grow up!" Olivia continued to showcase the toy, unfazed by Grace's protests. Anxiously, I scanned the restaurant, hoping nobody was paying attention to our conversation. In doing so, I caught Aileen's eye. She darted over, clearly noticing our animated discussion.

"Girls! My girls! How are you?" Aileen's cheerful interruption provided a welcome distraction.

Grace threw the tissue paper from her bag over Olivia's hands in a desperate attempt to conceal the toy. "Good, we're good. Great actually," she stammered, her face flushed with embarrassment.

I couldn't help but giggle at her distress, while Olivia remained composed as always.

"That's good. Would you like your usual?" Aileen's keen observation suggested she suspected something was amiss as she eyed the tissue paper. "Oh my gosh... is it someone's birthday?!"

"No! No!" Grace interjected hastily, her eyes widening in panic.

"Yes, it's Grace's birthday, and I was just giving her... her gift!" Olivia announced proudly, unveiling the toy from under the paper and presenting it to Grace, who looked as though she wanted to disappear into the booth.

Suppressing my laughter, I watched as her cheeks turned even redder with embarrassment. Aileen chuckled and walked away to put in our usual order, "Oh, I love it! You girls are such fun!"

"I can't believe you did that!" Grace's tone was a mix of disbelief and annoyance. She hastily stashed the toy deep inside her bag, covering it with her coat for good measure. Meanwhile, I gave my own bag one last glance before setting it aside.

Olivia burst into laughter. "Jesus, just try it out and let us know if you feel any better! You need to lighten up!"

I interjected, "Well, I appreciate the sentiment, Liv, even though you have probably stolen these illegally from your office and could have gifted them in a less public setting..."

"Anna, if any of us need a vibrator it's you. The talent in your work would have me horny all day long." Olivia fanned herself with a napkin.

I inhaled deeply, "I meant to speak to you about that...the man you met – that was Amir."

Her jaw dropped, "No fucking way."

"Who's Amir?" Grace asked, completely lost. I began to fill her in on my stupid office crush, detailing every interaction, my frustrations with him and then... "I kissed him."

"Oh. My. Fuck." Olivia's hand flew to her mouth, her eyes widening in shock.

Grace's mouth dropped open, a look of utter astonishment crossing her face, even wider than when she'd opened the sex toy.

"Well – technically - actually - he kissed me."

"When did this happen?" Grace gasped, her voice barely a whisper amidst the palpable disbelief in the air.

I buried my head in my hands, feeling the weight of their incredulity bearing down on me. "Last week. In the pouring rain… it was like something straight out of a movie, honestly."

I cursed at myself for romanticising the moment. Even though the kiss felt extraordinary…. *He was not my person.* I repeated this in my head, remembering my latest podcast episode on dating. **Dating is how you find out more about yourself - dating doesn't always lead to a soulmate.** I found out I like kissing in the rain. I realised I like when a man holds me extremely tight. I discovered that I like when he sucks on my bottom lip. I definitely like when he -

"This is so exciting! Did you have hot office sex?!" Liv questioned, her eyes wide with anticipation, wakening me from my daydream.

I lifted my head, shaking it slightly. "Nope. He left straight after. Told me he didn't want to be another storyline on my podcast."

Both girls' expressions showed a blend of shock and sympathy. "You're kidding," Grace's disbelief mirrored my own sentiments. "Wait, is he Mr Mysterious?"

"Y- yes… how the fuck did you figure that out?" I questioned.

"Mixed signals – duh." Grace explained.

I shook my head again, feeling a twinge of disappointment. "It doesn't matter anyways. He's in the bin now. I don't plan on talking about him again… On to the next."

"Under…" Olivia choked out.

"What?" I asked, puzzled by her sudden change in demeanour.

She wore a devilish smile. "Under… under the next…" Her words trailed off, leaving a mischievous glint in her eyes.

***

On Thursday, I brought both Olivia and Grace into the studio for a discussion on all things related to sex and self-pleasure, inspired by the recent vibrator gifting.

"There's no reason for it to be awkward," Olivia spoke with confidence.

"I agree," I chimed in, nodding in agreement. "The more open we are about sex, not just with our partners but with our friends, the better, I think. It needs to be less taboo."

Olivia sighed, her expression turning thoughtful. "I mean, I get it. It's difficult sometimes. I'm very confident talking about sex, and you can be harshly judged for it. My experience is that men can either find it incredibly sexy or call you a whore. And masturbation… is amazing. It makes your sex life better too."

"Look, men talk all the time about sex but if women do, we're made to feel shameful. I hold a lot of that shame and need to try get over it." Grace said, her cheeks flaming.

"Why do you think you feel shameful?" I asked, curious.

She paused, choosing her words carefully, "I think society makes us believe that women should be modest and pure. Like, think about 'losing your virginity' – I was told growing up that I should be extremely careful about who I chose to have sex with the first time. It had to be special, with someone I loved and really mean something. I was told that I should hold onto it for as long as possible. But with the guys I know, they weren't given that same talk? It's like a cool thing. They're encouraged to have sex. It's like… the sooner the better almost?"

Her words sat heavy in the air. "You're so right." Olivia gasped. "And I hate the term 'losing your virginity' because what are we losing? If anything, we're gaining. We're gaining experience… hopefully gaining pleasure too."

I sat in slight disbelief at how my life had shifted in a matter of a few weeks… from being a background worker at Spotlight to having my own show talking about women 'getting themselves off' and the shame surrounding that and our sex lives. But for some reason, it felt much more empowering than it did embarrassing. There was a sense of liberation in the air.

***

On Friday, Paddy sat across from me, looking a little more uncomfortable than usual as the pre-recorded conversation played on air. I couldn't help but tease him by making some exaggerated orgasm faces, trying to elicit a reaction. He chuckled and shook his head in amusement.

As the section ended, I switched on my mic to conclude the episode.

"So, this week has been quite enlightening. I've come to realise that self-pleasure and self-development are crucial acts of self-love. Perhaps, I just need to focus on loving myself a little bit more."

As my closing song began to play, wrapping up an empowering episode, Paddy shifted awkwardly in his seat.

I couldn't help but giggle. "Did you enjoy that one?"

"Uh, aside from getting some vivid pictures in my head that I never wanted to imagine?" he chuckled uncomfortably, scratching the back of his neck. "But, yeah, it was actually really interesting. And, you know, I was encouraged to lose my virginity. Felt huge pressure to do it, or my mates would take the piss out of me. It's kind of like society views it as women losing something – but men gain something."

"It's insane," I sighed. "But I do think the perception is starting to shift."

"You're a part of that change. It's a daring conversation to have. No one else is talking about it on air," he laughed. "That's for sure."

***

Later that night, I lay in bed, engrossed in a romantic novel, with the soft glow of a rock salt lamp casting a warm light across my room. Suddenly, my phone buzzed against the bedside table, breaking my concentration.

I stared at the email in utter disbelief. It was the first I'd heard from him in over a week, and surprisingly, it contained the first genuine compliment he had ever given me.

From: amir.davairi@apex.com
Subject: Well done.
"Best episode yet. Really honest."

CHAPTER FOURTEEN
On the lash

Definition: out drinking

The music in Ollie's was deafening, drowning out our attempts at conversation. Grace fought back yawns, exhaustion evident as the clock approached 2.30 am.

In a dimly lit corner, Olivia was entwined with a dark-haired man, lost in a passionate embrace oblivious to the bustling nightclub around them.

I grabbed Grace's hand, pulling her towards the dance floor hoping to liven our vibe. Amidst the pulsating beats – a mix of timeless club classics and current chart-toppers – we moved in rhythm.

Beside us, two men exchanged suggestive glances, indicating their desire to dance. To my surprise, Grace nonchalantly embraced one, prompting me to reciprocate the other's advances.

He was fair-haired and somewhat attractive, though I couldn't help but find his choice of wearing sunglasses in a dark club a bit of an ick.

Nonetheless, his hands found their way to my hips as I swayed against him, letting the music guide our movements. Meanwhile, Grace giggled awkwardly as she attempted to do the same.

As the next song started, I grabbed her hand and pulled her closer. "What are we doing?" I asked, feeling completely out of character.

"I don't know, but I feel like I need to loosen up a bit. Your whole 'not every man you date has to be your soulmate' bit on the pod inspired me," she shouted over the music. "So why not?"

I couldn't help but smile, feeling a sense of warmth. I admired Grace's willingness to step out of her comfort zone and explore. But as we turned to find our dance partners, they had vanished, and the club lights began to flicker on, signalling the end of the night.

We stood on the chilly street outside, scanning the bustling crowd for the elusive men, while Olivia waited for her new beau to retrieve her coat from the cloakroom.

"It's fucking freezing," Olivia remarked, rubbing her arms for warmth. She was dressed in an outfit that some might mistake for lingerie, but to her, it was the perfect Saturday night ensemble. She looked unbelievable.

"Where could he be?" Grace giggled, her eyes darting around the throng of people.

"I love this—" I hiccupped. "Are you going to go home with him?"

"Of course I am. He's a footballer," Liv interjected, misinterpreting our conversation.

"No— I'm actually talking about Grace. SHE DANCED WITH A MAN!" I exclaimed, still reeling from the unexpected turn of events.

Olivia let out a shrill scream. "WHAT?! Where is he?" Her eyes darted around the area, searching for any sign of Grace's impromptu dance partner.

But Grace, swaying slightly on her feet, giggled, and waved her off. "No, stop," she laughed. "I just felt spontaneous. I'd only have asked for his number, but there are soooo many more men out there." She gestured towards the crowd, the majority of which seemed to be male.

"I quite liked the one I was dancing with," I admitted quietly. "But I have that date with Tom, so..."

Olivia snorted incredulously. "So? I know he's Tom Beckham, but why would you stop yourself from seeing someone else? It's just a date."

"Isn't that unfair to him?" I pondered aloud. "He's interested, and it feels wrong."

Grace playfully punched my arm, nearly stumbling in the process. "Anna, shut up. He's not your boyfriend, so you don't owe him anything yet... And what if the date with him is soooo bad? Then what?" Her words were starting to slur together. "You're committing to him before you have to commit. And who wants commitment? Nooooo way."

"I can't believe you'd limit yourself, you stupid bitch," Olivia laughed heartily. "Have options. Create a roster. Be more carefree... How else will you realise what you like and don't? You both need to get on the apps."

"No, not the apps," I protested, grimacing at the thought.

I truly despised dating apps.

"I SWIPE RIGHT!" Grace suddenly yelled, darting across the road and almost getting hit by a taxi. Bewildered, we followed suit, wondering what had spurred her sudden decision, only to find her dance partner surrounded by a group of others, all still wearing sunglasses and matching T-shirts with the words 'Andy's Belfast Stag' printed on the front.

"So, which one of you is getting married?" Grace giggled, teasingly.

To her dismay, the men pointed to her dance partner. She rolled her eyes, laughed, and gave him a playful middle finger.

Olivia departed with her newfound companion, leaving Grace and I to walk back to my apartment together. We collapsed in fits of giggles on my bed.

"I don't think I'm ready yet," she admitted between laughs. "Honestly, what are the chances?"

And I couldn't agree more. "Men are fucking dickheads," I sighed.

"Hey! Not all of them... maybe we should sign up to the apps," she suggested, eyeing me mischievously.

So, in our drunken haze, we decided to take the plunge. We downloaded every dating app possible and took on the task of creating each other's profiles, hoping that maybe, just maybe, we could find a match or two amidst the chaos of online dating.

***

By Thursday morning, the pressure was mounting, and I found myself staring at my notes with a sinking feeling. There was nothing particularly captivating for my upcoming episode.

After two hours of fruitless brainstorming, I glanced down at the scribbles covering the pages and had a sudden realisation... Perhaps Tom could provide some inspiration. Maybe his age and our date could serve as the basis for an episode topic: dating older men, taking a chance on uncertain dates...

With a renewed sense of purpose, I started jotting down ideas, feeling hopeful that my evening plans could help lead me to an intriguing episode.

First date conversation topics – what are his goals? What makes him happy? Best thing he's done recently? Celebrity crush? Fave type of music? Best place he's travelled to?

How to combat first date nerves....

Chivalry – is not dead? I wonder if our date will be as extravagant as the flowers.

ANNA

Hi Mia, I'm still working on my episode notes. Is there any chance we could review session to tomorrow instead of today? I'm still polishing things up, and I think it'll be worth the wait. Sorry for the short notice!

MIA
No worries! I've an appointment tomorrow so you will have to review with Amir. He's available at 10.45am.

My heart sank.

***

As my nerves got the better of me, I decided to do some shopping on my lunch break, with the aim of finding something nice to wear. I paced around town, managing to pick up a simple but nice red dress. I couldn't completely remember what Tom looked like and I forced myself to avoid googling him.

I knew however, that I'd have to dress well and respectable as he was definitely a bit older than me and absolutely fucking minted. I couldn't show up in a cheapy number which I'd stored in the back of my wardrobe. As I walked back towards work, I decided to pick up a box of chocolates. He'd gifted me flowers, so it was only fair I bring him something as a surprise.

At 6.35pm, I sat on the toilet having my usual pre-date nervous pee (third pee in the last 20 minutes). I scrolled through my phone and decided 'fuck it' and searched his name on Google. Images immediately popped up along with hundreds, maybe thousands of articles listing his success. He'd been involved in the golf scene for years, setting a standard for Northern Irish players and then once retired, he'd written a book and joined the tourism board. AND HE WAS 37.

He looked older than I remembered in the photos. I paced around my living room for twenty seconds before my feet hurt. I'd chosen my nicest red heels; to match the dress. Olivia had borrowed them one time and described them as 'devil shoes' due to how much they hurt her feet, and as much as I agreed with her, I'd somehow convinced myself to wear them tonight.

At 6.45pm, I hadn't heard from Tom but assumed he was just running a few minutes late. At 7pm however, I started to feel a bit doubtful.

ANNA

Hey you, are we still on for tonight? x

I sent the text just after 7.10pm. He didn't seem like the type to stand someone up…

At 7.30pm, my gut was screaming at me to get into pyjamas and have a lonesome movie night. I called Grace for some advice.

"Are you sure he said 6.45 and not 7.45?" she hummed down the phone.

"Yeah, I've re-read all of our texts."

"When was the last time you spoke to him?"

"Uh like yesterday afternoon…" I sighed, wishing I'd text him earlier in the day to confirm we were still on.

Grace sighed, "Maybe he had an emergency or got into an accident or something…"

I could tell by her hesitation that she wasn't convinced.

"I don't know." I mumbled. "Do I wait?"

I looked down at my dress and heels. I'd put in so much effort, I'd even watched a 'How to contour like Kim K' tutorial on YouTube. My makeup was looking better than ever.

"It's up to you. I- maybe wait until 7.45? It's just very … strange that he hasn't text you back…"

My anxiety was beginning to manifest as nausea. *Why would he send me flowers and then not show up for a date?*

I began to overthink… *maybe this was all a practical joke? Maybe I wasn't even texting Tom… maybe it was a catfish.*

"I'll wait." I sighed.

"Have a glass of wine and pop on the TV. Occupy yourself. If he doesn't show, I'll pick you up and we can go for a drive-through McFlurry," Grace suggested, her voice filled with warmth and concern.

I couldn't help but imagine Grace, cosy in her fuzzy pyjamas, tucked up in bed with a book by her side. The thought of inconveniencing her weighed on my mind.

"Honestly, if he doesn't show up, I think I'll just crawl into bed," I confessed, feeling a wave of disappointment wash over me.

"Start swiping." She giggled, surprising me. "As Liv would say, onto the next."

"Under. She'd say under... but yeah." I laughed, "Maybe I should."

"Keep me updated babe. I'm here if you need me," Grace's voice reassured me.

"Will do, love you," I responded, the warmth of her support comforting me.

"Love you."

I hung up the phone, glancing at the time. 7:42 PM. Feeling a mix of disappointment and frustration, I decided to pour myself a glass of red wine and put on some music. As the familiar tunes filled the room, I couldn't help but feel like Bridget Jones, singing along to all the cheesy love songs. *How had I become the girl who gets stood up and feels like crying about it?*

I opened my phone and began swiping through profiles, hoping to distract myself. While no one particularly caught my interest, a few messages of interest helped fill the void of disappointment.

Unfortunately, I remained dressed and ready for another hour, waiting in vain. By 9 PM, I decided to call it a night. As I began to remove my jewellery, my phone suddenly buzzed with a new notification.

TOM BECKHAM
You about?

I stared at the text message in disbelief. It vibrated again.

TOM BECKHAM
Where are you?

ANNA
At home? You never showed up

TOM BECKHAM
I met some mates in town and I lost my phone. I'm soo sorry.

If my gut could shout, it was screaming on the top of its lungs. **RED FLAG.**

ANNA
Ok. Hope you had fun.

I replied bitterly.

TOM BECKHAM
Wanna meet me?

TOM BECKHAM
I'm in the Dirty Onion Bar

TOM BECKHAM
I still really want to see you. It'll be fun x

I stared at the messages on my phone, then glanced at my reflection in the mirror, weighing my options. I could stay in and spend the evening ruminating on "what ifs"... I could opt for a comforting McFlurry excursion with Grace... Or I could muster the courage to meet him, just for one drink.

ANNA

Not feeling up to it anymore. Have a good night

Then my phone buzzed again.

TOM BECKHAM

Come meet me. I was sooo looking forward to seeing u tonight

I had invested so much time and effort into my makeup; it would be a shame to let it go to waste. Plus, I did have a soft spot for The Dirty Onion... And let's face it, I badly needed content for my episode. The thought of writing about being stood up wasn't particularly appealing, especially knowing Amir would be scrutinising my every word.

ANNA

Ok, sure. I can be there in 15 minutes?

TOM BECKHAM

Ok gorgeous

I felt a knot of nerves tightening in my stomach as I hastily touched up my makeup in the mirror and swished some mouthwash. Grabbing my coat, I spotted the box of chocolates sitting on my hall table. Without pausing to overthink, I snatched them up and headed out the door.

During my walk to the bar, it dawned on me that not showing up for our date and then texting me almost three hours later was hardly deserving of a sweet gesture...

I was greeted by a long queue outside. Standing on the cobblestoned street, facing the entrance, I hesitated for a moment before deciding to text him.

ANNA

I'm outside but there's a long line...

Less than a minute later, Tom emerged from the crowd, calling out "Anna!" above the bustling noise of people.

He looked rather appealing, a bit dishevelled but in a charming way. His white shirt casually peeked out from his jeans, exuding a laid-back yet somewhat sexy vibe. Catching my eye, he waved me over. As I approached the entrance, the doorman graciously stepped aside, acknowledging Tom, while I couldn't help but overhear disgruntled comments from others upset about me skipping the queue.

"Thanks for getting me in," I smiled gratefully.

Tom snorted, "I don't queue. Ever."

His response stirred something uncomfortable within me. I suppressed my discomfort and scanned the bustling bar, alive with people and the strains of live music. The familiar surroundings provided a comforting sense of relief. As Belfast's oldest building, it exuded charm. Once a fishmongers in the 1600s, then a grocer's, an importer of tea, and finally a Jameson whiskey warehouse, its wooden beam structure held countless secrets. And I found solace in its timeless vibe.

"I brought you these," I said, handing him the box of Dairy Milks.

His eyes lit up as they fell on the chocolates in my hands, and a smile spread across his face, forming wrinkles around his eyes. "No wayyy! Thank you."

He hugged me tightly and planted a kiss on my cheek. "I don't think a bird has ever bought me chocolates before." His breath, a blend of spirits and smoke, wasn't particularly pleasant.

A bird

Definition : a woman

"Well, I've never bought chocolates for a man before. I just saw them and thought, because of the flowers and all..." I mumbled. "Thank you—for the flowers, by the way."

He looked puzzled for a moment, then seemed to recall something. Before I could analyse his thoughts, I was swept away towards the bar.

"You look gorgeous," he complimented me as we waited for our drinks. "Really, really gorgeous."

I felt my cheeks warm at the small compliment. It was refreshing to feel good about my outfit choice, for once.

"I remember you being so on edge at the party. Is this not your scene?" Tom gestured around the bustling bar. People danced and screamed along to the live band, the air crackling with energy.

"No, no. It was just Sebastian. He made me uncomfortable," I mumbled. "That's all."

"Yeah, he's quite something..." Tom chuckled, running his tongue over his chapped lips, softening them. "So, does that mean you're going to get drunk with me tonight?"

He casually draped his arm around my shoulder, drawing me closer to him. His hand squeezed my shoulder playfully, and I couldn't help but shiver, glancing down at my feet. I hadn't planned on getting drunk... But when I looked up and saw the playful smile on his face, I relaxed. He didn't mean any harm.

"I don't know. I have to work tomorrow," I replied hesitantly, mindful of the episode I had yet to plan.

Just as I finished talking, two shots of baby Guinness arrived alongside a pint of cider for him and a 'vodka something or other' for me. We clinked our glasses in a toast, and I felt a bit more at ease as the alcohol coated my throat. But the comfort didn't last long.

"Come," he said, placing his hand on my back. "I want you to meet my mates."

I thought it was going to be just the two of us... The sting of disappointment and an instant wave of anxiety washed over me, like a cold bucket of ice water. Nothing about tonight was going according to plan. I hadn't planned to meet his friends, but perhaps this was just a friendly thing? Maybe he had no romantic feelings towards me at all. Maybe we were just going to be mates.

"Oh, okay," I replied, walking with him towards the back corner of the bar. A wonderful guitarist played in the background as we navigated through the crowds of people. A few nodded at Tom, smiling as if he were a regular customer, or perhaps he was just more famous than I realised.

"Right, lads!" Tom yelled, interrupting the conversation shared between the four men sitting at the table. "This is Anna."

As I looked around, I felt like I was being thrown to the wolves. They were all older men; one looked old enough to be my dad. The table was littered with empty glasses, giving the impression that they'd been here for hours.

A slim, brown-haired guy stood up, wiped his hands on his trousers, and shook my hand. "Hi, I'm Greg."

"And this is Johnny, Adam, and Nolan," Tom said, pointing to each guy. I nodded along, smiling at them. "Isn't this sweet? She brought me chocolates!"

Tom pushed aside some of the glasses and stacked a few to make room for the box. Nolan snorted into his beer, and Adam hit his back to stop him from coughing—or laughing. Tom ignored them and pulled out a chair for me to sit on. "So nice to meet you," I said with a smile, hoping they wouldn't see through my facade.

It was awkwardly quiet at our table, and I wasn't sure what to say or do. "So, how'd you two meet?" Johnny quizzed.

I turned to Tom, who glanced at me and clicked his tongue off the roof of his mouth. "Well... I found her crying in my utility room..." he began.

I held my face in my hands, absolutely mortified, as he gave a detailed explanation of our first encounter. By the end of it, the guys were in fits of laughter, with Nolan even brushing a tear from his cheek from laughing so hard.

"S-s-so you told him he was a dickhead?!" Greg exclaimed.

"Yes, she goes 'whoever owns this house is probably a right dickhead!'" Tom imitated my voice.

"I do not sound like that!" I laughed. "And I don't think you are! I didn't know you owned the house!"

"Oh, just wait until you actually get to know him!" Adam chimed in. "He's a right tosser when he decides to be!"

I felt a sense of relief as our conversation flowed smoothly. After an hour, I found myself still sipping slowly on my second drink, while the guys were progressively getting more intoxicated. They kept making frequent trips to the toilets, and from the corner of my eye, I noticed a small white bag being passed around. I'd never taken any drugs and had no intentions of it, but from their wide eyes and alertness, I was positive they were sniffing something.

Toms' eyes gleamed with excitement, hinting at possible involvement. Another red flag... my subconscious screamed. Despite knowing the bar had a zero-tolerance policy, I found myself turning a blind eye.

I scrutinised his facial features—nice lips, big eyes, a charming smile. Yet, as I admired him, the question lingered: did I fancy him? *Kind of... like how I fancied the older cast of Mamma Mia.* However, did I want to sleep with him? Did I desire him in that way? The uncertainty lingered in my thoughts.

"I think I'm going to head home." I whispered to him.

He turned round, eyebrows raised, "But the night hasn't even started!"

It was after 11 and I knew if I stayed, things would get messy. "I know, I just have to work in the morning." I fake yawned, hoping he'd have some sympathy.

He rubbed his hand up and down my back, trying to pull me closer. "You should stay," he urged.

His eyes flicked between mine and my lips, and before I could react, he was kissing me. The taste of his mouth turned my stomach, and I kissed back for a brief moment before pulling away. "I-I really should go," I stammered.

Before he could respond, I stood up and wrapped my coat around me. Tom remained seated, sipping his beer, as I said my goodbyes to everyone. When I glanced back at him, he simply nodded. I had expected him to... I don't know, maybe stand up and walk me out? It bothered me that he didn't even offer a goodbye hug. Perhaps my mouth tasted bad too.

I made my way through the streets toward my apartment, each step a reminder of the discomfort my heels were causing. About three minutes away, I reached my breaking point. Balancing awkwardly on one leg, I removed my left shoe, then the right. Carefully watching the ground, I made sure not to step on anything unpleasant. Upon reaching home, I settled on the edge of my bath, washing the accumulated grime from my feet. Afterward, I called Grace to share the latest updates.

"I don't like the sound of him." She muttered. "Lots of red flags."

"Yeah..." I sighed, "I'm getting the same vibe."

"Don't get hung up on it. You've only met him... what... twice?"

"Yeah, you're right. I was just very surprised with the flowers, I guess. No one has ever bought me flowers before."

"You didn't even like the flowers."

"I did!"

"No you didn't!"

"Okay, so I didn't. They were just too much and so *not* tasteful. Oh god, do I sound ungrateful?! I'm not meaning to be, I just..."

"No, you're not ungrateful. I know you appreciated the gesture but just the choice of flowers…" I heard her shudder, "It was outrageous. A statement for sure."

I laughed. "Ugh, why can't I just find someone…"

"You will. Have you been swiping?"

"Oh my god, give over with the swiping. Have you found a match or something? Is that why you're so eager for me to?" I teased.

Give over
Definition : be quiet / stop yapping

She chuckled. "No, I deleted them all. But if you give it a shot, maybe it'll inspire me to redownload. Maybe."

"Christ," I sighed, shaking my head at the thought of chatting to or meeting another man.

I stayed awake until just after 3am, attempting to write my next episode, only I was slightly lost, and the pressure of reviewing it with Amir weighed heavy on my shoulders.

Remember when I said that dating doesn't have to lead you to your soulmate? It should however, definitely lead you to self-discovery…

Through recent experiences, I've discovered a lot.

I've realised I need to shift my perspective even further.

When I launched this show, I was nursing a broken heart, yearning to replace the connection I had with my ex — Mr. Fuckboy.

But you know what? When I was with him, I made him my entire universe. I catered to his every need, neglecting so many parts of myself in the process.

In the past month without him, I've experienced a newfound sense of liberation. I've been able to focus on my work, nurturing my career, and pouring energy into developing this show. No more pretending to be interested in Gaelic Football, no more sacrificing my comfort for someone else's.

I've loved wearing my comfiest, ugliest pyjamas and claiming the entire bed as my own. I've not shaved my legs in a while, and I love the fact that I don't have to ask someone what they want for dinner, even though half the time, he wouldn't bother to reply or show up anyways. My standards were buried six feet under ground...

So, my rollercoaster relationship with Mr. Fuckboy was like a crash course in boundaries, I guess. But you know what? Learning the lesson and actually putting it into practice are two entirely different beasts.

This week, I got asked out on a date by a man we're naming 'Mr. Millionaire.' I dolled up, feeling all those butterflies as I eagerly awaited his arrival. Only, he stood me up. I waited for what felt like an eternity. Just as I was about to give up and let my bed swallow me whole, a text came through—inviting me to a nearby bar.

And what did I do? I went. Ignoring his blatant disrespect and conveniently forgetting the boundaries I've been preaching about. Why, you ask?

1. My ego was bruised, and damn it, I looked good. I craved that validation after being left hanging for so long.

2. Convenience. It was just down the street, so why not?

3. And if I'm being honest, part of me was hoping for some juicy material to spice up this podcast.

In hindsight, it's clear I let my ego and the allure of 'potential' cloud my judgment. But hey, we live and learn, right?

Anyway, I ended up going to what I thought was our date, only to find him surrounded by his friends at the bar. To be honest, the night wasn't as enjoyable as I had hoped. Sure, there were some laughs, and I didn't have to pay for a single drink (despite my attempts), but I felt insecure and anxious the whole time.

Reflecting on it, I realise I'm upset with myself for going along with it after he stood me up. Instead of seeing the red flags, I could squint and see them as pretty pink flags...and I like pink. But eventually, the reality started to seep through... I could only paint the picture for so long.

Perhaps it's time for me to take a break from dating men and start dating myself?

My notes were as chaotic as my thoughts, but they held the raw truth. Unsure of what else to include, I glanced at the clock and realised sleep was imperative if I didn't want to resemble a complete wreck while reviewing them with Amir the next day.

CHAPTER FIFTEEN
'Up to 90'

Definition: stressed out

"Tea?" Amir asked, already heading for the 'tea-table'. I accepted with a smile.

My stomach churned with nerves. We hadn't really spoken much since our dramatic kiss in the rain. It felt as though it had never happened at all. But if he wasn't going to address it, then neither would I. I'd just have to forget it ever happened.

"You take sugar, right?" he asked, his expression soft.

I nodded. "Yes, just one, please."

A moment later, he placed the steaming mug in front of me on the boardroom table.

"I really enjoyed your last episode," he said, taking a seat beside me. His choice of seat caught me off guard; he usually sat across from me.

"Thank you," I replied, accepting the compliment. "Why did you like it so much?"

I briefly wondered if it was the thought of me masturbating that caught his attention, but I quickly pushed the suggestive idea aside.

He smiled, caught off guard by my question. "I just realised how much shame society places on women long before they even think about being intimate. It's like the longer a girl waits, the more 'innocent' or 'special' she's perceived to be."

"Yeah, exactly." I hummed.

"And you know, it got me thinking. The whole idea of 'losing your virginity' is pretty messed up. Reflecting on it, it feels gross to think of a man 'taking' something from a woman, as if he's gaining while she's losing. The terminology just doesn't sit right with me. Sex should always be a shared experience." His words tumbled out so quickly that I struggled to keep pace. The unexpected confession caught me off guard, and I tried to suppress the surge of desire welling up within me. Yet, listening to him speak so eloquently and with such emotional intelligence about such a sensitive topic turned me on more than anything. I wasn't sure how to respond.

He turned to face me fully. "I'll be honest, when I first heard about this podcast, I was quite apprehensive. I was worried it might be overly vulgar, maybe focusing on topics like the 'best positions' or the like. And discussing many of the subjects you cover is challenging because they often spark mixed opinions among the audience. Given the state of the station, we can't really afford too many controversial or negative opinions. But what you've been doing is truly beneficial. Not just for the station, but for our listeners as well."

I felt like I might faint. "Thank you. That's a surprising compliment."

It was unusual to hear him offer encouragement.

"So..." He paused, seeming to have more to say but holding back. "Um, right... What do you have planned for this week?"

I handed him my notebook, open and ready with my episode notes. "Sorry, I didn't have time to type it up. I hope you can decipher my handwriting."

He nodded, a hint of apprehension in his expression. "Alright."

As his eyes scanned each line, his expression remained unchanged. He gave away nothing, his lips pursed in thought as the notebook lay closed on the table, his humming filling the silence.

"What's wrong?" I asked, feeling a pang of anxiety.

He shook his head, blinking slowly, still lost in contemplation.

"Is it too heavy?" I muttered, nerves creeping in. "Too depressing?"

"No, not at all," he assured me. "I just sense there's more beneath the surface." He paused, then added, "But, you know, it's your personal journey. This is delicate territory." He gestured towards the journal. "Please, if I'm ever crossing a line or pushing too much, you have to tell me."

I nodded, curious about where he was leading.

"I think there's more to explore," he continued. "More you could uncover and perhaps share... if you're comfortable with that, of course."

I swallowed hard, bracing myself. "Okay, go on..."

"Why the decision to stop dating?" he queried. "I mean, I understand the 'date yourself' concept you mention at the end, but it seems contradictory to what you said at the start. You mentioned that every date should lead to self-discovery, right? So?"

I hesitated, uncertain how to respond. "I understand what you mean but... for me, dating feels like a constant source of anxiety. I'm tired of feeling anxious—before the first date, waiting for a text, wondering about his feelings, what comes next... I just feel like I'm wasting so much energy and keep getting disappointed."

He ran his fingers over his lips, contemplating. ""Yeah – those are all examples of *when* you feel anxious... have you ever wondered why?"

I chuckled nervously, feeling a bit uneasy. "I know why," I admitted.

His eyes met mine, prompting me to continue.

"Where do I even begin?" I chuckled, picking at the polish on my nails.

"Am I crossing a line here?" he asked, suddenly anxious. "We can stop if you're uncomfortable."

"No, no, it's okay," I reassured him. "I wasn't expecting a therapy session this afternoon, but it's fine," I said with a laugh.

"There's no pressure to answer," he said, chuckling himself. "I just think it might be helpful for you and your audience. We all have our own anxieties."

I took a deep breath. "Alright. So, why do I feel anxious?"

He nodded, his expression open and understanding.

"I worry that I'm not attractive enough... that he won't like me... that I'll stumble over my words... that I'm going to get hurt... that he'll cheat on me... that I'll spend so much time trying to get him to love me that I lose myself in the process and that..." My heart raced as I poured out my insecurities. But when his gaze locked with mine, it felt like time stood still. "That it'll all go wrong," I confessed softly. "That I'll end up too broken to fix. I hate the feeling of having to piece myself back together."

He swallowed, fully absorbed in every word I spoke.

"And, as much as I'm trying to heal from past relationships every day, it's hard to change my entire mindset all at once," I confessed. "I know I should focus on how I feel about my partner instead of constantly worrying about how they feel about me. I thought I had moved past it, but going on that date with Tom – I mean, Mr. Millionaire..." I chuckled, baring all my truths. "I still couldn't shake the feeling of wondering why he asked me out. He's super successful, handsome, and rich... I just don't measure up." I shrugged, my voice deflating. "And even when I met his friends, I found myself overanalysing every shared glance, wondering how they felt about me. I'm stuck in this loop of needing... needing..." My words faltered. "Umm... validation, I guess."

His eyebrows furrowed, and his dark eyes locked onto mine as I continued speaking.

"And, you know... I know what I should do, how I should act, and how I should feel. But sometimes, it's just so hard. So, I figure if I eliminate dating and stop obsessing over finding a partner, maybe that'll ease a lot of the anxiety?"

"No, it won't," he interrupted, his tone firm with conviction. "Dating might trigger it, but you need to address the root cause of why you ever felt inadequate and have this incessant need to please." His voice grew louder as he spoke, almost as if he was angry at me for feeling the way I did.

His words stung, hitting deep, but I knew they were true.

"Right," I laughed, though it felt uncomfortable, and tears threatened to well up in my eyes. I grasped at my notebook, wanting to escape the room, "I'll revise and rewrite."

His eyebrows furrowed. "No, what you have is good. Don't delete anything. Maybe just end it with some inspiration, if you can find it. Just..." He let out an exasperated breath. "Don't..."

He paused, shaking his head, grappling with his next words.

"Don't?" I prodded him to continue.

"Don't shut down because you've been hurt." He finally said, his eyes avoiding mine. His words hung in the air.

He shook his head, as if snapping himself out of a trance. "Shall we go over the updated notes after lunch?"

I was so intrigued. Maybe that's why his walls seemed so high... *had he been hurt in the past?*

"How about we do it during? Just in case I have more work to do after." I suggested. I stood from the table, gathering my belongings.

"Sounds like a plan. My treat," he replied.

***

I stared at my pages, ideas bubbling in my mind. The clock on my phone screen showed I had just under two hours. Lunch with Amir was looming on me. I was a tad more enthusiastic knowing I could go home after he reviewed the episode, but only if he approved it. I plugged my headphones in and began to write – and rewrite – and rewrite again, an honest and more meaningful end to my episode.

Something was brought to my attention... and it has made me question two things. Firstly... Why do I feel so anxious when it comes to dating? I'll be very honest, I'm insecure. Like most people, I look at myself in the mirror and poke and prod at the things I don't like. In fact, when I broke up with Mr Fuckboy, I spent over an hour in the mirror looking at every potential pocket of fat wondering 'is that why I wasn't good enough?' I replayed our conversations in my mind, wondering if I was too much or didn't speak enough. I re-read our texting chains, checking for any potential mistakes or icks on my part.

I felt unwell. Admitting it felt more embarrassing than the act itself.

I have this annoying need to please, to impress, to make people like me. But now, when I reflect on my relationship with him, I feel sorry for myself that I even bothered trying.

I was enough.

He messed up. He slept with other girls, and what I've learned is that it wasn't my fault. It had nothing to do with how I look or the person I am. He led me on, he manipulated me and he's just a bad person.

If he wasn't interested in me, he could have said so. If he thought I wasn't good enough, he could have told me. BUT it actually wasn't anything to do with me.

But instead, he strung me along and made me a pawn in his game. He decided that instead of a delicious, fulfilling, and satisfying main course, he also wanted a starter, dessert, and multiple drinks... and he even desired whatever the table beside was eating too. He'd never be satisfied. And it wasn't my fault.

Each week I'm able to detach myself from the situation and look at it with new perspective.

Every word I wrote helped me break free a little more.

I've only just come to realise this now... and it's helped me understand why I felt the need to dress up so much and try to perfect myself for Mr. Millionaire. I didn't want him to see my flaws because I feared he wouldn't like me, and I worried history would repeat itself. But the thing is if he doesn't like me then he's just not my person. I need to try to understand and believe that rejection is just redirection.

But even though all of this sounds good, it's all positive... I still have so much work to do.

One of my biggest issues is my insecurity over my appearance. This fuels my anxiety more than anything else. I've placed too much value on what I look like—what size my waist is, how pouty my lips are... the list goes on. Constantly wondering what people think of me... and comparing myself to other women.

I've been overly focused on external validation. When, in reality, I need to prioritise internal validation. How I feel about myself, instead of obsessing over how someone else feels about me.

When it comes to confidence in dating, I've heard that it often comes with experience.

But can I truly date without constantly obsessing over my perceived flaws?

Is it possible to embark on this journey of self-healing and personal growth while trying to find my person?

"So, where do you want to go?" Amir appeared at my desk ten minutes early for lunch.

I began packing my handbag, contemplating. "Uh, maybe..."

"How about Established?" he suggested.

I felt a blush creeping up my cheeks. Taking a deep breath, I met his gaze. "Maybe not..."

He grinned knowingly, teasing me.

"But seriously," I stood up, "I'd rather not... you know, relive any memories." I let out a sigh, my words barely audible.

"Ah, I'm sorry," he started to say.

"Don't apologise," I interjected, playfully squeezing his arm. But he tensed up immediately, taken aback by the gesture.

"Sorry," he quickly responded, shaking his head. "I still don't know Belfast that well, so I was just suggesting it because I've been there before... I haven't explored many places for lunch. Usually, I just grab something from the deli or order Uber Eats."

My lips parted, feeling a flush of embarrassment. Of course, he wasn't suggesting Established to revisit our previous encounter. I mentally scolded myself for jumping to conclusions. "Okay, well, there's a Cuban sandwich bar about a 5-minute walk away. It's carb-heavy though... are you on a special diet?" I teased.

He rolled his eyes. "I don't diet. Food is one thing I'm not willing to sacrifice."

We walked in sync toward the elevator. "I honestly thought you were the type to cut out all carbs, gluten, sugar-"

"And happiness?" He laughed. "No, I do work out though..."

The elevator doors closed.

"Really? Couldn't tell," I teased.

"I should start wearing tighter shirts," he bantered back.

"Please don't. I'll file a complaint," I quipped.

He snorted. "What would you be complaining about?"

I paused, weighing my words. It was just banter... not flirting. "Distraction in the workplace."

The elevator doors opened at the perfect moment, allowing me to step off before he could respond.

Okay, maybe a little bit of flirting.

CHAPTER SIXTEEN

Giving Out

Definition: complaining

For the first time since meeting Amir, I had left him speechless. We walked quietly towards the Cuban Sandwich Factory, a quirky, yellow-coloured shop in the heart of town. It was a bright day; the sky, though blue, was adorned with fluffy clouds, but fortunately, the sun was shining through.

"I've passed by here on my runs," he finally spoke, gesturing down Queens Arcade. The beautiful shopping hall, adorned with expensive jewellers, looked like it belonged in a posh part of London rather than Belfast.

"You also run? Shocking..." I teased, allowing my eyes to casually roam over his body, feigning disinterest. He squinted at me.

"Yeah, I do... actually! Are there any shirt shops around here?" He stretched his arms out, causing the fabric of his shirt to strain against his chest.

"Maybe wait until after we've had our sandwiches. You might need a bigger size, not smaller," I winked at him, relishing in this playful banter.

My mouth watered as the sexual scent of sandwiches enveloped me. I ordered a classic Cuban for both of us, with extra pickles, along with some lemonade, and Amir kindly paid, despite my offer to split the bill. "Business card-" he quickly flashed a bank card at me.

"Thank you," I smiled, grabbing two seats in the corner while he waited for the receipt.

Pulling out my notes, I prepared for him to review them. It seemed essential to tackle this task before our food arrived, to avoid any grease drippings on paper and give us something to talk about.

He strolled over and pulled out the chair opposite me, removing his black blazer and hanging it on the back of the chair before taking a seat. He certainly didn't need a smaller shirt. I swallowed nervously and slid him the notes.

"Was my questioning too much earlier?" he asked before diving into the notes. "I feel like it was too much."

"No, it was fine," I assured him.

"Not too intrusive?"

"Amir..." I chuckled. "My podcast is um… purposeful intrusion into my personal life — but I control what I share with the audience. You pushed me this morning to delve deeper. It was challenging but… beneficial."

He began reading. I observed closely as his eyes skimmed over my words, hoping to glean his thoughts. He breathed in and out, never too deeply to betray shock or distaste. His jaw twitched for a brief moment, but then stopped, denying me the ability to guess his impression.

"Our food will be here soon. They're very fast," I interjected. It had only been about two minutes, but I felt the urge to hurry him along—not for the food's sake, but for my own mental well-being.

He sighed, handing me back the book.

"What?" I asked, feeling a prickling sensation on my skin.

He pursed his lips, anger evident on his face. "You didn't answer the question," he said bluntly.

I was taken aback, confused by his reaction.

"Look, maybe it was too much to ask, so don't worry about it," he continued, his tone softening slightly. "But I like what you wrote about validation and appearances. No one wants to date a beautiful person if they have an ugly soul," he added, catching me off guard with his comment.

Cheesy. But true.

An uncomfortable silence enveloped us as I pondered his words. He was right. Reflecting on it, I realised that the reason I chose to date James was for an ego boost—I valued physical appearance far too much. He didn't attract me with his personality or emotional connection. I was seeking something in him that I lacked within myself: confidence.

"Are you okay?" he asked softly, concern evident in his eyes.

"Oh—yes. Sorry. I just had a realisation," I replied, looking down and taking a sip of my lemonade, allowing my hair to fall and conceal my flushed face. The sharp, lemony liquid made me cringe as I drank.

He took a sip of his own drink. "You don't have to tell me if you don't want to," he offered.

"You probably don't want to hear," I chuckled. "You read and listen to my life enough as it is—"

"I do want to," he interrupted gently.

I sat up in my chair and crossed my legs, realising I had been slumping down without noticing. "Nah.. I just—I realised that—I realised why I've chosen the men that I've previously dated. Literally, just for validation," I confessed with a sigh. "I always felt happy about myself when an attractive man thought I was good enough to be on his arm... to hold his hand... to be in his—bed," I continued, feeling a wave of shame wash over me. "So ridiculous." I concluded, covering my face, unable to bear the weight of my embarrassment. "Or because they seemed to have more confidence than I did..."

Our sandwiches arrived, interrupting the conversation. We ate in silence, our thoughts heavy with unspoken words.

"You're infuriating," he choked out, his voice strained with frustration. "Absolutely infuriating."

"Sorry?" I stammered, taken aback by his sudden outburst.

His eyes bore into mine, searching for something. "I'm infuriating?" I repeated, feeling a mix of shock and confusion at his accusation.

"Why are you the way that you are?" he continued, shaking his head. "Why are you... so insecure?"

My stomach churned, threatening to empty itself of the food I'd just eaten.

"What—" I began, but he cut me off.

"You didn't answer the question about what makes you anxious... where the people-pleasing and need for validation comes from? Instead, you've just focused on more insecurities instead of addressing them," he snapped.

"I can't just wave a magic wand and have all the answers or a solution. Plus, recognising it is the first step..." I snapped back.

He rolled his eyes in frustration. "Yeah, of course. But..." He huffed out a loud sigh. "I just don't get it. How can you be insecure?"

"Everyone is insecure," I replied, my voice barely above a whisper, completely shaken by his incessant questioning.

"But you—" He mumbled, throwing his hands in the air. "You're confident on air. You're good at your job. You speak really well. You never mess up your words. And... and you're beautiful, Anna. So, all this talk about pinching rolls of fat and not liking what you see in the mirror is confounding to me."

I sat there, stunned into silence as shock seized control of my senses.

"Any man would be lucky to have you," he said softly. "You should know that."

"So why don't you want me?" The words spilled out of my mouth before I could stop them.

His expression faltered, taken aback by my unexpected question. He avoided my gaze, unable to meet my eyes. "We can't do this—"

My fingers dug into my thighs unconsciously, hanging onto every word he uttered. "Why?" I interjected.

His lips pressed into a thin line, withholding words that I sensed would stir up emotions I'd been trying to suppress. "I said... we can't do this, Anna," he replied, his tone abrupt and commanding, a stark contrast to its previous softness. The butterflies in my stomach began to fade, retreating into the shadows.

I remained silent, afraid that anything I said would be something I'd regret.

"I don't date," he added, his words final.

"You don't date?" I responded incredulously.

He nodded, a wry laugh escaping him. "It could never happen. I'm your boss."

I fell silent.

"And I'm going back to New York," he added.

"So, let me get this straight... you encouraged me earlier to not give up on dating but you don't date?" I held my breath before snapping, "And you don't want to be another storyline on my podcast. I forgot."

He sighed, his hands clenched into fists. "I'm sorry I said that. It was wrong."

"I'm not going to fall for you," I declared, crumpling up my napkin and gathering my rubbish from the table. "So don't worry about it. Forget I said anything."

"Hold on a seco—"

I bit the inside of my cheek to stop myself from speaking any further and stood up, ready to throw the bits of rubbish in the bin so I could escape.

"I'm not trying to get you to fall for me—why would you—why did you think that?" he asked, venom coating his tongue.

His words stung, piercing through my emotions. Unfortunately, I had already kind of fallen... but at least I knew that I could pick myself back up. It annoyed me how I constantly was having to remind myself that he was never someone I could consider dating.

"Maybe the fact that you kissed me?" I retorted, turning back to our table. He clicked his tongue against the roof of his mouth, chuckling to himself. It irked me.

"You kissed me back," he countered, glaring at me. "And don't say you didn't want to. I know you wanted to."

I huffed in frustration, closing my eyes briefly. "You are so infuriating!" I exclaimed, drawing the attention of some other customers inside.

"I'm infuriating?" he shot back, rising from his chair, and looming over me. "Do you know how infuriating it is for me to have to read your notes each week? To listen to your show?"

"Then why have you spent most of today talking to me about it and trying to give me some sort of therapy session?!" I challenged.

He didn't respond.

Nausea bubbled in the back of my throat. I began to regret eating the sandwich. "You know what? I'm honestly glad that you're going back to New York soon. I can't deal with this." I declared, turning on my heel and heading for the door, refusing to give him any more of my attention.

Fury surged through me like a wildfire, consuming every rational thought in its path as I stormed out of the shop and down the street. He called after me once, his voice barely registering amidst the tempest of my anger.

Instead of returning to the office, I fled home—I needed the solitude to calm the storm brewing within me and to gather the shattered remnants of composure.

He made no attempt to reach out—no calls, no texts, no emails. And as I returned to the studio, ready to pour my heart into my show, his absence loomed like a shadow over my resolve.

I quickly scanned over my notes as the countdown began. My heart was still racing, but when I caught Paddy's encouraging smile, I felt a wave of calm wash over me. I started speaking, stumbling only once or twice, and then it was over.

The episode, filled with profound truths, proved to be my most challenging one yet.

Thankfully, Paddy didn't bring up Amir, and I couldn't help but wonder if he already knew everything. After leaving the station, I headed straight to my bed. The thought of going out for drinks or meeting up with anyone was the last thing on my mind. All I craved was some peace and quiet. Snuggled up in my duvet, I scrolled through social media, absorbing mention after mention.

@greyivy
Don't mind me... just shedding some tears after listening to Belles of Belfast. The truth hurts, but I needed that tonight @spotlight_belfast

@melanieirish
Even though we're halfway through the year, I've decided to make a New Year's resolution... no more seeking validation from crappy guys. I can create my own love.

@christina_cowell
Feeling all the self-love vibes after tuning in to @spotlight_belfast - this show needs to be on every night.

My pillow was damp with salty tears as I finally allowed myself to release the emotions I'd been holding in. Tomorrow was a fresh start, and I was determined not to give up on dating and to work much harder on myself. I knew that unequivocal love and happiness were out there somewhere; I just needed to find them... first within myself.

***

"Nah, girls I can't cope with this!" I shouted, clutching my jacket tightly.

The wind howled, threatening to topple me over.

"Quit complaining!" Olivia yelled, striding ahead.

I sighed, trailing after her. "Can't we just grab coffee instead? I can't stand this wind, and there's already sand in my shoes," I grumbled.

Helens Bay Beach, usually delightful on a sunny day, felt less inviting under today's dismal weather; the wind was biting, and ominous clouds threatened rain at any moment.

"Better to burn calories than consume them!" Olivia retorted. "Step it up."

Grace and I exchanged worried glances before hastening our pace to match her stride.

"You know, I agree, I think we should just go grab coffee," Grace moaned, her eyes scanning the grey, grumbling clouds above.

Olivia stopped abruptly and turned to us, her face flushed and eyes glaring. "I NEED this. I need cardio, or I'm going to look like an elephant."

My laughter died down as I realised, she was serious, judging by the intensity in her eyes.

"You could never look like an elephant," I reassured her. "God gifted you with an insane metabolism. It's actually unfair."

I spoke the truth. Olivia could devour everything on the McDonald's menu in one sitting and somehow still lose weight. She was gifted.

She responded by rolling her eyes, "Can we at least do some interval training for 10 minutes? Like a little running, then a slow walk, and then run again?"

Grace burst into laughter at the suggestion, and I couldn't help but join.

"What's gotten into you?" I questioned.

"Seriously, Liv? I've never seen you run in all the years we've known you," Grace added.

Spits of rain began to hit us.

Tucked away in the corner of Joxer, a coffee shop in Holywood town centre, we sipped on hot matcha lattes to warm us from the failed beach cardio.

Joxer exuded cosy coffee shop vibes with its dimly lit booths scattered throughout the space. The sound of rain tapping gently against the windows added to the comforting atmosphere, creating the perfect backdrop for catching up.

"So, I'm quitting my job," Grace said, tears welling in her eyes as we sat in the coffee shop, enveloped by its cosy vibes.

"You're what?" I couldn't believe it.

"Me too!" Olivia chimed in, clapping her hands together in celebration, "Honestly – I am so done!"

I continued to stare at Grace, shocked. She loved her job. She worked her ass off. "What happened?" I asked.

"Oh nothing really happened – I'm just bored of the stories I'm writing." Olivia spoke nonchalantly, "I feel like I need to write more juicy tabloid style journalism but… but… my boss is limiting me. She doesn't really spotlight my stuff."

"That's exciting." Grace swallowed her emotions.

"I applied for a few places already. I'm kinda stressing about it – actually speaking of which – I'm going to have to pass on going to Galway now. I'll need time to prepare." She picked at her fingernails, admiring her new manicure.

I glanced at Grace who was staring into space, her eyes glazed over.

"Ok." I spoke for us both, "Ok that's fine – but what about your hotel room?"

"Yeah, don't worry about the hotel room – maybe ask what's his name

– Paddy? Ask Paddy to go. Or better yet, ask that sexy American guy Ammar? Amir?… use *my* hook-up room as your own." She giggled.

I shuddered at the thought. "I won't be asking Amir to go anywhere."

"Well ask… someone." She shrugged her shoulders at me and reached for her coffee, taking a long sip. "Tom!!"

I ignored her. My focus returned to Grace, who's eyes were still staring at nothing. She hadn't been listening at all to our conversation and I'd totally blanked her job quitting admission, thanks to Olivia's distraction. "Grace?" I spoke softly.

She shook her head, blinking to clear the water in her eyes, "Sorry – yes – can't you just get your money back?" She asked Liv.

"No, it's too late notice. Already checked."

"You should have just stayed in our room."

"No fun in that – I couldn't bring a sexy Irish man back to bed." Liv fluttered her eyelashes and pulled her hands through her curly blonde hair, "It was only 90 euro."

Only 90 euro. I shuddered. That would get me a lot of groceries in Lidl…

"When's your interview?" Grace asked her.

"Oh – a few days after Galway. But… okay so there's another reason I'm dropping out." Olivia hid her face in her hands and let out a small squeal. "Ahh – okay so.."

"What?"

"I'm going on like a REAL date." She peaked up from behind her hands, "Mini golfing."

I snorted and took a sip of my tea, "aye right."

Grace giggled along with me.

"I'm being serious! The hot barista from Established…he must have witnessed how bad my lunch-time speed dates had been."

Olivia began to glow as she explained how he asked her out. She had been sitting in the coffee shop, frustrated beyond belief after another week of less than satisfactory lunch-time dates. They'd laughed, exchanged IG handles and he texted her details for a date. He didn't ask her. He didn't give her an option to say yes or no. He just told her a date and time.

"I love this!" Grace smiled, genuine excitement gleaming in her eyes.

"I agree – it's exciting that you're going on a proper date… do you know how to play mini golf?"

She giggled and wiggled her eyebrows, "Wellll let's just say – I'm pretty good at getting a hole in one."

"Christ-" Grace facepalmed, blush spreading across her cheeks.

"Oh for fuck sake." I giggled. *Only Olivia…*

We all shared a laugh at her stupid joke before reality set in. *Grace. Her job…*

"So…" I spoke, instantly lowering the tone, "Grace – why are you quitting?"

Her smile instantly dropped as she confided, "I'm really burned out, especially with the constant traveling and long hours. It feels like all I do is work, and when I have time to socialise, my actual social battery is non-existent. I have to really force myself to be social. After our last night out, I sat in bed crying at how tired I felt. And when we go out, I drink alcohol to keep myself going, trying to have fun like everyone else, but I constantly feel like my mind is focused on work and work only. I'm forever stressing about my to do list."

I nodded in understanding. "I get you. That's for sure the right decision then, but… what do you think you'll do next?"

She stared at me, eyes glistening over, "I have no clue. But I need to leave. The show I was excited about isn't going to be green-lit either, so I just feel like I've been working for nothing. I'm going to hand in my notice this week I think."

"Do you still want to work in production?" I asked, "Tv?"

"I don't know. But I don't know what else I'll be good at."

Silence fell between us as I didn't know what to say or do. I gulped the last remaining mouthful of my matcha and stared at our empty plates that had previously been filled with sugary French toast and strawberries.

"What about Spotlight?" Grace asked, shaking away her negative expression. "How's the show?"

"Oh my god, I forgot!" Olivia interrupted, shoving her phone in our faces. "Someone actually tweeted about my voice on your show! Finally!"

@333felicity9
Miss Sensuality is a vibe. END. OF. STORY.

The tweet was nice, but the moment felt ruined. We had sat listening to Olivia's job woes, but she'd totally disregarded Grace.

Olivia sat up straight, a smile forming across her face, "So, what's your update Anna? How's the American? Please tell me you shagged him. God does not put a man like *that* in front of you without reason."

Both girls giggled, immediately lightening the mood. My stomach was knotted, however. I didn't want to drone about my problems and worries when Grace had a much bigger hill to climb.

"Fine." I shook my head, letting out a soft contented sigh, "All is good."

"Just good?" Olivia pleaded, eyebrows furrowing, "You haven't shagged him?"

"I think if she would have…" Grace's nose turned up as she spoke, "shagged him… she would have told us immediately after."

Dimples formed in my cheeks, "Ahh – I don't think I'll be…shagging…him anytime soon."

"What about Tom?"

"Is Tom Mr Millionaire – yes.. right?" Grace asked, trying to align my dates with their code names.

"Yes and I don't think I'll be 'shagging' him anytime soon either."

"Well it's a good thing I bought you that vibrator!"

I buried my face in my hands, red from embarrassment. The whole café had probably heard that. "Jesus Christ Olivia."

"I think we all need to use them more! Orgasms help lower anxiety you know? They also help you sleep better... slow down aging... and also might help you live longer."

Grace and I looked at her trying our hardest not to laugh.

"You're welcome bitches."

CHAPTER SEVENTEEN
Straight in, no kissin'

Definition: diving straight in / no fucking about

Monday morning arrived faster than I anticipated, signalling the start of our team bonding day. We found ourselves reluctantly heading to We Are Vertigo. Stepping into the massive indoor inflatable trampoline park, it resembled a cavernous room filled with bouncy castles. Normally, the sight would have filled me with excitement, but at 9:15 am, all I craved was my warm bed. The atmosphere was chilled, with a biting coldness in the air. I hugged myself, tugging my sleeves down to shield my hands from the cold.

My mood dipped further when I noticed Amir, clad in grey sweatpants and a snug black gym top.

It took a moment for me to find my balance as I stepped onto the inflatable surface. Despite wearing the 'sticky socks' provided, I still slid around precariously. Balancing was never my forte on solid ground, let alone on a mammoth inflatable trampoline that wobbled with every step someone took near me or with any slight movement I made.

"Alright everyone, gather round," Amir's voice commanded attention. "Today isn't just about fun; it's about strengthening our team. These days help us build trust, communication, and camaraderie."

A fake gagging sound broke the seriousness, eliciting laughter from the group.

"But remember," he continued, undeterred, "failure is part of the journey. When you fall, laugh it off and get back up. It's how we respond to failure that defines us."

"How inspirational," I whispered sarcastically, catching his eye.

His attention lingered on me, a flicker of a challenge in his eyes.

"So, we have to embrace the challenges today, support each other, and have a laugh along the way. Yeah?" His attention returned to the group.

Everyone nodded in understanding.

"So, we have two teams, with ten people on each team," Amir announced, scanning the group as he spoke. Although there were supposed to be 24 of us attending, conveniently, 4 people had called in sick. I couldn't help but wish I had also opted for the same excuse. I steadied myself by gripping Paddy's shoulder, feeling a surge of anxiety as Amir's smile morphed into his trademark smirk. I could almost anticipate what he was about to say next.

"Anna, would you like to be a team leader?" he asked.

I glanced around to find many expectant eyes trained on me. "No," I mumbled, wishing I could disappear. Paddy chuckled at my response.

"Sorry, what was that?" Amir inquired, seemingly amused.

"No. Not a chance," I asserted, my tone firm. I shot him a glare, still irked by our lunchtime 'date.' His teasing felt completely unwarranted.

"Too bad," Paddy remarked, giving my back a tap. Despite its gentleness, I nearly toppled over.

"Okay, so on Anna's team, we'll have..." Paddy began, assigning people to my 'team' while I shot daggers at him. "And on Amir's team, we'll have…"

I was determined to outperform Amir in whatever game lay ahead.

Thankfully, after ten minutes, I had regained my balance and was managing adequately. However, I wished I had worn a sturdier sports bra as I bounced around. I had only slipped once, nearly knocking out Dillon as we raced from one end of the trampoline to the other. Thus far, my team was lagging behind in every obstacle course.

While everyone else seemed to be revelling in the festivities, I found myself seething with anger. My competitive nature had taken over, leaving me feeling anything but jovial. I could practically feel my hair standing on end, my face flushed and undoubtedly unattractive.

"Okay, okay," Amir shouted, still trying to catch his breath. "Next up - and personally, what I've been most excited about…" His gaze bore into mine, his eyes seeming to ignite a fire within me. "Dodgeball."

"How very American." I grumbled.

My team lined up on one side of the inflatable arena, while Amir's team assembled at the opposite end. As staff members arranged soft dodgeballs in the centre, we locked eyes, each of us emanating a palpable aura of determination. My blood surged with adrenaline, ready to unleash every ounce of competitiveness I possessed.

As the whistle blew, signalling the start of the match, both teams lunged forward to grab the soft, foam balls scattered across the arena. I swiftly grabbed one, feeling its squishy texture in my hand. Across from me, Amir mirrored my movements, his eyes narrowing with focus.

The game erupted into chaos as balls flew back and forth between us. Dodging, ducking, and weaving became second nature as we all attempted to evade the incoming projectiles. I launched a throw towards Amir, but he deftly dodged it, sending a ball hurtling back in my direction. I managed to dodge it at the last second, feeling a rush of exhilaration as I narrowly avoided elimination.

"Anna, watch out!" Lisa's urgent shout snapped my attention back to the game just in time to see Amir taking aim at me again. With reflexes honed by adrenaline, I leapt aside, narrowly avoiding the incoming ball that instead struck Lisa's ankle, eliminating her from the game. Guilt washed over me as I turned to her, offering an apologetic expression.

"Get him," she spat, her eyes narrowed with determination as she bounced off the court.

Determined to avenge Lisa's elimination, I seized a ball and took aim at Amir, my resolve burning fiercely. I wanted nothing more than to wipe the cocky smile off his face. He raised his hands in a challenging gesture, silently daring me to do my worst.

As I prepared to throw, another ball flew towards my side, thinning our team's ranks. Glancing around, I realised we were down to only four members. With a surge of determination, I hurled my ball at Jillian from Amir's team, knocking her out of the game. Amir rushed forward, attempting to retaliate, but his throw missed me entirely, earning a laugh from my lips.

"Do you have ANY hand-eye coordination?" I taunted, revelling in the moment.

But karma seemed to have its eye on me as well. In a twist of fate, I slipped and fell onto my backside, much to his amusement. As I struggled to regain my footing, the game continued around me, each throw and dodge intensifying the battle between our teams.

The sound of a ball bouncing echoed through the arena as Greg was eliminated, leaving my team with just three members against Amir's six. The odds seemed stacked against us, and frustration boiled within me.

"G'wan, Amir! Get her!" Paddy's cheer from the side-lines only fuelled my irritation, and I shot him a glare.

"Paddy! You were my friend before his...!"

"Aye, but I'm on his team," he replied with a shrug, sending a surge of anger coursing through me. Channelling my frustration into action, I grabbed another ball and aimed it at Suzanne, striking just below her knees. She fell theatrically, and I turned to face Amir, mirroring his trademark smirk. His expression darkened as two more members of his team were eliminated, inching us closer to victory.

"You don't know who you're messing with!" he teased, tossing a ball casually from his left hand to his right.

As the match unfolded, the tension between us crackled in the air like electricity. Every move we made seemed calculated, each dodge and throw a subtle challenge to the other's skill and determination.

I glanced around for a ball to throw but came up empty-handed. Another one of my team members was ejected from the game.

Our eyes locked repeatedly, conveying a silent but intense rivalry that fuelled our actions. It seemed like everyone was avoiding the two of us, as if we were engaged in our own separate childish game... and I was determined to win.

I ducked. "You might want to aim a bit lower next time."

I picked up a ball and aimed it towards his feet, but he jumped, narrowly avoiding it.

"And you might want to aim a bit higher!"

Suddenly, we were both alone on the court; our teams watched from the side-lines. Music blared through the speakers as adrenaline surged through my veins.

He jumped, allowing the ball to pass beneath his feet again. I cursed and grabbed another, eagerly planning my next hit.

"Oh, come on, is that all you've got?" he taunted, throwing a ball in my direction, but I slid the opposite way, avoiding contact.

With a burst of speed, I dodged to the side and unleashed a powerful throw, sending the ball flying towards him with all the force I could muster.

Time seemed to slow as the ball soared through the air, and for a moment, it felt as though the entire arena held its breath. Then, with a satisfying thud, the ball connected with his shoulder, sending him out of the game.

A victorious cheer erupted from my team as I stood there, adrenaline coursing through me. Despite the exhaustion and the lingering frustration from earlier, I couldn't help but feel a sense of triumph wash over me.

My team leapt back onto the court, their cheers filling the air with celebration. Hugs and high-fives were exchanged, and I felt a surge of pride. Sure, it was just dodgeball, but defeating Amir felt fantastic.

Heading over to where he sat with Paddy, I couldn't resist a teasing remark. "We can't all be winners," I quipped.

Amir's eyes flashed with annoyance as he glanced up at me. "You only won one game," he shot back.

"But the victory tastes sweet!"

My delight continued through the rest of the day, even as Amir scowled at me from across the table at lunch. He was very bothered, and that made me even happier.

"You two are completely ridiculous," Paddy remarked, sliding into the booth with a slice of pizza in hand.

Amir's eyes locked onto mine, annoyance brewing beneath their surface. "She's ridiculous," he retorted with a snort.

"What? How am I?" I asked, genuinely puzzled.

He shook his head dismissively, taking a bite of his pizza and ignoring my question.

"You're just moody because I beat you at something," I retorted, feeling a surge of defensiveness.

Amir's arrogant smile only intensified. "I'm not moody. If anyone should be moody – it should be you. You only won one game."

I scowled at him, ready to launch into an argument, but Paddy's interruption halted the brewing confrontation. "For fuck's sake, will both of you just shut up?" he interjected, frustration evident in his voice. "Stop being pissy at each other for just one moment! You've both made this entire day about beating each other. It's embarrassing! We're supposed to be bonding as a team, not tearing each other apart! I swear, if I have to lock you two in a room together to work out whatever this… drama… and pettiness… is, I will."

Feeling a pang of guilt, I looked down at my greasy pizza slice, suddenly losing my appetite. The victory that had felt so sweet now turned sour as I realised the toll our constant bickering was taking on Paddy. I wondered if anyone else had noticed, and anxiety gnawed at me as I fretted about my unprofessional behaviour.

With a heavy sigh, I slid out of the booth, discarding my plate of pizza in the bin. "Sorry," I muttered to Paddy, my voice heavy with regret. "See you tomorrow."

The day, meant for bonding and fun, had been ruined by our petty rivalry.

***

"I did it," Grace sighed, her voice trembling with a mix of disbelief and liberation. "Oh my, I actually did it!" Her stress dissolved into relief as she clicked the send button, dispatching her resignation email into the digital ether.

She sank onto the sofa beside me, her body trembling with the weight of her decision.

I reached out, pulling her into a tight embrace. "No turning back now," I whispered softly, trying to offer reassurance.

She nodded, a single tear tracing a path down her cheek. "Yeah. Yeah. Oh, wow."

"How do you feel?" I asked gently, my hand rubbing small circles on her back.

"Surreal. I feel like I've been wanting to do this for so long… I can't wait to actually have a life outside of work," she confessed, her voice breaking with emotion. "I feel like I'm finally free."

I hadn't anticipated her reaction, the sudden rush of tears catching me off guard. Hastily, I rose to fetch some tissues, returning to wrap her in my arms once more.

"I'm so proud of you, G," I said, sincerity lacing my words. And truly, I was proud, though underneath lay a layer of apprehension, worried about her leap without a safety net. "How much notice do you have to give?"

"14 days according to my contract, but they'll probably demand 30," she groaned. "I can't believe I finally did it… I need to make a list of how I'm going to actually enjoy my life now. Maybe hot yoga… or I might start hiking."

"Yeah," I replied cautiously.

"Actually, let's be realistic, hiking's not really my thing," she chuckled, wiping away her tears.

"Thank feck for that," I quipped, giving her a playful nudge before getting up and heading to the kitchen. "Tea?"

"Yeah. I hate saunas too so maybe just regular yoga?"

***

We lounged on the sofa, mindlessly scrolling through our phones as a familiar movie played in the background. Suddenly, Grace broke the silence. "I think I'll redownload… the apps."

I snorted in disbelief. "The day you actually join a dating app is the day I'll skydive."

She laughed, her eyes sparkling with determination. "I'm serious! Now that I might actually have time to date!"

"The man ban is finally ending?!" I gasped dramatically, feigning shock.

Her eyes rolled playfully. "Maybe. What are dating apps like? Any good?"

I chuckled. "Why don't we find out…"

I tapped on the app icon, opening it to a couple of notifications. As I explained how it worked to Grace, she wrinkled her nose, clearly unimpressed by the concept.

"It seems a bit superficial, doesn't it?" she remarked.

I shrugged. "I suppose. Unless you take the time to read everyone's bio, but even then..."

"Oh, he's cute!" she suddenly exclaimed, grabbing my phone from my hand. "Alexander... what a name!"

She swiftly swiped right before I could even react. "Oh my god, I've fallen for it already!" she exclaimed, a mix of excitement and disbelief in her voice. "He's cute though – oh you MATCHED!"

She yelped, flapping her hands around in excitement and dropped the phone onto her lap.

I lifted it for a peek of the screen. Alexander was a nice-looking man, tall-ish from what I could see, with brown hair.

"He's a doctor," I mused, a smirk playing on my lips. "My parents would be peeing their pants if they saw this."

"What does his bio say?" Grace asked eagerly, grabbing the phone back. "29, I'm an Intensive Care Doctor – so you know I can take care of you."

"Ick," I chuckled. "That's a bit cringe."

"Shut up! Love podcasts – oh, I wonder if he listens to yours?!" Grace nudged me excitedly. "Self-development and the gym."

"Sounds like he takes care of himself," I remarked.

We both let out a scream as a message popped up, causing her to accidentally send the phone flying across the room.

"GRACE!" I screamed, rushing to pick it up. "Oh my god..."

ALEXANDER:

Hey Anna, how you?

"How you?" Grace giggled, mocking his message. "Reply, 'me fine. How you Alex?'" Her voice took on a playful tone, acting like a cave-woman.

ALEXANDER:

Sorry, how are you? Big thumbs!

I smiled at the message and began typing my reply.

ANNA:

Hey! I'm good, how are you?

ALEXANDER:

Oh, you know. I'm either saving lives or watching people die. Bit of an emotional rollercoaster over here... need someone to help stabilise me lol

"He's really playing up this whole doctor thing," Grace commented with a groan.

"Yeah, a bit," I agreed.

ALEXANDER:

Have you any plans this week? Anything exciting happening?

"God, he's keen," Grace chuckled. "Let me reply."

Before I could protest, she snatched the phone and darted across the room, a mischievous smile on her face.

"What are you going to say?" I asked, feeling a mix of excitement and anxiety.

Her fingers danced across the screen, her smile growing wider with each tap.

"Grace?" I called out, chasing after her as she dashed to the opposite side of the room, giggling mischievously. I sprinted to her, grasping the phone.

ANNA:
Apart from you taking me on a date? No...

I shifted my attention from the phone to Grace, who stood nervously watching. "No, you did not!" I exclaimed, then leaped, pushing her onto the sofa. Playfully, I hit her again and again with a pillow. "You can't just invite someone we don't know to set me up on a date!"

She giggled uncontrollably. "I'm going to pee myself!"

"So much for making a man work for it! You just offered me on a silver platter!" I laughed.

The phone buzzed, interrupting our playful scuffle.

ALEXANDER:
Straight in, no kissin' – I like it! How's Thursday night looking for you? We could go for a late-night hot chocolate at Daisies?

Grace yelped, attempting to grab my phone. "You're welcome!! And that is SUCH a cute date idea!! I want to go for a late night hot chocolate…"

"Why don't you just sit in the corner and watch us?" I teased, nudging Grace playfully. "You orchestrated this! If I'm not feeling it, we can swap seats."

ALEXANDER:
If that doesn't suit, we could grab coffee on Saturday? Or... on Thursday, I'm also happy to meet in a bar. I don't drink alcohol but could have a few 0% beers haha.

"He's SO KEEN," she screamed, excitement radiating from her. "The options! He's giving you options!"

As I read his messages, a thought nagged at the back of my mind. Why was he giving options when he didn't know anything about me?

"Wonder why he doesn't drink." I hummed. "Rare you meet a sober Irish-man."

"Maybe because of his work?"

I laughed, "Nah I know plenty of doctors that love the sesh."

The Sesh
Definition : Partying / drinking / going 'out out'

Grace snatched my phone to reply, only I pushed her off, "Piss off!" I laughed.

ANNA:

Hot chocolate on Thursday sounds lovely. I've never been to Daisies before! What time suits?

I'd heard of the quaint basement chocolate store but had never visited.

ALEXANDER:

Let's do 6:30 pm? So, tell me more about yourself? What makes you happy?

I couldn't help but smile at his message. It was a thoughtful question, unexpected. My past experiences on dating apps were abysmal, with opening lines such as 'if you were a zombie, what part of me would you eat first?' or just 'nice tits' …

"I like him. I approve." Grace announced. "Good vibes so far."

CHAPTER EIGHTEEN

You're worth ten of him

Definition: You're worth more

My boxes were being ticked. It all seemed almost too good to be true.

"What are you smiling at? It's getting a bit creepy," Paddy's voice interrupted my excitement.

"Nothing," I quickly replied, shaking my head, but my attention quickly returned to Alexander's texts.

I was completely glued to my phone. Every time I sat it down, it seemed to buzz with a new message moments later.

"Didn't realise you hated me," he spat, dripping with sarcasm.

I looked up at him, noticing his relaxed posture with his legs propped up on his desk, clearly not in the mood for work. "Why would you think I hate you?" I asked, genuinely puzzled.

He shrugged nonchalantly.

"Paddy?" I pressed; my curiosity piqued.

"You don't trust me with your secrets anymore?" He asked.

I tilted my head to the side, trying to read his expression.

"I just matched with this guy, and he's... funny... he's got a good personality. That's all," I explained, feeling a bit defensive.

He hummed thoughtfully. "Ah."

Without saying anything more, he left, heading for the breakroom, leaving me feeling slightly confused and wondering about his reaction.

Later that evening, I found myself on the treadmill of all places, still engrossed in conversation with Alexander. Despite the bustling noises of the gym around me, our texts created a cocoon of intimacy.

He mentioned that he studied the same course in Uni as my parents and currently worked at Daisy Hill Hospital in Newry. I could almost envision my dad's reaction to me dating a doctor; he'd be absolutely thrilled.

Alexander revealed his love for travel, sharing that he had a solo trip planned to India in November. I found his independence incredibly attractive.

Furthermore, he had a passion for cooking, particularly Mexican cuisine, and boasted about his ability to whip up an amazing mocktail margarita. HOT.

He also mentioned that he didn't drink alcohol because he disliked how it made him feel afterward, prioritising his mental well-being. He emphasised that he didn't need it to have fun. HOT and... aspirational.

I couldn't help but feel the butterflies fluttering in my stomach as he continued to impress me with every message. At 3:48 am, I finally forced myself to say goodnight and reluctantly turned off my phone. Yet, even as I drifted off to sleep, my mind was filled with dreams of our upcoming date.

***

The next afternoon, as I strolled to Established to grab some lunch, I spotted Amir at the cash register, picking up a coffee. My initial instinct was to turn on my heels and avoid any confrontation, but instead, I walked inside with determination and stood behind him.

He laughed, engaging in conversation with the barista, before turning to face me. There was a momentary flicker of surprise in his eyes, quickly replaced by his usual, almost stern expression.

"Hi," I greeted him with a subtle smile.

He simply nodded and briskly walked past me, heading straight for the door.

His dismissive attitude stirred frustration within me. I had tried to be friendly, yet he gave me nothing in return.

As I simmered with annoyance, a familiar giggle caught my attention. Glancing over, I spotted Olivia seated at a table in the corner, accompanied by a man. It was a reminder of just how small Belfast could be.

I ordered a latte and a toastie and decided to interrupt her little date whilst I waited.

"Oh my gosh!" I giggled, approaching their table. "Are you that famous reporter? Olivia? I love your work-"

Before I could finish, her laughter grew louder, and I could see shock in her eyes. "Oh, shut up, you bitch you!" she exclaimed, a mix of surprise and amusement in her tone.

She stood up, pulling me into a quick hug and whispered in my ear, "This is the man I told you about. Be nice."

I looked at her, confusion evident across my face. *I'm always nice...* I felt slightly taken aback by her reaction.

"Cormac, this is my best friend Anna," Olivia introduced, beaming at him.

He stood briefly to shake my hand. "Nice to meet ya," he greeted me, his southern accent catching me by surprise.

"Where you from?" I inquired, curious about his background.

"Ah, Kilkenny, but studyin' and uh... werkin' up 'ere," he replied, gesturing towards his apron. "Well, tryin' to anyways, but yer friend Olivia here is a welcome distraction."

Olivia blushed at his compliment, seeming even more smitten than she usually would be.

"What are you studying?" I asked, finding him quite pleasant.

"FinTech management," he replied with a smile. "It's good, like. Always interesting. One sec, sorry."

He excused himself and headed behind the counter to fix something.

"FinTech management?" I repeated, a hint of curiosity in my voice.

Olivia shrugged and then rubbed her fingers together in a gesture that insinuated money.

I laughed. "So, are you on a date now? Did you go mini-golfing?" I asked, feeling a bit puzzled. She had been unusually quiet since our last meet-up, and I felt overdue for a catch-up session.

"The date is on Saturday... we're going for ice cream, mini-golf, and then dinner," she replied.

"Jeez, that's a marathon of a first date," I remarked. "Won't you run out of things to talk about?"

She bit her lip, looking uncertain. "Hadn't thought about that."

"I'm sure you'll be fine," I reassured her.

"I see him every few days in here, and we always have a good chat, so hopefully..." she trailed off.

"Takeaway for Anna!" the man behind the counter called out.

"That's me. I'll chat with you later," I said, acknowledging him before pulling Olivia into a quick squeeze and heading to collect my order.

***

ALEXANDER:

Why do I have first date nerves when it feels like I know you so well already?

I felt my cheeks flush as I read his text. It had only been 48 hours, but the connection felt remarkably intense. We had been texting non-stop, and it was as if we had known each other for much longer.

He'd already started laying out ideas for a second date – a trip to a 'special ice-cream spot' in Donegal.

"Anna!" Grace stood in front of me, holding up two outfit choices. "So, this one is more casual obviously," she said, holding up a pair of denim jeans and a knitted sweatshirt in one hand. "And this is more dressy." In the other hand, she held a knee-length chocolate brown dress.

I shook my head, decision paralysis taking over. "I have no idea."

She thrust the dress in front of me, choosing for me. "You can wear your black boots with it."

"You sure?" I asked, suddenly feeling more nervous. "It's not too much?"

She shook her head. "No, it's cute. Plus, he's been close to perfect already... dressing up will only make him like you more, right?"

"I just hope I like him in person... what if he's a total catfish?" I laughed, but the thought made me anxious.

"Well... only 24 hours until you find out!"

***

My eyes felt like they were hanging out of my head, and I looked like I'd been dragged through a hedge backward. Another night of late-night texting had left me totally exhausted.

I stirred my second cup of coffee and sipped on it slowly, hoping it would wake me up.

"Hey," he spoke monotonously as he walked into the breakroom and lifted out a mug.

"Hi," I replied, unsure of what to say.

I moved to the other side of the room, allowing Amir to make his cup of tea. We didn't speak further.

Sipping on my drink, my eyes darted around the room uncomfortably. I could have left, but I wanted something from him. I didn't know what… but just… *something*.

He poured a dribble of milk into his mug and stirred before dropping his spoon into the sink. As he walked towards the door to leave, I felt compelled to speak, but as I made a sound, he did too.

We faced each other, unspoken words lingering, the energy uncomfortable.

"What are you going to be speaking about on your episode tomorrow?" he asked, his voice strong.

My heart sank. *Tomorrow?* TOMORROW. I'd been so distracted from texting Alexander that I'd lost track of time. I mentally slapped myself.

"Uhm, I can review it with you tomorrow afternoon," I suggested, trying to cover up my unpreparedness.

Amir nodded, accepting the suggestion without pressing further. The tension between us lingered. With a nod goodbye, he left the breakroom, leaving me to ponder my situation.

I returned to my desk, knowing my episode would revolve around first dates. My own experiences and maybe even Olivia's, as her first date with the barista boy was fast approaching.

I quickly composed a message to Olivia:

ANNA

Hey babe, fancy being a guest on the pod tomorrow night?

I hit send and waited for her reply.

***

"You look insane!" Grace beamed as we stared at my reflection in the mirror. "Hold on, one second." She returned and pushed a bobby pin into the back of my head, securing my 'messy bun' in place.

My look was a mixture of casual and dressy, a perfect blend for a first date over hot chocolate.

"I'm sweating," I exclaimed, fanning my face. "Fuck, I'm sweating."

I lifted my arms up to review the damage, checking for any wet patches through my dress. Thankfully, there were none. Grabbing toilet paper, I folded it into squares and shoved it underneath my arms to catch any future droplets.

"I can't wait to hear everything!" She gushed, "I'm almost tempted to take up your original idea and sit in the corner so I can watch."

I laughed, "God, why am I so nervous?"

My mind flashed back to my talk with Amir about my nerves and anxiety, momentarily making me feel worse. I shook the thought from my mind.

"It's only natural!" Grace squeezed my shoulder. "Plus, he seems really nice and genuine. The type of man you deserve."

"Not helping," I laughed.

Grace drove me to Daisies, dropping me off outside the front around 6:35. I couldn't appear too keen, and I thought it wouldn't hurt to make him sweat a little.

"Okay, so if you need out or he's a total catfish, text me BLUEBERRY and I'll fake an emergency phone call," Grace instructed.

"Why blueberry?" I asked, finding humour in her protectiveness.

"Because when else would you text me blueberry?" She replied, as if it was the most logical thing in the world.

"Right, okay."

"And you've shared your location with me?" she asked.

"Yep. But I doubt I'll be moving anywhere. I can't imagine hot chocolate leading to a hook-up at his place."

She laughed. "Okay, okay, go on. I'll be parked around the corner."

"You're going to wait on me?"

"Yeah, I have a book and some snacks." She smiled. "Plus, I'm already excited to hear how it goes!"

As I walked down the concrete steps to Daisies chocolate shop, it felt like I was descending into a secret underground hideaway. The large black door at the front was heavy to push and led me into a white cavern, and another door. I pushed it open, and the smell of chocolate hit me immediately.

The space was small. Very small. And all the tables were empty but one. Two young girls sat reading, sipping their hot drinks.

"Table for one?" a friendly man behind the counter asked.

"Two, please," I requested and was led to a cosy little corner. The walls, floor, and ceiling were all white, adorned with shelves sporting various handmade chocolatey treats.

As I sat, he handed me two menus and suggested I try their home-made pistachio gelato.

My stomach began to sink as I looked at my phone and saw it was 6:43. He was 13 minutes late. Or maybe he wasn't coming at all.

ANNA:

hey, I'm here!

Goosebumps appeared on my skin as my gut plummeted. The message only had one tick instead of two, meaning it hadn't delivered.

"Some water for the table," the man set a jug and two small cups in front of me.

"Oh, thank you. Is the service okay down here?" I asked, refreshing the app.

"Should be?"

"I'm just going to run outside to check and come back, is that okay?"

He nodded. "Of course."

As I stood outside, the cold air whistled around me, and I waited impatiently, praying my luck would change. After two minutes of waiting, I gave up and returned inside.

"Sorted?" he asked.

"Yeah, all good. I might try that gelato you mentioned," I smiled, figuring I could treat myself while I waited.

Light background music lightened the atmosphere. It was silent otherwise as the girls beside me were captivated, quietly reading their books.

Suddenly, my phone vibrated against the wooden table. I opened it, seeing a text from Grace. Still nothing from Alexander.

GRACE:

No blueberry? I had to move further down the street as I spotted a traffic warden.

I sighed, typing my reply.

ANNA:

He's not here yet. Starting to think that I've been stood up. Keep you updated xx

The gelato was the only thing giving me hope as I tasted it. Once the bowl was finished, I texted Grace to let her know – he still hadn't shown.

A few minutes later, she walked in through the door. "Come on, let's go. You're not waiting around for a man who shows up..." she looked down at her watch, "almost twenty-five minutes late without a text to apologise. You're worth ten of him."

***

Shame. Embarrassment. Anxiety.

Emotions I felt heavily when Tom hadn't showed up for our date the week before.

Anger. Frustration. But... Relief.

Emotions I felt even heavier now that Alexander hadn't showed up this week.

He'd completely ghosted, going as far as to unmatch me on the app and block my phone number, and it had all happened in the six-minute timeframe of Grace and I driving to the date.

I lay in bed, my notebook on my lap, feeling like I was repeating a cycle but with more realisation.

Another day. Another failure?

For what reason does anyone think it okay to ghost someone?

I recapped my experience on paper, letting all the emotions out.

The thing is, because I'd invested so much time this week into speaking to the man, who would inevitably ghost me... is that... I'd built up expectations in my head.

I had designed a vision of a man who may or may not actually exist. I'd visualised a potential future after only a few days.

That's the first mistake.

But it's hard not to let your mind wander, especially when he sends you ideas and promises. Mine wanted to book me in for the second date before we'd even had our first.

That's why I'm even more confused as to why he ghosted?

Second mistake – I spent an hour re-reading our messages, searching for answers and criticising myself.

What did I do wrong?

But here's the truth – him ghosting isn't about me at all. Maybe he's already in a relationship. Maybe he actually is a catfish. Maybe he's not ready to meet a woman like me? Maybe he simply changed his mind? Who knows? And who cares!

I don't want to be with someone who can't even send a simple text to cancel a date. I don't want to be with someone who offers zero respect.

It's not hard.

The fantasy he provided me with this week was wonderful. It's given me more understanding of the type of man I want to be with, the values I admire and conversations I like to have.

But his words mean nothing. His actions have left me empty.

Yet, amidst the disappointment, there's a silver lining. In a way, his ghosting has been a valuable lesson—a stepping stone toward finding someone who truly values and respects me.

Oh and … men can be fucking dickheads.

I scribbled out the last sentence, trying to be positive even though I'd been let down once again. My ego was feeling very fragile.

***

"Here," Paddy said, tossing a bag onto my desk.

I looked down, puzzled.

"What's this?"

"Lidl bakery goods," he grinned.

Opening the brown bag, the aroma hit me instantly. Fresh pain au chocolats. "I feel like I could cry," I admitted, my eyes welling with tears. Hastily, I plucked one from the bag, relishing the crisp pastry as it crunched in my hands, and took a bite. "T-fahnk- you" I mumbled, mouth full.

He chuckled. "What's the full life update? Things have been so hectic with work that I feel out of the loop."

I sighed. "Don't even get me started."

We sat for thirty minutes as I poured out everything. Talking about it helped, yet it also made everything feel more tangible, the weight of recent events settling heavily within me, stirring a maelstrom of conflicting emotions.

"You seem different from a month ago," he remarked, reading through my episode notes.

"Yeah. I feel different."

"Just don't get too caught up in trying to 'figure out' how to get over the emotions you're feeling – sometimes we do that to avoid actually feeling them." He sighed.

"What do you mean?"

"It's.. okay... to be sad, you know? It sucks that he ghosted and you don't always have to turn struggles into something empowering," he stumbled over his words. "I mean it's amazing if you do feel empowered but just know, no-one would think less of you if you were actually just... sad."

His words hung in the air, leaving me uncertain how to respond. I'd never considered it from that perspective before.

Perhaps I had been burying my emotions beneath layers of empowerment narratives, striving to emerge stronger from every setback. But in doing so, had I denied myself the opportunity to acknowledge the pain?

I offered a faint smile, grateful for his insight. "I am sad." I admitted. "And I did spend hours wondering why he'd done it. I spent ages thinking how undeserving I am of a relationship. And it's annoying, because even though – deep within me, I know that's not true, every time I get rejected... I feel it a little more."

"Okay, so THAT is what you need to include in your episode." He smiled, "I love seeing how much you've grown in the last month, but I just worry the pressure of the pod is making you feel like you always HAVE to have the answers... you don't. I think it's more real if you don't."

I nodded, "I know you're r-"

"Anna... Paddy," Amir called out as he approached my desk, his voice carrying a dark edge. "How's things?"

He maintained his characteristic stern demeanour, clad in a sharp suit with polished shoes.

"Hey, good. Good. Just catching up." Paddy said. They exchanged a peculiar glance, laden with understanding—a look that made me a little anxious.

"Um, I need to edit my episode a bit. Mind if we go through it later today?" I asked, noticing his expression darken slightly more.

"Sure. 2pm," he replied, his tone more of a request than a question.

Before I could respond further, he left.

I inhaled a deep cleansing breath, "I hate when he does that."

Paddy laughed, "Does what?"

"The way he just walks off..." I added, "He's so annoying. What if I had something to say?"

Paddy shrugged, "You can tell him at 2pm."

And then he left me alone too.

***

After staring at my notebook for two hours and downing three cups of coffee, I ventured outside for a breath of fresh air, hoping for inspiration. Yet, despite my efforts, my mind remained blank.

However, an hour later, as I sat outside in the sun, it finally came to me in a sudden rush of clarity.

Isn't it interesting how we can feel empowered yet still experience moments of sadness simultaneously?

Perspective is everything.

I try to keep in mind that there's a whole bunch of opportunities waiting for me down the road. Yeah, this current situation sucks, but hey, I've been through some tough stuff in the past and I've always bounced back even stronger. Right?

Admitting that I'm feeling down isn't a sign of weakness—it's just being real. We all want to steer clear of going through old heartaches again, and sometimes we think showing our emotions makes us seem fragile.

But really, it's a sign of how far we've come. A testament to growth.

There are other men out there.

And I deserve better. Undoubtably.

And also... I'll become better myself. I'll get tougher, more in tune with how I feel, and hopefully, I'll make smarter decisions.

I re-read my episode notes as a whole and even though I could see the positive in the narrative, my body felt heavy as the sadness settled.

OLIVIA
Mr. Millionaire strikes again. I'll be over in 5.

I stared at the text from Olivia, feeling a twinge of anxiety. As she walked through the doors carrying a large box, I couldn't help but laugh.

"Just when I'd almost forgotten about him," I chuckled.

"Chocolates," she snorted, dropping the present onto my desk, "and a note."

'Sorry for our less than stellar first date.
How about a second above average one?
No mates. No bars. Just me, you, and dinner?
TB x'

"He's quite the charmer," she gushed, standing over my shoulder as I read.

I sighed, unsure of what to make of it. It was a nice gesture, and at least he acknowledged that our first date fell short.

"It's probably because I brought him chocolates. He's just returning the favour," I reasoned.

"Anna, if you don't go on the date, I will," she rolled her eyes, opening the box. Again, like the flowers, the gift was extravagant. There had to be over 200 artisan pieces inside.

"I didn't plan on seeing him again..." I contemplated.

"It's just dinner. Only an hour of your life and it could provide some content," she spoke persuasively.

"I'll think about it. Speaking of content, you never replied to my text

291

about being on the show?"

Her face twisted. "I'm not feeling it. Unless Spotlight wants to start paying me for my time."

"Anna?" I turned to see Amir standing there, expectantly. "Your review?" he appeared visibly frustrated.

I jumped, realising the time. "Sorry." I glanced at Olivia, and she took the hint, leaving instantly.

"What's this?" he asked, approaching the desk, curious.

I watched as he lifted the letter. His face twisted, shocked. "Sorry, I shouldn't have intruded." He dropped it back onto the desk.

"No, it's fine," I laughed.

"I didn't think-"

"It's fine. Honestly. Olivia just dropped it off a second ago and yeah… don't worry about it."

***

"This is good," Amir hummed, sitting across from me.

"Really?" I asked, my tone tinged with uncertainty. "It feels a bit depressing to me. I feel like all my episodes are so heavy, and all I wanted was a fun one on first dates for once, but now this…"

He looked up from the pages, surprised by my outburst of frustration. "Okay…"

"Sorry, I—just…" I paused, feeling the weight of his gaze. "I just feel like such an imposter talking about this sometimes. Who am I to give advice? And this one… it feels fake. Yes, I'm empowered. At this moment in time. But what if it hits me tomorrow, and I spend all day crying in bed?"

The words tumbled out of my mouth; my vulnerability laid bare.

He raised an eyebrow. "Are you not going to Galway tomorrow?"

I paused, taken aback. "What? Yes, why?"

He shook his head, ignoring the question. "Also, what about

Millionaire guy? Why would you be crying when he's asked you out again?"

"I don't even know if I'll go on the date but also, that's not part of my episode. I don't want to talk about it."

He caught himself, realising the intrusion, "You don't have to talk about any of this…" He handed me the notebook. "You can just do a fun episode on first dates, it's okay. You don't have to give a weekly life or dating update, especially if you don't feel ready to share it."

I nodded, feeling a sense of relief. "Sorry, I—"

"Stop apologising. This is all really good information. It's a good episode, and maybe you can save it for another day. Do you think you can prep something else for tonight?"

"I have no choice," I said, chuckling lightly.

He shook his head. "Why don't you just ask your audience to phone in their dating stories? Dating nightmares?"

And so that's what I did.

***

"That was fucking brilliant!" Paddy exclaimed, wiping tears from under his eyes as my outro song played.

I sighed a breath of relief, removing my headphones. "I literally have the best listeners and thank GOD. That was so fun."

"I nearly snorted Red Bull out of my nose when that story with the priest—" Paddy began, breaking into fits of laughter.

"No… I couldn't breathe. Imagine talking to someone for months only to find out they're about to enter the priesthood."

"I reckon he just said it to get her into bed… last fling before celibacy?" We laughed hard, unable to contain it. "Or the man who said he'd pick her up for the date and showed up on a bicycle…"

"I was just picturing her in heels, holding her dress up trying to throw a leg over."

Paddy clapped his hands together. "Ah, brilliant!"

"Right…" I smiled, starting to pack my headphones into my bag. "I still haven't packed anything for Galway. See you in the morning?"

He nodded. "Bright and early!"

***

As I contorted my arm in ways I didn't think were possible, attempting to dab fake tan onto the middle crevice of my back, my phone buzzed.

The email on my screen infuriated me.

amir.davairi@apex.com

I think the old episode would have been better. It had much more depth instead of those stories. Talk Monday.

I breathed heavily through my nose, feeling the tension coil tighter within me, until a scream of frustration escaped my lips, prompting Grace to knock on the door.

"You okay?" she shouted through.

"Yeah. Just… tanning," I replied, trying to steady my breathing.

"D'ya need me to do your back for you?"

CHAPTER NINETEEN

Galway Girl

Definition: a girl from Galway.

It was 7:46 am. Paddy was supposed to arrive at 7:30 am and he wasn't answering his phone. I paced up and down the footpath while Grace sat on the wooden bench outside my apartment building. Our overnight mini suitcases sat beside her, along with a bag filled with road trip snacks we'd picked up the night before.

"He'll be here soon," Grace reassured me, stretching her hands above her head before succumbing to the yawn she'd been suppressing. "Probably just running a little late." She wrapped her arms around her body, seeking warmth against the cold air. It didn't help that my apartment was right beside the water; the sea breeze was brutal.

I shook my head and started redialling Paddy's number. We had agreed to meet early as Galway was about a 4-hour drive away, and we wanted to make the most of culture day.

"Y'ellow," he answered, sounding chirpy.

Thank the Lord. I was half expecting him to still be in bed.

"What sort of time do you call this?" I started off strong, but a yawn caught my throat. This was definitely not a normal time to wake up on a Saturday.

"Alright, alright…" I mentally pictured him rolling his eyes at me. "Just stopped at a red light. We'll be there in 2 mins."

The call ended before I could respond. We?

I turned on my heels to face Grace. Her head shot up from her phone, eyes narrowed. "What?"

"Paddy said 'we'," I said, feeling my heart quicken. Surely not.

"We?" she tilted her head, confused.

"Yeah, like there's someone else in the car with him…"

Grace puckered her lips, deep in thought. I imagined my expression mirrored hers. "Did he tell you he was thinking of bringing someone else?"

I shook my head, a knot forming in my stomach.

"Did you tell him to invite someone else?"

Again, I shook my head, anxiety creeping up my spine.

"Does he have a girlfriend?"

I snorted, my voice trembling slightly. "Jesus no. All he does is work."

"Well, maybe he's just giving someone a lift down there. Dropping them off in that direction…" She suggested, but her words did little to ease my rising panic.

My skin prickled as I ignored the growing feeling in my gut, praying I'd be wrong. "I feel like he would have told m-" My voice trailed off, anxiety gripping me tightly.

I was interrupted by the beeping of a car horn and turned to see his black BMW pull up beside us. He rolled his window down and glanced at Grace and me… and our luggage. "How many nights have you packed for? I thought it was just one."

I clenched my fists, feeling a surge of anxiety coursing through me.

"You're late. Don't test me."

"Here, I'll help!"

My stomach plummeted as Amir jumped out from the passenger door. Dread washed over me like a tidal wave. He swiped a hand through his hair, displaying an array of rings and his nails – black in colour. No chips.

"What are you –" My voice caught in my throat, my anxiety reaching a crescendo. "Paddy, what is he doing here?"

I bit my tongue, trying to contain the panic rising within me. I had been hoping Galway would offer a useful distraction from him… yet here he stood, bright-eyed and bushy-tailed. Based on how he bounced on his feet, a smile covering his face, I assumed he was an overly cheery morning person. The opposite of me.

Paddy responded by ignoring me and rolling his window up. Grace snorted back a laugh as she handed Amir her mini suitcase.

"Amir, is it?" She smiled, "Thank you so much."

He lifted our cases with ease as I stood frozen in the spot. *This was not happening…* I inhaled a deep breath and looked towards Grace for help, but she was already jumping into the back seat behind Paddy. I couldn't get out of this… there was nothing I could do but accept it.

Amir lifted my suitcase from the footpath and placed it into the boot of the car. "Are you carrying rocks in here?"

"Just a few weapons, no rocks though," I replied, attempting to lighten the tension.

He rolled his eyes. "I hope you don't mind… I haven't really seen much of Ireland…"

I wasn't sure what to say to him, so I jumped into the car beside Grace, trying to push aside the unease settling in my chest.

The drive was long. Four hours in a car would make anyone a bit uncomfortable, but I felt completely claustrophobic. I shielded my eyes with sunglasses and tried to snooze, avoiding catching Amir's eyes in the reflection. Paddy played chill tunes, and conversation flowed, with Grace leading most of it.

Two hours in, just as I'd begun to doze off, finally feeling my body relax, Paddy screamed loudly. Grace and Amir joined him, and I jolted awake, fearing the worst. A crash. He'd hit someone. The engine had blown up. But it was just a practical joke to shock me awake and provide them with some much-needed entertainment.

Three hours in, we stopped at a service station for a pee break and to refuel. To entertain myself on the last stretch, I decided I'd tell Amir some fake facts about Ireland, which only caused us to bicker back and forth as he didn't believe a word that was coming out of my mouth.

We left our bags at the hotel reception, arriving too early to check in. Eager to explore, we ventured into the waking city. The streets buzzed with life. Drunken, smiling couples swayed to traditional music, their carefree spirits contagious. Flags of various nations adorned every shop, pub, and restaurant, painting the scene with a vibrant tapestry of diversity. It felt like a St. Patrick's Day celebration, but with an embrace of all cultures from around the globe, not just Ireland.

A tantalising array of aromas wafted through the air as food vendors lined the streets, tempting us with crepes, paella, and bockwurst. My mouth watered.

Amir led the way, capturing moments with an impressively pretentious film camera. Paddy and Grace lagged behind, engrossed in reminiscing about past trips to Galway and Grace's family in Cork. Their conversation faded into the background as I immersed myself in the tapestry of the city.

The sun beat down upon us, and I regretted not bringing a hat as I felt my scalp starting to burn. Scanning the surroundings, I searched for a stall selling hats, but instead, my gaze landed on a quintessentially Irish pub. Its warm glow beckoned, drawing us closer. Outside, patrons sat at whisky barrel tables, sipping drinks, and enjoying the lively atmosphere.

A couple, tipsy on their toes, exited the pub, laughter and the strains of 'fiddly dee' music trailing in their wake.

I picked up my pace and reached for Amir's arm. He turned, surprised. "Fancy a pint?"

Despite it being July, the first thing to greet us was the warmth emanating from a burning turf fire and the lively banter of old Irish men.

"Oh, sure you know I will John-boy!" One man gloated, lifting his pint.

"Aye, right!" His friend laughed.

Inside, a guitarist with a husky voice, tinged with the remnants of too many cigarettes, serenaded the bustling crowd. Every seat was filled, and people stood along the old brick walls, soaking in the atmosphere. He was joined by a fiddler and a box drum player, who skilfully multitasked by playing the tambourine.

As we ventured further into the bar, navigating through the dense crowd, we found ourselves pressed closer together, jostled by the throng. Amir turned, checking to see if I was still following behind. I nodded at him, and he reciprocated with a nod of his own before reaching out to grasp my wrist. Grace and Paddy trailed behind; their closeness evident.

"Do you think there's something going on between them?" I shouted above the chanting, trying to make myself heard over the din.

"What?" Amir mouthed back, struggling to hear. He pulled me closer to his side, our bodies touching. "I can't hear you."

For a moment, discomfort surged through me, a pang of unease at the proximity and intimacy, but I pushed it aside as Amir's arm slid from my wrist to wrap around my waist, drawing me closer to him.

"Oh—do you think there's something going on?" I repeated.

He looked at me puzzled. "What?"

I rolled my eyes and leaned in to shout into his ear, "Like romantically?"

He pulled back; lips open in shock. "Between us?"

My heartbeat thundered in my ears. "No—no! Them." I pointed to

Grace and Paddy, who were just a few steps behind.

He nodded, his shoulders beginning to relax as he gave me a cheeky smile. "I hope so."

Vintage, empty liquor bottles adorned the wooden cabinets that lined the walls, a familiar sight in Irish pubs. These relics showcased the passage of time, proudly displaying our history and heritage.

"Yooo!" Amir exclaimed, pulling me into a two-step. "Are you guys heading out?"

The men nodded, affirming, "Yeah, all yours mate."

In a stroke of luck, we secured a wooden but slightly wobbly table in the bar's corner. "Let's leave the lovebirds to it. Take a seat beside me, I promise not to bite," I teased.

Whilst I didn't really fancy him sitting next to me, my primary goal was to observe the unfolding dynamics between Paddy and Grace. I slid onto a chair.

Amir rolled his eyes, placed his hand on the table, and leaned down, his face inches from mine. "Not sure if I should trust that."

I needed a drink immediately. He settled into a chair beside me, casually draping one arm around the back of my seat. I subtly squeezed my legs together, attempting to make myself small and calm the fluttering sensation his proximity ignited.

I harboured A LOT of lingering resentment towards him – at least in my mind. My heart, more often than not, shared the sentiment. Yet, my body... felt different.

Paddy and Grace arrived and took up place facing us. "Guinness all round?" Paddy shouted above the music.

"I don't drink bin juice, sorry." Grace laughed.

"Bin juice?"

"That's what I think Guinness tastes like. Water for me please."

He raised his eyebrows at her, "Am I fuck buying you water..." He declared, heading to the bar with a laugh.

"Personally, I love a Guinness. Liquid gold," Amir laughed.

"I prefer a baby Guinness shot. Tia Maria and Baileys." I licked my lips.

"Shots?" He arched an eyebrow, "Noted. I'll make you regret saying that."

"I can't believe Olivia is missing out on all of this. She'd be in her element." Grace scanned the bar, her eyes lighting up. The atmosphere was truly electric, an experience unique to Galway. Irish vibes reverberated from the pub's walls. While every country in the world may boast an Irish pub, none could hold a candle to this one. Not even close.

"I know," I sighed, cosying into my chair.

"Do you think people assume I'm Irish when they look over?" Amir questioned; his tone deadly serious.

"Are you jokin'?" I shot him a look as if he had ten heads.

"No." Grace chimed in simultaneously.

He wasn't joking.

"I feel Irish just sitting here." He leaned back on his chair which caused his arm to press further into my back.

I rolled my eyes. "Shut up."

"It was just a question. No need to be rude." He teased. "She's so rude to me, don't you think?"

Grace stayed silent, diverting her gaze towards the bar, likely summoning Paddy for help, sensing an argument brewing.

"Stop acting like a child." I huffed. "You're always rude."

He inhaled deeply through his nose, "How am I rude? Give me 5 examples."

I closed my eyes in frustration, "I could give you 50."

"50 examples?"

"Probably 500."

A hearty laugh rumbled from his stomach, "You're so easy to piss off."

I turned to him, clicking my tongue, "You-"

Paddy arrived back, cutting me off as he sat a tray with two Guinness and two G&Ts onto the table. Grace lifted a G&T from the tray and took a surprisingly long sip, "Oh thank god you're back. I can't listen to these two."

I laughed. Amir laughed. I shot him a glare for finding it amusing.

"Paddy, do you think I look Irish?"

He lifted an eyebrow in response and took a seat at the table, "Aye. Hundred percent." Sarcasm dripped from his words.

I shook my head, lifting a Guinness from the tray. I gulped down four large mouthfuls and sat the pint down, savouring the taste. The Guinness in Galway surpassed that of 99% of places.

"That was my drink." Amir hummed.

I slid the pint over for him to finish, "Go on then." I took my G&T from the tray and lifted it to cheers him, "Sláinte."

Sláinte
'To health' - a drinking toast when you cheers your glasses together.

"I don't want your germs." He remarked, eyeing his remaining drink.

Paddy bellowed a laugh, "Well you've swapped spit with her before, and you're still alive. Will you two stop acting like children?"

I wished the ground would swallow me up right then and there. I buried my face in my hands, afraid to look at Amir. I didn't know how he'd react to that revelation. Grace joined Paddy in laughter.

"Swapped spit?" Amir questioned.

I peeked an eye out from behind my hands, seeing confusion across his face.

"Kissed. You two kissed. Did you forget?" Paddy teased.

I dropped my hands to my lap as Amir turned to me. "No, we didn't." He said defensively, playing dumb.

"Funny, I'm pretty sure each of you confided in me about said kiss after it happened."

"Stop," I warned him.

"Please continue." Grace giggled. I observed as she edged closer to him, detecting a certain energy between them.

"I have no idea what you're talking about." Amir stretched out, sinking deeper into his chair. He shot a glance at me, his face turning red as a beetroot. I found strange satisfaction in his discomfort.

"Was it really not that memorable?" I teased, feigning offense, and swivelled around in my chair to fully face him. Panic flickered in his eyes. "Or maybe you thought it was so bad that now you're pretending it didn't happen at all!"

"I-" He paused, uncertain of his words.

"You what?"

He offered an awkward smile, "Are we really going to talk about this now?"

A disquieting feeling started to churn deep in my stomach. *What did we have to talk about?* I stared at him, searching for emotions he felt but wasn't expressing.

"See, that's how you know you aren't Irish," Paddy cackled, interrupting the tension, "You can't take a joke…"

The conversation shifted. My mind did not.

***

We spent a few hours immersed in the welcoming atmosphere of that charming pub, occasionally joining in on the live music. Amir and I had, for the most part, set aside our bickering, and I was thoroughly enjoying the afternoon – until the conversation veered towards his impending return to NYC.

"So, what are the odds of you getting me a job in the Big Apple?" Paddy asked. I observed as he downed the remainder of his fifth, maybe sixth drink, licking his lips after.

"I came here to help Spotlight, not take away one of its biggest assets." Amir responded nonchalantly.

"A compliment. Wow. That's rare coming from you." I teased. "I'd take that and run with it, Paddy."

"But seriously, sometimes I wonder what life would be like further afield? Belfast is so small. Everyone knows someone who knows someone," Paddy mused.

"That's the beauty in it though – don't you think?" I asked, "I think New York would be such a lonely place to live."

"It can be at times, but so can everywhere." Amir sighed, "New York is so full of opportunity though. You wouldn't try it?"

I paused, thinking for a moment. "No – what would Spotlight do without its second biggest asset?" I joked.

"I think you would thrive." He hummed into his drink, eyes beating into mine.

My face twisted. I couldn't help it. I was barely surviving in Belfast, never mind thriving in New York.

"I'm serious." Amir sat his drink onto the table and pulled out his phone. Unlocking it, he slid his finger over to the camera roll app. "This is Apex."

He handed me his phone, gesturing for me to scroll. Pictures of a vibrant office, a bright kitchen stocked with snacks and interesting meeting rooms filled the screen. It was as if 'Spotlight 'was black and white and 'Apex' embodied every colour of the rainbow.

"Look." I shared the phone with Paddy.

"I've seen before."

I continued to scroll, "God, we really have been neglected." I remarked, injecting a touch of humour, though the contrast between the two offices was a stark reality.

"Well, I'd take a job anywhere. Belfast, New York… Lurgan if need be." Grace chimed in, laughing. "Know of any?"

"What do you work as currently?" Amir asked, intrigued.

"It's really exciting actually. Every-day is different. It's called unemployment," she giggled. "I just quit my job as a researcher. Long story. I won't depress you with it... anyone have any good news?"

I reached across the table and squeezed her hand.

"We're getting a revamp... hopefully." Paddy added, "Well – if all goes to plan."

"Seriously?" I asked, ears perking up.

"Yeah – it's in my plan." Amir sighed, "I'm firstly focused on convincing the board to keep the station going, obviously. That's step one. Step two is understanding what budget we'll have and where it'll go. A more – colourful workspace would help with more colourful ideas."

I replayed his words. *I'm firstly focused on convincing the board to keep the station going...* I hadn't realised how serious the stakes were.

"We have some colourful characters." A laugh escaped Paddy's throat, "Anyways, it's the weekend... none of this work chat."

The condensation that had built on the outside of my drink felt wet against my hand. I took a long sip, thoughts buzzing around my head.

"Sounds like you're doing a lot of good for the station." Grace spoke, eyes wide with interest. Amir smiled back at her graciously and nodded his head slightly.

"I'm trying."

I still questioned his intentions, mainly because I didn't understand his reason why. Why was he so interested in 'saving Spotlight?' What was in it for him? Grace shifted the conversation and began talking about the show she was working on before she quit; but all I could focus on in the moment was understanding Amir.

As he spoke with Grace, his eyes darted towards me. He smirked, only slightly when he realised, I was watching him. Every nuance in his eye and every shift of his smile – I caught it all. Doubt slithered into my stomach once again. *Why was he so interested in Spotlight?* His intentions seemed genuine on the outside, but I wondered if there was a motive behind it.

***

Music vibrated up the walls and poured out onto the streets as we stepped outside many hours later. People hurriedly covered themselves with umbrellas, jackets, bags, and any available waterproof items. The sky had opened up, transforming a once bright and sunny day into a wet affair.

"Ah for feck sake." Paddy exclaimed as we ventured onto the street. "It's raining cats and dogs."

"We should go back and wait it out." Grace suggested, shielding herself with her handbag.

Silently agreeing, we turned back towards the pub.

"We're full." The doorman shrugged, offering a sorry smile, "Nothing I can do – sorry."

Inhaling deeply through my nose, I pivoted on my heels. Amir stood a few steps behind us, eyes closed, face turned towards the sky, allowing raindrops to saturate his hair and cascade over his lashes. He was thoroughly soaked and noticeably drunk.

"You're getting soaked!" I screamed. He paid no attention, letting the rain continue to drench him, a surreal moment amidst the downpour.

"Mad man." Paddy strode into the rain, improvising cover by pulling his t-shirt over his head. He reached out and tousled Amir's wet hair, sending raindrops scattering.

Both guys erupted in laughter. The sound caught a butterfly in my stomach like a fish on a rod, awakening the irritating feeling of desire.

His laugh.

His smile.

His love for the rain.

The last time we stood in rain like this, we kissed.

I stood outside the pub door, letting the rain cascade down my face. Fuck emotions. Fuck every emotion. Every single one of them.

Fuck the confusion.

Fuck the desire.

Fuck the hatred.

Fuck the frustration.

Fuck the fear.

Fuck it all.

Fuck Amir for walking into my life and making me feel emotions that were different than I'd felt before. All-consuming, completely distracting, and utterly confusing. Watching him in the rain, carefree and drunk – I felt all of them. Every emotion.

"-'mon" Grace grabbed me by the arm as we followed after them. "Ye-alright?"

I nodded, my focus on him. When his eyes finally attached to mine, I knew exactly what he was thinking. We both chose to ignore it.

***

The hotel staff generously offered extra towels upon our return, recognising our soaked-through attire. Such was the unpredictable 'charm' of Ireland, where the weather danced to its own rhythm every day of the week.

"How about we clean up and meet for some dinner in an hour?" Amir suggested, his eyes carrying a gentle haze from the alcohol.

I nodded, feeling a touch of insecurity as rain-drenched strands of hair framed my face and mascara subtly threatened to pool under my eyes. I shook the towel through my hair, attempting to salvage some dryness. "I might need a bit longer – it'll take at least 30 minutes for me to peel myself out of these clothes."

***

"A few drinks and you're like two dogs on heat!" Grace's playful remark echoed through the bathroom door. A tad more intoxicated than the rest of us, she chuckled at her own observation.

I turned the shower on and stuck my hand underneath waiting for the water to warm. My body was still tingling from the chill of the rain.

"What d'you mean?" I screamed back at her as I shed my clothes and stepped into the hot, welcoming water. The muscles in my back immediately relaxed as I melted into the soothing heat.

I poked my head around the shower curtain, hearing Grace enter the bathroom. She looked at me, a mischievous smirk planted across her face. "Don't play dumb."

She started washing her face at the sink, still clad in her drenched clothes. "The two of you never quit! It was quite entertaining, I have to say."

"Agh!" I pulled the shower curtain back, refusing to look at her.

Silence fell between us. Just the sound of water running, splashing, and bouncing; and the distant melody of the bedroom radio. I lifted some fragrant body wash and massaged it into my skin.

"Do you really think-" I tried to frame my thoughts, worried I'd sound stupid, "Never mind."

"You never quit annoying each other." She laughed, "Honestly – I've never seen you so bothered by a man – but at the same time, I can tell you're infatuated with him."

I rolled my eyes and slid the curtain back to show her my face, "I am NOT infatuated with him! Jesus Christ."

The curtain slid back again and I scrubbed some shampoo into my scalp. It smelled like fresh oranges which was calming my nerves.

"Why not give it a chance?" She mumbled, still cleansing her face. "I recon he'd be all over you."

I scrubbed the suds from my hair, sighing in frustration. "This is the least peaceful shower I've ever had."

She didn't respond. I peeked my head from the curtain once again, and Grace's eyes met mine in the mirror reflection, as she wiped her face with a towel.

"Nothing will ever happen between Amir and I. It just won't. Yes – we kissed once, but afterward, he ran off making his 'feelings' very clear. I'm not going to allow myself to fall for a man who has no intention of respecting me or caring for me how I deserve. He can't give me what I want."

I let my head fall back under the water. Grace stayed quiet, probably unsure of how to reply to my outburst. I grabbed the conditioner and lathered it on to the ends of my hair.

"So, what do you want?" she asked, seemingly deflated.

I swallowed the lump in my throat debating how to answer her question, "Not this." I washed my hair one last time under the water, "I'm getting out now."

I grabbed a towel and wrapped myself in it, trying to avoid exposing myself completely, even though we'd both seen each-other naked plenty of times throughout our years of friendship. She sat on the closed toilet seat as I walked towards the mirror and began to apply cleanser to my face and neck.

"Look - I don't know him well enough to form an opinion, but I know you."

I stared at her, begging for the conversation to end. If we didn't talk about him, then hopefully I'd stop thinking about him.

"I know when you fancy someone – and you clearly like him."

I pinched the bridge of my nose, "YES! I do- of course I do, but I also HATE him. I don't know why we're even having this conversation. He's going back to America, he's also a dick – I thought you would have seen that! You usually spot dickheads miles before I do."

I washed my face once more and dried it with a fluffy face cloth.

"I think you're avoiding your feelings."

"I'm avoiding this conversation." I walked into the bedroom and sat on the edge of my bed. I melted into the silky sheets and started scrolling on my phone.

"Anna!" Grace groaned, following me. She sat across from me on a vintage-looking armchair. Legs crossed. Arms crossed. Face stern. "What's going on with you?"

I sighed and allowed myself to fall backwards into the bed. I stared at the ceiling, unable to form the words to explain. "I don't know." I mumbled, "I don't know."

I pinched the bridge of my nose and threw my phone behind me, releasing a sigh, "I...I don't know Grace... he's leaving soon, so there would be no point in pursuing anything. It would just make my life more difficult than it already is."

"So, you do have feelings?" She stood up from the armchair, "I knew it..."

I peeled my eyes from the ceiling and glared at her, "I have – a lot of feelings – not just desire – it's complicated."

She raised her eyebrows, "He definitely likes you."

Yanking a pillow from behind me, I placed it over my face and screamed. After my momentary release, I sat up once again, "We sound like school children right now. Also he hates me. We fight constantly."

"Look, I'm not going to tell you what to do. Make your own decisions. HOWEVER – I saw how he was looking at you today. It wasn't a look of hate..." She left in the direction of the bathroom and moments later, I heard the shower begin to run. I closed my eyes, feeling like I could nod off to sleep. At least that would distract me from my emotions – if he didn't haunt my dreams.

Instead of sleeping, I began to comb through my hair. Frustration bubbled beneath the surface of my skin at how much I desired Amir but also how complicated it all was. I felt *things* every time he looked at me, but I couldn't accept his reaction after our first kiss. I wasn't going to pursue a man who clearly didn't want me enough to be with me. Not again. Not after James. His hesitation was enough of an answer. I wanted someone who was sure of me. Who knew they wanted me, completely, and made it known. Maybe Tom… he made it known. For sure.

CHAPTER TWENTY
On The Lash

Definition: to go out drinking

An hour and 22 minutes later Grace and I descended the weath-ered wooden staircase toward the hotel bar and restaurant. We were 22 minutes late… thanks to my meticulous attempt to achieve symmetrical winged eyeliner and the extra effort I'd invested strategically stuffing toilet roll into my bra to make my boobs stand taller than usual.

As we climbed down the staircase, I noticed the two men sitting on armchairs conversing and chuckling. Unfortunately, Amir had his back to me, eliminating any potential for a cinematic 'Cinderella descending the staircase,' moment. Paddy nodded his head towards us, prompting Amir to turn around. He rolled his eyes immediately upon spotting us, kindling a fire deep within me and unsettling my composure before I even reached the bottom step. *What was his fucking problem this time?*

I huffed heavily through my nose, trying to breathe through the discomfort crawling up my spine.

"What's wrong?" I snapped, jokingly. He was wearing a tight black t-shirt, black jeans, and a seductive leather jacket. "Are your skinny jeans too tight? Cutting off circulation?"

He looked down at his jeans and back at me, "They're not skinny jeans. Jesus."

I stared at his eyes and then glanced down, "Look pretty skinny to me."

His eyes rolled to the back of his head once again, "You're thirty minutes late and you're already giving me shit? Can you quit it for a night?"

"You rolled your eyes before I'd even uttered a word!"

His lips flattened together, "Because you're thirty minutes late."

"Twenty two minutes actually. You're being a bit dramatic."

"I'm dramatic?" He laughed.

"Grace-" I turned for back up but she was nowhere to be seen. I glanced around me, looking for her signature curly hair. She was gone. "Where-"

"They must be in the restaurant." Amir walked off then turned his head and nodded at me to follow him.

Surprisingly enough they weren't in the restaurant when we arrived and were ignoring our phone calls, texts and for all we knew – they could have left Galway entirely. "This is your fault. If you wouldn't have been so rude!"

"Yer table is 'dis way sir." A waitress interrupted, eyes twinkling… clearly taken by his good looks.

"Coming?" Surprisingly, he turned towards me and extended his hand. I bit my lip, dismissing the gesture, and walked ahead of him. My pettiness was off the charts, but he had this knack for getting under my skin. No way in hell was I holding his hand. *CHRIST.*

Reaching the table, which was set for four, he skipped a step and pulled out a chair, gesturing for me to sit. "How chivalrous. Didn't know you had it in you."

"Oh shut it." He groaned, jaw clenched as he battled with my bitching. Part of me was satisfied that I could provoke him just as much, if not more than he provoked me. We bounced off one another. Shot after shot. Dig after dig.

The waitress awkwardly cleared her throat which startled me a bit. I'd forgotten she was still here. "Hav y-eaten wid us before?" her accent was so thick that I wondered how much he could understand.

"No." We both replied in unison, our eyes locking.

"Ok well – tis t'ree courses fer t-irty euro. Start, yer main and dessert. Colm will be lookin' after ya, ok. He'll be over in just a min to take yer drink order."

I nodded. "Thanks."

She departed, her gaze still lingering on Amir. If we were dating, it could be considered a little disrespectful for her to stare for so long.

"What did she just say?" He inquired and reached for the black leather menu.

"Three courses for thirty euro. Starter, main and dessert. Although I'm not hungry enough for three. Someone will swing by to take our drink order in a minute." I translated. "I wonder where they went to…"

My eyes roamed the restaurant, praying Paddy and Grace would make an appearance now that our bickering had cooled down.

"What's boxty?" His eyes squinted at the menu.

"Like a pancake."

"Shouldn't that be for dessert?"

"It's made of potato, so no."

"So, like a hash brown?"

"No." I shook my head at him, feeling overwhelmed.

"Oh."

Silence fell between us. I didn't feel hungry at all, but I was dying for a drink. The restaurant was darkly lit. Old Irish paintings hung on the walls. A maroon carpet coated the floors. I couldn't help but wonder about the wisdom of carpeting a restaurant – what if someone dropped… mashed potatoes? The thought of how they cleaned it up made me cringe.

It was very busy. Conversations blended with the clinking of cutlery and glasses as people either dined or congregated by the Irish flag-studded bar. In a corner, a group of men gathered, pints in hand, engrossed in a sports game playing on a TV screen.

Amir's phone vibrated against the hard wood table. "Paddy." He sighed with relief, unlocking the phone.

"What about him? Where are they?" I gazed at him expectantly, eyes curious and waiting. "What's he saying?"

Frustration etched across his face as he read the text message. "Try not to kill each other tonight. Neither Grace nor I will defend either one of you in court." Rubbing his eye and pinching the bridge of his nose, he let out a loud, defeated sigh. I pursed my lips, keeping my emotions in check. *What was I thinking?* I couldn't possibly fancy this man on an emotional level. We'd only spent 10 minutes together, and already, irritation radiated from me. He made my blood boil.

I reached down beside the table and grabbed my bag. "I think I'll just go spend the night in my room."

"No." He stood, rattling the cutlery. "Look… I call truce."

"You call truce?"

"Do you seriously think we're incapable of having dinner together?"

I shook my hands in frustration, "Well it's not going great so far!"

He glared through me, smoke practically exploding from his ears.

"Hiya folks – can I take some drink orders?"

I broke our intense eye contact and took a seat back at the table. "2 shots of tequila, please, a water, gin and tonic, and a Guinness."

"All for you? And what will yer man be havin?" The waiter, Colm, questioned.

Amir eased back into his seat, his eyes watching my every move, "That'll be all. Thank you." He said, addressing Colm, his stern demeanour unyielding, devoid of any hint of a smile.

I released a breath, attempting to expel all the negative energy from my lungs in an effort to calm my anxiety. A dinner. A one-on-one dinner with Amir. It was a lot to take in. I fidgeted, tugging my dress down and absentmindedly picking at a loose thread to distract myself. While I busied myself, I noticed Amir remained silent. Glancing up a few moments later, I found his intense gaze fixed on me.

"So, tequila? We're on the hard stuff tonight." He remarked.

I swallowed; my mouth suddenly dry. "Yep." I replied, needing something to ease my nerves and unwind. My heart still raced, and a touch of queasiness lingered.

He huffed and stroked a hand through his hair. Glancing around our quieter corner of the restaurant, even though it was relatively empty, the whole situation felt suffocating.

"Look-" He hesitated and held onto his breath for a moment. "Let's put everything behind us. Have dinner. Have drinks. Charge it to the business card… and then call it a night."

The idea sounded tempting.

"Separately-" He added, panic evident in his eyes.

I glanced at the vacant table to my left, "You want me to move to another table? Jesus…"

He was probably right to be fair. It was for the best. We'd eat each other's words and spit them back out all night long. I grasped my cutlery, ready to make a move when…

"NO! Christ!" He pinched the bridge of his nose. The thing he always did when he was stressed.

"What? What now?"

A low laugh, rumbled from his throat.

"What?" I asked again.

He laughed louder, unsettling me, "I meant..." he managed to say between laughs, "I meant go to bed..." more laughs, "separately."

Oh. OH.

My cheeks heated, "Obviously." I replied nonchalantly.

An awkward, intense silence hung between us. He shuffled in his chair, adjusting his t-shirt that clung to his body, teasing me with glimpses of the abs underneath. "So... uhm... tell me about your life before Spotlight?"

As the drinks arrived, and maybe thanks to the tequila, a normal conversation finally began.

***

To keep our conversation flowing, I kept the drinks flowing. Honestly, it was more about calming my nerves than really craving the booze. He was good. He had a way of asking questions and pulling answers out effortlessly. It got under my skin. By the time dessert rolled around, my hormones were doing somersaults. How could such an intelligent, interesting man also be so irritating and impossible? He even suggested we order two different desserts and split them both. *Dreamy.*

"Oh look at that..." He grinned when Colm sat a chocolate lava cake in front of us.

"You aren't getting a bite of it." I declared, diving my spoon into the cake like it was the last one on earth.

"I'll be right out with yer apple pie in just a moment." Colm promised before disappearing.

The chocolate melted in my mouth and I couldn't help but moan in delight. "Mmmm – ah – no!" I swatted away his spoon with mine, and suddenly we were in a full-on dessert battle.

"You agreed to share." He pointed out.

"That was before I tasted it." I shot back, savouring each bite like it was a revelation.

He dug his spoon in, fighting mine and picked up half the dessert before shoving it into his mouth. I huffed in response.

"That was a childish move."

He rolled his eyes, savouring the victory and chocolatey goodness. Without missing a beat, I lifted the remaining cake and defiantly finished it off.

"You know – " he said, wiping his lips with a napkin, "I would've responded earlier, but my mouth was too full."

I covered my mouth, trying not to choke as he made me laugh.

"If you're trying to hide the chocolate on your lips, I already saw it." He said with a grin.

My eyes widened as I laughed, still covering my mouth, "You're lying."

He shook his head, passing me his napkin. "There you go."

I furiously wiped at my lips, noticing the white cloth napkin go brown, a surge of embarrassment washing over me. Licking at my lips behind the cloth, I couldn't detect any lingering chocolate. "Is it gone?" I slowly pulled the napkin away, praying I wouldn't embarrass myself further.

"Yep. You got it." He reassured, a soft smile on his face.

Colm arrived interrupting the moment, "Here is yer apple pie folks. Sorry for the wait."

"I don't think I can eat another bite." I said, almost simultaneously with Amir's, "Maybe we should get it to go?"

He nodded, "Alrighty – I'll get it boxed up. D'yas want coffees or teas? Or just the bill?"

"Just the bill, please." Amir replied.

A few minutes later, Colm returned. Amir pulled out his wallet and stared counting euros. "Here you go." He slipped the cash into the black leather case holding the bill.

"Perfect. D'yas want a receipt?"

"No. All good. Just the pie." Amir responded.

Colm nodded and vanished.

"Do you not need the receipt to expense it?" I questioned.

"I'm not expensing it." He replied, finishing his drink.

"What?"

He shook his head casually.

"I'll give you half then." I fumbled in my bag, searching for my purse.

"Anna-" The sound of my name instead of the usual teasing nickname 'belle' made my toes curl. "My treat. I had euros to use anyways…"

I bit my lip, uncertain how to respond. I appreciated him paying, of course, but I didn't want to give him any kind of upper hand. I didn't want to owe him anything. His gesture also made the dinner unintentionally feel like a date.

"Ok well… lets head out into town then and I can buy us a few drinks?" I suggested, attempting to level the playing field.

"Perfect. Let's go." He stood up, pulling on his leather jacket. "We need to get you a coat first."

We.

"Here's yer change and pie." Colm appeared, handing Amir his cash.

"Oh no keep it." He insisted, placing a hand over Colms. The gesture evolved into into a solid handshake.

"Ye sure? It's thirty euro too much."

"Mhm. Best meal I ever had." He smiled, patting Colm on the back, "Thanks so much."

***

"Take the pie." He forced it towards me. I lifted my hands in response.

"I don't want it." I turned towards my door and slid the room key in. "You keep it."

"You'll want it later when you're drunk."

I paused for a second, he did have a point, but then again, he footed the dinner bill, so the pie was rightfully his. "I typically don't crave apple

319

pie when I'm drunk. I prefer chicken nuggets."

He rolled his eyes and shoved the pie towards me again, "Aren't you supposed to be a vegetarian?"

"FLEX – Flexitarian."

"That's not a thing."

"It's a thing for me."

He huffed, "Ok – fine! I'll keep the pie, but if you're drunk later – don't come begging for it. You had your chance."

I hesitated, contemplating whether I should accept it. His eyes playfully teased me. "Fine." I said, opening the door to my room, giving him no satisfaction. "I'll meet you in five. I need to find a coat and fix my makeup."

"You might want to get rid of the chocolate on your chin too." He chuckled, sauntering down the hall, "Meet you in reception."

"What?" I called out. I closed the door behind me and rushed to the mirror, where I saw, there was in fact a sizeable blob of chocolate on my chin that he had allowed me to parade through the entire hotel with. If I didn't laugh, I'd might have cried.

***

A knock on the door interrupted me as I was in the middle of fixing my foundation.

I walked to the door, already knowing Amir would be standing outside. "It's been twenty minutes." He huffed as soon as it opened.

"I need two more." I turned my back, letting the door fall behind me. He stopped it and followed me into my room.

Back at the bathroom mirror, I began dabbing pressed powder over my chin and cheeks. He stood at the door, watching me.

"Stop staring." I glared at him through the reflection.

He swung on his heels and walked into the main bedroom. "Are you fucking kidding me? You have two beds? Paddy and I have to share one."

"Karma." I laughed, picturing the scene in my mind, "Don't go looking through my stuff." I shouted after him, jokingly.

"Hard not to look when it's all over the floor and bed."

Fuck. In my quest to find an outfit earlier, I'd scattered the contents of my suitcase across the room. Grace however had neatly unpacked her belongings and hung her outfit options onto hangers. I wished I could be like her… but alas. I quickly grabbed my lipstick and tossed it into my purse before following him into the bedroom.

He sat on Grace's bed, which wasn't cluttered in clothes… unlike mine.

"They're Grace's." I lied, "She couldn't find what to wear earlier… she's messy."

He nodded, still sitting. "Hmph."

"What?" I questioned, standing above him.

"I didn't take Grace as a lacy black lingerie type of girl." He pointed towards the underwear sitting on my bed, which I'd brought, just in case of emergency.

I inhaled, struggling to find words, "Okay – that's enough sight-seeing, let's go."

Finally, he got up from the bed and followed me out of the room.

As we exited the hotel with no particular direction in mind, I racked my brain for things to talk about. We'd not really spent that much time one on one, especially without arguing. My skin prickled. A reaction caused by the breezy air and the awkward silence which was brewing. It wasn't too cold, but it was Galway so it obviously wasn't too warm either.

Amir cleared his throat, "So does Grace usually wear stockings with that lingerie or-…"

A laugh escaped my throat, not expecting his silence breaking question, "Stop it."

"I'm curious, you know…"

A group of older teens overheard his question as they passed by us, and casted amused glances our way. They giggled just as I did. I slapped his wrist, embarrassed.

He nudged me back, playfully shoving me to the side, "Just so I can prepare Paddy – you know. I wouldn't want him to have a heart attack from the sight."

"It would be a shame not to add some stockings and heels." I added, relishing in the playful, childish banter. The thought of dressing up for Amir crossed my mind, and I felt a flutter in my stomach, wondering about his reaction.

He raised his brow and puckered his lips in contemplation. "Hmmm…"

I averted my gaze to the starlit sky, avoiding eye contact with him to prevent my cheeks from turning crimson. The sky was cloudless, but stars shone brightly.

"Do you think Paddy has a thing for Grace?" I thought back to their flirtation.

"Do you not?"

I shrugged, "I kind of got that vibe, but – who knows. I've never seen him with a girlfriend before. He's been single for as long as I've known him."

"You might be jumping the gun a bit. Just because he flirted with her doesn't mean he's making proposal plans." Amir chuckled. I shoved his arm again.

"Hmph…You're the one thinking he's going to see her in lingerie and stockings."

"Touché." He replied, as American as ever. No-one in Ireland ever said 'touché,' and I couldn't help but enjoy his unique phrases.

The melodic tones of folk music poured out from a pub across the cobblestone street, blending with ambient singing, shouting and cheers.

"Anyway, let's grab a drink." He suggested, gesturing towards the pub. I followed, my mouth watering at the prospect of another gin.

Among a small crowd outside the pub, we waited to get in. A diverse mix of accents filled the air – North and South Irish, English, Australian, and, of course, Amir's unmistakably… but also deliciously American one.

"It's so busy." He remarked, checking the time on his phone - 10.50pm.

"Shall we try the next spot?" I suggested, surveying the stagnant crowd.

He nodded.

The next three bars proved just as packed. At one spot, a bartender handed out pints of Guinness through a small window hatch, allowing people to drink in the street. Everywhere was bustling. I scanned the surroundings, trying to decide our next move, and spotted a Tesco Express. "This way."

Trailing behind me, he sighed, "I doubt anywhere will have space. Maybe we should head back to the hotel. It wasn't as busy."

I paused, facing him. "We're going to do something totally Irish."

He tilted his head, "Okay?"

"We're getting a carryout and drinking in the park."

***

We scanned the shelves debating what alcohol to buy. "Is this even legal?" Amir asked, lifting a bottle of red wine.

"Totally." I assured, flashing a not-so-innocent smile as I took the wine from his hands and returned it to the shelf. "How about some cans?"

"Didn't peg you as a beer drinker."

I lifted a can of premixed pina colada, "They have other cans too…" The can, not refrigerated, felt warm against my hands. *Perhaps not the best choice…*

"Trashy," he coughed into his hands.

I shot him a questioning glance. "What was that?"

He shrugged and walked back towards the wine. "Nothing."

"This entire situation is a bit trashy... any suggestions to make it less so?"

Amir scanned the aisle and, without a word, headed towards a fridge stocked only with white wine. He gestured for me to join him. "See if you can find...a... New Zealand... Sauvignon Blanc."

I snorted in response. "Seriously?"

"What? It's the best type of white wine." He shrugged nonchalantly and continued his search. The air of pretentiousness exuded from him, but in an obnoxiously alluring way. He grasped at the fridge handle, breaking the vacuum seal. "Here..."

His hands presented a cold, condensation-drenched bottle of wine. It made my mouth water, even though I'd never tried that specific wine before. He turned to me, holding the bottle. "This looks good to me."

I nodded, saliva building in my mouth. A drink was definitely in order after our bar-hopping adventure.

"No complaints... That's a first." He mumbled under his breath, just loud enough for me to hear. The smirk on his face hinted that he wanted me to catch it.

"I haven't tasted it yet. But I'm open-minded."

"Oh yeah?" He raised an eyebrow and snorted.

Without uttering another word, I walked off towards the checkout, with him following behind, wine in hand.

"Do we need straws?" I asked, glancing back at him.

"No." he looked at me as if I had five heads, "Why? Are you afraid of... how did Paddy say it... swapping spit?"

Ignoring his remark, I continued walking. The cashier greeted me with a tired smile. It was late, and the shop was relatively empty as most people lingered in the bars and restaurants. Not many, I presumed, were opting for a carry-out in the park when they could be dancing in a pub surrounded by culture and craic. Amir joined me a moment later, holding the wine and a large packet of salt & vinegar crisps – as if we hadn't already eaten enough. "Just these, thank you."

She scanned the items, "D'ya wanna bag?"

"No – it's okay." I replied, sliding the items into my handbag. Before I could pull out my purse, Amir had already paid with his Apple Pay.

"Oh – you didn't have to do th-" before I could thank him, he interrupted.

"Thanks." He said to the cashier, throwing his arm over my shoulder and pulling me out of the store. We walked back over the cracked pavement, his arm still draped over my shoulders, in a comfortable silence. I led us towards a park not too far from our hotel.

"Looks a little damp." I commented, leaning down to feel the grass. Thankfully it wasn't too bad... but before I could say anything further, Amir had taken off his large coat and placed it on the ground.

"We can lie on this." He suggested, spreading it out.

"Won't you be cold?"

He shrugged nonchalantly and sat. It wasn't too bad outside. The evening air was mild, without breeze and the sky was empty of clouds, adorned with a multitude of stars. Thankfully, there were no signs of another rainstorm. I lifted my handbag between us and pulled out the wine. Amir opened the packet of crisps.

"I don't know how you can eat another bite." I laughed, unscrewing the top of the wine. I lifted the bottle to my nose. It was sweet and delicious, but I had no clue what it smelled like specifically, as I was as clueless about wine as I was about... sports.

Amir swallowed his mouthful of crisps, "Couldn't help myself. Your chips are just better here."

"They're called crisps." I corrected. I lifted the bottle to my mouth and took a swig. It tasted as nice as I expected.

"Chips." He bickered, taking the bottle from my hand. A smile graced his face as he drank a mouthful. He looked at me, his eyes glowing. "So good."

"I give you credit – the wine is great. But these are crisps. Not chips." I said, taking one from the packet and crunching. The salt tingled my tongue.

"Agree to disagree." He rolled his eyes.

I laughed and looked up at the gorgeous sky. The fresh air smelled like the grass had recently been cut. It was a perfect night.

"Have you any thoughts about your next episode?" He asked, curious.

"I only recorded my last one 24 hours ago." I lay down fully, covering my eyes with my hands, "I don't even want to think about it. I feel like it's all my friends ask me these days. It's all I think and talk about." I peeked from behind my fingers to see him watching me. He leaned down onto his side.

"Although, what's with your comment on yesterday's episode? You told me to change it to funny first date stories and then didn't like it."

He shrugged, "You don't always have to take my advice. I'm not... always... right. I am 99% of the time but-"

"But you're my boss, so of course I'm going to take your advice."

He laughed, "your boss." He repeated the words on his tongue, as if tasting them.

He took a sip of the wine and passed it back to me. I sat up for a second to drink and then reclined, gazing between him and the stars.

"I actually thought it was good advice too. It's hard turning my actual life-experiences into life-lessons." I sighed, feeling the weight of other people's expectations on my chest, "I don't know – I'm not complaining by the way – I'm so grateful for the show and I absolutely love recording it." Panic washed over me, he was my boss, and here I was moaning about my problems.

He laughed and stroked a hand through his hair before aligning his eyes with mine, "Relax. You don't need to reassure me of that. This isn't a performance review – it was a genuine question. Friend to friend."

"Oh, so we're friends now? Interesting." I was sickening myself with the constant refusal between the two of us to call truce, but it entertained me how frustrated he got at my denial. I smiled, enjoying the irritation that washed over his face.

He pointed his finger and narrowed his eyes. The look he gave me lit a fire deep below my belly button. "Anna."

I swallowed.

"Do me a favour?"

I nodded.

"Shut the fuck up." He said, not breaking a smile.

I hesitated for a second, words on the tip of my tongue dying to be said. We stared at each other, energy flowing between us. I took a long, thoughtful deep breath, calming the nerves somersaulting through my veins and said it.

"Make me."

He shook his head, a smile breaking his calm, collected exterior. A moment of silence began, where neither of us knew what to say, do or what came next.

"You have no idea how… badly I want to…do that." His voice deepened, resonating with longing. He leaned down, closing in some of the distance between us. "So…" My breath caught in my throat as he placed his thumb over my lips, "so – so bad." He admitted, still holding back from the desire of something unknown.

His thumb traced a path from my lips, past my chin and unexpectedly wrapped his entire hand around my throat, applying pressure that stopped me from moving. My nervous system went into overdrive, awakening every part of me that I'd been fighting to hide. Struggling against the mild constriction, I instinctively tilted my head upward, silently urging him to bridge the gap with a kiss. The teasing had worn thin; I craved resolution. As he released the pressure on my throat, I grabbed his shirt and pulled him closer to me. "Do it." I stressed, breathless.

He teased me for a moment, keeping his lips a centimetre from mine while our breaths mingled together. "No." He mumbled, releasing his grip. "We can't."

The desire between us, mixed with the heightened beating of my heart was so intense it made me feel like I could pass out.

"We can." I breathed.

Finally, his lips sweetly graced mine, slow and cautious, making my whole body beg for more. A jolt of electricity surged through me as his hand came to cradle the back of my head. His fingers tangled in my hair, anchoring me in place as our mouths engaged in a deliberate, sensual dance. He held the reigns, orchestrating every movement.

My whole body, mind and soul needed this. It was tangible. NOT a figment of my imagination. He pulled back for a fleeting moment, eyes closed, and I immediately went into panic waiting for him to run off or end things. To my immense relief, he took a shaky breath and resumed our pursuit but with such fervour that it made my body shake. I moaned as he pulled on my hair and sucked on my bottom lip, hungry, as if to draw blood. My hands wandered. One behind his head and the other grasped his shirt, which I was yearning to tear apart. I needed us to be closer, to dissolve the space between us. Amir withdrew again, gasping, and mumbled, "fuck..." before crashing his lips to mine once more. His dark and dirty accent echoed through me, sending tingles down my spine.

I lifted my leg to the side, and wrapped it round him to eliminate the remaining distance. He slid his hand underneath my back, effortlessly lifting me towards him, and in an instant, he skilfully flipped us so that I found myself on top. The transition felt seamless, leaving me with a weightless sensation, accentuated by the breathlessness from my relentless pursuit of his lips.

I could feel the heat emanating from his body, which only fuelled the fire within mine. As time passed, our desperation deepened. Each second felt like an hour as we lost ourselves in the moment, completely consumed by the fiery passion between us. I wanted nothing more than to succumb to him, completely, but the sudden realisation dawned on me – we were in a park, in public and anyone could be watching us. I reluctantly withdrew my lips, gasping for a much-needed breath. As Amir looked into my eyes, I couldn't help but feel a sense of anticipation for what was to come. Something much more intense.

CHAPTER TWENTY-ONE

Sure look

Definition: it is what it is

He sighed and gently eased me off his lap. I sensed a subtle energy change and began to wonder why. Another, more frustrated sigh escaped him "Fuck." He mumbled, his voice low and shaky.

I wasn't sure what to say. If he was regretting the moment we shared, I didn't want to know. I looked up at the starry sky and closed my eyes, needing a moment to reflect on what had just happened. Walls began to rise within me as I overanalysed every nuance of his reactions.

"Anna?" His voice drew my attention, and I turned my gaze towards him. He was already staring, a fixed look of concentration on his face. "You okay?"

I nodded, "Are you?"

He exhaled deeply and paused before speaking which made an uncomfortableness creep up my spine., "I just don't want things to end badly between us."

I sighed and sat up to face him. Whilst I understood his reasoning, I also disagreed. "Why think about it ending? It hasn't even started."

"No – I" He stopped himself, deliberating his words heavily before he spoke. "I don't think we should – start anything."

My heart sank, settling heavily in the pit of my stomach. "What do you mean?"

"I'm leaving soon... like really soon and we work together and you're seeing that millionaire guy and-" his words tumbled out in a hurried rush. "And on that dating app-"

I stopped him, "I'm not seeing anyone. Especially not Tom. I went on one date with him... but that's all."

"His name's Tom?"

I nodded. "Yeah, so that's irrelevant."

"I just don't see how this would work." He shook his head, "Your show is all about dating."

I knew what he meant. I hated that I understood what he meant. My cheeks burned with embarrassment.

"I wouldn't want you to talk about me. But also, I get that that's your job. Selfishly... I also couldn't stand hearing you talk about dating other people if we were to start something here. I'd obviously want you to myself."

I took a swig of the wine to alleviate the growing soreness that was building at the back of my throat. Crocodile tears. I was fucked. "I understand." My voice sounded as deflated as I felt inside.

"I also have my own issues to work through too." He lifted the wine from my hands and took a sip. The confession surprised me, and I wanted to know more. "It's not you. I'm not looking to date anyone."

I reclaimed the wine back from his hands, downing two large mouthfuls. "We should have bought a few more bottles."

He laughed. A low chuckle.

"Do you want to talk about it?"

He sighed, "I never have."

Curiosity bubbled in my body, dying to know the details. I stopped myself from prying. "You don't have to." *But please do.* I wanted to understand him. "But you did previously say that... um... you don't date at all. Why?"

The air hung heavy with silence for a while before he decided.

"Uhm." He began, and his Adams apple moved up and down, "My mom passed away when I was six. Cancer." He avoided looking at me as he spoke, "Then my dad re-married."

My heart ached for him. He was usually emotionless, cold, and dead-pan. But now, I could tell by the crease upon his brow and how he bit the inside of his cheek, he was suffering.

"Uh – so – my stepmom raised me until I was twelve... and then one day I came home from school and she'd disappeared. We never saw her again but after months of searching and involving the cops – my dad discovered she'd ran off with someone else and was living in Texas." He laughed, as if still in disbelief. I placed a hand on top of his clenched fist, only for him to shiver and pull away almost instantly. "There were no signs. She just left."

Uncertain of what to say or do, I acted on impulse and shifted, strad-dling him. I wrapped my arms around him, giving him the tightest hug possible so he couldn't move. He sucked in a deep breath, "I – you don't have to – I'm fine."

I lifted my face from his shoulder and looked him dead in the face. His eyes showed me a shattered soul who had not only lost one mother figure – but two. I didn't speak, just pressed my lips gently to his. He responded for a brief moment before pulling away, whispering, "We can't do this Anna." I nodded and swallowed my feelings instead of speaking them.

"I never want to end up like him." He confessed, his eyes hardening,

"I can't."

As Amir attempted to push me away by placing his hands on my hips, I cradled his face. "I wouldn't do that to you."

His fingers tightened on my thighs, "He was broken. Not once, but twice. He didn't deserve it." Shaking his head, he entered a reflective state, "He provided everything - our home, money, food, love. He gave them everything. Yet, no-matter what he provided; it didn't stop him from being left broken. Completely utterly broken."

"That's just awful. I can't even imagine…"

I knew in that moment, no matter what I would say – nothing would be right. Nothing would alleviate his pain.

I sensed his chest rising and falling with deep breaths. It seemed like he was resisting fully feeling the pain in my presence.

His hand moved up my back before gently pulling my neck backward so I could face him. He crushed his lips into mine, kissing me deeply, fiercely. I returned the fire and tangled my hands in his hair, forcing us closer. His fingers burned into me, pushing my crotch into his and sending electric currents through my body. I kissed him hard, sending signals of the words I didn't know how to speak. We expressed ourselves through passion, an exchange of energy.

His hand ventured up my thigh, gripping my ass with intensity. His body communicated desire, but the anger and frustration behind his movements signalled that it shouldn't be happening. It felt wrong.

As much as I didn't want to, I pulled away, extinguishing the fire that burned between us. "Sorry." He mumbled, his tone devoid of emotion. He placed his thumb on my swollen bottom lip, eyes still drawn to them. I held his hand against my face.

"You don't need to say sorry. I understand."

It frustrated me to no end. I understood completely. He carried the weight of a deep fear. A fear of getting hurt just like his father had. And he was moving back to New York. There was no point in pursuing anything. We'd both just end up broken.

I shifted out of his lap and stood up, stretching my body.

"Oh shit." He grumbled, realisation hitting him. "The wine."

The spilled wine adorned the grass, leaving only a few sips in the bottle. I lifted it, shaking out the little liquid that was left. A smile broke across my face. We'd been too consumed by each other that we hadn't noticed anything else around us, including a half bottle of wine seeping into the soil.

"Why don't we go pick up another bottle and then go back to the hotel?" Amir proposed.

"Yeah – it's a bit chilly." I replied, although truthfully, I wasn't feeling the cold at all. What I really needed was to retreat to my room, away from him, so that I could fully process everything.

"I think I've drank enough today to be honest." I added. More alcohol would only cloud my thoughts and intensify my emotions. I sighed and pulled out my phone to text Grace and inform her that we were on our way back.

"Yeah. Probably best to call it a night. It's been a long day."

We walked back towards the hotel and silently observed the people we passed along the way. The streets were alive with celebration, but I felt as if I were mourning. The lingering sensation of his lips on mine persisted as we walked side by side, resembling strangers in the midst of a lively crowd.

***

An Irish folk band were performing in the corner of the hotel bar, flooding the entire venue with music. I breathed in, hoping for some mental clarity.

We walked towards our rooms, making small chat – talking about nothing of importance, he moaned about the worn décor of the hotel corridors. Dull. Faded. In need of a revitalising touch.

Amir insisted he walk me to my room, even though I assured him I'd be fine alone.

"Maybe we should eat that left over dessert." He chuckled.

I forced a smile, "I couldn't eat another bite. You can enjoy it and your crisps too." I presented the packet from my bag.

"Chips." He playfully snatched them from my hands. "They're chips."

I rolled my eyes, too tired to partake in another battle. "Ok, well enjoy your chips. I'll see you in the morning? I think breakfast is served until 10am." We paused outside my door.

"I'll be too full." He teased and munched on another 'chip'.

I laughed, "Can you hold this?" I asked and passed him a handful of lipsticks, lipliners, a mini mirror and comb. "I just need to find my key."

A sinking feeling settled in my stomach. I knew in that moment that I'd left it in the room. "Shit."

"What?" He asked, looking at me with wide-eyed confusion.

I bit my tongue and pulled out my phone to call Grace. It went straight to voicemail.

"You forgot your room key, didn't you?" A teasing smirk appeared on his face – the expression I liked least. It usually meant he was gearing up to take the piss out of me…

"Don't." I pointed at him.

He lifted his hands in defence. They were filled with items from my bag and the crisps, which made the situation slightly funnier. "I won't." His eyes crinkled in the corners as he tried to stop himself from laughing. "I wish I was surprised, you know."

"Shut up." I banged on the door, hoping Grace was inside.

Immediately, I was met with a response – that neither of us were expecting.

Moaning. Headboard banging. Skin slapping.

I swirled around, my eyes widening in sheer disbelief and instinctively clapped my hands over my mouth.

"Is that- " He murmured, his eyes as wide as saucers.

"Shhh!" I slapped his arm. My heart pounded uncomfortably in my chest.

Amir pressed his ear against the door, attempting to confirm the reality of the situation. When he tried to speak, only a small chuckle escaped his lips, accompanied by a disbelieving shake of his head.

Another loud, feminine moan echoed through the closed door. I panicked and pulled at Amir's arm, inadvertently causing the items he held to clatter loudly to the floor.

"Dickhead," I scolded, dropping to the ground to retrieve them. The sounds from within the bedroom abruptly ceased, "Fuck." I whispered. "Come on!" We gathered the scattered items and hastily retreated down the hall. The absurdity of the situation made me giggle. "Oh my god." Amir exclaimed, "I can't believe it."

I shook my head, bewildered. "I can't cope! This is so unlike her."

Grace, essentially the reborn Virgin Mary, rarely engaged in such activities. If she met someone, she'd totally make them wait at-least five dates before anything got remotely spicy.

"He's obviously doing something right – I mean – did you hear that?"

"Shut up, shut up, shut up. I don't want to think about it." I covered my ears and squeezed my eyes closed, "I can't deal with two of my best friends – well – you know…"

"Fucking?"

I shuddered. "Mhm."

Amir, finding amusement in my discomfort, stroked his chin in contemplation. "So…"

"So?"

"So, if they're occupying your room. Where are you going to sleep?"

And then it dawned on me. I shook my head, "I – I'll just have a cup of tea in the bar and… I can wait it out."

He raised his eyebrow, "Wait it out? You really think they'll be finished anytime soon?"

I bit my lip.

"Because I know, for a fact, that Paddy hasn't been laid in a hell of a long time. He's not leaving her anytime soon."

I pinched the bridge of my nose. Amir looked at me all cocky and American. It irked me.

"What are you suggesting?" I asked.

He cocked his head to the side, "You can sleep in my bathtub."

"Thanks for the 'kind offer' but I'll just pay for another room." I rolled my eyes and walked off, leaving him in the corridor.

"You think I didn't try that this morning when I realised, they'd given Paddy and I a bed to share?" He shouted after me. "They're fully booked. It's culture week!"

I bit my tongue so hard, I thought I might draw blood. I turned on my heels to face him. "Fuck." I whispered, seeing the amusement painted across his face.

He strolled towards the lift and pressed the button going up. It opened two seconds later, and he gestured from inside. "You comin' or what?"

I hurriedly ran up the hallway, muttering curses under my breath, and stepped into the lift, accepting the reality that I was stuck with him for at least another eight hours.

He supressed a laugh, lips pressed together. I shook my head at him, then focused on the lift doors. Two floors later, the doors opened, and I followed him to his room. His cologne lingered in the air, and I swallowed, attempting to squash any flicker of desire within me.

Yes, I was in his room.

Yes, we were alone.

Yes, typically this would be an opportunity for something... more.

BUT.

Despite past desires, I needed to Ctrl+Alt+Delete any hope for the future.

"Could I get a pillow or something for the bath?" I asked.

He emptied his jean pockets, tossing his wallet and phone onto the hardwood desk. "Yep." He chucked a pillow my way, a teasing smirk playing on his lips. "Bathroom's right there- "

Amir pointed to the only door in the room. "I'd never have guessed that." I teased.

"Enjoy your sleep in the bath. You can run the hot water if you get cold." He laughed and began to pull off his shirt. My cheeks went red, seeing a slight glimpse of his skin.

"Goodnight." I turned on my heels immediately and opened the bathroom door, preparing myself for the most uncomfortable sleep of my life.

I closed my eyes and took a deep breath, unsure which curse word to unleash. *There was no bath.* Only an old, shitty, standing shower.

CHAPTER TWENTY-TWO
Parful

Definition: a big compliment

"You okay there?" Amir's voice echoed, and I turned to see him leaning against the doorframe, looking infuriatingly tall and handsome. It angered me. He swallowed his laughter, sensing the annoyance on my face.

"This isn't funny!" I shook my head, frustration boiling within, and chucked the pillow at him.

He struggled to stop himself from laughing as it collided with his bare torso. Nothing could make a dent in his abs, never-mind a damn pillow. I made a conscious effort not to let my eyes linger on him.

"Look, it's fine. I'll crash on the floor." He raised his hands in defence.

I pulled at my hair, feeling a pang of guilt. He brushed off my non-response and moved towards the sink. "Need some toothpaste?"

I nodded, extending a finger for him to squeeze a drop onto. Side by side, we stood at the sink. I did my best to brush my teeth with my finger. He shot me a foamy toothpaste smile, making me laugh.

"Stop that. I'm mad at you." I glared at his reflection.

He threw his head back in laughter, spitting the remaining toothpaste into the sink. "Mad at me? Be mad at Grace and her lingerie and stockings…" He winked before exiting the bathroom. "And heels! Can't forget the heels!"

I stopped myself from screaming. *You told me there was a bath I could sleep in!*

"You can leave if you want, I'm obviously not forcing you to stay. BUT I think you'd sleep better in a bed than the hotel bar." He shouted from the main room. "And we're both sensible adults, right?"

I took a deep breath. The woman in the mirror blushed, courtesy of either the wine or the half-naked man who had been the subject of many inappropriate daydreams. Maybe, just maybe, this was meant to happen. Perhaps he had dreams too. Why else would he strip off his shirt so swiftly? I debated.

Bracing myself, I asked, "Do you have a t-shirt or something I could wear. This outfit won't be too comfortable to sleep in."

Peeking around the door frame, I saw him grabbing a bottle of water from the mini fridge. Pausing, he raised an eyebrow at me. "Sure."

"If you don't mind-" I added, nervously.

He threw me a dark navy t-shirt without another word, and I disappeared into the bathroom to change. I stripped down to my bra and panties – before slipping the t-shirt over the top. It fell just below my ass, meaning if I was to bend over… accidently of course… he'd get a decent view. I lifted it to my nose. It smelled exactly like him.

I pulled my hair into a high ponytail; thanks to the bobble I'd left on my wrist from earlier in the day and tried to make myself a little more desirable. Amir was making a pathetic excuse for a bed on the floor, which made me laugh.

"I think we're capable of sharing a bed, don't you? As you said… we're both sensible adults… right?" I asked.

He'd removed his jeans and was only wearing a pair of black boxers. I refused to over-analyse his appearance as I knew I'd lose the game I was playing. He looked up at me, eyes wide. A smile appeared on his face, and he laughed as he shook his head, "Oh Anna…"

"What?" I played innocent.

He lifted a pillow from the ground and threw it at me. "Go to sleep." His eyes devoured me up and down, telling me that if I didn't sleep, I would be in trouble. Curiosity bubbled low in my tummy.

"Mhmm…I'm really tired…" I fake yawned and stretched my arms above my head, lifting the t-shirt in the process. I watched him through squinted eyes. His eyes widened taking in my lace underwear underneath.

I walked towards the bed, ignoring his eyes that were following me. "Do you have a spare phone charger by any chance?" I asked and swung round to face him.

He was right in front of me, our bodies inches apart. His hand fluttered to the back of his neck as he took a step back. My breath caught in my throat. My heart stopped thumping.

He lifted his finger and pointed it at me. His breath shook as he spoke, "Don't."

I shook my head, "What?"

He stepped back again, cautious but calculated. A smirk formed on his face, giving away the teasing thoughts that were running through his mind, like mine.

"What?" I repeated and took a slow step towards him. I wondered if my heart was beating at all. All I could hear was the exchange of our lustful breathing. He looked warily at me.

He shook his head at me and inhaled deeply, debating his next actions. "It's taking… all… ALL… of my self-control to not…"

"What?" I whispered for the third time, closing the distance. I looked up at him.

His eyes glared into mine, and then to the wall behind my head. I carefully pressed my hand against his arm, hoping to draw his attention back to me.

"Anna…" His voice was dribbling with desire. *Oh-so-sexy.*

"Amir." I responded, full of expectation.

He lowered his face to mine and hesitated to close our lips together. "We should go to sleep." He whispered, "I don't want to hurt you."

I nodded and gently removed his hand from my face. Embarrassment flooded through my body. There I was, half naked, with a look in my eyes that practically begged him to fuck me.

"I just wanted a phone charger." I replied, monotone. Reality sunk me again, and I felt embarrassed at my disrespect towards him, especially after learning about his history less than an hour earlier. But the way he walked me to his room… took off his shirt… the way he looked at me. I couldn't help but wonder.

He bit his lip, "right" and turned to dig through his bag.

As soon as some distance was created between us, I felt an immediate coldness within the room. I climbed into the bed and under the duvet to try warm myself up.

A moment later, Amir passed me a charger and I plugged it into the socket beside the bed. "Thank you." I smiled. "Sorry for overstepping."

His expression was dull and depleted, matching the new energy shift in the room. "You're not overstepping at all. Are you okay with me sleeping there?" He asked, gesturing to the opposite side of the bed.

"Yeah of course. Are you okay with me here? I can take the floor?" I sat up fully and crawled out from beneath the duvet.

"No – shut up – it's fine." He laughed, settling into bed beside me, taking up twice the amount of space.

"Just don't hog the covers and we'll be fine." I teased, trying to lighten the mood.

"Okay but just stay on your side of the bed." He warned. I rolled my eyes in response.

He chuckled and turned off his bedside lamp, leaving only the dull yellow light from the lamp on my bedside to illuminate the room. I laid my head on the pillow, facing him, our faces just inches apart. "This feels strange for me." I confessed.

He laughed, "Because I'm your boss? You've told me 100 times already."

Rolling my eyes once more, I replied, "To be honest, I'd forgotten all about that. I wasn't thinking about work."

"Oh... What was it then?"

"It sounds stupid now." I hid my face under the covers as my cheeks went red.

"Tell me." He insisted, trying to lift the cover but my grip was tight. "Anna!"

"I've just never slept beside a man... who didn't want to... be intimate with me." I confessed, the unease settling in my stomach. The weight of instant regret pressed me into the sheets.

I heard him take a deep breath, likely debating how to respond.

"Anyways - goodnight." I interjected and turned the opposite direction.

He sighed grumpily, pausing with words lingering on the tip of his tongue, "I want to. But I'm... struggling right now." He admitted, gently stroking my hair, "Battling between desire... and... my moral compass."

I turned back towards him, "what does that even mean?" It embarrassed me how frustrated my voice sounded, clearly revealing my longing for him.

"I want you - fucking - badly. But if we were to start this, you know it would only have to end. And then we'd both be hurting." His eyes held only the truth. "But also – if we did. I'd never let... our first time... happen like this. I have way more respect for you than that."

I wasn't sure how to respond.

"So don't think that I don't desire you. It's important we have this conversation. We're both adults and have to make adult decisions sometimes that suck. I'm sorry." He sighed.

"Yeah."

"Let's be sensible and get some sleep." He leaned forward and planted a kiss on my forehead, "goodnight."

"No. No. No." I scolded him, playfully hitting his chest under the covers. "You can't kiss me on the forehead and expect me not to fall in love with you." I laughed, half joking, half serious.

He laughed heartily, "I can't believe you just said that."

"I can't believe you just DID that." I jested.

He groaned and buried his head under a pillow. "Oh, shut up. Go to sleep."

I rolled to the other side and flicked my light off. Unsurprisingly, I felt like I spent half my night gazing at the ceiling, hesitant to move in case I disturbed him, and anxious to sleep for fear of snoring or talking unconsciously. Meanwhile, Amir lay beside me, softly breathing and occasionally emitting light snores. At some stage in the early hours of the morning, I faded into a light rem, only to wake up a few hours later to an empty bed.

I jumped up feeling the void beside me. My initial thought was that my snoring could have woken him and drove him out of the room. He was nowhere to be seen. I slid out of the sheets and lifted my phone. It was almost 9am, but I didn't focus too much on that. He'd text me.

AMIR
In the gym – in case you wake up.

He'd sent the message 40 minutes prior, so I decided to quickly shower before he returned. As the hot water trickled down my spine, it seemed to wash away the remnants of my troubled sleep. The tension, stress, and anxiety I was previously feeling seemed to gradually dissipate, as if being carried away by the steam rising around me.

I could sleep beside Amir. We hadn't crossed any boundaries. We navigated through the initial awkwardness and defined our non-relationship. It was fine. I was going to be... fine.

Anticipating the softness and cosiness that awaited me, I stepped out of the hot shower and reached for a towel. *There's just something about hotel towels.* These ones were larger and much fluffier than the regular towels I owned. I grabbed a second towel and shook some wetness out of my hair. It was damp and beginning to curl, which meant I'd need to get back to my own room asap or else risk Amir seeing me resembling a wet, frizzy dog.

My skin surprisingly looked good, considering the alcohol I'd consumed. My eyes were a tad smoky from left over eyeliner, but nothing I couldn't handle. I tapped my phone, seeing ten minutes had passed since I'd checked his text and decided I'd need to quickly get changed and make my escape.

As I opened the door, the unexpected happened, shattering my plan. Amir entered the hotel room precisely as I emerged from the bathroom in nothing but my towel. My cheeks flushed crimson, my stomach plummeted, and my feet felt rooted to the floor. He was covered in sweat; his black gym shirt sticking to him.

"You're awake." He acted unfazed, but also didn't move.

I nodded, swallowing the saliva that had built up in my mouth. A sliver of light trickled in from a break in the curtains, lighting his face beautifully. He really was crafted by god. This was a dangerous game... That I thought we'd stopped playing. I was 100% we had stopped playing.

He shook his head and ran his tongue along his teeth. It felt like he was eating me with his eyes. I contemplated dropping my towel to give him a better view.

Suddenly… "Fuck it."

Before I could fully process his words, he had me pressed against the wall and our lips collided. An invisible magnetic force seemed to draw us together. His tongue intertwined in mine, as one of his hands clawed at my wet hair. The air around us crackled and popped with electricity as we pulled each other closer, inhaling the scent of passion and surrender.

My hands roamed freely, exploring the contours of his body. This was it. *We surrendered.*

"Oh…fuck." He moaned against my lips, pushing my body further into the wall. I pulled at the bottom of his sweaty t-shirt and in a swift movement he removed it.

He sucked on my bottom lip, making me moan, before moving his lips to my neck. I felt like I couldn't breathe. His fingers toyed at my towel as he mumbled, "I think this needs to go."

Without a second of thought, I dropped the towel, revealing my fully naked body. His eyes darkened looking me up and down before he attached his lips to mine once again. "So beautiful." He moaned. "So fucking beautiful."

I replied with a moan, wrapping my arms around his neck.

Suddenly his hands grasped my ass and he lifted me, allowing my legs to wrap around him. He pressed his body into mine, allowing me to feel his erection through his shorts. *This was fucking glorious.* "Oh my god, Amir." I mumbled, in between his tongue fighting with mine.

"OI! Is it safe to come in?" A voice echoed through the door, startling me to my core. I gasped in shock and Amir dropped me to my feet.

Our eyes widened and suddenly I felt way too naked.

"One minute Paddy." He rasped, pinching the bridge between his nose. "Shit." He whispered, panic-stricken eyes darting towards me. "I'll get rid of him. Pretend you're in the shower."

I nodded and closed the bathroom door behind me. The hot water couldn't soothe me this time, not even if I was to place the showerhead between my mother fucking legs. The desire within me burned only for Amir.

CHAPTER TWENTY-THREE

Can't cope!

Definition: Unable to comprehend/deal with a situation

I looked like a shaggy dog, but my hair – was the least of my worries. Even with my ear pressed to the door, I couldn't quite hear Paddy and Amir's conversation thanks to the running of the shower behind me. The door slammed closed a few moments later and Amir knocked to tell me to get ready for breakfast.

He huffed as we walked down the corridor, visibly frustrated. "Don't tell Paddy anything happened between us. He just asked me, and I said no."

"Yeah, okay." I found it strange but accepted his request.

He pressed the elevator button and we waited in silence. Something uncomfortable was lingering in the air. "Are you alright?" I asked.

"Yeah, yeah." He replied quickly, shaking his head.

I began to panic, wondering if he was already regretting our kiss, but decided not to press him further.

We walked into the buffet to find Paddy and Grace sitting in silence. Something was up. Large cups of coffee sat in front of both of them, a refreshing sight after a day full of booze. Paddy had an almost empty plate, just a few toast crumbs leftover, and Grace looked to be struggling through a plate of plain pancakes. No syrup. Not even butter. I giggled realising she was sporting her first ever proper hangover.

"Good morning." I said, attempting to sound as cheery as possible.

Grace looked up at me through her heavy lashes. She looked woeful. "Morning." Her voice croaked as if all her energy had been sucked out of her. "Why are you in such a good mood?"

"Anna, coffee?" Amir asked.

I nodded, "please."

He headed to the coffee machine in the corner. I took a seat at the table facing Paddy. "I'm not saying you look bad but maybe walk around backwards today so you don't scare anyone."

He responded with his middle finger, whilst taking a large gulp of coffee.

"You struggling?" I asked Grace, trying to hide the smile on my face, "Drink a lot last night?"

She nodded her head and with a shaky hand lifted some water to her chapped lips, "I don't want to talk about it. I might throw up."

"Which part do you not want to talk about? You two having loud, passionate sex for the entire hotel to hear or the alcohol?"

She spit out her water and began to choke loudly. Amir appeared back at the table, quickly sitting our coffees down before patting Grace's back to help her breathe.

"What shite are you talking?" Paddy asked, shock across his face.

Grace shook her head and continued to cough into a napkin. It took her a minute to breathe as normal, but once she could, she set the facts straight. "We didn't have... sex."

I rolled my eyes, "Amir and I both heard you – it's fine."

"Well, that's impossible considering it never happened." She replied, totally serious.

"Yeah – we didn't have sex." Paddy laughed.

Amir cleared his throat, "Respectfully…" he gestured towards Grace, sitting down at the table, "We did hear you… but we left as soon as we realised what was happening."

He passed me my coffee. I elaborated, "Last night, Amir walked me back to my room and I was trying to find my key outside when we heard through the door you two… you know… loudly. So, we left and I stayed in his room." I spared the details, not wanting to embarrass Grace further.

She looked at Paddy and back at me, "Babe, I can assure you… whatever you're insinuating… didn't happen. We didn't get home until after 5 am this morning."

Now I was really puzzled, "So-"

"Someone else was in your room?" Amir asked, eyebrows furrowed.

"It sounds like you've got the wrong room." Grace asked. "405?"

I nodded… but now I was questioning my own sanity. I was still unsure if I believed them or if this was a big elaborate lie to hide their truth.

"I walked Grace back as she could barely stand up, made sure she got in okay and then I went to my room… only to find you two in my bed. I lay on a sofa in the reception. I've not slept yet." Paddy elaborated.

Amir bit his lip, holding back a laugh.

"No. no. This can't be right." I shook my head in denial. "I called you, you never answered." I pointed at Grace, frustration building.

"My phone died." She shrugged, "I didn't think you'd have any problem finding our room…"

A waiter momentarily interrupted our dilemma by setting some toast and butter onto the table. I had zero desire to eat.

"I don't understand. You're both lying!"

Paddy laughed, "Nope."

"I was the most drunk I've ever been last night, but I can assure you – I'd remember that happening." Grace's face went red. "You went to the wrong room."

I buried my face in my hands as the feeling of total embarrassment crawled up my neck. Amir was probably raging at me. "I can't cope." I mumbled. His laughter echoed over the table and warmed me slightly. He rarely laughed. I looked up from behind my hands to see him with a smile on his face, taunting me.

Raging
Definition : angry

"Did you know I was at the wrong room?" I asked, completely flustered.

"Obviously not!" He replied and rolled his eyes, "I thought you'd know your own room number. I wasn't even looking."

I released a frustrated sigh and stuffed a piece of toast into my mouth, attempting to stifle the urge to scream. "Sorry." I apologised, my words muffled by the food.

"I'm not." Paddy's grin could be seen from 10 miles away, "You two hated each other 24 hours ago, and somehow, without us directly meaning to, we got you to share a bed."

He raised his hand, and Grace joined him with a high-five.

"Nothing happened-" Amir interrupted their celebration, raising his hand at Paddy. In it was the butter knife he used to butter his toast. It was mildly threatening but carried an innocently sexy vibe.

"Yeffah- we just sflepfttt-" I mumbled and swallowed my toast. "Sorry-" I wiped my mouth with a tissue. "We just slept." I reiterated, much clearer than the first time. "Obviously."

Despite the fact that I sensed their scepticism, I let Amir steer the conversation in a different direction whilst I continued to shove toast into my mouth. It would take some time for me to shake off the embarrassment caused by my room number blunder. Amir chuckled heartily as he regaled Grace and Paddy with the details of our unexpected adventure to Tesco and a carryout in the park the night before – an experience far from the Galway encounter he had anticipated.

***

I lay in the hotel reception, notebook in hand, debating if there was anything I could write for my episode whilst Grace sat peacefully on an armchair beside me, reading a gossip magazine.

"I feel as woeful as the stories in here." She held it up, "This is why I don't drink." She moaned, flipping the pages. "Why on earth does anyone drink… when you know you're going to feel like this the day after?"

Her revelation made me snort with laughter. I tapped my pen on my notebook, struggling to conjure up any interesting thoughts. "At least you slept. Poor Paddy."

After breakfast he retreated to his room for a nap, eyes hanging out of his head. The only problem was that we were due to check out in two hours, so his slumber wasn't going to last long. Amir had decided on a walk to take some photographs of the city, which Grace and I had declined, deeming cups of tea and a morning after recap to be more important.

"We were blitzed." She burst into laughter, "It was such a funny night. He dropped his chips and goujons on the way home and we ate them off the ground. I almost choked from laughing so much."

"You what? Who are you and what have you done with my best friend?" I laughed.

This wasn't like her at all. Miss Sensibility needed a new nickname.

"It was such good craic." She struggled to stifle her laugher. I couldn't help but relish seeing her in such high spirits. "Anyways, your turn…. Be honest. Did you and Amir… you know? Sleep together?"

I shook my head, "Nope. I mean – we had a moment. Moments, I guess. We kissed, but that was it."

"That was it? Anna, that's still significant. You were biting each other's heads off before Paddy and I ghosted."

I rolled my eyes, "Thanks for that by the way."

"The KISS?" She waved her hands, pushing me to elaborate.

I shrugged, feeling deflated for some reason. "I don't know. It was like a moment of weakness."

"What are you on about?" She sat up fully, placing her magazine on the coffee table. "Elaborate?"

"He's afraid of commitment." My mind retraced our conversations. "And everytime something… happens… between us, it's like he instantly regrets it."

"Anna…" Grace sighed, disappointment evident in her tone. "What's right for you, won't go past you. Don't shut down to the idea. He might just be a slow mover."

"No – I just." I paused, unsure of how to explain my thoughts, "I want someone who knows that they want me completely and jumps head first… not someone who desires me sometimes but other times isn't sure." I explained. "Like, one minute we're kissing and it's the best feeling I've ever felt, but in the next minute he's shutting down and has me questioning everything. That's not how… love… should feel? Right?"

She nodded, biting her lip in contemplation. "Right."

"I thought you'd be proud of me for realising all of this?" I replied, "I'm trying to be sensible and avoid getting hurt."

"No. No – I am proud. I've been telling you this for a year… but" she hesitated, "I just thought this was different. The way he looks at you."

I shook my head. I'd started biting my nails without realising. "I'm just trying to be realistic."

"Yeah. I get you. God… I thought I was going to hear a 'sex-pidition story' as Olivia calls it." She laughed lightly, trying to brighten the mood. "Didn't expect you to have a revelation overnight."

I shrugged, unsure what to respond. Grace got up to refill our pot of tea at the bar, leaving me alone with the blank pages in front of me.

Maybe it was the alcohol that was probably still in my system that was making my mind think so deeply, but I began to scribble all of my realisations down, unleashing a major truth.

I'm not satisfied. I'm extremely fed up with the relationships I'm allowing myself to get into. I know what I want now. More importantly, I know what I don't. I've reached a point where I'm ready for a meaningful relationship. It's taken me some time to decide what I truly desire, but I'm determined to leave behind the 'realm' of unsatisfying connections and men who wouldn't DIE for me.

"Am I interrupting?" I looked up to see Amir looming over me. Hastily, I slammed my book, praying he hadn't caught a glimpse of my notes.

"No. How was your walk?" I asked.

He took a deep breath and sank into a chair beside me, "Cold. It's chilly out this morning. Managed to capture some cool shots though." He gestured towards the film camera in his hands.

My mind was racing, I wanted to write. I had so many thoughts running through my head and he consumed many of them.

"Have you enjoyed your first time in Galway?" I inquired.

"Yeah, for sure. It's gorgeous..." He trailed off, then lowered his voice to almost a whisper before continuing, "Listen, can we talk about this morning?"

My heart quickened, bracing for whatever he was about to say. "Yeah...it probably shouldn't have happened. Right?" The words stumbled out of my mouth uncontrollably.

He looked taken aback, casting doubt on my own words. But then his gaze intensified, hardening "Yeah." He admitted, affirming my thoughts, "We need to nip this whole... thing," he motioned between us, "in the bud."

I nodded. As his words sank in, my heart sank too, stung by the reality of it all. But deep down, I acknowledged the truth. Our back-and-forth wasn't healthy; it was for the best. I was no longer going to offer myself on a silver platter to someone so emotionally unavailable. He wasn't going to provide me with what I truly wanted.

"Hey guys." Grace interrupted, tea in hand. I was beyond grateful for her presence, but the tension lingered in the air. "Back from your walk already?" She asked him.

"It was cold."

***

Paddy groaned as he dragged his luggage to the car out front. "I still think we should stay an extra night." He mumbled through a yawn.

"That's because you've only had around two hours sleep… some of us have work to do today." Amir chuckled.

"But it's gods day. We don't work on Sundays." I joked.

"You're not driving, sit in the back." Amir ignored me and took the car keys from Paddy, who obliged instantly, seemingly ready to fall back into a slumber.

"You have a licence?" I teased Amir.

"Yes, and I'm also insured on this company car – any more questions?" He snapped unnecessarily, eyebrows creasing.

I raised my hands in defence, "Jesus, I'm just kidding with you. Calm down."

"Funny." He said, deadpan.

He turned to Grace and lifted her luggage into the boot of the car. She thanked him and then slid into the back seat beside Paddy… leaving me with no option other than to take the seat beside Mr Grumpy Pants.

"How come Paddy gets a company car?" I decided to keep prodding him, wondering what was bubbling under the surface to make him so reactive. I thought we were on good terms.

"Tax avoidance probably." He shrugged; his expression devoid of emotion. I debated if I should push him further but decided to keep my mouth shut.

Grace interjected, "Who's hungry? There's a great seaside spot not far from here."

"Me." Paddy mumbled. His eyes were closed but apparently his ears were awake.

The next hour was spent mostly driving in the wrong directions, until we eventually found the little café she had mentioned. It was old and quaint, didn't look like anything special, but it served the best Irish stew I had ever tasted.

With our bellies full, all three of us dozed off on the drive home as Amir took the wheel, tuning into an entrepreneurial podcast while he drove. Whilst I normally would have been interested, fatigue took over, and I didn't want to be the only one awake, fearing either awkward conversations or more bickering between us.

***

Tom Beckham? I rolled my eyes, seeing a display of cards and a couple of boxes on my desk. I assumed that the arrangement I arrived to on Monday morning was from him, because, well, no one else had ever sent me presents. However, I was extremely shocked to find them addressed to "THE BELLE OF BELFAST." I hesitated, holding off from opening the contents for a moment, panic settling in – how had he figured out my identity? This would end my career.

I glanced around the almost empty office. Only Lisa: an editing assistant, sat live listening to our morning show which was being recorded in Studio C. It was only 8.12am, and I had arrived early, eager to continue planning for my upcoming episodes. No one was nearby to offer me any information on how the letters and packages had ended up on my desk, so I opened the first one, hoping for answers.

Dear Belle of Belfast,

I fucking love you bitch.

I paused. The letter was definitely not from Tom… unless he had turned into a young, probably 20-something-year-old woman.

Sending a tweet is not enough so I wanted to write a letter – yes a letter, are we back in the 1900's? I don't know, but it seemed fitting to express my gratitude! Thank you for your honesty, thank you for your stories, thank you for your advice. I've been going through a really tough time, getting over my ex of 3 years. He cheated and I lost a lot of my self-worth after finding out. I honestly was debating taking him back, as I missed his company. I was feeling incredibly lonely… especially late on a Friday night, when Netflix wasn't cutting it and I felt sick scrolling my phone. All I wanted was to cuddle him and have someone to tell my secrets to again. Lying in an empty bed each night depressed me and I kept wondering 'what's wrong with me? Why did he do that?' But then, every Friday night I began listening to your show. And last Saturday morning, I woke up feeling different. I had the realisation that nothing is wrong with ME. HE was in the wrong. HE cheated on me. HE made the decision to ruin our relationship. Nothing changed. I'm the same person I was when we first started dating. I've found peace in that realisation. Just because I feel lonely, doesn't mean it's bad to be alone. So much growth has come from me being alone, girl! I'm a work in progress and that's OKAY! Listening to your show has made me feel a little bit less lonely and a lot more hopeful.

Anyways, I hope this reaches you and you realise you're making an impact with your show. Thank you,

Shannon. X

Tears streamed down my face uncontrollably as I stood in complete shock, my heart swelling with gratitude for Shannon and her kind words. Glancing at the pile on my desk, I felt a tremor in my hands. If every piece of mail contained such heart felt messages, I knew I wouldn't be able to compose myself. Seating myself, I gingerly began opening the envelopes, unable to restrain the tears that mingled with the ink on the pages. A few unopened boxes remained, revealing skincare products, a wellness journal, and even vitamins from brands wanting promotion?

"Who are you trying to impress coming in here so early?" Paddy's voice startled me, causing me to drop a bottle of apple cider vinegar gummies that clattered to the floor.

"Shut up," I muttered just audibly enough for him to hear. "I just – I have so much work – my episodes." I couldn't string a sentence together.

"What's all this?" Paddy questioned, raising his eyebrows as he examined the scene. He lifted a candle I hadn't noticed and took a sniff. "Does this smell like 'birthday party' to you? It just smells like cheap vanilla to me."

I smelled the candle and shuddered at its sweetness.

"Hold on a minute…" He took in my appearance, "Why do you look like you've just finished reading one of your sad romance novels?"

I shot him a playful glare, but his words struck a chord. In that moment, I became acutely aware of the mascara stains on my cheeks and the lingering puffiness around my eyes. "Stop."

"Wait, let me guess…did you finally start watching Greys Anatomy?" his expression a mix of mock concern and amusement.

I couldn't help but snort, shaking my head at his stupid antics. A nervous chuckle escaped me.

"Right, what's the craic? What's wrong with ye?" he enquired, his tone shifting to genuine concern.

I bit my lip, glancing towards my messy desk. "I'm fine."

His curiosity got the best of him as he started lifting some of the letters, but I swiftly snatched them away, guarding them like precious secrets.

"Private!" I scolded.

"Oh, love letters? From whom?" He snatched them back.

"No! Uh…" I grabbed them from his hands.

"Then what?" he pressed.

"Fan mail… I guess." I shrugged, attempting to downplay the significance of the unexpected flood of attention.

Paddy paused for a moment, his brow furrowing, and then a wide smile took over his face. "Fan… mail?" He questioned, a tinge of disbelief lingering in his voice.

"And PR packages…" I attempted to hide my excitement. "That questionable candle was from a brand wanting to get involved in my podcast… and so is this." I lifted a t-shirt from the pile on my desk. "and these…" I passed him some discreetly packaged supplements, a glimmer of mischief in my eyes.

"Sexual enhancement." He halted his reading, eyes widening further. "You're having me on…"

You're having me on

Definition : You're joking

I laughed, "what the fuck?"

"What the fuck is right…" He squinted at the small print on the back and then back to me, "let me read a letter."

"Absolutely not."

"Anna…"

"Paddy."

He unleashed the full force of his puppy dog eyes.

"No."

***

No more settling for subpar men. No more ignoring red flags. No more sacrificing my own desires to please others. No more being left feeling confused or insecure at the actions of those I like. No more wondering am I good enough?

The heartfelt fan letters had sparked a serious sense of introspection. Seated on my sofa at 8.52pm, I crafted and revised my episode notes. A gentle backdrop of meditative music accompanied me, aiding in weaving my thoughts together. I took a moment to think about what I truly desire.

I've always focused on wanting to be loved… but never thought in depth about the type of person I would like to receive that love from.
- *What are his values? Do they align with mine?*
- *Do our long-term goals and aspirations align?*
- *How well do we communicate with each other?*
- *What do our conversations consist of?*
- *What common interests do we share?*
- *How does he emotionally support me?*
- *How does he express affection?*
- *How can I trust him?*
- *How can I depend on him?*
- *How do our lifestyles align?*
- *What are his habits or routines?*
- *How does he handle our fights or disagreements?*

I had always treated this unknown future partner as a prize I'd have to achieve and win over, but maybe I should flip the switch and start thinking the other way around.

This made me reflect on my parents' relationship. They met in school, and my dad won my mum over with dinner dates, cinema outings, and walks in the park. No late night 'booty calls' or drunken regrettable kisses. Instead, he expressed his affection through heartfelt letters, surprise sticky notes hidden in her car, homemade dinners, and the occasional bouquet of flowers. Effort. It was all about genuine effort – a demonstration of his love for her. I loved hearing about their relationship as I grew up. My pen hit paper again.

When I envision having children someday, I want to share with them the story of how I met their father — a tale of respect and genuine care.

I refuse to recount a narrative where he played games with me or casually chose me from a pool of options. I won't tell a story of uninspired Netflix and chill invitations instead of thoughtful, well-planned dates.

My writing created a moment of clarity that prompted me to reflect on my self-worth.

I want my future children to understand that their mother held high standards. Maybe not in the beginning, but she learned.

Over time, she made the decision on what she would and wouldn't accept and she decided that she was worth more than what was being offered to her.

A teardrop landed in the midst of my words, marking an ending and a new beginning. It was a transformative tear, that turned into a full-blown emotional sob, cleansing and empowering, paving the way for a journey of self-discovery and renewed strength.

CHAPTER TWENTY-FOUR
Jesus, Mary and Joseph

Definition: when an Irish person feels compelled to use the Lord's name in vain, they often use the entire holy family

On Tuesday evening, around 5:30 p.m., Grace and I lounged on her sofa, disappointed by a text from Olivia cancelling our dinner plans. There was no excuse attached, but we assumed she was with her 'new boo.'

Grace yawned, stretching herself out. "They have me working overtime until my notice period is up. I'm wrecked," she said, her eyes fluttering closed.

Then my phone buzzed again.

"What's she saying now?" Grace mumbled. "If she's changed her mind, tell her I don't want to go anymore."

But the message wasn't from Olivia.

TOM BECKHAM

Hey Anna, just wanted to reach out and see if you received the chocolates? I'm really sorry that our first date happened the way it did. I've been cursing myself ever since. I'd really like to see you again if you'd give me the chance x

"Grace…" I passed the phone to her. "Read this."

She yawned again, sitting up to view the phone. "Oh."

"I don't know what to do." I admitted.

"Those words would make anyone want to go on a date." She chuckled, "But remember his actions… the red flags."

I huffed and began typing a reply.

ANNA

Hey, thank you for the gift. I'm not sure that we should see each other again, but wish you well x

"Oh, I didn't think you'd actually send that." She grasped at my phone. "He's typing."

TOM BECKHAM

I totally understand why you'd say that but the person on our 'first date' … if you can even call it that… was not the person I am. I stupidly got drunk after bumping into old friends, after a really hard day. Would you consider meeting me for dinner and I can show you what I mean?

I bit my lip, flattered by his chase "Maybe I should?"

Grace stared back at me, equally contemplating the option.

"I mean… it's just a dinner." I added. "I feel like a hypocrite though, I just wrote my episode for this week and it's all about standards… here look."

I pulled out my notebook from my bag and flipped to the page with my questions on it.

"I get what you mean." She shrugged, "But you... everyone deserves a second chance. You can't determine the answers to these questions from one date. Also, it's good he's even acknowledged that the first date was a bit... shite."

I paused, thinking about it. "True."

"Plus, our plans tonight just got cancelled, see if he's free?" Grace suggested.

"Am I too keen offering myself tonight?" I debated.

"Not for the right person."

ANNA

Okay. Second chance... don't blow it. I've just became available tonight? Last minute bite?

He replied within an instant.

TOM BECKHAM

Thank you. I'll have my driver pick you up for dinner at 6.15pm? or is that too soon?

ANNA

Okay. Sounds good.

"His driver?" Grace giggled, "How fancy."

I rushed home and quickly shed my casual work clothes. As I pulled on a pair of leather trousers, I noticed the fuzz on my legs... I only had around thirty minutes; I didn't have time to shave, and besides, he wouldn't be seeing me naked anyways. I changed my bra from comfort to push-up and tied a blue silk top around me. Adding a trendy gold necklace and earrings, I slipped on a pair of simple black heels and managed to quickly fix up my makeup and add some curls to the bottom of my hair before receiving a text informing me that a car was outside.

After swishing some mouthwash around, I dashed out the door. An all-black BMW awaited outside my apartment building. I stood awkwardly at the side of the road, wondering if this was for me. The driver rolled down the passenger window.

"Uh, hi, for Anna?" I asked.

"Yes, sorry!" He hurried out of the car and opened the back door for me to slide inside.

The interior was all leather, emitting a musky scent, but in a good way. "Are we picking up Tom?" I asked the driver.

"I've been told to drop you at his home," he responded, catching my eye in his rear-view mirror.

His home? Like... Portrush? That was over an hour drive away..

"Oh, okay. Thank you." I pulled my phone from my bag, wishing I would have solidified plans with him.

ANNA
I assumed we'd be having dinner in Belfast haha x

TOM BECKHAM
I'm not in the city centre, hence why I sent a car. I've a surprise for you when you arrive. It'll be worth the journey. I promise babe x

Babe? My stomach grumbled, a blend of hunger and anxiety twisting inside me. *This wasn't how I envisioned spending my night... How would I even get home?*

As we drove down the long driveway to his home, it appeared even grander than before.

Tom awaited outside his front door, clad in black trousers and a baby blue polo shirt. With the car's halt, he descended the steps and graciously opened my door. I stepped out, trying to maintain some semblance of grace with his assistance.

"You look stunning," he murmured, leaning in to kiss my cheek.

"Thank you," I replied, surprised I could hear his words amidst the thunderous pounding of my heart. "So do you."

He did look good, undeniably so, but not quite Amir's calibre. I quickly dismissed the comparison from my mind.

He led me inside his home, which felt even emptier than I remembered. The hallway lacked the bustling presence of people this time, and only faint music played in the background.

"I bought a plant," he said, gesturing to an aloe vera plant that seemed dwarfed by its oversized pot.

"Nice." I replied, mustering enthusiasm. "I love aloe vera."

He seemed genuinely pleased with his plant, so I didn't want to dampen his spirits.

"I had a friend come over and prepare us some dinner," he added, his hand gently guiding me towards the kitchen. "Thank you again, for giving me a second chance."

A friend? I thought tonight would just be the two of us...

As the heavy door swung open, my senses were enveloped by the enticing aroma of whatever was cooking. A dinner table stood in the centre of the room, adorned with a white tablecloth, and graced by a vase filled with pink flowers, evoking a scene straight out of a romance movie. My heart fluttered at the sight.

"Anna, this is Jean Ocreux. He's a local chef. The best, in my opinion," Tom introduced.

A short, bald, and plump man turned towards us. With a name like Jean Ocreux, I was expecting a French or perhaps Italian accent, but...

"Awhk here, ya tol' me she was a beaut, but lord jaysus, where have you been hiding this one?" He asked Tom, with the most outrageous

Northern Irish country accent. I had to listen closely to even understand him. It gave me a flash back to my dinner with Amir a few days earlier. I quickly shook the thought from my head.

Tom laughed, "That's for me to know, and for you not to find out."

I smiled, finding Jean very endearing.

"Right love, hope you're starved!" he said, rubbing his hands together.

"Very." I replied, feeling a bit lightheaded from hunger.

"Sit yourselves down sure. I'll be over in a minute with your dish and then I'll be on my way, so I will."

Tom turned to me and wiggled his eyebrows, eliciting a laugh from me. He pulled out a chair and gestured for me to sit down. As I settled in, a thought crossed my mind: *one positive aspect of dating an older man... how chivalrous they tend to be?*

"Would you like some wine?" Tom asked.

"Ah, yes. That would be lovely," I replied.

"Red or white?"

"Give that girl anything other than white wine and I'll have your head!" Jean shouted from across the kitchen.

I'll have your head
Definition : I'll kill you (joking, of course)

Tom chuckled and rolled his eyes. "White... okay?"

"Yes, perfect," I giggled.

He poured my glass as I pondered what to talk about. "Thank you for sending me chocolates," I said. I'd already thanked him by text, but it was the only thing that came to mind.

"It's the least I could do. We didn't exactly start off on the right foot," he replied with a smile.

"Right, so I hope ye like fish. D'ye like fish?" Jean shouted.

"I do," I giggled, deciding that admitting I was almost always a vegetarian would be an insulting idea.

"Well, thank Christ for that!" Jean exclaimed as he lifted two plates and walked towards us. "Fettuccine with seared scallops and prosci- prosciu - HAM."

"He asked me what I wanted him to cook, and I just said something impressive and tasty," Tom laughed.

"Well, get eating! There's a chocolate torte in the fridge for after. If it's shite, don't bother telling me!"

I snorted and laughed into my wine, rather impolitely.

"Thanks, Jean," Tom replied, rolling his eyes.

And with that, Jean left through the back kitchen door. When Tom and I were alone, I could hear the soft jazz music playing in the background. The pasta looked delicious, so I couldn't resist diving into the dish.

"Wow," I breathed, savouring the flavours. "I give you credit... I've no clue how you threw this together so fast."

Tom nodded, his eyes rolling back in satisfaction. He seemed to be enjoying the food as much as I was. He waited until he swallowed before he spoke, "Gorgeous."

I nodded in agreement.

"And Jean's the best. Always comes to my rescue."

"Do you cook much then?" I asked, my eyes darting to the expansive kitchen.

"Do you count toast as cooking?" he laughed, taking another bite of scallop.

"No," I replied.

"Fair enough. I can barely cook that without burning it..."

Our evening continued with effortless conversation. He spoke passionately about his deep love for Northern Ireland and his work within the tourism board. As he shared his visions for the future of the country, I couldn't help but feel a surge of hope and pride. We transitioned from the dinner table to the sofa, where we enjoyed some coffee alongside our dessert. Jean had kindly left a caramel sauce, which we drizzled over the indulgent chocolate torte. I felt at ease with this version of Tom; he was a far cry from the man I'd met in the Dirty Onion.

He fed me a piece of dessert on a spoon, then leaned in... slowly. My heart quickened as his lips met mine. He tasted almost as divine as the food we'd just enjoyed. The absence of cigarettes and the presence of chocolate was a welcomed surprise. In a swift motion, he pulled me onto his lap, so I was straddling him. His hands pressed into my back, drawing me closer to his body as we kissed. He withdrew his lips from mine and began to trail gentle kisses down my neck and along my collarbone. Opening my eyes, I felt him harden beneath me.

I panicked, realising one major pressing issue... I hadn't shaved. I couldn't have sex with him if I hadn't shaved!

Lifting my palm to his cheek, I gently moved his head towards mine, attempting to pause the moment. However, he interpreted this as a signal to resume kissing me, so I allowed it. I let him explore my mouth while his hands began undressing me, starting with my top. He flipped me onto my back, hovering over me, and began placing fervent kisses along my breasts, which were spilling out of my bra.

"You're so sexy," he mumbled, his words sending a shiver down my spine.

I pushed my body into his, savouring the compliment.

His hands continued to explore lower down, brushing up and down my thighs still confined by my leather leggings.

"Do you want to go upstairs?" he asked.

Did I? I wasn't sure...

I pulled his face back to mine and kissed him again. He was a great kisser.

"Let's go upstairs," he said, standing up and extending his hand, making the decision for me.

As I followed him up the staircase, I realised that I did want to do this. I wanted to have sex tonight. My only reservations were our age gap and how he had acted on our last night together... but maybe older meant more experienced... and maybe more experienced meant I'd finally get my first orgasm from a man?

***

Unfortunately, I wasn't so lucky. I lay beside Tom in bed as he panted, trying to catch his breath.

"That was - that was amazing," he said, wiping sweat from his brow.

I lay in silence, covering my body with the quilt. He had lasted approximately two minutes and seemed completely unaware of my clit or any other sensitive spots on my body.

"Let's go again. Get on your knees! I'm going to use you until you explode all over me... you want that?" he questioned, spanking me. "I want you to cum around my cock. Understood?"

Shocked at his newfound stamina, even though his words made me feel totally 'icky,' I decided to go along with it, hoping I'd get more pleasure as he took me from behind. But alas, one minute later, he was spent... and I was growingly frustrated.

"Fuck..." He moaned, rolling onto his side. "That was something."

My eyes darted around taking in the sheer size and emptiness of the room. An armchair sat in the far corner, but that was the only furniture besides the bed and bedside tables. A huge TV was hanging from the wall, pointing directly at the bed.

My thoughts were interrupted as Tom let out a sigh and leaned over to kiss my shoulder. "You're so great. We should make this a regular thing."

I turned to him, perplexed. "What?"

He didn't respond. "Tom?"

"Like, you come over a couple of times a week," he replied, opening

370

his eyes. They were hazy, clouded by the aftermath of our encounter. He placed his lips on mine, preventing me from asking any further questions. His hands began to massage my breasts as we kissed, but my mind couldn't focus. I was overwhelmed by the entire night—the car journey, the chef, the disappointing sex...

"Tom..." I pulled away briefly, but his lips chased mine, kissing me deeper and pushing me harder into his bed. He removed his hand from my breast and pressed it between my thighs, massaging... *oh, maybe he does know where my clit is after all—never mind, spoke too soon.* He inserted a finger inside me.

"You like that?" he mumbled against my lips.

Yeah, I suppose... I thought, but my clit would be preferred. He continued kissing me, breathing deeply against me as he pumped his individual index finger in and out.

"Mmm, you're so wet for me."

If you keep dirty talking like that, I'll dry up...

Suddenly, he pulled his lips from mine and began to dive under the covers. He kissed along my stomach, which made me feel totally self-conscious, and then placed a kiss directly on my clit. *Oh wow.* Before I could enjoy the feeling, he moved his mouth further down.

"Oh no, go back." I moaned... but he mustn't have heard me as he continued to move lower. As he pumped his one finger in and out of me, he flicked his tongue lightly from side to side. "Up." I instructed, wrapping my fingers in his hair, hoping I could move him towards my clit. He stayed positioned in the same spot however, which quite honestly, wasn't doing anything for me.

"You like it rough don't you, dirty girl?" He mumbled. "I'm not sure you're ready for two."

He withdrew his index finger and then proceeded to enter two fingers inside of me, which honestly didn't make much of a difference. Usually, I'd be moaning for his satisfaction and faking an orgasm to make it end...

but that was the old Anna.

I lifted the covers up fully, catching his eye.

"This isn't working," I sighed.

He continued pushing his fingers in and out of me, but it made zero impact. His smirk made my stomach twist—not from pleasure, but from distaste. "How about this?"

He lifted his fingers from within me and then flashed three of them, insinuating that would be better.

I closed my legs, halting his access. "No."

"No?" he questioned, confusion covering his face.

"You aren't doing it right," I explained, opening my thighs, and pressing my fingers on the most sensitive spot in an attempt to demonstrate.

He raised his eyebrows and licked his lips. "Oh I like that..." He sat up, tossing the duvet onto the floor behind us. "Keep doing that," he instructed, starting to play with himself while watching me.

I bit my lip and closed my legs again. *That wasn't the aim.* I sighed and wiggled my way off the bed, wrapping myself in a sheet.

"Where are you going?" he moaned.

"To pee."

At first, I took the wrong door and ended up in a walk-in closet, but eventually found my way to the marble bathroom. As I sat on the toilet, I willed the pee to start flowing, trying to mask the sound by humming. The room was undoubtedly huge, with marble his and hers sinks overlooking the back garden, a luxurious bathtub with golden taps, and a massive rain shower... very fancy indeed. My appearance was a bit worse for wear. I washed my hands in the sink and used the water to fix the slight mascara that had run from my eyes.

Returning to the bedroom, I saw Tom sitting up, scrolling through his phone.

"Hi," I greeted.

"Hey," he breathed, tossing his phone under his pillow. "You really had me going there..." His eyes were alive and needy.

"I-I'd love to stay the night, but I have to work tomorrow," I said awkwardly, not allowing him to finish.

His eyebrows shot up in surprise. "Oh." He moved to the edge of the bed, the sheets just about covering him. "My driver can bring you back."

I wiggled on my feet. "Are you sure? I hope you don't think I'm rude."

He sighed. "After what just happened, I can only think of you as a goddess."

I'd never been called a goddess before.

"Here, I'll help you find your clothes," he offered, standing up, completely exposing himself. A flaccid penis was never something I wanted to look at, and especially not now. I turned in the opposite direction and focused my eyes on the floor, scanning for my clothing. I dropped the sheets to my waist in order to put my bra and top back on.

"Here," Tom said, handing me my trousers.

"Oh, I just need to find my underwear now."

I scanned the floor, unable to locate them. Then, I fluffed the duvet, covering the bed... but they weren't anywhere to be seen.

"Do you see them anywhere?" I asked.

"No," he replied, lifting a pillow to check underneath. Something told me he knew exactly where they were... and I didn't know whether to be flattered or disgusted at the idea of him wanting to keep my underwear.

"It's okay, if you find them... uh... let me know," I said, dropping the blanket and quickly pulling the trousers over my legs. *Leather trousers and no underwear. Nice.*

"Will do," he nodded, handing me my heels.

I looked down, dreading putting them back on my feet.

"Could I borrow a pair of socks?"

"Sure," he replied, walking into the closet.

If he was going to steal my underwear, I was at least stealing a pair of socks.

"Do you want a hoodie?" he shouted from the closet. "It's cold out."
Even better.

"Yes, please, that would be great!" I called back.

He returned with a pair of black socks and a navy hoodie. I couldn't imagine him ever wearing it. "Thanks for this, I'll return it soon," I said, pulling it over my head.

He began walking towards the door to the hallway, and I followed. "As I mentioned, we should make this a regular thing."

"What... dinner and sex?" I snorted.

He turned to me as we walked down the staircase. "Yeah, exactly."

"Hmmph," I hummed.

I politely pecked his lips when we reached the bottom of the staircase and began to comb my hands through my hair as he phoned his driver. "He's just at the garage down the road getting a coffee, won't be long. Would you like a bottle of wine to take home?"

I thought about it for a moment but politely declined. He had already gone to great lengths: arranging transportation for me, inviting me over for dinner, trying his best to... make me cum... in his own way. I felt a pang of guilt for my negative thoughts about him. He was a good guy, just not the best in bed. I pressed my lips onto his, expressing gratitude for the night.

Our conversation was interrupted by the sound of a car pulling up onto the driveway. "That was fast," I remarked.

Tom nodded and kissed me once more. I hoped he would walk me to the car and open the door like he had when I arrived, but he stood watching as I hopped down the steps and tiptoed my way across the gravel, wearing his socks. The driver jumped out as he saw me approaching and opened the back door, allowing me to slide inside. I hoped I didn't smell of sex. Tom waved as I placed my head on the window and prepared for a long, quiet journey back to the city.

CHAPTER TWENTY-FIVE

Deadly

Definition: In a positive sense, meaning excellent or fantastic

Honestly, it never really hit me, not even a smidge. I'd often forget that people were tuning into my podcast as I rambled on during recordings, just letting all my thoughts spill out in full-on oversharing mode. But isn't that the whole point? Oversharing, raw and unfiltered?

Then came Wednesday, and my desk looked like a paper storm hit it, all thanks to the Instagram story I shared about my Monday fan mail… thanking everyone who had taken the time to send. The PR packages? Well, they were also piling up, triple to Monday's amount.

Mia was over the moon. She had assigned a sponsorship manager to fire off some emails to the brands enquiring about paid podcast promotion. And as for my afternoon plans? I had a few hours of (anonymous of course) interviews with local news. Can't say I saw that coming. *Deadly.*

Then as my day was about to end...

"I'm at work, can this wait until later?" I hissed down the phone.

"No, it absolutely cannot," Olivia snapped. "You need to tell Tom that you don't work here!"

I chuckled, realising I hadn't informed her yet about seeing him... and my 'sexpedition'.

"He's sent you another present! Some lady dropped it off this morning!" She screamed, clearly aggravated. "I'll bring it over in ten minutes."

"I don't know why he'd send me something when could have just given it to me last night." My mind jumped to the missing underwear, *surely not...* "I'll tell him to stop. Sorry, Liv."

"I'm sorry – did you just say LAST NIGHT? You were with Tom... Tom Beckham last night?"

I rolled my eyes, bracing for her outburst. "Yes..."

"I thought we were friends, Anna! Why didn't you tell me?!" She moaned, "You wee bitch!"

"It was very last minute; he sent a car for me..." I confessed.

I imagined her, sitting at her desk looking utterly shocked. It wasn't typical of me to act impulsively; she'd be impressed.

"HE SENT A CAR!"

"And hired a chef." I added.

"HIRED A CHEF?!"

"We had..." I glanced around, ensuring no one was nearby, then whispered, "sex."

The phone went quiet. I started to worry if the information had shocked her into silence.

"Liv?"

"You're such a fucker! How dare you not tell me this!" She screamed, "I can't believe you!"

I chuckled, "I fell asleep on the way home... I -"

"No excuses. You'll simply have to make it up to me with cocktails."

"Now that I can do… Have you opened what he sent?"

"No, but it looks lavish as usual."

"It's probably a razor and some shaving cream…" I giggled, "I didn't plan on sleeping with him, so I didn't shave."

"Well… no point in peeling a potato if you don't plan to mash it." She giggled. It took me a minute to understand the meaning of her statement. "He probably thinks you're a big feminist." She laughed.

"I mean… I am…but…"

***

Olivia arrived shortly after, a mischievous grin on her face. "You can't NOT open it in front of me," she teased. "I came all this way to deliver it to you."

(She'd caught a 4 and a half minute long uber).

I glanced at the bag she held, heavy with tissue paper.

"Alright, alright," I said, feeling eager to see what was inside.

I carefully removed a neatly wrapped box from the bag and began to unwrap it. As I lifted the lid to peek inside, I immediately closed it with a giggle.

"Oh my god," I exclaimed.

"What? What is it?" Olivia leaned forward, curious.

I lifted the lid again, revealing the lacy red lingerie set nestled inside.

"Oh my fuck!" Olivia gasped, then quickly covered her mouth, realising we were in my workplace.

I couldn't help but continue giggling. "This guy…"

Olivia pointed to a card resting inside the bag. "What's that?"

I opened the red envelope and extracted a plain gold card. Another addition to my growing collection…

Anna,

Figured you'd need a new set

because one went missing.

There's also a gift card, in-case
this isn't your style.
TB x

My jaw dropped to the floor.

"You know, I think I'd accept that gift card as payment instead of cocktails," Olivia quipped.

I was speechless, too shocked to respond. I'd never had a man spend money like this on me. I felt honoured but a little unworthy. Olivia took the card from my hands and scrutinised it while I discreetly stashed the bag under my desk, not wanting to risk anyone seeing anything.

"You must have given him one hell of a blowjob," she whispered.

"Liv! Not the place," I whispered back, mortified. "And if you must know, I actually didn't. Just sex, twice... and then... he went down on me... well, he attempted to go down on me. Honestly, the sex was woeful, but this kind of makes up for it?"

Her eyes widened in disbelief. "I don't get it."

"Don't get what?" I practically jumped out of my skin as Amir appeared behind me. My heart raced... *How long had he been standing there?*

"Nothing," I said, my voice sounding much higher pitched than I expected.

Amir raised an eyebrow, clearly not believing me, but I didn't have the time or energy to entertain him today. I glanced at Olivia, silently plotting my escape. "I'll walk you out."

She arched her eyebrows and refused to humour my plan. "No, no. I know the way. See you tomorrow night."

As she disappeared, I hoped Amir would do the same.

"Are you going to tell me now?" he questioned, still determined to pry the information out of me.

I rolled my eyes and sat back at my desk, ignoring his persistence.

"Come onnnnn."

"It's none of your business – a private conversation. I was literally about to leave the office when she arrived." I replied, attempting to brush him off as I began clicking through my emails. His presence unnerved me, especially when he loomed over me. I avoided making eye contact, or even looking at him.

"Anna... figured you'd need a new set," my head shot up to see Amir holding the golden card. I leaped from my seat, attempting to snatch it back.

"That's private," I snapped.

"It was lying on the floor..." He looked down, noticing the box... which was also open, proudly displaying the red lace lingerie. His face turned from amusement to bright red. "Have your personal gifts delivered to your home address from now on."

"Olivia just dropped it off. I didn't know what it was." I grabbed the card from his hand and dropped to the floor, hastily covering the box with tissue paper and its lid.

I looked up at him towering above me as I dropped to my knees to fix the box. It was an uncomfortably suggestive position. His eyes darkened, and I could sense that both of us were probably thinking the same thing. My lungs felt like they burst. Exploded. Combusted. **Holy fuck.** I quickly averted my gaze back to the floor and stood up, hastily fixing my composure, trying to ignore the pulsing between my legs. He walked off without saying another word.

***

My notebook pages stared at me, covered in scribbles as I tried to organise my thoughts and create a digestible plan for my episode.

What can I say? Where do I start? Mr Millionaire may be kinder than I thought. I'm feeling a bit overwhelmed to say the least. I've never been treated like this before... Wined and dined doesn't even cover it. In the last 24 hours, he's made it impossible for me to forget him; From a romantic dinner date, to random surprise presents.... I'm not sure how to feel. I felt sickly after our 'first date' but this week I feel... kind of different.

I scribbled out the line, realising I still felt a bit sickly. But I just couldn't understand why.

I've never dated a man more than a couple years older than me and I've never had someone buy me gifts. I'm not sure what I've done to end up in this situation.

When I was with him however... It felt like I was going through the motions but not really present in the moment.

I've been asking myself why ever since...

I'm very overwhelmed by the gift giving and the attention to detail... however I don't have the connection I desire with him but these things just take time to grow, so maybe I'm just expecting too much too soon. There's just something holding me back... something keeping my walls up.

I wanted badly to write about Amir as Mr Mysterious; to open up and tell my audience that my head was in a spin because he was haunting me. Every time I saw him, it infuriated me how he was completely untouchable. That we would never be together, we would never share another kiss or another flirty moment.

No-one makes me feel like Mr Mysterious. I don't want to be with him but...

I scribbled out my writing.

I know we will never be together, but I just don't understand him.

And again, I crossed out my words.

I need to constantly remind myself of my new standards and who fits into them. I know one thing for sure – Mr Mysterious isn't cutting it. He never will. So maybe... maybe I need to give Mr Millionaire a bit of a chance? At least he's showing me some effort and upfront about his feelings towards me.

As much as I wanted Amir, I could never act on it or write about him ever again.

Thursday came, and luckily, it was just a half-day for me. My brain was a bit fried from interview questions and the sudden spotlight, so what I really craved was some downtime with Grace and Liv. We decided to meet up at Maggie Mays, sipping on milkshakes and soaking in the atmosphere filled with students. It took me back to our school days, reflecting on how much had changed, yet some things always managed to stay the same.

"Yes, he's lovely, of course he is, but I'm not looking for anything… you know that." Grace said, her eyes rolling dramatically back. She put on the act of annoyance and indifference, but the subtle blush playing out on her cheeks betrayed a different story.

Olivia finally diverted her attention from her phone, placing it face down on the table. "Wait, who are we talking about again?"

"Paddy and Grace! They ditched us for their own little adventure… ended up eating chips off the street, right Grace?" I giggled watching her squirm.

"Ditched us?" Liv inquired.

"Amir and Anna." Grace explained, "We just wanted them to stop bickering and start – I dunno… something."

Olivia's interest piqued, "Hot Amir, from the office?"

I let out a little huff. "How many people called Amir do you know?"

She tilted her head to the side, pausing to think. "Fair point… I know a lot of men but none called Amir. Just hot Amir from your office. And he is H.O.T. Hot!"

"Anyway…" Grace diverted, "Paddy and I are not a thing. So just… bury that thought."

A sudden buzz echoed through the table. Olivia eagerly grabbed her phone, but her excitement deflated seconds later. Mine was tucked away in my bag. Grace's, however, lay on the table. She picked it up, shaking her head, a smile breaking through. It seemed the universe had its own plans for her.

"What?" I questioned.

She turned her phone towards us, revealing a text from the man himself.

PADDY
Fancy a drink on Friday night? Or tea... I know you don't really drink and probably don't ever want to drink again after Galway!

I nearly choked on a sip of my milkshake, "Oh my god!"

"Did you tell him to text me?" She moaned.

"No – I didn't – that's the universe sending you a signal." I giggled.

She shook her head, exclaiming, "No! No! I hate this! How do I let him down?"

Olivia and I couldn't help but giggle at the sheer coincidence of the situation.

"It's just a drink..." Olivia chimed in, "Or a tea... though that might be a bit boring. Go for a cocktail! Get dressed up!"

Grace shot her a frustrated look, her eyes filled with exasperation. "I don't have time for a relationship. I still need to find a new job! And when I find it... I'll need a month or two, at least, to adjust and impress. That's my focus. No men."

"Does it not get boring?" Olivia asked.

"What?" Grace replied.

"Being on a man ban? I worry that just one man would have me bored... I've always kept... a few... on my roster," she said, flicking her straw back and forth, her words hiding something behind them.

"No, it's healing. Cleansing. Peaceful."

"Lonely?" The word slipped out of my mouth before I realised it.

After my unintentional question about loneliness hung in the air, there was a brief moment of silence. Grace looked at me, her expression a mix of surprise and contemplation.

"Lonely?" she echoed, chewing on the word for a moment. Olivia leaned in, curious to hear Grace's response. She sighed, breaking the silence, "Maybe sometimes, but it's a different kind of loneliness. It's intentional, you know? A choice to focus on myself and my goals. And... I'd be okay to get a drink with Paddy and keep it casual, but I wouldn't want to give him false hope for more than that."

False hope. The word struck me for a second, but I chose to ignore it.

Olivia grinned, "A cocktail doesn't mean you're signing a contract for a relationship. Just have some fun without overthinking it."

Grace nodded. "I know, I know. It's just, I've had guys lead me on before and it hurts. The fact that I'm unsure of saying yes is an answer... right? I should be dying to see him."

I didn't know how to reply, but her words stirred something inside me.

"Now... enough about my Friday night plans." Grace, always perceptive, playfully nudged me, a sly smile on her face. "Anna, how's work? Amir? The date with Tom?"

"Oh yeah, what's your episode about this week?" Olivia questioned, still not looking up from her phone, "Give me every detail."

"I've just realised that I need to end things with Tom. The fact I feel so unsure about him..." I mumbled, still caught in a daze. "As for my episode... I've no idea. I don't even want to talk about it." I buried my head in my hands, an uncomfortable feeling rising up my spine.

"I don't think he's right for you." Grace squeezed me reassuringly. "I know you don't want to talk about it but I'm always here."

The sound of Olivia's phone vibrating as she tapped the screen filled the silence.

"Who is he?" Grace asked.

"Who?" Olivia looked up from her phone screen, caught off guard.

"The guy you're so busy texting."

"Cormac." She placed her phone back onto the table again, a sly smile on her face.

"The barista? The one you went mini-golfing with?" I asked, grateful the attention had turned away from my dilemmas.

She shrugged, "Yeah."

"And?" I pestered.

"It's nothing." She shook her head.

"Nothing?" Grace looked as confused as I felt, "what do you mean?" she laughed.

"I just – I don't have much to say. He's nice."

"Nice?" I asked.

My stomach did a somersault. It was unheard of – Olivia, not spilling the beans? Normally, within the first minute, we'd be knee-deep in the details of her latest crush, uncovering every facet, especially the intricacies of his prowess in bed. This unexpected secrecy left a lingering curiosity in the air, and I couldn't help but wonder what had her keeping things under wraps.

"Yeah… nice." She refocused on her phone, typing away with intensity.

Grace and I exchanged a puzzled glace. I gestured to her, silently miming "what the fuck?" She responded with a bewildered shake of her head.

"So… what makes him so nice? What's the appeal?" Grace inquired.

Olivia let out an exasperated sigh and tossed her phone onto the table. "Look – I don't know. Okay? He's too nice!"

I had no idea how to respond to her. She sunk her head into her hands and accidently hit the table. "Ow."

"What's going on babe?" I asked, stroking her head, concerned.

"It's stupid." She raised her head and took a long sip of her milkshake.

"You can tell us anything…" Grace encouraged.

Olivia inhaled a deep, frustrated breath. "He won't fuck me." She let out a cry.

The table next to us looked over in shock, a mixture of surprise and discomfort painted across their faces. The sudden revelation seemed to have disrupted the serene atmosphere of the café, and we found ourselves at the unintentional centre of attention.

Grace's eyes widened, and I'm sure mine did too. "Oh… uhm." She muttered, attempting to diffuse the situation.

Olivia rolled her eyes, frustration evident in her voice, "I can't remember the last time I… He just – he wants to…" she gestured with air quotes, "Get to know me… and respect my boundaries? I don't want that! But he's just… so nice?"

The two boys seated next to us snickered and exchanged glances, clearly taken aback by Olivia's candid revelations in a public space. Their amusement came to an abrupt stop when I shot them the middle finger however.

"That's a good thing! A sign of a gentleman!" Grace exclaimed, overjoyed.

Olivia's hands trembled as she ran them through her hair, panic creeping in. Her eyes, wide with surprise and vulnerability, started to water. "I've never dated a gentleman…" she gasped, the weight of her past experiences heavy in her voice, "I'm used to… I don't know…" She lifted a bottle of ketchup from the table, holding it as if it were a metaphor for her intimate history, "being shaken and smacked around in bed like someone's trying to get what's left from an empty ketchup bottle. And you know… once they have the ketchup, they move on to mustard or brown sauce or…"

I fought back laughter at her red sauce metaphor. Grace covered her chuckle with a dramatic cough.

"He – he wants our 'first time' to be special! He's barely even kissed me!" Olivia exclaimed, her distress evident. "I don't know what to do!"

"Just take it slow. Go with the flow." I advised.

She shook her head aggressively. "No, no. I think he's trying to trick me!"

"Why would he try-" I began to ask before being interrupted by Grace.

"He's not. He's probably just interested in you as a person and not you in bed."

"That makes no sense. How could he not want me in bed? I've never felt so undesired!" Olivia expressed, her confusion and distress palpable.

My eyes glanced around the café, spotting Aileen. I motioned for the bill.

"Anyways – I just need to find someone else, you know? Someone who isn't so…"

"Nice?" Grace asked, scared of the response.

Olivia nodded. "Maybe I need to go on a man ban like you, you know? I have that big job interview and I should be focusing on that… but instead I can't stop re reading his stupid texts and…" She dabbed under her eyes with a napkin. "and wondering why he didn't heart react to the titty pic I sent him."

"Titty pic?" Grace whispered, uncomfortable.

"As long as you didn't send him a … kitty… pic." I added, giggling. "That would be worse. Imagine…"

Olivia shot me a dirty look.

"Sorry."

"The cheque, my girls." Aileen interrupted us by setting the receipt onto the table. Grace handed her a tenner before we had the chance. "What's the plans tonight?"

A small cry escaped Olivia's mouth, "I'll probably just lie on my sofa and die alone."

***

Wrapped in my fresh bed sheets, I read through my notes. Shame, a feeling I thought I had overcome, resurfaced, coursing through me as I realised my mistakes.

I'm not satisfied. I'm extremely fed up with the relationships I'm allowing myself to get into. I know what I want now. More importantly, I know what I don't. I've reached a point where I'm ready for a meaningful relationship.

It's taken me some time to decide what I truly desire, but I'm determined to leave behind the 'realm' of unsatisfying connections and men who wouldn't DIE for me.

I screamed into my pillow, overwhelmed with disappointment in myself. Flipping to the next page, I contemplated tearing out the scribbles from the book as my eyes scanned each line.

What can I say? Where do I start? Mr Millionaire may be kinder than I thought. I'm feeling a bit overwhelmed to say the least. I've never been treated like this before... Wined and dined doesn't even cover it. In the last 24 hours, he's made it impossible for me to forget him; From a romantic dinner date, to random surprise presents.... I'm not sure how to feel.

As I revisited my notes, a realisation washed over me like a cold shower on a hot day... I didn't actually like Tom as much as I had convinced myself I did. The bubble burst, and reality hit me like a ton of bricks.

Sure, he had painted a picture of luxury and opulence, enticing me with his extravagant gifts and fancy dinner dates. But deep down, I knew there was something missing – a genuine connection, a spark that just wasn't there.

His actions and words left me feeling more confused than ever. The lavish gestures seemed to hint at a desire for something more meaningful, yet his casual proposition for regular sex left me cold.

That wasn't the kind of relationship I wanted. It wasn't fulfilling or satisfying in any way. It was just empty, hollow promises wrapped in a shiny package.

And sure, I could have casual sex with him to fight off the loneliness of being single. Or... I could see the loneliness as a positive thing. An opportunity for peace, a calm nervous system and no man drama. I could be like Grace.

So, I made the difficult decision to admit to myself that Tom wasn't the one for me. And strangely, it almost annoyed me to admit it – to acknowledge that I had been swept up in the romance he had created in my mind.

But just as I deserve someone who would give their all for me, who would be fully committed and devoted, Tom deserved the same. And I couldn't give him that. I needed to meet him and let him know softly.

***

Later that night, I found myself stretched out on Grace's cosy sofa, keeping her company. We indulged in some much-needed relaxation, binge-watching our favourite shows on Netflix whilst waiting on Olivia to show up… only she never did. We had no doubt she was with Cormac or under someone else… to get over him.

As I lay there, my phone continually buzzed, but to my discomfort, it was only texts from Tom. I had been unintentionally ignoring him, caught up in the demands of life and work. Moreover, my realisation loomed heavy, and I wasn't sure how to communicate it. I decided to accept his invitation for Friday night dinner in hopes of doing so.

CHAPTER TWENTY-SIX
Catch Yerself On

Definition: wise up / get a grip

"So, were you planning on telling me about your date with Grace... or?" I teased, poking Paddy's side.

He squirmed and turned, shooting me a playful glare. "I knew she'd tell you right away, so..."

He reached for two mugs and began preparing my favourite brew.

"I ship it," I teased.

"Oh, shut up," he rolled his eyes, pouring just the right amount of milk into my cup. "Anyways, now onto your personal life. I was thinking we could pre-record your episode this week... and take the whole evening off."

"Nope, no avoiding me. What's your plan for the date?" I responded.

"Anna, I'm not talking to you about this, but if you want me to be able to meet up with Grace then we *have to* pre-record," he replied, deadpan. "Now – about your episode?"

I felt a pang of panic. "Honestly, I'm still unsure what my topic is this week."

He shot me a disappointed look. "Aren't you meant to review with Amir in…" He glanced down at his watch, "Two hours?"

"Two hours," I confirmed. "That's 180 minutes to figure it out."

Paddy chuckled. "It's 120 minutes actually."

"Fuck." I sank into a chair at the breakroom table and covered my face with my hands. "I'm just – I'm having a lot of imposter syndrome. I feel like I NEED advice. I shouldn't be giving it."

He placed my cup of tea in front of me, and I took a long sip. His eyes reflected a mix of sympathy and frustration. "You don't have to give advice every week. Just tell a story."

I mulled over his words. "You don't think that'll be boring?"

"The reason you got this show in the first place was because of your ability to tell stories. Remember the man and woman in the stairway?" He chuckled.

My stomach lurched. Little did Paddy know… *the man in the stairway was Amir.*

I nodded. "Okay. Hopefully, I'll figure it out in the next 120… minutes?"

He laughed. "Amir and Mia are actually in Dublin, so you're in luck. You're reviewing it with me this week. We can catch up at the end of the day."

Relief washed over me. "You couldn't have told me that sooner?"

***

At precisely 5:58 pm, Tom arrived at my door, cradling a bottle of red wine in his hands. "Holy shit," he exclaimed, taking in my appearance as I opened the door. A gentle kiss on my cheek followed before he confidently made his way into my apartment. "Nice place."

I attempted to shrug off my embarrassment, though his bedroom alone surpassed the size of my entire apartment, complete with unwashed dishes left in and beside my sink. Perhaps it was a subtle strategy, giving him the "ick" before I decided to end things.

"Do you want to have a glass now, or shall we save it for later?" he inquired, gesturing towards the wine.

"Um, we should probably head out... before the town gets too busy," I suggested. "Our table is for 6, right?"

He nodded and placed the bottle on my kitchen table. "Come here," he urged, pulling me towards him with one arm around my waist and the other hand entangled in my hair.

Sensing an imminent kiss, I panicked, "Let's get going! Can't be late..." I flashed a smile and quickly manoeuvred my way out of his embrace.

***

The city's ambiance, a mix of distant laughter and bustling nightlife, surrounded us as we navigated towards our fancy destination. As I walked up the grand steps of the Merchant hotel, I felt the need to change myself to match the opulent exterior. My black dress and heels seemed almost inadequate, especially when compared to Tom's impeccably styled outfit and designer shoes, which effortlessly compensated for any shortcomings on my part.

Upon entering, my attention was immediately drawn to a stunningly large chandelier and intricate plasterwork detailing, adorning the ceiling and walls—a display of undeniable luxury. I couldn't help but wonder if this was what the Queen's dining room looked like.

"Your eyes look like they're about to pop out from their sockets," Tom teased, breaking my gaze.

I chuckled uncomfortably, attempting to compose myself. "This place is just so gorgeous."

"You haven't been here before?" he inquired.

I shook my head.

"But you live, like, two minutes away from it?"

"I shop in Lidl… not Marks and Spencer's." I laughed, though by the look on Tom's face, my joke didn't quite hit the mark. "Here seems expensive." I explained. He pretended to understand.

My eyes swept across the lavishly decorated, art deco surroundings. The walls, painted in a tasteful mix of black, gold, and chocolate hues, framed a room that boasted a large overhanging palm tree at its centre— something Gatsby would undoubtedly approve of. As we admired the decor, a suave, well-dressed gentleman approached us, fitting seamlessly into the hotel's luxurious aesthetic with his tall stature, brown slicked back hair, and refined attire.

"Good-evening. Are you a resident, or do you have a booking this evening?" the impeccably dressed man inquired, glancing down at the iPad screen on the desk in front of him. The air of sophistication was palpable.

Tom took a deep breath, "The reservation should be under Tom Beckham."

"Oh, of course! Mr. Beckham, apologies," the man responded, shaking his head in slight fluster. "This way…" He gracefully turned on his heels, signalling for us to follow him to our designated table. A fleeting thought crossed my mind—*did Tom frequent this place with his dates?*

Seated in a cosy corner of the dining hall, we were discreetly tucked away from any prying eyes. Almost instantly, a waitress appeared, presenting us with two leather-bound dinner menus and a drinks menu adorned with gold embossing. I couldn't help but marvel at the sheer extravagance of the place.

"What do you recommend?" I asked Tom, noticing he had taken a pair of glasses from his pocket and was deeply engrossed in reading the menu—an unexpectedly enticing sight.

"Uhhhh…" he hummed, leaving me in suspense.

I was hoping he'd say 'a side salad' and 'water' because my budget wasn't going to stretch too far.

"Depends. The lobster ravioli or Irish beef fillet are pretty amazing," he finally responded, casually mentioning the two most expensive items on the menu. *Of course.*

The waitress returned with a beaming smile, and I wondered if, by the end of the night, her cheeks would ache.

"Can I get you two started with some drinks?" she inquired.

"Dom Pèrignon. A bottle," Tom replied, catching me slightly off guard. I watched as he returned his gaze to the menu.

"Um, could I also get a water, please?" I interjected.

She nodded, "Water. Of course. Would you like a few more minutes to order food or?"

"No, we'll share the dipping breads and I'll have the Kilkeel crab to start, saddle of lamb for my main."

The waitress quickly scribbled down his order. "And for you miss?"

I panicked, "Uhm. Just a main please. The seabass?"

That'll be all," Tom waved her off with a nonchalant gesture.

Silence fell between us. At the opposite end of the room, my eyes were drawn to the back of a dark-haired man. Amir was in Dublin... I thought... so it couldn't be him. I needed to stop thinking about him.

"What's new with you?" Tom asked, snapping me back.

***

The food was amazing. Tom wasn't terrible. Our conversation spanned from a recent weekend trip he'd taken to Miami... and the one I'd taken, much closer, to Galway. He talked about the stress of the press and the challenges he faced in the dating scene. I tried, multiple times to interject and explain to him how I wanted us to be – just friends – but the timing wasn't right. Things just got worse as our conversation went along.

"You need to, you know, be prepared." He mentioned, taking a leisurely sip of his champagne.

"For what?" I asked, feeling a sudden tension that made the hairs on my arms stand up.

"You know – if we were to ever become serious – the press will probably write about you." He explained.

My heart raced, and a sense of unease settled in. "Oh… about that."

Before I could delve into the topic further, the waitress smoothly presented Tom with the bill. "I hope everything was up to standard?"

He nodded, slipping his bank card into the leather case, and handing her a £50 note for a tip.

"Thank you." I said, smiling awkwardly and squirming in my seat, "I can… send you half?" I suggested, pulling out my phone and opening my internet banking app.

He laughed, "No. Let's go. I know a spot for a nightcap. You can pay me back in other ways." He slapped my ass as I stood up to put on my coat.

My blood pressure spiked; I knew I needed to address things now. We descended the steps and found ourselves in the street. "Tom…" I hesitated, "I need to say something."

He turned, appearing confused, and I knew what I needed to say, but somehow my words had gone missing.

"Go on then…" he encouraged, swaying slightly on his feet, clearly affected by the alcohol consumed.

"I… I…" The streetlights reflected onto his face. I wished it were darker, so I wouldn't be forced to see his expression or for him to see mine.

"Spit it out, Anna," he chuckled. The normally bustling street now felt eerily quiet, as if it were holding its breath, waiting for the outcome of our exchange.

"I don't think we should see each other again."

"What do you mean?" he protested, his voice carrying a mixture of confusion and frustration.

I stared awkwardly down at my heels, feeling his intense gaze on me.

"Hello?!" he suddenly screamed, making me jump. His sudden outburst reverberated in the otherwise still night, making the atmosphere on the street palpably uncomfortable. Passers-by stole glances, their footsteps quickening as they navigated around our unexpected confrontation.

"I'm sorry. This just doesn't feel right to me. This relationship... it's just not what I'm looking for. You're lovely but - "

"Wow, wow, wow. This isn't a relationship." Tom laughed condescendingly. "We aren't in a relationship."

"I know we officially aren't in a relationship, but you know what I mean... this connection-"

He snorted, his tone dismissive, "No I don't."

I clicked my tongue off my teeth, feeling a surge of frustration. "Okay." I shrugged, refusing to give in to his dismissive demeanour. "But you literally just said how I'd need to be prepared if"-

"Can you explain to me... how WE are in a relationship?!" He continued mockingly.

I hesitated, feeling his words making me small. He started pacing back and forth, his condescending tone cutting through the night. "We aren't in a bloody relationship. Jesus Christ, would you look at yourself..."

I glanced down at myself. *Hold on a minute... If he was insinuating that I wasn't 'good enough,' he was in for a reality check.*

"You can't seriously have thought..." he looked at me with false disgust.

"Tom, I'm just going to stop you right there. We aren't in a relationship; that was a poor choice of words," I said assertively. I could see in his eyes that he was hungry for drama. He wanted an outburst. He wanted me to beg him for forgiveness. "What I essentially wanted to say was that... I don't want to see you again. I don't want this to go any further." His face dropped as I began to walk off. He grabbed my arm, stopping me in my tracks.

"I wouldn't want to be in a relationship with you!" He slurred. "I never asked you to be my girlfriend! I can't believe you even thought such a thing!"

I shook him off me, "Get off." And turned on my heels to walk towards my apartment.

"ANNA!" he shouted. "Where are you going? You're acting crazy!"

At this moment, I realised why this man had been single for so long… His ego was way bigger than his poor little dick.

"You know what…? FUCK YOU!" He screamed.

I turned back and flashed him a smile. As I confidently moved forward, embracing the empowering realisation that I went with my gut and deserved better, our tense exchange was abruptly interrupted by someone descending the Merchant steps.

"Hey, everything okay out here?" Amir's concerned voice cut through the heated atmosphere.

Tom, visibly taken aback, stammered, "Uh, yeah, everything's fine."

"What – what the fuck are you doing here?!" I responded, astounded.

My heart raced as I locked eyes with Amir, an unexpected and almost comical twist adding another layer of surprise to the already charged moment. It felt like a scene ripped from a movie or a page of fiction, incredibly cliché. But… Belfast was a tiny city, where things like this happened more often than not.

A tall blonde woman, her hair cascading in waves around her shoulders, donning bright red lipstick, emerged from behind him. She exuded an air of confidence, her gaze unapologetically meeting mine as if she had been unaware of the unfolding drama. I swallowed, realising I had indeed seen him inside the restaurant. It was his back, seated at the other end.

"You know this guy?" Tom questioned, "Is he the reason?"

I shook my head, "No. No, he's not. I just don't want to be with you," I said, maintaining a straight face. My sympathy for Tom had vanished after his ignorant, egotistical outburst.

"Anna, I'll catch you in 2 minutes, okay?" Amir shouted down the steps. I shook my head, confused. He turned to his date and gave her a hug goodbye. She reciprocated with a subtle smile that hinted at a shared understanding.

"You know what, I would never date you anyways." Tom persisted. I rolled my eyes. His words didn't pierce me.

Amir reached the bottom, squinting his eyes at me, concerned. "You alright?" he dismissed Tom, only staring at me.

I nodded, "I'm good."

"I'm heading to meet Paddy... he's in Muriels bar? It's just a minute away. He's with-"

"Grace." I smiled, feeling a sense of calm. "Bye." I waved at Tom and headed off in the direction of the cocktail bar with Amir beside me.

"Are you serious?" Tom screamed after me, "You know what, you CAN send me the money for the meal!"

I ignored him but made a mental note to send a letter containing cash to his house. I didn't want him to have anything to hold over me.

"What the fuck was that guy's problem?" Amir mumbled, concern etched on his face. "Are you actually okay? All I heard was a man shouting, 'fuck you' and a woman walking off."

"What are the chances..." I chuckled, unsure if I found it funny or uncomfortable.

As Amir and I began walking away, I couldn't help but steal a glance back at the tall blonde woman. She gracefully walked the opposite direction, her confident stride seemingly unaffected by the unexpected scene she had just witnessed. Even in that brief moment, her poise and composed demeanour intrigued me. *Was Amir dating her and was that why he'd rejected me?*

"So..." Amir pressed.

I shook my head, "Ah – that's, ehm, Mr. Millionaire. I ended things with him. Like, for good."

We paused at the traffic lights, waiting for them to turn so we could cross the street. Amir turned to face me, "ended things?" He seemed confused.

"I wasn't dating him… or in a relationship!" I clarified, stumbling over my words, "I just told him I don't want to… in future. I – I don't want to see him again."

He nodded. "He didn't take it well…"

I shook my head and laughed, "Nope."

Grace and Paddy were equally shocked to see us both land in the cocktail bar together. I briefly filled them in on the unexpected turns of the evening.

"Sounds like you need a very strong drink." Paddy jumped from his seat.

"I'm actually okay." He disappeared, ignoring me. I turned to Amir, lips pressed together. "Ah, I really don't want a wild one tonight."

"I'll see if he needs help at the bar." He got up and met Paddy. I noticed how his shoulders were clenched, and the outline of his muscles burned through his shirt. I tried to lip read but failed.

Grace sighed, "Are you okay?"

I nodded, "I think so. How's your non-date?"

She bit her fingernails, "Ah… It's good. He's a great guy, but you know that." She shrugged, "I have a question, how come you and Paddy never—you know—dated? Or got together?"

"No spark. He's like a brother." I responded simply, "I've just never felt any attraction towards him in that way. He's all yours."

She rolled her eyes. "How's things with Amir?"

I pondered, "I don't know. I feel a bit numb. I thought he was in Dublin and… I didn't expect to see him tonight, especially not on a date." The cosy ambience of the cocktail bar and soft glow of the lights created a warming vibe.

"A date?" Grace's jaw dropped, "You're joking. But he's moving back to New York?"

My stomach twisted. I hadn't filled Grace in on Amir's childhood and his fear of turning out like his father... I replayed everything he'd told me in Galway and began to question what was a lie and what was the truth. *If he was so afraid of love, why was he on a date with that woman?*

He stood at the bar, laughing along with Paddy. I felt hurt. If he thought I wasn't the right match for him, he could have told me straight instead of possibly inventing detailed, emotional lies.

"I love you." I nodded at Grace, "but I think I need to get out of here. My head is spinning..."

She sighed, "I get it. Get some sleep. You probably need an early night."

"Tell the boys I said bye... and sorry." I jumped up, pulling her into a hug. Before they could return with shots of some kind, I escaped the bar and headed home. The crisp night air outside offered a stark contrast to the warmth inside, providing a moment of clarity amidst my confusion.

***

I swapped my dress and heels for fluffy pyjamas and slippers. A cup of tea sat on the table before me as I opened my laptop and loaded up the Spotlight Radio website. Paddy helped me pre-record my episode, so we both could enjoy a Friday night off. It was uncomfortable listening to my own voice, but it turned out to be exactly what I needed to hear.

"I make mistakes regularly. I make them all the time. I've made multiple in the past week. But every time I make a mistake, I get closer to realising what's right. In life, we don't always do the right thing.

We date the wrong people.

We break up with them.

We lose a bit of self-worth.

We spend months rebuilding it.

We swear to be different.

And then we date the same person again.

Why?

It's a frustrating cycle. We often find ourselves repeating the same patterns, even though we've promised ourselves we won't. But why does this happen? Perhaps it's because familiarity feels safer than the unknown. Maybe it's because we're drawn to what's familiar, even if it's not necessarily what's best for us. Or it could be that deep down, we're still grappling with unresolved issues or insecurities that keep us stuck in these repetitive relationships. Whatever the reason, breaking free from this cycle requires introspection, self-awareness, and the courage to choose differently next time.

I know for a fact, I have always craved a romance worthy of novels or films – a courtship where a man takes a woman on enchanting dates, like a stroll along the beach, as cliché as it may sound, just so he can get to know her better. I need deep conversations that go beyond mere small talk on a sofa, a connection that's much more than ordinary.

So today, I want to mark a change. A shift. A shake.

The moment *we all* decide to stop accepting what we once believed was okay… was normal… is the moment the universe starts making moves to bring us what we want.

If you accept less, you will get less.

If you set a standard for more, you will get more.

So, let's break the cycle. Let's stop returning to old habits and choosing partners that deep down, we know aren't right for us. Instead, let's focus on finding love and validation within ourselves. Let's walk hand in hand with that inner power until someone comes along who is truly worth more than our peace."

The soothing ambiance of my home, the soft glow of the laptop screen, and the comforting warmth of my tea created a cocoon of solace, allowing me to reflect on the profound shift in perspective that the night had brought. I realised my Amir chapter had not yet been fully closed. Seeing him with another woman made me spiral so much that I'd abandoned my friends in a bar. This time however, I noted a change within myself. I wasn't spiralling because of comparing myself to the woman he was with…. And I wasn't feeling insecure. I just felt confused, like I'd been lied to.

I pulled out my notebook and began to journal—not for the benefit of future podcasts, but for myself.

Do I want to tell my future children that the first time I encountered Amir, he was half naked with another woman in a stairwell… at a funeral? No.

Do I want to tell my future children about the rude consultant who teased and provoked me each day? No.

Do I want to tell my future children about the man who kissed me and then changed his mind, leaving me confused and feeling insecure? Not once, but multiple times. No.

Do I want to tell my future children about the man who cried to me about his emotional unavailability, his childhood trauma and then I spotted him on a date just days later?

NO.

I shivered, reading over my notes, slamming the book closed. Fuck him. Fuck this. As much as I tried to resist wanting him, as much as I had a thousand reasons why I shouldn't, it wasn't easy. The weight of unresolved emotions hung heavy in the air, reminding me that closure was a journey yet to be completed. But I was going to really, really try.

CHAPTER TWENTY-SEVEN

Bleedin' Deadly Serious

Definition: for real.

The last thing I expected on Monday morning was champagne. Mia popped the bottle, liquid exploding over the boardroom floor.

"Oh shit – Amir." She muttered, realising the potential mess, "Pass me a mug."

Wearing a notably less enthusiastic expression, Amir handed her a pink coffee mug, which she promptly filled with the effervescent bubbles.

"I'm a bit lost here," I confessed, accepting the mug while remaining completely oblivious to the occasion.

"Maybe sit down for this." Paddy suggested, accepting a mug from Mia.

Perplexed, I settled into a chair at the boardroom table, my heart quickening with uncertainty. The room seemed to spin with an air of mystery, and I couldn't shake the feeling that I was caught in the middle of an elaborate prank.

Mia, seemingly amused by my confusion, exchanged glances with Paddy before revealing the surprising news, "You've been nominated for a Northern Ireland Entertainment Award! Best Newcomer in Audio Entertainment!"

The words hung in the air, and for a moment, my mind struggled to process. As the significance of the nomination sank in, a surge of excitement rippled through my body.

"What?" I chuckled, a hint of disbelief tainting my laughter.

Amir, opting for coffee over champagne for his morning sustenance, turned to pour a cup from the nearby side table. His expression remained unchanged—deadpan, seemingly emotionless.

"You deserve this!" Mia exclaimed, her eyes reflecting sincerity, "You share so much truth on your episodes."

Paddy nodded in agreement, adding a touch of humour, "A bit too much truth at times."

"What?" I repeated. I had no words. I felt totally speechless. "Are you serious?"

Mia smiled, "Bleedin' deadly serious."

"So, when is it? The awards ceremony?" I inquired, the information still struggling to find a place in my understanding.

"The 25th," She announced, taking a deep breath.

I paused, processing the timing, "Of this month?"

She nodded.

"Just over two weeks away?" I sought confirmation.

Again, she nodded.

"Right," I responded, a mix of excitement and nervousness settling in, "What do I wear? Is there an audience vote? And where is it?"

Mia paused, turning to Amir, who stood in the corner absorbed in stirring his coffee, seemingly lost in contemplation. His deadpan expression intensified, giving away nothing as he responded, "You can't go."

Confused, I probed further.

"If you were to attend," he continued, maintaining his emotionless demeanour, "You have to understand that people can't know your identity. You can't accept an award – if you win… which, I don't want to dampen your spirits, but it's unlikely. Your show hasn't been running that long… And you couldn't walk on stage? How do you expect to not show your face?"

My stomach sank. His words bore a stark reality that briefly clouded the excitement of the nomination.

"Of course," I sighed, "Sorry, I don't know what I was thinking."

I looked up at Mia, who had her lips pressed together. She wore an expression of both annoyance and sadness on my behalf. The dream of accepting an award, a moment I had momentarily envisioned, now seemed like an impractical fantasy.

"It's not about winning. It's a shame you can't attend… even with a mask on her face?" Mia turned to Amir, suggesting a solution on my behalf, "Or a wig? What about a wig?"

"You'd look hot as a blonde." Paddy suggested, sarcasm dripping from his words.

Amir shook his head, "No—no wigs, no masks. It's too risky."

"How about prosthetic makeup? We could make her nose bigger," Paddy laughed, the absurdity of the suggestion hanging in the air.

Amir's face twisted with anger, unable to find humour in Paddy's bizarre proposals. "Can I have a few minutes alone with Anna, please?"

Mia exchanged a nod with Paddy, and they exited the boardroom, leaving Amir and I alone. He took a seat across from me, running a hand through his hair as he sipped on his coffee, a cloud of uncertainty settling in the room.

"I'm not going to go, don't worry," I reassured him, but anxiety clawed at my stomach. His frustration puzzled me; being nominated should be a positive turn of events. It should alleviate the pressure from The Board, regardless of the outcome.

He remained silent, eyebrows furrowed.

"What?" I asked, hoping he'd grant me an insight into his clouded brain.

A deep inhale. He shook his head, dismissing his words. "Nothing – we're all good. Just don't get your hopes up."

His coffee threatened to spill over the edge as he stood from the table, moving so fast it caught me off guard.

"What? I'm lost." I stood up, matching his pace. "What did you want to talk to me about – alone?"

He shook his head, "It's nothing."

"What about the board, what did they have to say?" I asked.

He rubbed the stubble under his chin, his eyes holding a million thoughts behind them. I struggled to understand what was causing him to be so aloof and unexcited.

"It's a good thing." He nodded. "But all this press, I worry that…" he bit his tongue, "How many interviews did you do last week?"

I shrugged, "I don't know… like eight? Nine?"

"They'll be dying to know your identity… your Mr. This and Mr. That's identities. You need to be seriously careful." His eyes scolded me. "What about Mr. Millionaire? Does he know? He seemed furious at you on Friday night."

I was taken aback. "No, no. Of course, he doesn't."

Amir nodded, "Because if he did, you wouldn't be able to do your show anymore. It's a litigation nightmare. And I doubt any man would want to date you." He snorted a little at the end of his sentence, finding amusement in the situation.

My stomach sank. "I know. I'm extremely careful. And I'm sorry I even thought about going to the awards. I just got – excited in the moment!" My voice gained volume as I spoke.

His nostrils flared. Silence filled the room, suffocating us both. I stood facing him, eyes aligned.

"What's your episode for this week?" He asked, "What's your topic?"

I shook my head, "It's only Monday – I, I don't know yet." I lifted my journal from my bag and began reading through my notes.

"Uhm – I could do … Self Love Habits…" I turned a page, "Icks… not settling… Love bombing and breadcrumbing…" I mumbled, feeling the pressure.

He clicked his tongue against the roof of his mouth, "Tell your audience why Mr. Millionaire wasn't good enough for you? He's famous, rich, and quite handsome, from what I saw… what else could you want?"

I rolled my eyes and threw my notebook onto the table, "Seriously?"

He shrugged, "End his chapter? Your audience will be wondering who's on your current roster!" He suggested, his tone oozing with arrogance.

"You – you want to know who's on my roster!" I pointed at him, "Is this what your attitude is about? Seeing me with a man?"

He rolled his eyes, scoffing at the idea, and began pacing the room.

"Because I wouldn't mind an explanation on your date on Friday… actually."

He huffed, "My date? And why do I owe you any explanations?"

"Oh, I don't know… maybe because you CRIED to me in that fucking park in Galway about your Philophobia! How you didn't want to start something with me… only to end it when you go to New York!" My body radiated anger.

"What the fuck is Philophobia?" He questioned.

"Fear of love! You said that you're afraid and then I see you on a date? Just tell me you don't like me, for fuck's sake!"

His face dropped.

"Okay." He conceded.

"Okay?" My stomach plummeted, hitting the floor like a lead weight. The room fell into a stifling silence, and the air felt thin as if our bickering had sucked out all the oxygen.

He let out a loud frustrated sigh, "I've saved your show, by the way, The Board is fine – it's safe for broadcast, until they say otherwise."

I threw my hands in the air, "Why the fuck would you keep that from me?"

He maintained a guarded silence, withholding the explanation and simply shrugged in response.

"I don't get you." Pausing, I scrutinised him from head to toe. The excitement and relief I should have felt at my show being allowed to continue was overshadowed by the unease I felt from him. "Is this because of the stairway?"

He stopped pacing. "What?"

"The stairway. Me catching you with that girl? Are you afraid I'm going to tell someone? So you save my show?" I spat.

He shook his head.

"Because I won't. So, if you hate me so much, go ahead and tell the board to pull the plug! I'll quit entirely if you want!" I shouted, frustration boiling over. "What did I ever do to make you hate me so much?"

He remained silent.

"I don't know if you had to bribe someone... or? Oh my god." I paused, a sinking realisation coursing through my body. "That's why you kissed me..."

All the air seemed to evacuate from my lungs. The words barely escaped my trembling lips, "You— you pretended to like me... because if I told everyone, your reputation would be ruined."

"Shut up!" His scream reverberated, possibly audible through the soundproof glass door.

I gasped, my hands trembling. The fragments of the puzzle fell into place, revealing a picture I never wanted to see. His outburst, the salvaged show, the confusing array of emotions— it all made sense now.

"Fuck you," I uttered, almost a whisper, and stormed out of the boardroom.

He screamed my name as I left, making a spectacle of us both in front of the entire office.

I turned to face him, tears welling in my eyes. I shook my head, attempting to withhold my emotions.

He stared at me, his chest rising and falling. I waited. He said nothing.

The truth lingered, elusive and unsettling, as we stood in the aftermath of a storm that had yet to fully unleash its fury.

***

I berated myself for being naive, thinking there was something more between us. Months of self-coaching to suppress any feelings for him felt like a waste when it turned out he never felt the same way. Taking a much-needed hiatus from life, I declared a few sick days off work, replaying our fiery argument on an endless loop in my mind. Tears had been my companion until I felt utterly spent. My pillow was practically swimming by the time I pulled myself together.

Not that I expected to, but I heard nothing from him on Tuesday… or Wednesday.

Seated across from Grace in Maggie Mays, I refrained from indulging in my usual milkshake. The mere thought of it was enough to turn my stomach.

"I don't really know what advice to give you," she said, squeezing my hand across the table. "Have you considered going to HR?"

"No. I— I couldn't do that." My eyes welled up painfully for the hundredth time. "Unfortunately, he's actually really good at his job. He's saved the station and seeking revenge or damaging his reputation would only make me feel worse. In a way, I wouldn't have a job at all without him – I just – it's all so…"

"Fucked?" she whispered, shocking me. Grace rarely cursed. "But he emotionally manipulated you, Anna, just to protect himself?"

"I was just stupid," I sighed, my head falling into my hands. "I just need to figure out what to do next... I don't want to quit, but I don't know how I can ever work with him again."

"At least he's heading back to New York in a few weeks. It's not long."

"Why does everything feel like it's sort of falling apart? Me, my job. You, your job. Have you found anything yet?" I inquired.

A subdued smile graced her face. "Well, Juice Jar. It's not fancy or in production, but... it pays the bills... for now. Everyone who works there seems lovely."

I hadn't anticipated her taking up a position at our local juice shop. It was renowned for its top-notch, fresh acai bowls and overnight oats – not something I could easily envision Grace preparing, especially given her background in setting up locations for big-budget TV shows. Quite the contrast to her usual day-to-day.

"I mean it's still something right?" I said, "Think of all the people you could meet... I'm sure producers and what not stop there all the time. They do Pilates classes now, you know? Sounds like something a Hollywood producer would go to."

She giggled, "Yeah."

"Anyways, where the fuck is Olivia?" I questioned, scanning the half-filled café.

Grace shook her head. "I haven't heard from her. I texted about her job interview last Friday too and she never replied."

I was confused. I hadn't heard from her either.

"Same. I messaged her on Saturday and then on Monday about the awards nomination too... she never said anything." I pondered, "Oh – thank you for the flowers."

"You've already thanked me four times."

I laughed.

Aileen approached our table, placing a stack of pancakes in the middle for us to share. My stomach flipped at the thought of eating. "How are my girls?" she asked, sliding into the booth.

"Been better." I rested my head on her shoulder.

"Do you ever get in trouble for talking to your customers like you do with us?" Grace asked, turning to check out the other staff. They were standing bored as the café was nowhere near as busy as normal.

"I'd like to see them try shout at me." She scoffed. "What has you feeling so low?" She threw her arm round me. "Men?"

I snorted and lifted my cup of tea, the mug warming my hands. "Kind of."

"Break ups are hard." She squeezed me, trying to comfort me.

"How would you know?" Grace's mouth was half full of pancakes, "You've only been with one man and you married him."

"I'm not going through a breakup," I chuckled, "I just have bad luck. Really bad luck. Every man I seem to choose ends up being emotionally unavailable."

Aileen sighed and quietly slid out of the booth. Grace and I exchanged puzzled glances as she disappeared behind the cash register, only to return with a newspaper.

"Many men begin emotionally unavailable. Yes?"

I wasn't sure if she needed an answer, "Do they?"

She rolled her eyes, "Some men try therapy. Others say 'feck it, it'll be grand' to self-discovery and later face the harsh reality that they might die alone."

Grace sighed, "so true."

"Their metaphorical taxi light flickers to life, and essentially… the first woman who steps into their car, could become 'the one.' Are you with me?"

I nodded, "I think so."

"Then, as if a traffic light switching to green, they accelerate into the fast lane of marriage," she elucidated, gesturing towards the Belfast Buzz newspaper in her hand. She dropped it onto the table in front of us.

My eyes widened in shock as I took in the front cover.

TOM TAKES A SWING AT LOVE!

"No," I snorted, "there's no way."

And lo and behold, a photo of my 'Mr. Millionaire' at the Miss Northern Ireland Finals, arms wrapped around runner-up, the petite and stunning brunette beauty, Saoirse Ferry.

"The most emotionally unavailable man. It took him 40 odd years," Aileen said, sitting back down beside me and pushing me into the corner of the booth, suddenly making me feel suffocated.

Grace, unable to contain herself, swiftly lifted the paper from my hands, and her eyes widened in disbelief as she caught sight of the front cover. A gasp escaped her lips, and she began choking on her pancake. I handed her a napkin to spit out her food. Together, we found ourselves in an unexpected fit of laughter triggered by the irony of the situation.

"What's so funny?" Aileen asked, her curiosity piqued by our shared laughter.

I snatched the paper back from Grace and began to read the description. According to the paper, he'd been dating Saoirse for 8 months, and they could be getting engaged. She had hoped their engagement would take place on a recent trip... to Miami. Shocked at the surreal situation, I wondered what else the universe planned to serve me.

"I had a stint with Tom," I divulged, a wry smile playing on my lips as I chuckled at the irony. "Regrettably."

Aileen, always quick to share her opinions, scolded, "He's quite senior for you! I'm guessing it didn't end well?"

Shaking my head, I replied, "Uhm – no. He wasn't the right fit. Thank god."

Aileen leaned in, offering a sagely perspective, "You know, for a young woman like yourself, the allure of dating an older man may seem appealing in theory... but more often than not, they usually reveal why they've been single for so long. I'm relieved you didn't hop into his taxi."

***

The water exuded tranquillity, gentle waves orchestrating a dance with the sailboats in the Titanic Quarter harbour. Grace and I perched on the grass adjacent to Olivia's apartment building, anticipating her appearance.

Out of the blue, Grace disrupted the serene atmosphere with a candid confession, catching me off guard. "I think we're all a bit emotionally unavailable," she admitted, pre-empting any response from me. Her voice carried a hint of vulnerability. "I am. I know I am. I cover it by saying I'm on a 'man ban' but the truth is, I worry I'll find someone I love and then one day wake up and hate them... or have them hate me. Only to go through a divorce as horrible as my parents. They despise each other. Can't even sit in the same room together."

Moved by her openness, I wrapped my arms around her, pulling her into a comforting hug. We lay back onto the grass, gazing up at the cloud-strewn sky above.

"I worry I'll never find a love that measures up to what my parents share." I admitted.

"SORRY!" Olivia's voice interrupted our deep confessions. "I- Cormac- I couldn't get him to leave!"

I sat up, observing her clad in sweats and a hoodie. Her attire was casual, a departure from the usual, with limited makeup and her hair pulled back into a ponytail—the first time I'd seen her adopt such a laid-back style since I'd known her.

"Oh – so that's why you haven't been replying to either of us!" Grace laughed. "He's kept you locked up?"

Olivia rolled her eyes and slumped down beside us. "I'm stressed."

"What? Why?" I inquired.

She let out a deep, frustrated moan. "He's obsessed. He picked me flowers on a run the other day, baked me cinnamon muffins, and every time I go into the coffee shop, he makes a heart out of foam on my coffee."

"Those are lovely gestures! You're just frustrated because you haven't slept with him yet." I playfully pinched her side, eliciting a squeal.

"We've done... other things." Her voice sounded deflated, and she looked confused, and a bit grossed out. "He also made me a Spotify playlist!"

"Oh... was it just... not good?"

"The playlist was perfect!" She shook her head. "He's good at going down on me too... Great even."

Grace giggled, "So, what's the issue?"

"I don't know, It's just... too much!"

"I'm confused... this is what you wanted, right? You want to, you know, develop the relationship? You still want to have sex with him?"

"Yeah, but... now... now that we're almost at that 'stage'... I'm not sure!" Her face was filled with confusion. "He texted me 'goodnight, gorgeous' last night and 'good morning, beautiful' this morning!"

"What's wrong with that?"

Olivia grumbled, "Just... if that's how he is now, what will happen when we actually... have sex? He'll ask me to move in with him! Or worse, marriage!"

I giggled, and Grace joined in, sensing the brewing hilarity of the situation.

"Olivia... have you ever considered that you are absolutely, completely, without a doubt... emotionally unavailable?" Grace asked with a mischievous twinkle in her eye.

CHAPTER TWENTY-EIGHT
It is, so it is

Definition: when something is the way that it is... so it is

"One, two, one, two." I spoke into the mic, testing the audio levels, "Toast, Butter, Jam."

Paddy responded by giving me a thumbs up. I stared at my typed notes in front of me, ready to record a heavy episode.

"What makes someone ready for love? And are we ever genuinely prepared? Philophobia is the term for that fear, and it can come from various sources, with past trauma being a big one. Experiences of heartbreak, betrayal, and unhealthy relationships can create this fear. Perhaps you worry that love will make you vulnerable, leaving you open to rejection, hurt, abandonment... Love demands that we open up emotionally to another person. People grappling with low self-esteem, as I have at times, may question their deservingness of love. It's the fear of not being good enough, of feeling inadequate.

Maybe you're burdened by unrealistic expectations of what love should look like… or feel like. Our views of love are often shaped by the romanticised portrayals in films or fairytales we absorbed growing up. They often paint a picture of a flawless 'meet-cute,' followed by a happily ever after, riding off into the sunset.

Consequently, we hesitate, awaiting the arrival of the perfect, unflawed Prince Charming, or Princess, or the damsel in distress who needs rescuing.

Perhaps it's the fear of rejection, of loving someone more intensely than they reciprocate. There's also the anxiety of commitment, the daunting idea of sharing a future with someone… maybe marriage and family.

Sometimes we fear intimacy, both emotionally and physically. It's a big thing… having someone truly know you inside and out; all vulnerabilities exposed. What if you get rejected?

Is it worth it? Personally, I've decided yes. I'm willing to take the risk – the actual risk of meeting someone who ISN'T emotionally unavailable…"

My episode concluded with snippets from women across Belfast sharing their own fears when it comes to love and how they managed to find it despite them. Tears welled up in my eyes, and I noticed Paddy's eyes glistening with emotion as we listened.

***

A low-key weekend unfolded, and finally, I felt my energy unwinding. My emotions found a calmer rhythm. It had been almost a week since I last spoke to or saw Amir, but thoughts of our disagreement lingered. As I walked to work on Monday morning, my mind began to race again, wondering what could happen next. *What if he tried pulling me for another chat? What if he had my show cancelled?* Hundreds of "what ifs" clouded my brain.

Little did I anticipate what was coming.

Mia had called a companywide boardroom meeting, transforming the space into a sea of faces and hushed conversations. The room was definitely too small for the influx of employees. Seated confidently at the head of the table, Mia commanded attention. Her eyes, fixed on the laptop screen before her, hinted at the impending importance of the gathering. Neatly organised printed pieces of paper, containing vital information or perhaps a well-thought-out agenda, lay beside her.

"Alright, everyone! This meeting brings good news, unlike our last one," Mia announced, her voice carrying a tone of optimism. "The last time we gathered, I shared an unsettling update on the state of our station. Today, I'm thrilled to announce that things have taken a turn for the better. No more layoffs. Our budgets have increased, courtesy of new sponsors, brand partners, and an expanding listenership. This positive shift is a result of our enhanced online presence and the addition of exciting new shows to our network."

A wave of jubilation swept through the room.

"And for some even better news," Mia hesitated for a moment, "I'm sure some of you will be pleased to know that Amir Daivari has returned to the States and will no longer be breathing down your backs." An uncomfortable laugh escaped her lips, met with cheers and shouts of celebration from a few men.

Time seemed to stand still for me. My blood stopped pumping. Heart stopped beating. Lungs stopped breathing.

He'd left.

Internally, conflicting emotions waged war. Relief and happiness struggled against heartbreak and devastation. The chapter had closed with the most unpredictable ending.

"I don't understand why you're celebrating him leaving," Paddy's words punctuated my thoughts. He addressed Kevin, John, and William, who were still rejoicing. "None of us would have our jobs right now if it wasn't for Amir, you do know that?"

Silence descended upon the boardroom.

"We've lost twelve colleagues, but by doing that... he saved the rest of us from unemployment. And those twelve... in fact, more than twelve deserved to lose their jobs due to fucking around way too much." Paddy's eyes glared around the room, a profound sense of disappointment etched across his face. "We have eight times the number of sponsors, a completely new operating system, and even a new coffee machine, which is way better than our old shitty one. He pushed us all into a team bonding day, which most of you complained about, and it ended up being the best thing for our company, and everyone had the best craic. Yes, he was stern. Without question, he could get hot-headed. But imagine having the pressure he had on his shoulders. I doubt 99% of you could handle it. I think Amir deserves a lot more credit instead of everyone celebrating that he's gone. He should have been thrown a thank-you party." His words hung in the air, heavy with a mix of anger and disappointment, challenging the room to reconsider their perspective.

"Thank you, Paddy." Mia nodded, "Please can we all make an effort to send thank you emails to Amir for his time with us?"

Paddy shook his head, frustration evident, "Thank you emails? He— He was sent by Derek's family to SHUT DOWN Spotlight... to fire everyone. They wanted to stop all business outside the USA as it wasn't profiting them enough, but... but he saved us instead. He deserves more than a fucking thank-you email."

The glass door swung closed as Paddy exited the boardroom, vexed by the lack of gratitude in the room. Everyone exchanged worrisome glances, shock etched across their faces at the realisation... maybe Amir was the 'good guy' after all. Following him from the boardroom was my only option.

***

Paddy stood in ominous silence beside the steaming kettle, the air charged with tension as the water bubbled violently. I watched him intently, a sinking feeling in my gut. My mouth was glued shut; words held within it.

"What?" he exhaled, shooting a fleeting, wounded glance in my direction.

I swallowed hard, my throat tightening. "Are you alright?" I ventured, fully aware of the stupidity of the question. He wasn't alright, and we both knew it.

He shook his head, the silence stretching as he prepared to unleash a storm of emotions. A palpable rage smouldered beneath his calm exterior.

"You know what…" he began, pausing for emphasis. I sensed the impending eruption, a tempest of emotions brewing within him.

"What?" I prodded, a knot forming in my stomach.

"On your show, every week, you're brutally honest. You reveal your deepest vulnerabilities," he said, fixing me with an intense gaze, seeking affirmation. I nodded cautiously, feeling a shiver run down my spine.

The hairs on the back of my neck stood on end. I braced myself.

"So, what I'm struggling to understand," he continued, his tone simmering with restrained anger, "is why you were NEVER truthful off your show? Why lie in real life?"

I was hit with a wave of shock, the ground shifting beneath me as a brutal revelation tore through the fabric of our friendship. The impact left me staggered. "I don't understand." I stammered.

Paddy shook his head, as if in disbelief. This was unchartered territory – I had never seen him like this. He had never been angry with me before.

"You do Anna." He stared me down, his eyes piercing, "You do understand."

Without saying another word, he abruptly left the breakroom. This time, I didn't follow. The weight of his words had me stuck to the ground, my thoughts racing and my emotions in disarray.

***

Taking a sick day wasn't an option, my workload demanded attention, though my mind struggled to focus. Paddy's words lingered in my thoughts. He had left the office, so I couldn't pull him on it and he'd not responded to my texts asking if he could explain.

After a day of diving into administrative tasks—sifting through sponsorship requests, responding to emails, and meeting with the analytics team—I trudged home, deciding to call Grace along the way.

"I'm knee-deep in celery juice, can I call you back?" Grace's voice crackled through the phone, accompanied by the background hum of a bustling café.

"Amir is gone. Didn't say goodbye," I blurted out, the weight of the day pressing on me. "And Paddy is pissed at me."

"What?" she exclaimed over the blender's drone. "Hold on-"

I chuckled, picturing her multitasking with the phone cradled against her shoulder as she shoved celery sticks into the juicer.

"It's okay," I shouted, trying to be heard above the noise. "I'll talk to you after work. When do you finish?"

"7 pm. I don't understand why anyone needs juice so late," she laughed. "I've just got a delivery order for 40 celery juices… who in their right mind would drink that much celery?"

I laughed in agreement, "God… Call me when you get home."

"Alright, love you."

"Love you." The familiar exchange brought a fleeting moment of comfort amid the chaos.

The evening air had me shivering. The heaviness of the day settled in my bones.

Unlocking the door to my apartment, the familiar scent of home offered a momentary escape from the whirlwind of emotions that had accompanied me. I kicked off my shoes and sank into the welcoming embrace of my favourite armchair, my gaze fixed on the unanswered messages on my phone. Paddy's silence lingered. With a sigh, I wandered into the kitchen, absentmindedly preparing a simple dinner for which I had little appetite. As I sat alone at the dining table, the glow of city lights filtering through my window, I picked up my phone, contemplating whether to reach out again. The uncertainty gnawed at me, but the fear of pushing him further away held me back.

The night stretched and lost in the soft glow of the TV screen, the familiar voices of fictional characters provided a momentary escape from reality. But just as the storyline began to unfold, there was a knock at my door.

There stood Grace.

"Kale, spinach, cucumber, broccoli, carrot, beetroot, turmeric and ginger," she handed me a brown-looking juice.

"Oh, thanks." I was relieved to see her but nervous about the blended veg, "Isn't this supposed to be green?"

She walked past me, ignoring the question, and slumped onto my sofa. "Are you hungry?"

I looked at her and then at the juice before taking a small sip. I shivered; I didn't really like broccoli cooked, never mind raw and blended.

She snorted, taking in my reaction. "So..."

My nose flared as I swallowed. "Why is it spicy?"

"Pizza?" she continued.

"Anything that isn't this. I love you but god – never make me a juice ever again." I threw the cup into the sink, watching chunks of half-blended vegetables catch in the drain. "Is that on the menu?"

The smirk on her face told me the answer before she did, "No." Her eyes gave away a tell-tale flicker of guilt, "So... Pepperoni?"

"I literally just had some noodles..." I crawled back onto my armchair, wrapping a blanket around me. "How was work?"

"It's work." She shrugged, flicking through her phone. "Should I get a medium or large?"

I shook my head, "I'll just have a slice."

She rolled her eyes, "Yeah – okay. You always say that and then eat five."

"I do not!" I protested, "But yeah – get the large."

She shook her head, knowing me better than myself.

"So... work? How is it? Don't be so vague." I threw a pillow at her, trying to pull her away from her phone.

She glared at me, "It's temporary. I love the team but today I had to remake a matcha latte three times because it wasn't scalding hot enough. Like...I'm talking as hot as the earths core." She shook her head, reliving the memory, "I miss visiting cool castles and exploring old, abandoned buildings or fancy skyscrapers... I need to send out my CV to more production companies."

"I can help." I offered, "I'd like some distraction from reality anyways."

"Yeah – I bet." She smiled, solemnly.

"I don't even want to get into it right now." I sighed.

Grace nodded, "Okay, you can sit in your self-pity, but your time is up once the pizza arrives. Do you have any wine?" She stood and walked to the kitchen, effortlessly making herself at home. She opened the fridge, finding a cheap bottle of rosé. "Ah, you do."

I chuckled, "You drink wine now?"

The distinctive sound of the bottle being unscrewed answered my question.

"Where are your glasses?" I turned to see her exploring the cupboards.

"In the dishwasher." I pointed.

As she opened it, a burst of hot water sprayed her, prompting her to turn towards me, gracefully lifting the bottle to her lips. As usual, she shivered slightly upon tasting the alcohol. "Not bad." Her twitching eye said otherwise.

Finding her spot on the sofa again, I erupted into laughter watching her. A sight I never expected to see – Grace sipping wine from the bottle.

She smiled at me, looking from the corner of her eye, and passed me the bottle. I took a sip, and my heart began to crackle.

Galway. Amir. Sharing wine in the park.

I swallowed. "Have you seen this?" I pointed to the show on the TV. She shook her head. "Nope."

"It's decent." I turned up the volume, and we both began to watch in comfortable silence. I tried my hardest to follow the characters on screen and forget memories of the past.

Twenty-eight minutes later, a Happily Ever After scene began to play out in front of me, and I couldn't help but sniffle.

I'd dated so many men, and none of them offered a sliver of that.

For the second time, a knock at the door interrupted my distraction. I moaned and paused the TV. "Must be the pizza," Grace announced, eyes watery.

"I'll go." I jumped up.

"No!" She fought me, pushing me back into my chair.

"At least take some money for it- "

She ignored me and headed to the door. I lifted the wine from the floor and took a sip, waiting for that deliciously greasy smell.

But instead...

I heard hushed voices.

Loud footsteps.

And then he squeezed my shoulders, nearly sending me into shock.

"Dickhead." He teased, words dripping with sarcasm. He grabbed the wine from my hands, faked disgust written across his face. "At least drink from a bloody glass, you tramp!"

I gasped, "What the fuck!"

Grace appeared from behind Paddy, guilt drawn across her face. "Pizza arrived."

Her hands were empty.

"I actually wanted some pepperoni!" I exclaimed sarcastically, standing up. I pulled Paddy into a hug, not giving him any option to refuse.

He awkwardly patted my head, not used to this type of affection. "Okay. Get off now." He acted repulsed and slumped onto the chair opposite me. Grace sat beside him, and they both exchanged a knowing look.

"What's going on?" I narrowed my eyes, "Is Amir about to appear too?" I looked at the door, prepared to see him standing there too.

Paddy laughed, "No." And then his tone changed, "He's actually gone... I've not heard a word from him."

"Seriously?" I sighed.

He nodded, notably upset. "I'm sorry for snapping at you earlier. That's why I'm here."

Grace eyed me, observing my reactions.

"It's okay." I sighed. "I just don't understand... everything you were saying. What did you mean?"

He stared at me, eyebrows raised as if to test my truthfulness, then turned to Grace, who gave him a dumfounded look in response.

"You never told him how you felt." He sighed. "I mean – in ways – you did, from certain things you said on the podcast. Kind of. But..."

I shook my head in denial, "I don't even know how I feel... felt."

Grace snorted, "Pass me that wine."

I did.

"Okay, so I had feelings, a lot of them. I hated him one minute and thought he was everything and more in the next. But... I'm so glad I never told him that I liked him!" I admitted, anxiety building in my body.

Paddy looked confused. "Why?"

"Because he felt nothing." My voice was defeated, "I may not have told the whole truth. But he lied. He really lied."

Paddy failed to understand so I explained further.

"Remember the first day Mia suggested I have my own show?" I asked. "I was caught telling a story from Derek's funeral. One where I wanted to leave so badly, that I took the stairs... And in the stairwell – I met two half-naked... shagging... strangers."

Paddy began to laugh, shaking his head at my brief retelling.

"That was Amir." I concluded.

Grace spat out the wine and began to choke, "What?!"

Paddy tapped her back. "I know." He responded, shocking us both even more, "He told me. Like before you even figured out it was him."

My mind exploded. "What?"

It didn't make sense.

"He told me. He found it quite funny actually." Paddy elaborated, "We had a bet on how long it would take you to figure it out."

I shook my head in denial.

"Then why – why." I paused, unsure if I could reveal the things he confessed to me in Galway. Things I believed to be a lie. "Who was he on a date with?"

"Oh yeah..." Grace sighed, "On Friday night."

Paddy laughed, "What are you talking about? He wasn't on a date. He hasn't done anything but work since he got here."

"He was with a blonde woman in The Merchant." I bit my cheek, unsure if I wanted to know the answer.

"No – there's no way. He spent all week travelling North and South of Ireland meeting with sponsors and board members... I am telling you – the last thing he'd be thinking about is dating." Paddy shook his head, "In fact... hold on."

My heart raced. He pulled out his phone and began to type and scroll.

"Is this the woman?" He showed a picture on his phone and I nodded, afraid for what was coming next.

"I think so."

"Derek's sister." He explained. "She used to be involved in Spotlight... but lives in London...I think."

"But why would he meet with his sister? I'm lost." My eyes pleaded for further clarification.

Paddy shrugged. "I know – I know for a fact he wasn't on a date. She was probably thanking him for saving the station. Derek wanted to keep Spotlight alive and did so... for many years, whilst making a loss... everyone begged him to shut it down. When he was sick, Amir spent a lot of time with him, and promised him that he wouldn't let Spotlight die. His wife... The Board... they thought Amir was sent here to shut things down and they put huge pressure on him to do so. He's lied to them relentlessly... but he kept the station alive."

"So... was the sister angry or?" I asked.

"Yeah, or was this her goal too? Because... because she's from Northern Ireland too so maybe it was a shared wish?" Grace questioned, almost more intrigued than I was.

Paddy let out an exasperated breath, "Jesus, I don't know every fecking detail! Let me live." He laughed. "Why don't you ask him?"

The room fell silent.

"Anna..." he said my name delicately, waiting for a response. "Call him. Tell him the truth... see where he's at."

"I don't know." I shook my head. Uncertainty still clung to me like a shadow. I had already given myself a mental pep talk, preparing to make room for something better if he had left and wasn't planning to stay. "What good would that be? He's not going to come back."

"Christ." He lifted the wine bottle from Grace, who was nursing it rightly. He took three gulps finishing the bottle. "Stop being so difficult!"

"What do you want?" Grace asked, contemplative. "I know – what you said to me in Galway..." she paused, taking a beat, "but do you still think he isn't right for you?"

I swallowed, looking inward for a moment. I wiped a tear that escaped my eye, desperately craving clarity instead of confusion.

"Even so... I always think that you should tell someone how you feel about them," she added, "or you might live to regret it."

Her eyes turned to Paddy and they exchanged a knowing look.

***

I'd left my notebook in the office so instead of being able to write down my thoughts, they clung to the walls of my mind.

'Sorry.' I typed into iMessage.

I then erased it just as fast. My pillow suffocated my scream as I let out my frustrations. I pulled at my hair, unable to decide how I felt and what to say to him.

Impulsively, I pressed call. It rang four times and then went straight to answering machine. *Had he declined it?*

I hung up, not wanting to leave a voice message and began to type again.

I can't believe you've left. I'm at a loss for words, except to say that I'm sorry. I regret jumping to conclusions, but unfortunately, my mind went to the worst possible scenario. Maybe it's a self-sabotage pattern from being hurt in the past. But I want to be with someone who won't play games with my heart or leave me guessing about their feelings. However, in realising that, I also acknowledge that I haven't been entirely truthful with you. I played games to shield myself from your potential rejection.

So here's the truth.

I've liked you since the day we met.

I didn't anticipate liking or falling for you, but I admit it – I did. I fell hard. I tried everything to deny it because... I couldn't. For numerous reasons, I couldn't allow myself to fall for you.

You're my boss.

You're challenging.

You're hot-headed.

You're difficult.

You're frustrating.

You're like a goddamn Adonis.

You're an American and sometimes a bit of an arsehole.

You're emotionally unavailable.

You were always leaving Belfast.

And I, I have a podcast with the responsibility of creating entertaining episodes for an audience, expectant of wild dating stories and learning experiences from many different men.

I'm also an employee.

I'm challenging.

I'm hot-headed.

I can be difficult.

I can be frustrating.

I'm a Belfast girl, through and through, who can give shit better than she takes it.

And... I was emotionally unavailable, but now I think... (think being an important word here) I'm emotionally available, and I wanted to tell you the truth.

I'm sorry for assuming the worst when I've since learned you had good intentions all along. Thank you for saving Spotlight and everyone who works here.

I hope to see you again, but if I don't, I wish you the best in life. Call me anytime.

Anna x

I pressed send.

CHAPTER TWENTY-NINE
Boys a dear

Definition: a way of expressing shock. Used when something surprising or shocking happens.

FOUR DAYS LATER

He never responded to the text.

He never called.

And surprisingly, I was okay.

At first, I felt confused. I spent 24 hours checking my phone constantly, waiting on a notification or call that never came. But then reality set in, I'd said everything I felt I needed to say. I laid my cards on the table. If he chose to leave them be, then I'd guard them until someone else, much more deserving, came along.

It was okay to grieve the idea of something we could have created together. I allowed time for it.

But I refused to let myself feel misplaced.

***

On Friday evening, I found myself sitting across from Paddy, ready to record my episode.

"You good?" he hummed, already sensing the answer.

"I will be." I replied, offering a grateful smile.

"For what it's worth, I'm really proud of you," he nodded.

My eyes shimmered with tears for a moment. "Thank you."

"Now, go smash this episode before you undoubtedly win a fancy-ass award tomorrow night."

The countdown started, my intro song played, and I sucked in a deep breath. "Every setback is a new opportunity. Rejection is redirection. Every obstacle is a steppingstone to success. When one door closes, another door opens. Don't let the fear of striking out keep you from playing the game.' These quotes all echo the same sentiment – don't dwell on the past.

But how do you truly get over an ex? You stop allowing their memory to hold power over your present. You reclaim your mental space, filling it with positivity and self-love.

And how do you move on? You paint vibrant pictures of your future, imagining the endless possibilities that lie ahead. You focus on your own growth and happiness, rather than dwelling on what could have been.

When I first embarked on this podcast journey, I was lost in the aftermath of my breakup. Desperate for a remedy, the only solution that seemed remotely feasible was to seek out someone new to fill the void left by my ex. It felt like the logical step at the time, a way to distract myself from the pain and loneliness. Little did I know, this approach would only lead to more confusion and heartache.

So, I threw myself into the dating scene. I met new men, swiped through countless profiles on dating apps, and experienced the sting of being ghosted. But through it all, I began to establish new standards for myself.

It dawned on me that I have the power to fulfil myself. And even though, at this moment, my dating life is empty and unexciting, I'm totally okay with that.

Since I started this podcast, I've learned the concept of choosing myself wholeheartedly. Prioritising my own needs, desires, and well-being above all. Setting boundaries and refusing to settle for anything less than I deserve. I've also learned to listen to my intuition, to trust my instincts, and to cultivate a deep sense of self-awareness. Somehow, I've become my own friend, my own cheerleader, and my own source of strength.

Choosing myself isn't always easy. In fact, it's the opposite. There are moments of doubt, fear, and uncertainty. There are moments of loneliness, especially when I'm in bed at night, alone in my apartment, nothing but the hum of the TV to keep me company. But then I realise, I just need to find a better show to watch. A better way to fill my brain than thoughts of the past.

And my friends, I have the most incredible friends. Surround yourself with people that inspire and uplift you.

Each day that I remain focused on choosing myself, I feel stronger, and it becomes easier.

So, I guess I wanted to use this episode to empower anyone out there to treat themselves as if they are the main character. Stop being the side character in everyone else's story, and start writing your own."

As my outro music played, signalling the end of an emotional episode, I couldn't help but feel a sense of release and relief.

"Fuck yeah!" Paddy exclaimed, his enthusiasm infectious. "This is like therapy! But for free!"

***

I read her text with one eye open, and one still glued shut.

MIA – SPOTLIGHT
Are you awake?

Drool still hanging from my chin, I responded.

ANNA
It's 7.32am. On a Saturday.

MIA - SPOTLIGHT
https://www.belfastbuzz.co.uk/news/breaking-news/
belle-of-belfast-revealed

My gut sank reading the URL. As the web page struggled to load, I wiped my eyes and sat up in bed. A spinning wheel sat on the middle of the page, taunting me, making me wait. My palms started to sweat as another notification from Mia popped up on screen.

MIA – SPOTLIGHT
I'm on my way into the city. Call me once you read x

I hit refresh on the page, anxiety building. The text began to load, one torturous letter at a time.

WHO IS 'THE BELLE OF BELFAST?
An ordinary girl, living in an unordinary world.

Below the title was a picture of me, with Tom's arm wrapped firmly around my waist. I couldn't even recall it being taken. My stomach knotted as I read the photo annotation.

Anna Mulholland, pictured beside Tom Beckham, over ten years her senior.

I jumped when my phone rang, interrupting the screen.

GRACE

I declined the call immediately.

If you haven't heard of 'Belles of Belfast,' it's quite possible you've been living under a rock. The show has taken Belfast by storm. It's topics, while unconventional, have proved a huge hit with listeners near and far. One question every listener has, 'who is this Belle of Belfast?' Anna Mulholland, age 24, began her career in radio during her years of studying. Mullholland always had a passion for voicing her opinions, as we can see from her Instagram archive.

Three screenshots from my Instagram feed were plastered within the article. In one image, I was holding a sign at a Black Lives Matter protest. In another, I wore a 'blood stained' shirt at an event which was held to raise awareness for Period Poverty. The last photo, I was posing with Olivia in an Ann Summers store.

I felt beyond sick.

MIA - SPOTLIGHT RADIO

I declined the call.

Quite the overconfident activist, it's no question why Anna was offered the leading radio host role. Our source tells us that Anna almost turned down the position however, due to her inactive sex life and history of failed relationships.

How could they write this? My eyes began to pool with tears. Who was their source?

Anna however stepped into the presenter role and the world of dating; sharing weekly life updates on the show. In the past few months, we've met multiple interesting characters. Mr This and Mr That; code names gifted to each love interest, to protect their identities. We can now reveal a few of these flings, thanks to our source.
Tom Beckham played the role of Mr Millionaire. This comes as no surprise as we all know the pro golfer prefers younger women. When we reached out to Tom for a quote, he replied saying he could not comment on the matter, out of respect for Anna. We think it's probably out of fear she'd air more of his dirty laundry... Or maybe he's hopeful she'll take him back... as his girlfriend, Miss Northern Ireland runner up, Saoirse Ferry certainly won't.
One thing we're very aware of about our host Anna, is that her inexperience precedes her. When chatting about her infamous ex 'Mr Fuckboy', Anna shares her desperation for this man by detailing her actions after their breakup.
So, who is this 'Mr Fuckboy'?
An average man with an average name. When we called James to tell him the news, he was lost for words. When asked if he saw a future with Anna, he spilled the news that they had recently met and there was potential for rekindling their flame. So much for 'getting over your ex' ... huh Anna?

I choked on my tears reading James' lies.

In an effort to get over her relationship with James, Anna enjoyed a one-night stand with a man she labelled, 'Mr Bar Man.' This man has asked to remain anonymous, "To be honest, I don't remember much of that night, we were a bit drunk. She's a beautiful girl though and I would have seen her again, but not after this. What a psycho..."

Next, an image of Sebastian and I, mid kiss, was plastered on the site.

Our source was forthcoming with the identity of 'Mr Player,' Sebastian Reynolds. When introducing Sebastian to her audience, Anna explained, "his name has not been given to him because he plays golf...but because he plays women." Sebastian refused to comment on the news, but we can imagine he's replaying every episode on repeat.

Bile began to rise up my throat. I jumped from my bed and ran to the bathroom, afraid I'd vomit.

Now, there's one character we haven't been able to track down. We're on high alert to find out who this 'Mr Mysterious' character is and where he's hiding. Do you know? Send us an emai-

MIA - SPOTLIGHT

I answered the call, but a heavy silence hung between us, rendering me unable and unwilling to speak.

Mia's reassuring voice resonated over my speaker, "Anna, I'm on my way to your apartment now. Just stay calm."

Tears cascaded down my face as I let out a desperate cry. The weight of her words and what I had just read left me breathless.

"Oh, Anna, I'm almost there," she sighed. "5 minutes max. Stay on the phone with me. It'll be okay."

I clung to the phone, the sobs escaping me intensifying, as the world seemed to crumble around me. Collapsing onto the cold bathroom floor, I struggled to catch my breath. My day was supposed to be amazing, but it began in the worst possible way. I wrapped my arms around myself, squeezing, attempting to contain the shattered pieces of my world.

Her hair was tightly pulled back with rollers, and not a hint of makeup adorned her face. She appeared as though she had just woken up.

Silently, I sat on my sofa, tears streaming down my face, as she poured me a cup of tea. Her countenance was etched with concern, revealing a multitude of thoughts behind her eyes.

"Here." She handed me the mug, its warmth seeping into my hands.

"It's all over," I choked out. "How could this happen?"

She joined me on the sofa, wrapping her arm around me. "I don't know. But we're actively working on finding out. The article is disgusting. Cruel. You didn't deserve any of what they said."

At 8:10 am, I stood beneath the shower head, letting the water wash over my face. Citrus aromas enveloped my senses as I used a foaming shower gel to cleanse my skin. The brief respite provided a momentary escape before reality set in once again.

While I cleansed myself, Mia sat at my kitchen table, fielding one call after another from our PR department.

Exiting the shower, I wrapped myself in a towel and headed to my bedroom. My stomach grumbled, a combination of hunger and restlessness.

Upon returning to the kitchen, Mia turned to me, a sorrowful expression on her face. "We have no leads on who leaked everything yet."

I shrugged, feeling utterly defeated. "What now?"

"We will eventually identify the culprit. For now, we need to issue a statement in response to the article."

"I really don't feel like making a statement."

She sighed, squeezing my hand. "I really think you should mention something before the awards tonight."

"The awards...shit." I shook my head, realizing they had been completely overshadowed. I'd forgotten. "Does this mean I can't do my podcast anymore?" I asked, suspecting I already knew the answer. This had been my biggest fear. Amir warned me about how careful I had to be… *Amir*. My mind swarmed with worrisome thoughts, for a moment – wondering if he was to blame. I shook the thought from existence. Surely not.

"Honestly, I don't know what happens next." The uncertainty on Mia's face mirrored the growing dread in my stomach.

GRACE

My phone buzzed, providing Mia with an escape from the conversation.

"I should answer this," I sighed.

Mia nodded and rose from the sofa, giving me a bit of space to take the call. She squeezed the bridge of her nose, appearing visibly stressed as she leaned over the sink. She started handwashing our coffee mugs, disregarding my suggestion to use the dishwasher.

"Hey."

"Anna!" Grace's voice echoed through the phone, urgency, and concern evident. "Have you seen it? What's happening?"

I could sense a tinge of manic energy in Grace's voice, the urgency making her words rapid and breathless.

"Yeah I saw it. Mia's here."

"At your apartment?"

"Yeah."

"I'm going to come over now, do you want anything from the shop? Or perhaps a coffee or something?" she asked.

"No, I'm good. See you in a bit." I hung up the phone, feeling a little bit calmer knowing Grace was on her way. Her presence always had a reassuring effect on me, providing comfort and logical perspective.

Closing my eyes, I took in a long breath, holding it for four seconds before releasing. "I feel like I need to meditate or something," I mentioned to Mia, finding a slight sense of release after that steady breath.

Her eyes lit up, "Let's do it."

She grabbed a blanket from my armchair and started scrolling through her phone.

"Seriously?" I chuckled, feeling a little bit uneasy.

She nodded, "Absolutely."

The sound of calming music played from her phone as she sat beside me, covering us both with the blanket.

"I usually cross my legs, but we can lie down if that makes you more comfortable."

I opted for the latter, and we arranged ourselves on the sofa – topping and tailing. Listening to the guided meditation, my breath and heart began to slow. My nervous system relaxed, and unintentionally, we both drifted into a deep sleep.

CHAPTER THIRTY
A wee coconut finger

*Definition: a sweet dough finger / roll, dipped in icing
and topped with coconut. An ultimate irish comfort.*

An hour and 45 minutes later, Mia gently shook me awake. I opened my eyes, squinting at the living room light above me. "Please tell me it was all a dream," I mumbled.

"Unfortunately, not. But Grace is here," she said, stroking my head.

I sat up, still drowsy. Grace passed me a plate with a coconut finger on it. "No butter," she said, smiling, but her eyes revealed sadness and sympathy. "Psychopath..." She mumbled, "Mia has butter inside hers, by the way, like a normal person."

A laugh escaped me. "This," I said, lifting the coconut finger, "is essentially cake. It has icing on top. There is no need to cut it open and put butter inside it."

She rolled her eyes. "It tastes better with butter... that's the need."

"I'm not going to fight with you – again – on this," I snorted. "Pass me a cup. Please."

She handed me a cup of tea, and we nibbled quietly for a few moments.

"When did you get here?" I asked.

"An hour ago… but didn't want to wake you." she said in between bites. "I'd ask how you're feeling, but I already know the answer."

I nodded. "Yeah."

"We were talking…" Mia started, looking at Grace, "There's only one man, kind of, not mentioned in the article."

Grace hesitated, her eyes darting around the room as if searching for hidden answers. "Mr Mysterious." She sighed.

Amir.

My curiosity heightened. "What about him? Do you think it was him?"

Mia shrugged, and Grace gave me nothing.

The mention of Amir sent a shiver down my spine, and I couldn't shake the feeling that the storm I was in was about to intensify.

"Who is he?" Mia asked, her words laced with anxiety, probably afraid of overstepping. "I know you probably don't want to tell me, but it's important so we can rule him out…"

I set the plate onto the table, suddenly no longer hungry. I wiped at my lips with my sleeve, faced with the dilemma of revealing my feelings to Mia. I glanced at Grace, who was staring at me, anxiously waiting.

"It couldn't be him." I doubted my own words as I spoke.

"Anna-" Grace hesitated, "It could be… when you think about it. It lines up. I hate to say it."

I started to pick at the polish on my fingernails, contemplating the thought. My eyes began to water. "He wouldn't." My voice cracked. "I don't believe he would do that."

The anxiety tightened its grip on me. Thoughts raced through my mind, each one more unsettling than the last. The mere possibility that Amir, someone I thought I knew so well, could be involved in whatever was happening, sent waves of fear through me. My hands trembled, and I struggled to find the right words to convey the turmoil within.

"It's Amir." I choked.

I looked up seeing Mia's jaw drop. Her eyes widened, taking in my confession. "A- Amir? Amir Daivari? Like New York Amir?" She asked, "Apex Amir?"

I nodded, wiping my eyes with my sleeve. "Yeah."

She opened her mouth to speak but closed it again speechless.

"Do you honestly think he could do this?" I asked, looking at Grace. "You heard everything Paddy told us the other night... I-"

She shrugged, "I don't know for certain but who else? He knows your identity. He literally left the country after your argument without saying goodbye? Maybe he was after revenge after you... accused him of saving your show for other... motives." She tried to be careful as she spoke, not revealing the whole truth with Mia sitting in the room.

Mia shook her head, still in shock. "Also, he did read your show notes every week, which revealed more details than what we allowed you to broadcast." She spoke as her eyes glassed over, deep in reflection.

"Yeah but, I cut them down massively from what was in the journal." I defended, "I don't think he -"

Then my heart sank. *The journal.*

I stood from the sofa in a panic, "The journal..." Realisation dawned on me that I hadn't seen it in a few days.

"What?" Grace asked, observing me.

"I don't know where it is." I shouted, running into my bedroom. I began searching through handbags, my bedside table, under the bed. I returned to the living room, seeing them in hushed but panicked conversation.

"How much... extra... did you share in the journal?" Mia asked.

I paused, my gut sinking. "A lot. Everyone's names. A dramatic amount of details. So many details that... that it's embarrassing to even think about it."

I felt sick. The weight of the situation grew exponentially, my mind racing through the pages of that personal chronicle, realising the plethora of names, intimate details, and vulnerable confessions it held.

A sickening realisation gripped me as the truth slowly sank in – it dawned on me that I had, in fact, left my journal behind in the boardroom after my heated argument with Amir. It transformed a mere oversight into a daunting reality.

"Oh fuck." I screamed. "Fuck! Fuck! Fuck!"

"What?" Grace jumped up from the sofa, Mia following.

"What is it?"

My mind was at battle. I resisted accepting the notion that he could be responsible, but the arrows of suspicion were undeniably pointing in his direction. I shook my head, pulling at the ends of my hair. "I left the journal in the boardroom, after my argument with him."

"So, it might have been him." Mia nodded, "Ok…"

"I don't – I don't know. He might not have read it…he might not have even realised I left it. Anyone could have it." I added.

Grace shrugged, "that's true… anyone could have it."

I collapsed onto the sofa, screaming into a pillow, "I don't know what's worse!"

***

1pm rolled around and after much deliberation, I decided to text Amir with the link to the article. Immediately a blue tick appeared and underneath the message it said 'seen.'

"It's as if he was waiting on your message." Grace remarked.

I bit the inside of my cheek, an unsettling feeling still lingering. I watched my screen as a typing bubble appeared, but moments later, it abruptly stopped.

Mia returned from the apartment balcony, concluding her call.

"Okay, yes, sounds good… yeah, that'll do well. See you in a bit. Bye."

That'll do well

Definition : that will be fine / acknowledging that something will be sufficient

Her eyes met mine, "I'm sure it's the last thing on your mind but… the awards tonight… you could technically go now if you wanted? Without a disguise and any… risk." She delicately broached the subject, "I actually believe you're in with a good shot of winning."

She looked so hopeful, while my body felt like a lead weight, tethered to the sofa. I wasn't sure what to say.

"You know, I think – I – maybe I just need a few hours to myself to decompress," I sighed, "And then I might be able to pull myself together to go."

In truth, attending the awards was the last thing on my mind, but I didn't want to let her down.

Twenty minutes later, I found myself saying goodbye to them at the door.

"I'd imagine Olivia will be wanting to see you, so I'll give her a call and let her know you're having some alone time." Grace squeezed me into a hug.

"She's probably with Cormac anyways." I sighed, realising for the first time that I'd not heard from my other best friend. Or my mum.

"Call us if you need anything." Mia hugged me, "And, if you decide to come to the awards, the rest of us will be getting ready at 5pm."

I nodded, "Okay."

"And – Grace could come too!" She added. "And Olivia…"

Grace, whilst looking a tad shocked, went along with it. "Yeah, if you want. I've no plans."

***

I sat on the bathroom floor, patiently awaiting the hot water rushing into the bath. I had showered just a few hours prior but… my hair, a tangled and frizzy mess, had been left to air dry without the gentle guidance of a comb. The reflection in the mirror revealed my face was red, and my eyes swollen from incessant crying. I looked horrid.

Hoping the bath would bring some comfort, I stepped in, initially cursing the scalding heat as it made contact with my skin. However, with each passing moment, the warmth turned comforting.

I submerged my head beneath the water, feeling the weight of the day wash away as I swished my hair back and forth, then plunged myself completely under. As I held my breath, a fleeting thought crossed my mind… *What if I just don't come up from air again? My career was ruined. My hopes of finding love ever again had drowned with it.* I forcefully pushed the unsettling notion aside, gasping as I rose from the water.

I sat in the bath until the water went cold, my sanctuary gradually dissipating.

***

I drifted into slumber on top of my bed, still wrapped in my towel. Awakening in uncertainty and wondering what the time was, I fumbled for my phone with one eye half-open, only to discover its battery had died. In frustration, I flung it to the opposite end of my room.

I rolled over in the bed, attempting to return to sleep, my mind, however, refused to relent. Standing up, my head felt heavy, as if I was beginning to catch a cold. With damp hair clinging to my skin, I acknowledged the potential. Running a brush through the tangled strands, I applied serum, opting for a braid to let it air dry. Aiming for a refreshed feeling, I moisturized my face and brushed my teeth.

Gazing at my reflection in the mirror, tears traced silent paths down my cheeks.

I needed my mum.

Snatching my phone, I connected it to the charger. Within moments, it flickered to life, exposing a missed call from my dad and a message explaining that they were both en-route to emergency surgery, promising to call me as soon as possible.

I sighed, unsurprised but still upset. The demanding nature of their medical professions, compounded by a scarcity of doctors in the country, dictated their priorities.

And I'd been too occupied to catch his missed call… among many other messages.

PADDY
Come to the awards. We can get blocked once you win.

PADDY
I'll pay for every single round.

PADDY
And by that, I mean… I'll pay on the company card. It's technically a business expense.

PADDY
And then after that, I'll hunt down whoever wrote that article and make them drink their own piss. Deal?

I chuckled, grateful for his humour.

GRACE
Love you.

OLIVIA
You need to go to the awards because you will def win!! Not taking no

for an answer. Grace and I will both see you later xxx

MIA

I checked the office and... no sign of the journal.

2 hours later

MIA

I've called a local dress store and held a selection for you. Grace helped with sizing. There's also a hair and makeup artist coming to mine later. I just want you to know I have everything sorted incase you decide to come. I think it would be the best thing for you. x

I was grateful for her organisation and consideration, but my stomach churned at the thought of how people would look at me if I attended and what they'd be thinking.

AMIR (Missed call – 2)

A rush of air left my lungs as I glanced at his missed calls—one an hour ago and another 32 minutes ago. A single text accompanied them.

AMIR

Tried calling you. Call me back when you're free.

I immediately pressed the call button, only to be interrupted by a loud banging on my front door. Frustrated, I hung up, and the banging persisted, fists pounding. Peering through my peephole, I feared someone was attempting to break in, but to my surprise, there he stood.

He looked terrible. For the first fucking time since I'd met him – he actually looked terrible. His face was red and sweaty, his hair dripping and dishevelled. Clad in grey sweats and a crinkled white t-shirt, he seemed a far cry from his usual self.

Shock held me in place, pinning my entire body to the floor.

"I-I-where-" he struggled to catch his breath.

"What are you doing here?" I asked, my throat strained with emotion.

He clung to the doorframe, attempting to regain composure. My blood pumped fiercely through my veins, seeking an outlet.

"I – you're not getting ready?" he breathed.

Glancing down at my appearance, embarrassment warmed my cheeks. I was a mess. "What do you mean? Why are you here?"

"To check on you." He sighed, frustrated with my questioning.

"To check on me?!" I screamed, blood boiling. "You left. And then... th"

My voice cracked and any hopes at speaking shattered like glass. Shock shivered through my body. In his hand, he held the journal.

"You..." I croaked, tears immediately soaking my face. I let out a cry.

He moved into the apartment, pulling me into his arms. "It's okay. It's okay. We're going to fix it."

I pushed at him, shoving him away. "FIX IT? YOU CAUSED IT!"

His eyes met mine with confusion. "What?" He choked.

"You told them, didn't you? You read my journal." I pointed at it.

He lifted it up, "This? I didn't... I mean... I read a little bit but..."

I could taste the tears on my lips, "I can't believe you."

His brows furrowed deeper, and a perplexed expression lingered on his face. "But Anna- "

"GET OUT!" I screamed, pushing him towards the door.

He raised his hands in the air in defence. "ANNA!" He screamed, silencing me. "HOLD ON A SECOND!"

I went mute, shocked at the volume of his voice.

"What do you mean, I told them?" He asked for clarification.

I laughed, finding his pretending of ignorance typical, "BelfastBuzz! You told them! It's all in there and you told them!"

The confusion on his face grew more pronounced. He shook his head, a mix of disbelief and frustration. "I didn't tell anyone shit." he spat. "I would never! This has been my biggest fear all along. You think I'd ruin your career?"

I started to feel small.

"I thought you knew me better." His voice cracked. "I would never. EVER. I didn't touch this for days. I didn't plan on ever reading it... but you had left one page half ripped out and..."

I felt like I was falling through a black hole.

"I read what you said about me." He sighed, emotion welling in his eyes. He opened the book and flicked to the end, staring at the half ripped out page that I had intended to crumple up and throw away. He cleared his throat and began to read, "Do I want to tell my future children that the first time I encountered Amir, he was half naked-"

"Stop." I cried, "I know what I wrote. Are you trying to embarrass me or something?"

"No. I need to explain to you." His face hardened, "I was in that stairwell with a woman, whose name I do not know, who's face I cannot remember – as a distraction from the loss I was feeling. I don't deal well with death. That day... was the worst day. I'd been dreading it for weeks, I'd flown across the world – and as well as watching my close friend and boss be laid to rest, I also had the heaviness of the journey I was about to embark on. I had humongous pressure on my shoulders. I had to fulfil a promise that I'd made to him, to make sure his legacy would live on in his hometown. The woman in the stairwell... I was extremely drunk and it was a stupid way to take my mind off of everything, but it was working, until you walked in."

I choked back my tears. "Why are you telling me this now? You left!"

"Anna! For once, please don't argue with me! Please hear me out." He looked down at the book again and continued to read, "Do I want to tell my future children about the rude consultant who teased and provoked me each day?"

"You did." I cried, "every single day!"

He shook his head from side to side, visibly upset and angry. "Do I want to tell my future children about the man who kissed me and then changed his mind, leaving me confused and feeling insecure? Not once, but multiple times."

I started to walk away, afraid for what he would say next. He pulled me back. "Wait." He begged. "Do I want to tell my future children about the man who cried to me about his emotional unavailability..." His voice strained, "his childhood trauma and then I spotted him on a date just days later?"

I shook my head, feeling the pain of the words I'd previously written.

Taking a deep breath, he squeezed my arm and his eyes begged me to listen, "First – I wasn't on a date, but I hope you already know that. I was meeting with Derek's sister."

I nodded, "Paddy explained."

Tears dripped from my nose. He wiped his hand across my face.

"Secondly - Anna, I teased you because I loved seeing your reactions each time. It made me understand how your brain worked." He explained, eyes focused on mine, "And I kissed you, not on impulse, but because the thought had lingered in my mind since the first day that I saw you in the break room...how frustrated you got trying to find out if I wanted sugar in my tea." He laughed softly, recalling the interaction. "But, after our kiss, I found myself running from you because I felt something. Honestly, it scared the shit out of me. What started as desire morphed into anxiety. I have a lot of demons in my closet. Everything I told you in Galway was true. The childhood, losing my mom... has made me feel like I can't allow myself... to fall. I have been absolutely terrified to let myself fall. For I've learned that love, someday, inevitably turns into loss."

Tears began to fill his eyes as he held my face in his hands. "But here's the twisted reality, Anna. The real fucked up part of this is… if I don't allow myself to fall in love with you, then I've already lost you."

His voice turned to a whisper, "But love – *our* love, it won't mirror the flawless 'happily ever after' fairy-tales that you find in your books or what's portrayed on screen. I might need your help sometimes and your reassurance that you won't leave when things are tough."

I sobbed. Overwhelmed.

"So, please give me a chance." He cried. "Give this a chance. I'm sorry for everything, I'm sorry I confused you but hopefully now you have clarity… that I want you. I came here to tell you that I want you. Fully. I'm all in – I…"

I crashed my lips urgently into his, abruptly halting his anxious rambling. The taste of his minty mouth mingled with the saltiness of our tears. A low moan escaped me as I instinctively wrapped my arms around his neck.

This, I thought, was the craving that had lingered since our last encounter. I had denied myself this desire out of fear, fearing the vulnerability it brought. As his fingers dug into my back, creating a delicious ache, our bodies pressed together with an almost painful urgency. In that heated exchange of passion, I had a revelation.

He wasn't perfect, I wasn't perfect, and our story certainly wasn't perfect. But to hell with perfection. To hell with waiting for the ideal moment. Life is imperfect, and love? Love demands risk. Love is a daring dance, a risky plunge into the unknown. As our bodies entwined, I embraced the imperfections, realising that it's the messy, unscripted moments that make life and love truly worthwhile. If we were to end up 'happily ever after' or not, I was willing to take the risk.

He pressed me firmly against the wall, effortlessly lifting my legs and encircling them around him. A thrilling jolt coursed through me as I felt his hardness against me.

"Sorry," he muttered against my swollen lips before trailing wet kisses down my neck. I couldn't help but moan, pulling him closer in a desperate embrace.

Suddenly, thoughts of my open front door and nosy neighbours invaded my passion-fogged mind. "Amir..." I pushed at his shoulders, and instantly, he released me from his grasp.

"Are you okay?" he asked, his eyes aflame with desire and concern.

I chuckled, more than okay. "Yes—yes—yes." I pecked his lips. "I just don't want my neighbours catching us. We should close the door."

"Fuck the neighbours," he laughed cheekily, giving me another quick peck.

"Pause... close the door... and resume." I squeezed his arms, my heart pounding in my chest.

He paused, his eyes absorbing me for a moment before releasing his grip. Turning to the door, he then looked back at me, shaking his head with a smile. "We might need to resume a little later..."

I raised an eyebrow, intrigued.

"I need to get you in a dress. We have an award show to attend," he continued.

"Did Mia send you then?" I asked, my heart fluttering.

"No, she doesn't even know that I'm in Belfast. I spoke with Paddy though and he told me where to find you," he replied. "But... the awards... now that everyone knows your identity... I figured... why not? You should be there."

"Mia said that too." I nodded, feeling a sudden weight on my shoulders. "I'll go."

He pulled me close, planting a kiss on my forehead. "I never left... you know..." He sighed.

"What?" I questioned, confused.

"I was in a hotel five minutes away the whole time. It's taken everything in me not to come see you."

"So why didn't you?" The confession made me feel unsettled.

"Fear," he admitted. "But when I read the article, I needed to make sure you were okay. I can't imagine how you're feeling."

His fingers stroked my hair, momentarily distracting me from the complexities around us. However, reality struck.

"I'm just confused." I swallowed the tears building at the back of my throat. "If you didn't write it... who did?"

CHAPTER THIRTY-ONE

Great Craic

Definition: a great time

A flutter of nerves gripped my stomach. "It's okay," Grace reassured me, squeezing my hand.

We were greeted by fire-eaters and offered glasses of champagne; the air was alive with anticipation.

"Everyone's already inside," Mia chimed in, expertly fixing a loose strand of my hair. "You look incredible. The hard part of getting ready, especially on short notice, is done. Now all you have to do is enjoy the event."

The awards ceremony unfolded in the iconic Titanic Museum, its exterior shimmering in the evening light. Above us, the sky was a vast canvas, clear of stars, adding a touch of mystery to the atmosphere. Cameras flashed incessantly as glamorous individuals struck poses on the red carpet before making their way inside.

"Olivia is running five minutes late, but she'll be here shortly," Grace added. "We're all here to support you. You've got this." The words resonated, instilling a sense of confidence as we stepped into the glamour and excitement of the awards night. I smiled, grateful for their presence and support.

Inside, Amir and Paddy engaged in conversation with some of our board members. Unnoticed, we entered the building, and I couldn't help but appreciate Amir's rare and genuine smile as he nodded enthusiastically during their discussion. Grace abruptly grabbed my arm, bringing me to a halt.

"Hold on," she said, looking a bit frantic. "Do I have something in my teeth? I had a salad earlier, and... can you check?" Her eyes darted anxiously from me to the boys as she flashed her teeth for inspection.

"Nothing there," I assured her with a smile. "You're all good."

"Girls?" Mia inquired, already a step ahead of us.

"Is my hair okay?" Grace asked, running her hands through it. "Or do I need more powder on my face? You know how I have oily skin sometimes."

"Grace," I said softly, "you look beautiful. What's this about?"

Her anxious rambling unsettled me.

"Nothing," she shook her head. "It's nothing."

As her eyes darted towards the boys again, I began connecting the dots. Rather than questioning her, I opted for reassurance.

"You look gorgeous, honestly. You have nothing to worry about," I added.

"You're stunning, both of you! Now come on," Mia exclaimed, pulling my hand and guiding us over to the group.

Paddy's eyes subtly widened as Grace approached, a faint but noticeable spark lighting up in them. Though he maintained the ongoing conversation, there was a slight shift in his body language—perhaps a subtle straightening of posture or a softening of his expression.

"Jesus ladies!" He whistled, "You scrub up well."

"Nice to see you in something other than sweatpants and a hoodie Paddy." I responded.

Grace nudged me. "What Anna means to say is that you all look great too."

"Enough compliments – where's the bar?" I giggled. Anxiety had begun to bubble up in my stomach as I noticed people staring. A few people even pointing at me.

As Amir laughed, the warmth in his eyes reached me, and he casually moved closer. With an easy, affectionate gesture, he pressed a reassuring hand into the small of my back, his thumb gently rubbing up and down. The touch was comforting, grounding me in the midst of the attention.

As Mia and Gerry, a board member, chatted about Spotlight's nominations, the stares and occasional pointing from onlookers continued to make me uneasy. I couldn't escape the feeling that all eyes were on us. Whilst Amir's touch had provided momentary comfort… the nervous flutter in my stomach began to build again. Spotting the bar in the corner, a subtle wave of relief washed over me. Without giving it much thought, I decided it was the perfect excuse to make a quick escape from the scrutinising gazes.

"Guys I really need a fucking drink… I feel like a zoo animal." My eyes darted around the room, "Does anyone want anything?" I asked, feeling a bit breathless.

"We have champagne at our table, we'll be heading into the dining room soon." Mia suggested, "Don't worry."

I shook my head, panic building, "Right… right… ehm I just need a- a water." I began to manoeuvre through the crowd, my steps quickening as I felt Amir's presence following closely behind. The sounds of conversations and laughter seemed distant, muffled by the persistent thud of my anxious heartbeat. Glancing back, I caught Amir's eyes and he nodded, reassuring me that I was okay.

Reaching the bar, I exhaled a sigh of relief, the cool surface providing a momentary respite. As we stood side by side, the clamour of the event fading into the background, I found solace in the shared silent understanding between us. Sometimes, a quiet moment away from the spotlight was all that was needed to ease the grip of anxiety.

"It's going to be okay," he reassured, casting a quick glance around the room. "Ignore anyone staring. It'll stop soon."

I sighed, "It's just a bit much. I didn't think it would be like this."

He nodded, "Think of it this way... your show clearly had a huge impact. People listen in because they care about your life, your learnings, and your updates. They probably had an idea of who you were in their minds and are now discovering more information. I'd be more worried if no one was interested at all."

He had a point. "Thank you. It's just overwhelming."

Suddenly through overhead speakers, a voice requested we make our way to the grand dinner hall for the awards to begin.

***

Gratitude surged through my veins as I stepped into the opulent room. "Opulent" felt like an understatement; the banquet tables were resplendent with bottles of champagne and wine. Overhead, flowers and sparkling lights adorned the ceiling,

The focal point of the space was a replica of the iconic Titanic ship staircase, its grandeur capturing the essence of a bygone era. Positioned in front of this architectural marvel was a small stage adorned with a gleaming microphone. Massive LED screens, suspended from above, played a captivating promotional video for the awards. Animated text danced across the screens, announcing categories and nominees, leaving me in awe.

As I walked beside the man who had become my anchor, I felt a surge of euphoria—a stark contrast to the heaviness that weighed me down earlier in the afternoon.

Amir's voice broke through the mesmerising display. "There's Mia," he pointed. She was already seated, accompanied by her husband Phillip. On the opposite side of the table, Rory, a board member from Spotlight, was engrossed in the unfolding video. We approached the table, and with a gallant gesture, Amir pulled a seat for me before joining my side. Light conversation filled the air.

Jenna, another Spotlight Executive, took a seat opposite me, her excitement radiating through a beaming smile. Unable to resist, I found myself smiling back, swept up in the contagious enthusiasm of the evening.

Grace and Paddy sat, deep in conversation. I watched, carefully admiring every action. "They like each other." Amir whispered.

I nodded, "I think so too. Although Grace will deny it."

He chuckled, "sounds familiar."

The ambience transformed as the lights dimmed, casting a hush over the entire room. Abruptly, the red curtains that adorned the sides of the stage gracefully parted, revealing a fully-fledged orchestra. A wave of anticipatory stillness fell upon the audience, only to be shattered by the enchanting strains of music that erupted, captivating everyone present.

A single spotlight descended onto the grand staircase, illuminating a man and woman descending each step with grace. "Welcome, ladies and gentlemen, to the ninth annual Northern Ireland Entertainment Awards!" she announced into the microphone as the music lightened.

The applause resonated through the hall, but my nerves danced beneath the surface. Glancing around our table, I noticed the empty seat. Olivia's seat. A mix of worry and disappointment settled in as I searched the room, hoping to spot her familiar face. *Nothing.*

"We are thrilled to have you all here tonight. I'm sure you all agree, it's been great craic already… but the night is yet to begin!" the man added.

Amidst introductions and shared jokes from host to host, the judges panel took the stage. Recognising some impressive names among the six judges, excitement and nervous anticipation bubbled in my stomach. Thoughts of their discerning ears critiquing Belles of Belfast added a layer of tension. Under the table, Amir's hand found its way to my thigh, offering a reassuring squeeze, as if he could sense my escalating heartbeat.

A video began to play, showcasing the category as 'Best Comedy Star.'

"And the winner is, Shane Todd!"

A recognisable face hopped onto the stage, shaking the hands of the judges and accepting his award. Taking the mic, he began to speak "Thank you so much. I'm shocked, truly. I feel like I should make a joke or something, as that's how I got here I suppose. But I'm afraid it'll not be funny and you'll take this off me. So... cheers." He held the award to the crowd, who erupted into laughter.

I took a thoughtful sip from yet another glass of champagne, my eyes following him as he gracefully exited the stage.

"I can't wait to hear your speech when you win," Amir whispered in my ear. Suddenly, my eyeballs dropped from my head when the realisation hit me like a tidal wave—*holy shit, I hadn't prepared a speech.*

"I- I don't have one..." I stammered, feeling my blood thicken in my veins. "I didn't prepare anything, I..."

Amir's reassuring squeeze on my leg interrupted my escalating panic. "You'll be fine."

"But what if I win and I don't have a speech?" My throat felt like it was closing over. "Oh my god, what if I win..."

The orchestra played another quick tune, mercifully interrupting my spiralling thoughts.

"If you win, you'll walk onto that stage and own it," Amir whispered. "Every person in here will be staring at you."

I felt like they already were... and not in a good way.

As time marched on, my heart pounded faster and faster. I continued to sip champagne, attempting to wash away the bile that bubbled at the back of my throat. Nervous was an understatement.

A video played for the award category, 'Outstanding Writing for a Limited Series, Movie, or Dramatic Special.' I recognised a few shows I'd watched from the comfort of my sofa at home and wondered who the winner would be. The tension in the room built up; it was undoubtedly a tight draw.

"Aidan Largey!" the woman announced with exuberance. "For his multi-award-winning series, 'Sharp Sugar!'"

I stood to my feet, applauding, and felt Amir's amused yet seductive gaze on me. I had always been an avid admirer of Aidan's work, having binged his show multiple times.

"Big fan, huh?" Amir remarked, rising to his feet beside me, his voice tinged with a playful hint.

I nodded, enjoying the subtle undertones of jealousy. As Aidan began his speech, a moment I had witnessed on screen countless times, a discreet yet tantalising pinch on my thigh interrupted my focus. My hand instinctively moved to cover Amir's, halting his attempt to explore further up the slit of my dress. "Stop," I whispered, a playful giggle escaping my lips.

In the periphery, I caught Mia's eyes on us. A mischievous smirk graced her face, and her eyes seemed to acknowledge the growing connection between Amir and I. Suppressing laughter, I met her gaze as she shook her head in mock disapproval. I refocused my attention on the screen as another pre-award video began to play.

"Best Newcomer in Audio Entertainment!" The male presenter's voice resonated through the room. Instantly, my heart seemed determined to escape from my chest. *This was the moment.*

As the anticipation intensified, I could barely focus on the video playing on the screens, my mind racing as I scrambled for words I would say if I were to win the award.

The table held its collective breath as the presenter slowly approached the envelope. With deliberate anticipation, he delicately opened it, unveiling the name of the winner. The suspense hung in the air, thick and palpable, as the audience awaited the revelation that would shape the next moment of my evening.

"Belles of Belfast by Spotlight Radio!" The female presenter's jubilant scream echoed through the room.

I sat frozen, the realisation sinking in. I desperately tried to recall all the names of people I needed to thank. The entire table erupted in joy, and Amir, gripping my arm, helped me rise to my feet. I stared at them, feeling strangely detached from my own body. *This couldn't be real—there was no way.* Paddy enveloped me in a tight hug, passing me over to Grace, whose eyes glistened with tears.

"HOLY FUCKING SHIT ANNA! I knew you could do it!" she screamed over the orchestra and cheering. "I FUCKING NEW IT! Go get 'em!" With a push, she guided me through the jubilant crowd toward the stage. My mind grappled with extreme shock— A) from winning the award and B) from Grace's unexpected swearing.

Approaching the stage, I reminded myself to stand tall and smile. The female presenter handed me the award, and for a moment, I feared I might drop it due to my sweaty palms.

As I stood on the stage, a rush of emotions surged within me. The room, filled with expectant faces, seemed to blur at the edges as I took a deep breath to steady myself. My eyes scanned around, overwhelmed beyond belief, as the audience took their seats, patiently waiting for my speech.

"Hi," I mumbled into the microphone, the surrealness of the moment sinking in. "I honestly can't believe I'm standing here. Shock doesn't even cover it."

A soft ripple of laughter swept through the audience, but my throat tightened with a mix of nerves and sincerity.

"This morning, there was no way in hell I thought I'd be attending these awards because some news broke... that we'll not mention," I continued, the weight of the unspoken article lingering in the air. "But the reason I'm standing here, in this dress, in these shoes, and with my hair in anything other than a greasy, messy bun, is because of that table over there." I pointed to the group that had been my unwavering support. "Grace, Paddy, Mia, Amir, and all of my incredible colleagues at Spotlight."

A swell of cheers and applause filled the room, energising me to share a message that extended beyond this moment.

"We live in a world where women are often judged for being too confident, too emotional, or too opinionated," I continued, my tone impassioned.

The room hushed, and my gaze lingered on the faces before me.

"Often, we're made to believe that our voices don't really matter…" I declared, sincerity in my voice. "But 'Belles of Belfast' provided a platform for women to use their voices and be heard. A place to discuss taboo topics and make them feel normal because they should be normal. From the intricacies of our sex lives, pleasure, and intimacy to the complexities of relationships, we delved into body image, confidence, self-doubt, and the sometimes difficult but crucial conversations about mental health and consent."

A few people clapped and shouted in support from the crowd.

"The past few months have been a journey of self-discovery for me, the most significant lesson being that I possess the power to make myself happy, independent of others. That realisation is incredibly empowering. I am enough. You are enough. We are all enough. And if someone ever tells you that you are 'too much,' implore them to go find less. This award is for the women who rise above it, who say 'yes' to their dreams despite the 'no' they've heard. To all the brave women who live unapologetically, embracing their authentic selves without fear or shame."

My eyes scanned the room, landing on Mia.

"Lastly, but most importantly, I want to express my deepest gratitude to Mia," I continued warmly. "You saw potential in me, provided an opportunity, believed in my vision, and supported 'Belles' from the beginning. This award is as much yours as mine. Thank you for being a beacon of support and inspiration."

The room erupted into applause once again, the acknowledgment of her influence drawing a powerful response. As I descended from the stage, my heart swelled with a sense of purpose, knowing that this moment wasn't just about an award—it was about fostering empowerment, breaking barriers, and inspiring women to navigate their own journeys unapologetically.

Tears blurred my vision as my feet struggled to carry me back to the table, adrenaline coursing through my veins. I found myself being pulled in different directions, embraced by quick congratulations from strangers.

Mia enveloped me in her arms, her eyes filled with genuine emotion. "Oh Anna! I have no words."

"Congratulations!" Paddy enthusiastically high-fived me before proudly showcasing the engraved award around the table.

Amir, taking notice, remarked, "That was some speech. Did you come up with it on the spot?"

I chuckled. Grace, beaming with pride, poured more champagne into my glass.

"Yeah, kind of. Earlier today, when news broke about my identity, I started thinking about what I'd want to say on my last episode next week — how I'll conclude the show for good, you know? So, I pulled inspiration from that," I explained, a tear escaping my eye.

The thought of ending my show weighed heavily on me; there was so much untapped potential. "I just can't believe it's going to end." I whispered.

Amir, sensing my emotions, placed his arm on the back of my chair, gently tracing a finger up and down my arm. "Maybe it doesn't have to."

Music from the orchestra began to swell again as they announced the next award.

"I have a few ideas." He whispered. "Enjoy tonight and we can talk about it later."

Four awards later, an entertainment interval ushered in a delightful showcase of local talent – Irish dancers weaving rhythmic patterns, a lively band embracing the essence of the night, and a young choir enchanting the room with their soulful voices. As the performances continued with another dance group and yet another singer, the night began to feel a bit long, succumbing to the typical pace of most award shows.

Amir, seemingly disinterested in the last act, let his hand wander, teasingly playing with the strap of my dress on my shoulder. Engrossed in their performances, those around us remained oblivious to his subtle antics. Feeling his touch, I swiftly placed a hand on his thigh, squeezing with a subtle warning signal, attempting to rein in his playful distractions.

Turning my head towards him, I sucked in a deep breath as my eyes locked onto his, desire coursing beneath them.

"Stop," I mouthed, giggling at his distraction.

He raised an eyebrow and removed his arm from the back of my chair.

I sighed with relief and returned my eyes to the stage as the singer began repeating the chorus of the song. Just as I thought he had finished his teasing, his hand landed on my knee, squeezing gently. I tried to focus on the stage as he traced his hand upwards underneath the table-cloth, inching closer to the slit in my dress. My stomach fluttered, and I couldn't help but squeeze my legs together with anticipation.

His finger pushed underneath the fabric, and my breathing halted. Suddenly, the room erupted into applause, bringing me back to earth. He removed his hand and clapped.

I turned to him, my eyes conveying everything I was feeling—the frustration, the desire, the need.

***

"Oh thank fuck that's over with." Paddy sighed, rising from the table.

Mia snorted, erupting into laughter, "Paddy!" She scolded.

He rolled his eyes, and Grace joined in with a giggle.

"But seriously, you've got to admit, that was a drag! Way too long," he complained. We all laughed in agreement. Paddy, a little tipsy, swayed as he stood. His laughter was louder, and he was unquestionably drunk.

A singer took centre stage, performing alongside the orchestra. Upbeat dance tunes filled the room, creating a magical and uplifting atmosphere. Drunken attendees flooded the dance floor, swirling each other around and laughing.

I stood up, placing my hand on Amir's shoulder for support. I wiggled my feet and stretched my body, feeling the need to loosen up after sitting for so long.

"Are you okay?" Amir asked, eyeing me.

"Just checking if my feet still work," I replied, staring at my heels. They were taller than what I was used to. "All good."

"Great, you owe me a dance." He pulled at my hand

I burst into laughter, looking at him as if he had ten heads. "No chance."

Grace, still giggling at the table, stood up. "I want to dance."

"Are you drunk?" I asked, noting her glossy eyes, hiccup, and slurred speech.

"Come on, Paddy, let's dance," she said, ignoring me…and taking his hand refusing to give him a choice.

Wide-eyed, he followed her, glancing back at our table with fear etched across his brow.

"Come on. If Paddy can do it, so can you," Amir urged.

And suddenly, I found myself being pulled into discomfort. Mia continued to laugh heartily, thoroughly enjoying the unfolding spectacle, while her husband chuckled beside her.

"I have no idea how to dance like this," I admitted as he gently guided my hands and placed them on his shoulders, before wrapping his arms around my waist.

"It's easy. Relax," he reassured me, a warm smile playing on his lips, finding joy in my anxiousness. "Just sway to the music."

The music had shifted to a more relaxed tone, a soulful melody that wrapped around the room like a warm embrace. Couples gracefully took their places on the dance floor, creating an intimate setting under the soft glow of dimmed lights.

"This is cheesy," I teased, feigning annoyance. "I feel like I'm at a school dance."

In reality, my heart was fluttering.

He rolled his eyes. "Will you just try to enjoy it? Look up."

I followed his instruction and found myself captivated by the grandeur of sparkling chandeliers above us. He squeezed my hips, pulling me back into the moment.

"Beautiful," he whispered softly, his words merging with the smooth notes of the orchestra.

I nodded, a sense of wonder lingering in the air. "Ok...and?"

He threw his head back, laughter bubbling up. "You're impossible. There's an orchestra, a soulful singer, we're dressed all fancy, standing in front of a replica of the Titanic staircase, underneath an insane chandelier. This shit only happens in movies."

"I'm going to throw up," I giggled.

"Oh shut up." He laughed loudly and without warning, he leaned in and kissed me softly. The room seemed to fade away, leaving only the gentle melody of the music and the warmth of his lips against mine. I giggled against his lips.

"I said shut up." He mumbled, sharing my laughter before kissing me harder. One of his hands found its way into my hair, ensuring I couldn't move to talk or laugh further.

Our tongues met in a dance as we collapsed into our desires. The world outside the magical bubble we had entered ceased to exist.

When we finally pulled away, there was a shared understanding between us, a silent acknowledgment. He nodded and squeezed my hips once again, savouring the moment.

Those around us began to clap as the song finished and a new one began. I caught a glimpse of Mia, her husband holding her hand as they observed the dance floor. A sudden shock crossed her face as she pieced everything together.

"We've been caught." I giggled.

"I know. He's giving me the thumbs up behind your back right now." Amir replied.

Confused, I glanced behind me, seeing Paddy who instantly looked in the opposite direction. Grace was in his arms, swaying drunkenly to the music, a wide smile across her face.

"I actually meant by Mia, but…" I laughed, returning my focus to Amir. He looked in her direction and smiled, feigning innocence. She shook her head at both of us, and a mix of surprise and delight painted her expression.

"Kind of want to kiss you again just to make it clear," he said, eyes darkening.

"Make it clear?" I questioned, tilting my head.

He nodded, "yeah, that you're mine."

My heart skipped a beat, feeling the shared desire we'd both been trying to ignore for months. His words carried a lot of weight, and my breath became shaky as I wondered what to say next.

"That's only if you want? And I'm not saying that in an… I own you… kind of way… because you're very much your own person," he scrambled, his sincerity evident as he anxiously waited on my response. "But I'm done playing games. It's your choice. And I understand if it's too much. We can figure it all out though, I know it. But-"

"Shut up," I answered, pressing my lips into his, "shut up, shut up, shut up," I mumbled.

"You shut up," he mumbled back, smiling against my lips as we kissed.

"I'll fight you," I giggled.

"I hope so," he squeezed me and moved me around the dance floor, the playful banter continuing amidst the enchanting atmosphere.

As the song came to a close, Grace ran over interrupting our dance. "Olivia's here!" She exclaimed, pulling me away from the floor.

In the dimly lit room, Olivia stood, a vision in a floor-length dark green dress with perfectly curled, bouncy hair. She enveloped me in a hug. "Congratulations on the award."

I smiled, "Thanks babe… where have you been? You look insane." I stood back, taking in her beauty.

Her eyes darted around nervously as she shook her head. "Oh, you know… I was afraid you'd be mad and not want me here."

For a moment, everything froze within me.

"What?" Grace questioned; her curiosity piqued.

My gut tightened as nerves raced through me, an uneasy feeling settling in. "Why would I be mad at you?"

Olivia bit her lip, clearly troubled by what she was about to reveal. "I didn't expect them to write the article babe. I just said what I needed to say to get the job, but I never thought they'd actually use it." She placed her arm onto my shoulder, squeezing.

A sudden wave of nausea swept over me as the weight of her confession sank in.

Her dark, watering eyes cleared suddenly. "But – I did get the job! You are looking at the new Head Gossip Columnist for Belfast Buzz!"

She smiled widely, expecting joyful screams from us. But I was rendered mute, unable to comprehend the betrayal from one of my closest friends. The room seemed to close in, and the air became heavy.

"You fucking bitch!" Grace screamed, snapping me out of my trance. She was practically shaking with rage.

The colour drained from Olivia's face. "Oh, come on. It's not that bad. She won an award for christs sake!"

I shook my head, struggling to process the situation, and turned, desperately searching for Paddy and Amir.

Amir caught my eye, immediate concern etched on his face. My eyes welled up, and my throat tightened. "I can't believe this," I choked, my voice trembling, the shocking revelation unfolding before me like a dark, unexpected storm.

"Why are you making this a bigger problem than it is?" Olivia responded, half laughing, "I got the job?!"

She shook her head as if bewildered by why Grace was so angry.

"Congrats," I breathed, all the energy draining from my body, leaving me unable to yell, "I lost mine." Tears began to roll down my cheeks. "All thanks to you."

Olivia rolled her eyes, "Oh, catch yourself on, Anna. You weren't meant for it anyway. You nearly wet yourself every time you have to talk to a man, never mind sleep with him. Your stories are hardly interesting."

The realisation hit me like a tidal wave, my emotions raw and unfiltered.

Paddy appeared, handing Grace and I our glasses of champagne from the table. I waved my hand, unable to take the glass given how much my body was shaking.

"What's happening?" Amir questioned softly, placing a hand on the hollow of my back.

Olivia huffed, crossing her hands over her stomach. She shook her head, visibly frustrated, as if she was the victim in all of this.

"She did it," Grace choked, her eyes hazy, "Olivia told the press. She handed them it on a silver platter to secure her new job... as...."

"Head Gossip Columnist at Belfast Buzz." Somehow, she still glittered with pride while announcing her new title for the second time.

I clutched Amir's hand, unable to comprehend the depth of the betrayal from someone I had considered my best friend.

"Sorry, what?" Paddy choked out.

Amir's grip tightened, his stance shifting as he towered above me. His features hardened, the anger in his eyes was palpable, a fiery intensity that spoke volumes without a single word.

"I had no choice, though. In my interview, I had to give an example of some gossip no one in Belfast knows about… well… knew about. I didn't think they'd go and publish it." She attempted to justify her betrayal.

"You're so selfish," Grace spat. "This is why you've been so quiet lately!"

"Oh, hush up, you prude!" Olivia narrowed her eyes at her.

Amir pulled me closer and wrapped his arms around me, attempting to stop my anxious shaking.

"Olivia, I think you should leave," I requested calmly. She didn't deserve my politeness, but I knew her too well. She thrived on confrontation. Any sense that someone was angry at her, she'd explode and say anything to hurt them and worsen the situation.

Seemingly unscathed by the tension in the room, she tilted her head defiantly. "Leave? Are you serious, Anna? After everything, you're kicking me out?"

My gaze met hers, unwavering. "After everything? Our friendship is done," I choked out, "Clearly, it meant nothing to you anyways."

"Oh, fuck off!" She yelled, "You're blowing this way out of proportion. You should be happy for me! This is an amazing opportunity for me, and instead, you're both being bitches!"

Grace's anger flared, her voice cutting through the charged air. "You don't get to play the victim here."

Olivia's eyes flashed with a mix of frustration and resentment. "You always think you're better than everyone, don't you?" She shot a venomous glance at Grace.

"Better than everyone?" Grace questioned.

"But you need a reality check." Olivia spat, "you're not only working in a cafe with no career potential, but you also have no potential of finding love either. The reason you're on a man ban is because you know that, deep down, no man would fancy a boring girl like you. It's okay, you can admit it."

In an instant, Grace's anger reached a boiling point, and without warning, she unleashed a resounding slap across Olivia's face. The sharp sound echoed through the room, momentarily silencing the chaos.

Olivia recoiled, her cheek stinging from the impact. The shock on her face mirrored the collective astonishment that rippled through the onlookers.

My jaw dropped in disbelief. I'd never seen Grace utter a bad word at someone, never mind hit them. Paddy, reacting swiftly, intervened, and pulled her away from the escalating confrontation.

Amidst the stunned silence, Amir stood on edge, anticipating Olivia's potential retaliation to Grace. However, instead, she raised her full glass of wine and launched it at me, the liquid drenching my dress.

"That's it!" Amir responded decisively, forcibly pulling her away from me.

"Oh, Anna, look, even your man wants me!" she yelled.

Security appeared within a moment. As Olivia was escorted out by bouncers, I stood there, soaked and stunned, feeling the weight of the collective eyes upon me. Droplets of wine hit my toes, and the room's atmosphere shifted from celebration to an unsettling spectacle.

I darted for the exit. The once joyous night had transformed into a heartbreaking nightmare, leaving me with a mixture of humiliation, shock, and the bitter taste of betrayal.

***

Outside the venue, the cool night air provided a sharp contrast to the heated turmoil within. Amir followed closely, his comforting presence a silent reassurance. "Anna, are you okay?" he asked softly.

I shook my head. My steps were a blur as I navigated through the emotional wreckage, each tear mirroring the shattered remnants of trust and friendship left behind. The surroundings seemed to echo the emotional upheaval, with the distant city lights flickering like muted witnesses.

Paddy and Grace emerged, catching up to us, their expressions a mix of concern and disbelief.

Grace, still seething from the confrontation, spoke first. "I can't believe she did that! You should have let me fight her! I'd have torn her extensions right out of her head!"

"Calm down Conor McGregor." Paddy teased, attempting to lighten the mood as always. "You nearly knocked her out with one slap."

Grasping at the metal railing, the sight of the moonlight reflecting off the water's surface and the distant sound of lapping waves created a surreal backdrop. It was beautiful but gave me no peace.

Amir's hand on my shoulder provided a grounding presence as I looked between the water and the cityscape. He nuzzled his neck on my shoulder and wrapped his arms around me. Tears continued to stream down my face.

"I need to go home." I cried, defeated. "Today has just been way too much."

"Do you want us to come with?" Grace asked, softly.

I shook my head. "No, no it's fine."

"We can go to mine if you want?" Amir suggested. "I'm staying nearby."

We hailed a taxi. As the city lights blurred past, I leaned into his comforting embrace. The night had unravelled in ways I couldn't have anticipated, leaving scars that ran deeper than my wine-stained dress.

CHAPTER THIRTY-TWO
Delira and excira

Definition: delighted and excited

"A re you kidding me?" I exclaimed as the taxi came to a halt. Amir handed the driver some cash before gracefully exiting the car. He held the door open, a sly smile playing on his face. "What?" he asked, anticipating my reaction.

"You've been living on the same street as me this entire time?" I questioned, my disbelief evident.

He shrugged, "It's a really small city. Tiny compared to New York." Amir scanned a fob, effortlessly opening the entrance door to his apartment building. "I'm surprised you haven't seen me on my morning runs."

"You run?" I inquired, eyebrows raised. He nodded. "Like every morning."

Again, he nodded, casually pressing the button for the elevator.

"You're a psychopath," I laughed. The momentary banter provided some relief. My eyes, still sore and red from crying, had finally stopped

471

leaking.

"Oh, thanks," he rolled his eyes, "So kind of you."

I smiled momentarily, following him into the elevator. I sank into his arms as the lift climbed up floor by floor. He held me tightly, planting a tender kiss on the top of my head. My eyes watered, but with gratitude for the moment instead of upset.

"Here," he said as the doors opened.

My eyes rolled to the back of my head as we landed on the top floor. "The penthouse?" I asked, deadpan. "Are you kidding me?"

He shrugged nonchalantly and unlocked the door, "Yeah? So? Keep your panties on."

I slapped his arm. "This is so typical, you know."

The interior resembled a Manhattan-style apartment, transplanted into the heart of Belfast. The kitchen exuded a sleek, metropolitan charm with its matte black surfaces adorned with gold trimmings. Flowing seamlessly into the open-plan living room and dining area, luxury furnishings adorned the space. Plush contemporary sofas beckoned in the living area, accompanied by a large coffee table which was covered in books. The overall ambience felt like a page out of Architectural Digest.

"Jesus." I breathed.

He walked towards the sink and began pouring two glasses of water. "You're okay with tap, right?"

"Huh?" I was too focused on the floor-to-ceiling windows that framed a breath-taking panorama of Belfast.

"Tap water? I don't have any bottles left."

I snorted, "You did not just say that... everyone in Belfast drinks tap water. It's full of... like calcium and stuff. You're so American."

"You're so annoying," he laughed. "I swear to God."

I perched myself up on his marble kitchen island, "God doesn't like swearing."

He clicked his tongue on the roof of his mouth and handed me my glass. "Well, if God doesn't like what I'm saying, he'd hate what I'm thinking."

I tilted my head, sensing the hidden meaning behind his words. "Oh, do tell…"

My mood had shifted dramatically just by being in his presence. My problems, still very much present, had been blurred.

He sighed, shaking his head. I sipped on my water as he downed his glass within seconds. "Do you want a t-shirt to wear?"

I couldn't peel my eyes from him as he poured another glass of water and brought it to his lips, soaking them.

"Anna?" he asked, his accent thick.

I slid from the counter and turned away from him. "Unzip me," I requested.

He obliged, running a hand down the back of my dress, freeing me from the still-damp fabric. It pooled at my ankles, revealing my red lace underwear and stockings underneath. I felt hypersensitive to his touch, every caress sending shivers down my spine.

He breathed into my neck, kissing it gently. "You're gorgeous."

I held onto the counter in front of me as I gently swayed on my heels, pushing my ass into him. Teasing him.

"Turn around. Face me," he mumbled, demanding.

I did as I was told. Without another second spared, he lifted me onto the counter, spreading my legs and standing in between. His eyes were glossy, and his lips looked parched. "My god." He whispered, drinking me in.

I pulled his face towards mine, our lips colliding in a fierce embrace that hinted at the longing we had both suppressed. The kiss, hungry and desperate, sparked a wildfire of passion between us.

"No, wait," he murmured, gently pulling back.

"What?" I protested, already missing the touch of his lips.

"We need to talk about everything that happened tonight. Are you sure you're okay?"

I shook my head. "No, I'm not okay. The man I've wanted to kiss for months just stopped kissing me."

He chuckled, a tender smile playing on his lips.

"That's all I want right now. I don't want to talk," I whispered before reclaiming his lips with my own.

He pressed his body into mine, his hands wrapping around me. His fingers dug into my skin, pulling me as close to him as possible... but not close enough. The air crackled with an electric fervour as he removed his lips from mine and began attacking my neck down to my chest. His hand grasped at one of my breasts, squeezing it tightly whilst his other hand undid my bra. His lips found their way to my nipples. sucking and biting, he swirled his tongue around sending electric-like pulses down my body.

"Oh wow." I moaned, the intensity of my desire growing as I grasped at his hair, entwining my legs even tighter around him. "More. I need more of you." With a sense of urgency, I pulled his head up, craving the taste of his lips once again.

His hands on my thighs gripped even firmer, a delicious mix of pleasure and pain. "More," I pleaded, feeling a relentless throb between my legs.

He sighed, his lips leaving mine, and confusion clouded his gaze. "Anna..." he began, but I couldn't wait.

"What? What?" I begged, my need escalating.

"Are you sure?" His eyes bore into mine. Concern and desire battled beneath them. "I don't want you to do anything you'll regret. It's been a heavy day..."

I nodded, a sense of urgency pulsing through me. "I wouldn't regret it." I bit my lip, hesitating as reality settled in once again.

His eyes searched mine, trying to find the truth.

I sighed, "But you're probably right."

His head lowered onto my shoulder, kissing my collarbone gently.

Silence filled the air, the tension between us thickening. We both knew there was more to explore, but I needed a moment to process the overwhelming emotions of the day.

"I mean," I began, my voice husky with desire, "We don't have to do everything. But we could do some things."

He lifted his head, a mix of confusion and curiosity in his eyes. "Some things?" he echoed.

I pressed my lips onto his, my words a seductive murmur against his mouth. "Yeah... some things... I want to..."

His fingers silenced my words as they traced the lace of my panties. I moaned, the sensation sending shivers down my spine.

"You're soaking through the fabric," he whispered, his voice thick.

I nodded, very aware.

Without warning, he slid my underwear aside, spreading my legs wider. "Is this one of the things?" he demanded. "Answer me."

I nodded, unable to form words as his fingers danced over my most sensitive spot. My legs involuntarily squeezed together, the desire intensifying.

"Anna," he murmured, biting at my earlobe. "Answer me."

"Y-yes. Yes." I moaned, my head falling against his chest.

"Then stop trying to close your legs," he insisted, forcing them open and pressing my body down onto the cold countertop.

The apartment echoed with the symphony of my moans as his mouth lowered, immediately finding my clit with ease. I felt an overwhelming surge of pleasure as he skillfully teased and pleased me, his actions pushing me to the brink. His tongue flicked over me, sending shockwaves of pleasure through my entire body.

"What the fuck," I breathed, unable to cope. I looked down, astounded by the unbelievably hot sight before me as he ate me out. His relentless movements had me teetering on the edge.

"Behave," he scolded, tearing himself away, a glint of hunger in his eyes. "Stop moving, or I'll have to tie you up." The threat hung in the air, adding an extra layer of heat to the already scorching atmosphere.

My hands found their way into his hair as he passionately indulged. I pulled on strands involuntarily as my nervous system exploded with waves of pleasure. His movements were deliberate, each touch heightening my sensitivity. It was as if he was discovering my body, inch by inch, and every caress sent sparks of pleasure through my core.

"Fuck me," I begged, "Fuck me..." I could feel the pressure building inside, "I want you inside me."

He ignored my pleas, instead inserting two fingers inside as he continued flicking his tongue.

I struggled to breathe, desire crawling tantalisingly up my spine. "Ah – Amir," I moaned, "Oh my god."

I pulled at his hair, my legs closing involuntarily. He forced one thigh open with his hand while the other pumped in and out of me.

"Good girl." He mumbled against me. "That's it."

Seconds later, I came. Hard. I bit my hand to try to dull the scream that escaped my mouth, and as hard as he tried, he couldn't keep my legs open any longer. My orgasm washed through me, covering my body in bliss. I pushed relentlessly at his head as he kept going, making my body shake all over. "Okay – okay – okay," I moaned.

He persisted, and a moment later, it happened again. The feeling travelled up my spine, up my legs, ending in a release that the entire hotel would have heard, if not all of Belfast.

He finally pulled away, using his pocket square to quickly wipe his face.

I lay, unable to move, my body still shaking from the two orgasms he'd given me. I shook my head at him and covered my face, embarrassed at how loud I had been. He began to laugh and pulled my hands away from my face. He lowered his face to mine, "Can I kiss you?"

"Are you stupid?!" I screamed and pulled his face to mine. "You are —
that was…" I was left speechless.

He paused, looking deep into my eyes, his gaze smouldering with a
mix of desire and admiration. The connection between us was palpable.
His lips met mine in a slow, lingering kiss, a fusion of passion and affection that left me yearning for more. His fingers found their way inside
me once again.

I inhaled, feeling more tender than before. "My god."

Releasing his lips from mine, he pulled his now wet fingers up and
inserted them into his mouth, tasting me. I melted at the sight. It was
unquestionably the hottest thing I had ever seen.

My body still thrumming with the aftermath of pleasure, I found
myself breathless and utterly satiated. "Wow…" I gasped, feeling a wave
of vulnerability and intimacy wash over me. "How are you still clothed?"

He stood in front of me, still in his full tuxedo. Meanwhile, I lay with
my bra on the floor, panties to the side, heels nowhere to be seen but
stockings somehow still in place. He shrugged. "That's not something
I'm worried about right now."

His hands ran up and down my body, admiration written in his eyes.
I had never felt more desired.

I sat up, facing him, and decided to wrap my legs around his waist.
"I think it's your turn now?" I pushed him into me, feeling his arousal
beneath his trousers. My hand wandered, and I gently cupped him.
His breath was heavy, eyes narrowing into mine as he shook his head.
"Uh-uh."

I moved my hand up and down. "I want to."

I jumped from the countertop, immediately feeling small beneath
him, and slid onto my knees, still toying with him. I looked up at him
through my lashes, sensing uncertainty in his eyes. "What?" I asked,
feeling his hesitation.

His hand found its way into my hair. "You don't have to," he spoke softly.

"I know I don't have to... but I want to."

I genuinely did want to; unlike any man I'd been with before where I felt obliged. This was different.

He placed his hand over mine, pulling me to my feet. "Another time."

His lips met mine, gentle and reassuring.

"I don't understand," I giggled nervously. "I'm good at it. I promise."

He laughed, a smile covering his face. "I have no doubt. But I want tonight to be about you."

I felt confused, appreciated, loved. I'd never had a man be selfless when it came to sex. His focus was entirely on my pleasure, and it stirred a mix of emotions within me. I stared at him in wonder before kissing him once again.

***

4:38 am, I awoke to the emptiness beside me in bed. The city lights spilled through the curtains, casting a glow as the cold night air whispered around. Feeling a sudden chill, I stood up pulling the sheets closer to my body.

Stepping out, I headed towards the balcony, spotting him standing in the darkness.

"Hey," I whispered, trying not to startle him.

He turned. "Hey, I didn't wake you, did I?"

I shook my head. "No, are you okay?"

Approaching him, I noticed him only dressed in his boxer shorts. "You're going to freeze." I opened the bedsheet I was draped in and pushed myself into him.

"Just thinking," he said, his arms enveloping me. "Mhmmm... How are you feeling?"

The cold balcony floor made me shiver. "I'm okay."

"I love this view." He turned from me, gazing at the city below, his eyes reflecting a complexity of emotions.

I agreed, taking it all in. "What's bothering you?"

He shook his head, keeping his turmoil to himself. His lips met mine, a sweet kiss that hinted at deeper thoughts. "Just thinking about what comes next."

My nerves pinched; there was a lot to consider. "Let's go inside," I suggested, leading him towards the bedroom.

He followed, and we crawled back into bed. He spooned me, holding me tight. His hands found their way into my hair, gently stroking, and I sensed the weight of his emotions in the tender touch. "We're going to figure it out," he whispered and began placing delicate kisses down my neck. His teeth toyed at my ear, "You know that, right?"

I nodded. "I know."

He squeezed me, pulling me closer, my ass pressing into him. I turned around, wrapping a leg around his waist. Our lips met, tongues dancing together. I moaned, finding comfort in our closeness. I began to grind my hips, hoping to turn him on and distract him from the thoughts in his mind.

"I have an idea," he whispered against my lips.

"What is it?" It was hard to focus on his words with the desire growing between us.

"Come to New York," he mumbled, holding my head in his hands and kissing me with intensity. I froze, uncertain if I'd heard him correctly.

"What?" I asked in disbelief, pulling away.

He swallowed, looking more anxious. "I need to figure out the details, but you could come to New York and work for Apex."

My mind spun. *No, I couldn't.*

"I can't just give up my entire life here. My friends, my family…" I didn't mention Spotlight as I had no idea where my career was headed.

He sighed, realisation dawning. "Yeah, you're right. I'm just…thinking out loud." Disappointment melted in his eyes.

We lay face to face, unsure of the future and navigating the unspoken emotions that lingered between us.

"Are you still going back?" I asked, afraid of the answer.

He nodded. "Yeah. Two weeks."

I swallowed, feeling a burning in my throat. "Oh."

He stroked my hair, attempting to comfort me. "I just thought… I was thinking you could start over in New York. There's so much opportunity there."

He spoke with enthusiasm, careful not to pressure me too much.

"I- I don't know." I spoke. "I'm a Belfast girl... I can't imagine it."

Silence enveloped us before Amir finally broke it, his voice tinged with a raw honesty that mirrored the tumult within him. "I just feel that I already wasted so much time refusing to allow myself to give in to this… and now I don't want to be without you. I really want to try."

I reached out, tracing the contours of his face with my fingertips, attempting to convey reassurance.

"We'll find a way," I whispered. I cupped his face in my hands, my thumb gently brushing away the traces of worry etched on his forehead. "You won't be without me. Maybe New York isn't the solution, but we'll figure out what works."

He nodded. As dawn began to break, casting a soft glow through the curtains, we clung to each other.

***

The next afternoon, the scent of mildly burnt toast hung in the air as I discovered that despite residing in Belfast for a few months, he hadn't explored much of the city.

"You haven't been to Botanical Gardens?" I questioned, a playful glint in my eyes.

He chuckled, spreading butter on another piece of toast. "No."

"Belfast Castle?"

He shook his head.

"Um… St. George's Market?"

"I have no idea what that is," he mumbled, taking a bite of his bread.

My eyes widened with incredulity. "Okay, we're having a tourist day today."

He rolled his eyes. "No. You don't have to do that."

"Oh, but I insist…" I teased, my voice carrying a hint of mischief. "Maybe I'll lock you up in Belfast, so you don't have to go back to the States."

"I have a better idea… I think I should lock you up in this apartment. We could have a day on the sofa, or…" he walked towards me, spinning the chair I was sitting on at the kitchen island, "we could have a bed day… or I could just repeat what I did last night… right here." He said, placing one hand onto the cold marble and the other on my naked thigh.

His fingers began to toy at the edge of the t-shirt I was wearing, brushing underneath, sending shivers down my spine. My breath caught in my throat, anticipation building.

"Anna?"

I nodded.

"Open your legs," he pleaded, guiding me. I did as he asked, rendered speechless. "Oh, you're listening for once? Good girl."

His affirmation had the opposite effect; I wanted to tease him as much as he was teasing me. His fingers brushed over my panties tantalisingly slow, and a current of desire surged through me, making my skin tingle.

Surprising him, I slid off the chair and perched myself on top of the island. As he approached to play with me, I pressed a foot against his chest, stopping him. "No. You don't get to touch. You just get to watch."

His jaw dropped, and an eyebrow raised, surprised and intrigued. "Go on…"

I let my hand find its way underneath my panties, feeling how wet I was just from looking at him. I entered a finger, moaning, imagining it was him. Our eye contact was unbreakable as he watched in total shock.

"Oh…" He breathed, "Are you wet?"

I removed my finger, bringing it up to show him. It glistened.

He shook his head, taken aback by my unpredictability. "Fuck." He grasped my hand, bringing it towards him.

"No touching," I said, tapping his lips to quickly leave a taste.

I removed my panties completely, making sure to take my time as he watched. Once they were in my hands, I threw them at him, hitting his bare chest. He clicked his tongue off the top of his mouth, watching my every move.

I began to explore myself, rubbing up and down and entering two fingers in and out. He grew uncomfortable watching, unable to touch me. The air was thick with desire, a palpable tension that electrified the room.

"It's a shame you can't feel how tight I am," I moaned, "so tight."

He breathed heavily, his nostrils flaring as he took it all in. "Anna…" he said, almost warning me.

I moaned in response. "Shame you can't taste me."

He leaned forward, his hand gripping the countertop.

"It's a shame you…" I moaned loudly, "can't… fuck me. I've waited so long for you to… fuck me."

He leaned over me, but I pushed him back with my foot once again.

"Come on… while this is the hottest thing I've ever seen, you're being unfair." He spoke, his voice delicious and dark.

My breathing heightened as I began to touch myself faster. "Watch me."

He laughed, "I can't take my eyes off you."

I pushed my fingers in and out. "It's a shame…"

"Stop." He warned.

A smile made its way onto my face, enjoying my teasing. "It's a shame… you can't… *fill me.*"

"That's it." He demanded, grabbing my thighs, and pulling me to the end of the counter. "You have three choices… my mouth, fingers, or cock." Desire blazed in his eyes as he laid out the tempting options.

I felt a magnetic pull, a yearning that left me breathless. For a moment, I debated letting him take full control, surrendering to the intense desire coursing through both of us.

His hands tightened on my thighs, his eyes holding a promise of pleasure. But instead of yielding, a mischievous glint sparked in my eyes. I wanted to tease him further, prolonging the electrifying tension between us.

With a sly smile, I leaned back, propping myself up on my elbows. "Hmm, decisions, decisions," I purred, letting my fingers dance along the curves of my body. His gaze followed my every move, hungry and fixated.

"Maybe a taste first," I suggested, my voice a sultry invitation. I shifted on the countertop, granting him an unobstructed view. Slowly, deliberately, I ran my hands over my skin, trailing down towards the apex of my thighs. His eyes darkened with anticipation.

He licked his lips, clearly enthralled. "Anna, you're driving me crazy."

I chuckled, the sound a wicked melody in the room. "Isn't that the point?" I whispered, teasingly biting my lower lip. His desire surged, evident in the way he clenched his fists.

"But," I continued, drawing out the word, "I want you to watch, just watch." I lowered my hand, teasingly grazing the sensitive skin. His breath hitched, and I revelled in the control I held.

As I traced delicate patterns on my body, his eyes remained locked on mine. A symphony of yearning filled the air. I revelled in the power of anticipation, relishing every moment before surrender.

His voice, husky with desire, broke the silence. "Anna, I can't take it anymore. Let me—"

I silenced him with a playful grin. "Not yet" I murmured, enjoying the dance of desire between us. My fingers continued their enchanting exploration, leaving a trail of fire in their wake.

The magnetic tension grew stronger, an invisible thread connecting us. I was in control, revelling in the intoxicating power of the moment. The room was stifling, each heartbeat echoing the anticipation of what was to come.

As the teasing dance continued, I knew the line between control and surrender was thin, and the next move would determine the trajectory of our shared ecstasy.

"Okay," I moaned.

"Okay?" he nodded, eager for more. He lowered his head between my thighs, "Let me." He begged, his breath hot against my skin.

I nodded, "Just a taste."

His mouth devoured me, instantly sending shockwaves through my body. I moaned in pleasure, hands in his hair.

As his lips and tongue worked their magic, a symphony of pleasure echoed in the room. I arched my back, surrendering to the exquisite sensations he stirred within me. His skilful touch, guided by both passion and restraint, elevated the dance of desire to new heights. I gasped, caught in the whirlwind of pleasure. The room seemed to shrink, the world narrowing down to the intoxicating connection we shared.

His name escaped my lips in a breathy sigh, a plea, and a celebration all at once.

"Oh, yes..." I moaned.

He continued his exploration, his movements deliberate and unhurried, allowing the tension to build gradually. I clutched at the edges of the counter; my senses heightened by every subtle shift in pressure.

As the crescendo of pleasure approached, I could feel the magnetic energy intensify. The dance between us reached its zenith, "s- stop." I moaned, realising I'd lost at my own game.

"Anna," he whispered, his voice a sultry melody in the charged air.

"Tell me you want more."

I gazed into his eyes, the flames of desire flickering between us and surrendered. "More," I murmured, my voice a desperate plea.

With a final surge, a wave of pleasure washed over me.

He rose, his eyes locking onto mine. With a tender smile, I whispered, "Fuck you."

He laughed loud, "I win."

I giggled, still feeling euphoric. "I mean… I think I won. Three orgasms in less than 24 hours. I've never had a man make me cum before."

He looked at me like I had ten heads. "You've never had a man make you cum before?"

I shook my head, "Nope."

"You've dated the wrong men then," he mumbled, "I promise to always make you cum first."

As he traced his finger up the inside of my thigh, I squirmed slightly under his touch, revelling in the residual tremors of pleasure that still echoed through my body.

"Why?" I asked again, my curiosity mixing with the afterglow.

"Because there's no better feeling than when you're warm and pulsing," he murmured, his eyes locked onto mine, filled with a mixture of desire and genuine admiration. Without hesitation, he slid two fingers inside me, and the sensation sent a shiver down my spine. "But when you're as tight as this… I'm not sure how long I'd last."

My breath caught in response, the raw intensity of his words igniting a renewed flame within me. "Show me," I whispered, inviting him to explore the depths of our shared desire.

With an electrifying intensity lingering in the air, he gently lifted me off the countertop, my legs wrapping around him instinctively. Our lips found each other in a hungry, passionate kiss as he carried me to the living room.

As he placed me on the soft cushions, his hands explored the contours of my body. The warmth of the sofa enveloped us, creating a cocoon where time seemed to stand still, and only the intoxicating connection between us mattered.

Yet, in the midst of our kissing, a spark of determination ignited within me. I decided to reclaim a bit of the power I had willingly surrendered earlier. Gently pushing him back, I looked into his eyes with a coy smile.

"My turn," I whispered, my voice a sultry invitation.

Confusion flickered in his eyes, replaced by an eager curiosity. I straddled him, rocking back and forth slowly, whilst kissing down his neck and collar bone. The air crackled with anticipation as I took command of the moment, revelling in the newfound power.

My fingers traced patterns along his chest, "Let me show you what I can do," I whispered, a promise that hung in the air like a tantalising invitation.

"Okay." He chuckled. His eyes darkened, "Use me."

The power dynamic shifted, and I revelled in the pleasure of being both the provocateur and the captivated. I lifted myself off from him, the T-shirt swallowing me once again. Taking my place on my knees in front of him, I ran my hands up and down his thighs, massaging him over his boxers, which were damp from my grinding.

He inhaled sharply, throwing his head back. "Mmmmm…"

Placing my hand under the waistband, I whispered, "Lift."

"Are you sure?" He mumbled.

I rolled my eyes, "Completely."

He obliged, lifting himself slightly so I could peel off his boxers. His cock sprung free, shocking me - thick, shaven, perfectly sized. My mouth watered in anticipation.

"Are you okay?" He asked, breaking my trance.

I nodded, my cheeks warming, and opened my mouth. Staring at him with unbreakable eye contact, he watched as saliva fell from my tongue onto the palm of my hand. I wrapped my hand around his length, squeezing and began to move up and down.

He moaned, taking in the sight. "Fuuuuck."

Starting slow, I gently let my thumb run over his tip, then my entire hand grasped at his length, moving in a rhythmic dance. Up and down. Up and down. Meanwhile, my mouth kissed at his thighs, sloppy and wet. Looking up at him through my lashes, he moaned my name.

Lifting my head, I employed my second hand to pump him in opposite directions.

"My God." He breathed, watching me.

I pursed my lips, letting saliva drip onto his tip. Catching it in my hands as it dribbled down, I increased the speed of my movements, a seamless fusion of desire and skill.

He lifted his hand, pushing his thumb against my lips. I swirled my tongue around his thumb before sucking, teasing him for what was to come next.

"Put your hands back." I requested, my voice low and demanding. He obliged, a sly smile on his face, completely captivated by my every move.

I released his cock from my hands and pulled my hair back behind my ears. "Hold." I demanded. He took my hair into his hands, clearing it from my face.

"You're a goddess." He praised.

I lifted myself up slightly and dribbled onto the tip of his cock, soaking it. His breath caught in his throat as I ran my tongue over the fold of his tip and then ran my lips down the side, dribbling as much as possible.

I began to massage him, up and down, with both hands as I focused my mouth on the top. His breathing became erratic as he moaned my name as I sucked, creating the perfect movements.

I slid my hands away, taking him into my mouth entirely, feeling him pressing down my throat. Involuntarily, I gagged at his size, creating more saliva. His grip on my hair tightened as he lifted me off. "Don't hurt yourself baby." He spoke, breathless.

His free hand wiped under my eyes, which were watering. Leftover mascara from the night before dribbled down my face. "Oh fuckkkk Anna."

"Relax." I insisted, pushing him back.

I resumed, sucking, swirling, dribbling. As much as possible, I pushed him down my throat, thriving off his reaction each time.

His breathing heightened. His grip on my hair tightened. "I'm gonna..."

I kept up pace, both hands massaging, my mouth sucking.

"I'm going to cum." He called out, pushing my head up. I opened my mouth wide, sticking tongue out, waiting to catch it.

His eyes rolled back in euphoria at the sight. My hands continued their rhythmic motion, maintaining a firm grip as his release unfolded. He shuddered with pleasure, and I marvelled at the intensity of his reaction. As the last waves of his climax subsided, he slumped back on the sofa, breathing heavily.

With a satisfied smile, I leaned back, wiping my mouth with the back of my hand. His eyes, still filled with a mix of ecstasy and admiration, traced my every movement.

"Fuck, Anna," he whispered, his voice laden with awe.

I chuckled, "Not bad?"

He laughed, a rich, throaty sound that filled the room. "Understatement of the century."

Revelling in the afterglow, I rested beside him on the sofa. The air buzzed with a blend of passion and intimacy.

"That was incredible," he confessed, his fingers gently tracing patterns on my skin.

I grinned, "Glad you enjoyed it." A playful spark flickered in my eyes.

He moved closer, reclaiming the power dynamics with confidence. As our lips met in a hungry kiss, I revelled in the delicious taste of shared desire.

CHAPTER THIRTY-THREE
Now we're suckin' diesel

Definition: when things start to go right

I had no idea what to expect as I walked into the office on Monday morning. Settling onto my desk with a steaming cup of freshly brewed coffee, I waited anxiously.

Mia, always the early bird, was the first to arrive. "Morning, doll," she greeted, waving briefly before gracefully disappearing into her office.

Nervously, I started tidying my desk and meticulously organising my drawers, a sense of uncertainty lingering about the day's tasks. Apart from preparing for my last episode, I felt rather underutilised. Perhaps I wouldn't even be allowed to record a final episode…

Paddy, late for once, strolled in at 9:23 am, appearing somewhat lost in thought.

"Morning," I greeted with a warm smile.

He nodded, mumbled a greeting, and proceeded straight to the break room.

Sensing an unusual atmosphere, I decided to follow him. There was no trace of the usual cheeky remarks or banter; he seemed genuinely off.

"What's going on?" I questioned immediately.

He chuckled nervously. "Why would something be going on?"

Crossing my arms, I pressed, "Paddy."

He absentmindedly scratched his head, avoiding eye contact as he focused on the fridge. It was clear that something was amiss.

"Patrick," I said more firmly.

"I'm sorry," he squeaked, avoiding my gaze. "Don't hate me."

My nerves went into overdrive. "What did you do?"

He pulled his head out from the fridge, finally meeting my eyes. Confused by my apparent naivety, he twisted his head. Silence fell between us.

"Grace," he mumbled, trying to hide his smile.

"What?" I paused, confused. Then, suddenly like a tidal wave- the realisation hit me. I gasped, covering my mouth in utter shock. "You... did... Grace?!" It came out louder than intended.

Panicking, he shushed me. "Say it louder, why don't you?"

"Oh my god. Oh my god!!" I squealed with excitement, jumping up and down. "YOU AND GRACE?!"

His expression shifted to confusion. "You're not mad?"

I shook my head. "No! Why would I be mad? When?"

"I'm not getting into this with you. Ask her."

He closed the fridge, leaving emptyhanded and left the breakroom. I followed him like a puppy, eager for more information. "You can't do that. When did this happen? Saturday?"

I stood by his desk as he unpacked his backpack, trying his best to ignore me. "Leave me alone."

I huffed, sitting on a rolly chair and sliding over to him. "After the awards, obviously?"

He lifted his middle finger in response.

"Come on, you have to tell me something!" I asked.

Hands on my shoulders interrupted my begging. I turned my head, seeing Amir standing behind me, in a full suit. *Oh my.*

"Hi." He said, glancing around the office quickly, before pecking my lips.

"In the office, really?" Paddy moaned.

Amir shrugged in defence, "No one was looking."

"I was!" He lifted his hands.

I giggled. "Paddy slept with Grace."

Amir's eyebrows raised in surprise. "Oh really?"

Paddy narrowed his eyes at Amir and then turned to me, "I told him yesterday."

I turned to Amir, my eyes wide with curiosity. "Why didn't you tell me?"

He nonchalantly flipped Paddy off. "Dude! Are you tryna get me in trouble?" Then, he squeezed my shoulders. "I thought Grace would have told you."

"Told you what?"

The rhythm of our banter was suddenly interrupted, and I turned to see Grace standing a few feet away. In her hands, she held a carry case filled with an array of fresh juices, each one boasting vibrant colours.

Dressed in a stylish denim jumpsuit, she effortlessly melded casual comfort with a touch of urban chic. Her eyes sparkled with a blend of confidence and subtle playfulness, mirroring the mischief that Paddy wore on his face.

"What are you doing here?" Paddy asked, clearly surprised to see her.

She lifted the juice in her hands. "I thought I'd bring you all juice. I've been working since 4:30 am, so I needed a break."

Amir left my side and assisted her in distributing the cups around. I hesitated, taking a red-looking liquid from his hands. "Thanks... what's in this one?"

Grace shrugged. "Beetroot. I was just planning on dropping these off and leaving... but it seemed like an interesting conversation was being had?" she asked, pulling up a chair.

Paddy and her exchanged a knowing look, a silent communication that spoke volumes.

"You two slept together," I announced, making her choke.

She nodded slowly, her eyes revealing a mix of vulnerability and uncertainty.

Paddy, surprising me to my core, placed a comforting hand on her knee. "She wasn't mad. Don't worry."

"Why would I be mad?" I asked. "This is the greatest news ever."

Grace's eyes widened with a mixture of anxiety and relief. "Really?"

I nodded. "Of course. I don't know why I didn't set you both up sooner... I-"

"What about you two? Huh?" Paddy teased, his eyes darting between myself and Amir. He wiggled his eyebrows up and down, hinting that he knew something.

Grace too, had a knowing look on her face.

"Did you finally fuck?" Paddy asked, brash as always.

Grace turned round, hitting him with a slap on the wrist. A look of horror painted across her face. "Paddy!"

He laughed loudly.

"No... No, we didn't!" I defended, rolling my eyes.

Amir coughed behind me, his fingers gently brushing against my arm. "True...technically." The subtle touch sent a warm shiver down my spine.

I looked up at him, our eyes locking in a silent understanding, a shared secret about our passionate activities.

"Are you serious?" Paddy groaned. "Anna, let the man get some action... he's waited long en—Ouch!" His teasing was cut short by yet another playful slap from Grace.

"Dude, knock it off," Amir warned, his tone a mix of amusement and mild threat.

"I'm just relieved you two finally gave in. It's been painful watching you fight all the time." Grace rolled her eyes.

"No more fighting," Amir declared.

Without a second thought, I leaned in and kissed him gently. The ambient sounds of the office faded away, replaced by the sweet melody of an unexpected moment.

"Fucking get a room," Paddy moaned, faking disgust.

"We should..." Amir smiled cheekily. "Don't want to distract anyone."

"Who would have thought?" Grace broke the moment, laughing to herself. "At least Olivia was wrong about one thing... I might not have the career that I want, but at least I found someone... special."

Paddy melted, appreciating her kind words instead of mocking them.

"She's wrong about the career thing too. This juice is solid." Amir sipped, "One of the best I've tasted. Plus I was think-"

"Morning, morning," Mia appeared, interrupting. "Amir..." She hinted, tilting her head towards the boardroom.

He nodded, sharing a knowing look with her. "I'll catch you all later. Meetings..." He squeezed my shoulder, sensibly deciding against kissing me goodbye.

"What am I meant to work on today?" I asked Paddy.

He shrugged, "I don't know... why don't you two catch up over coffee until I get a chance to speak to Mia?"

Grace smiled, "I still have thirty minutes left before I'm back blending carrots."

***

Established welcomed us as usual, the familiar hum of conversation and the rich aroma of freshly brewed coffee enveloping the air.

Our conversations were flavoured with frothy matcha milk and the disappointment of a friend turned enemy. As we navigated through the shock of Olivia's betrayal and the surprise of her unsettling silence… *neither of us had received a text or phone call since the awards.* And for the first time in years, she had been absent from all social media platforms.

In an attempt to shift the atmosphere, I turned the conversation to lighter realms, asking about the beginning of Grace's newfound connection with Paddy. Her eyes glimmered, revealing a tale of buried feelings surfacing into the light, "I don't know – he's something. Who know's if it'll go anywhere but I like him."

I related to how she was feeling.

"I'd been thinking about it a lot. Lots of pros… that I tried to overshadow with meaningless, petty cons. And I… I can't let my parents failed relationships stop me from trying to create my own. The reality is, I do fancy him and alcohol… alcohol helped. And the adrenaline from slapping Olivia. That too. I just gave in…" She continued.

We laughed, indulging in the warmth of shared mirth and the adrenaline of a slap delivered to Olivia.

"I saw the way you and Paddy looked at each other and had an inkling feeling something was brewing." I smiled, sipping at my drink.

She sighed, "Just had to take the risk and go for it."

Her words echoed in my mind.

"You need to fill me in on everything…" Her smile widened with excitement. "No details spared."

As I recounted Amir's unexpected appearance at my door, the diary, and the shared moments of vulnerability and passion, the ambience of Established transformed into an intimate cocoon, holding our secrets close.

Grace, slightly emotional, nodded in understanding, connecting with the essence of taking risks and embracing the unpredictable nature of love. "It's crazy. I know so much is falling apart for both of us, but at the same time… so much is coming together."

"Yeah. Suppose you're right." I sighed, "There is one thing though… he's still returning to New York in two weeks."

Grace paused; her uncertainty reflected in the furrow of her brow.

"He asked me to go with him… To work for Apex," I finally admitted, breaking the silence. Her eyes widened in realisation, and I nodded, acknowledging the weight of the decision.

Before sharing my choice, I hesitated. "I said no… because that's crazy, right?"

Grace, equally tentative, responded, "Yeah, crazy."

I nodded in agreement, "I couldn't just throw my life away at home. I'd miss you and my family. Paddy too… And I love Belfast! So, I told him, it's not even an option. I mean, I've no idea what I'll be doing in Spotlight, but I can't just move across the world."

A thoughtful expression crossed Grace's face; her internal deliberations evident. After a moment, she spoke, her tone carrying a subtle shift. "Anna, I get it. It sounds crazy… it is crazy. But…" she paused, choosing her words carefully, "it's just another risk."

"What do you mean?"

"Belles of Belfast was a risk… and it's changed you as a person and the outcome of your life. Dating Amir, that's a risk, but you said it's one you're willing to take."

Her unexpected wisdom resonated with me.

"So… New York isn't too dissimilar. At least it would offer you a new job, a fresh start…" Grace continued, "And let's be real, long-distance is tough. Maybe this is your chance to see what could be. If it doesn't work out, well, at least you won't wonder 'what if.'"

As I traced the rim of my cooling cup of matcha, her words lingered in the air, weaving through the trepidation within me, inviting… *contemplation.*

"Well then…" I chuckled, caught off guard by her unexpected statement. "I didn't expect you to say that."

She looked at me, her expression mirroring my own bewilderment. "Life is a risk."

"Honestly!" A voice from the neighbouring table interrupted, drawing our attention. Two men sat across from each other, sipping iced drinks. "Mate, she's mental." One of them shook his head. He looked familiar, but I assumed it was due to how much I visited Established. "I don't know how I'm going to escape her."

His companion chimed in, "I told you never to date a customer."

Grace and I exchanged glances, our interest piqued, and we couldn't help but giggle as we carefully eavesdropped on their conversation.

"The sex was awful. She was acting like a crazed pornstar. Mental scenes."

I covered my mouth in shock, and Grace's eyes widened in disbelief.

"I shouldn't have waited so long to have sex with her. She practically begged me every day, but I tried to be a gentleman... look how that worked out! Terrible shag and now she's obsessed with me because of-"

"The hearts you made in her coffee each day?" the man seated across from him asked, with a teasing tone. "Or was it the muffins? Or the flowers?"

The man facing the dilemma buried his face in his hands. "You know, during sex on Saturday night, she hopped off me, saying she was mad at me... I asked why, and she said it's because I didn't 'heart react' to a picture she sent me of her tits... weeks ago! What the fuck is a heart react?"

Grace snorted, trying to stifle her laughter as she covered her mouth, while I couldn't help but gape at the unfolding drama.

"Cormac give us a hand, would ye?" A barista called out to his table, and he hopped up, rolling his eyes in the process.

Realisation dawned on me, and I exchanged a stunned look with Grace, our shared reaction evident. We couldn't contain our amusement as we giggled.

Cormac was Olivia's fixation. And unfortunately for her, he was no longer interested.

Karma. Karma's a wonderful bitch.

***

As I strolled back to the office, my phone vibrated, revealing a text from Mia.

MIA

Hey, feel free to take the rest of the day off. I'm meeting with The Board to plan our next moves. Let's catch up tomorrow afternoon. How about 1:45 pm?

I replied, confirming my availability to meet her then.

Uncertain about how to spend the remainder of the day, I tidied up my apartment and found myself searching Netflix and scrolling on my phone until 6pm when Amir called.

"Have you had dinner?" he inquired.

My gaze shifted to the coffee table, where a half-eaten yogurt and a handful of grapes rested.

"No, actually." I had failed to have a proper lunch either.

"How about some Chinese takeout? I'm just leaving the office and can bring it over to your apartment."

He arrived 25 minutes later, and we sat at the table, sharing noodles and salted chili chicken.

"How was your day?" I asked.

He smiled, pausing for a moment. "This feels strange."

"What does?"

"Having someone ask about my day over dinner," he admitted. "It's unusual."

I shook my head, "I feel like this whole thing is unusual. It feels like a total whirlwind but also doesn't at the same time."

He laughed, "I get exactly what you mean."

"And the drama from Saturday, I'm not over it."

"About that… I spoke with our lawyers today," he began, clearing his throat.

"Oh?" I questioned.

"I think they need to reach out to Olivia, to prevent her from sharing any more secrets," he said. "Just a gentle warning. Or not so gentle… depending on how much of a risk you think she is."

I contemplated for a moment. "Yeah, go full throttle. She can't be trusted at all."

He sighed, taking out his phone to text them and give the go-ahead.

"Thank you for sorting that. It wouldn't have even crossed my mind," I said, turning to peck his lips.

"You're welcome. We also need to probably do the same with any of the…men… too," he continued, discomfort radiating from him. "The only one they haven't written about is Mr. Mysterious. So, they'll be trying to find him… and make him talk."

I chuckled, analysing to see if he was serious or not. "So, what are you going to tell them?"

He raised his brow at me, "What do you mean?"

"The press."

"Huh?"

"Well… you're Mr. Mysterious," I smiled.

Amir's eyes widened in surprise, and his expression shifted from confusion to realisation. "Wait, what?" he stammered, genuinely caught off guard.

I chuckled at his reaction, "How did you not realise? Didn't you read that in the journal?"

He blinked a few times before bursting into laughter. "You're joking, right?"

I shook my head, still grinning. "Nope."

"I only read that page that was half ripped out." Amir's laughter continued, a mix of amusement and disbelief. "I can't believe this... this WHOLE TIME! I'm going to have to listen back on every episode now."

I joined in his laughter, feeling a sense of playfulness in the revelation.

"If you've said anything bad about me, you better run." He tickled my sides, making me scream.

"Don't threaten me! I – I have a great team of lawyers." I giggled.

***

I sat in the boardroom, awaiting my future. Amir squeezed my shoulders, "It's going to be okay."

He headed to the corner of the room, pouring us cups of tea. Moments later, Mia entered looking flustered. "Sorry I'm late."

She sat her designer bag onto the table, pulling out an array of newspaper articles and printed screenshots of gossip websites. "So..."

"So..." I breathed, heavy with anticipation.

Her face dropped, sympathy covering her. "These are all of the pieces that have been written so far. You don't have to read them."

Amir appeared from behind me, lifting them out of my reach, "Don't read them. It won't help anything."

He was right. Anyone else's opinion of me was none of my business.

"So, I've been speaking with The Board... and it's not good news." She sighed, "This Friday will be your last episode. I know you already expected that. From Monday, you will be returning to your old role. I'm sorry Anna."

I swallowed, accepting my fate. "It's okay." I felt beyond disappointed as reality set in.

Amir took a seat beside me and gently took my hand squeezing it. "Imagine all your new experience that you can bring to your previous role though." He said, trying to find the light in the dark.

I faced him, my eyes meeting his. Darkness and disappointment. I hesitated for a moment before asking, "What about Apex?"

His breath caught in his throat, "What?"

"New York?" I asked, curious.

"You said no." He scrunched his brows, confused.

"New York?" Mia asked, interrupting.

I turned to her, debating the ideas running through my head. She looked beyond confused.

"I – I don't know." I said, addressing Amir, "What's the option? What would my job be?"

For a fleeting second, he seemed almost breathless, as if the weight of the possibilities hung heavily on his shoulders. His voice, when he finally spoke, carried a genuine mixture of surprise and gratitude, "I need to discuss it with the team. I'll make a few calls and get back to you… are you serious?" His lip twitched, revealing a subtle smile.

"I can't promise you anything but let me know what they come back with." I replied.

"I'm going to go make the call right now." There was a palpable sense of hope in his words, a hope that went beyond the professional realm and touched on the personal aspirations he had harboured. He jumped up, leaving the room.

"What on earth is going on?" Mia asked, growing frustrated.

"I'm considering moving to New York… with Amir," I admitted, saying the words out loud for the first time.

Her face changed dramatically, registering immense surprise, "What?!"

"I'm just thinking about it."

She pinched the bridge of her nose. "Anna… how long has this… thing… been going on between you both? How long have you been seeing each other?"

My stomach swelled, embarrassment climbing up my spine. "I know it's crazy… but we've liked each other for months…"

I began to share the intricate details of our evolving romance, peeling back the layers of our relationship like chapters in a book. The hate-to-love dynamic, where our initial clashes transformed into a profound connection. The moments of resistance, the verbal sparring that gradually gave way to shared laughter and understanding. The decision to embrace vulnerability and give in to the undeniable chemistry that simmered beneath the surface. Each step, each shared glance, felt like a risk we willingly undertook, knowing that it could either lead to something extraordinary or unravel in unforeseen ways.

"I love this for you, I do… but I don't think following him or any man across the world is a good idea. Especially when you're just getting to know each other." Mia spoke.

"Honestly, this isn't really about him," I admitted. "This is about me. My future happiness. New opportunities. My career."

Mia's initial surprise lingered in her widened eyes, as she tried to process the unexpected revelation. Her brows furrowed, and a hint of worry creased her forehead. "Anna, I get it's about you, but… moving across the world is a big step" she said, her voice carrying a note of genuine concern. "I want you to be happy, but consider the risks, both personally and professionally. Really think on it."

Her concern was palpable, echoing through her words and the subtle lines etched on her face. Despite her support for my happiness, Mia couldn't hide the worry that lingered beneath the surface, emphasising the magnitude of the decision I was contemplating.

***

It wasn't until Thursday afternoon that he dropped a meticulously crafted proposal onto my desk.

"What's this?" I questioned, lifting the weighty stack of paper.

"New York," he confirmed, his expression tinged with a mix of anticipation and anxiety. "I know you like to visualise everything. So, this is that. The job, first and foremost. The lifestyle. Where you'd live. Good places to eat. Things to do on weekends."

I was rendered speechless. "You're joking."

He shook his head, encouraging me to delve into the possibilities. "Open it."

BELLE IN THE BIG APPLE
A podcast by Anna Mulholland

My breath caught in my throat as I absorbed the title. He pulled a seat over to my desk, immersing me in his vision.

"So, essentially, this would be your new show. Documenting everything you learn as a 'Belfast belle' but living in New York. It wouldn't be anonymous. You could share weekly updates, tales of life in the big city. I haven't worked out all the details yet, but I feel like you could manage that…" he explained, his enthusiasm radiating and infusing the air with a sense of thrilling possibility.

I flicked through the pages seeing photographs of local places and descriptions.

"That's Amelia – she works at Apex and would essentially be your new Paddy." He continued, pointing at the photos. "And Travis… he's my best friend. His girlfriend Jackie is super nice too… You wouldn't be alone."

My eyes watered as I flicked through the pages, "I appreciate all the effort you've put into this."

"Why are you crying?" Paddy appeared, concern covering his face. "Amir, why is she crying?" He spoke with anger.

"It's fine." I wiped the few tears that had escaped my eyes.

"If you've hurt her already, so help me god." Paddy warned, directing evil eyes at Amir.

"Paddy! It's fine!" I reassured, "I was just looking at something."

He tilted his head, intrigued. "What are you hiding?"

I held my breath as I passed him the proposal. Paddy's initial anger softened as he flipped through the pages. A thoughtful frown creased his forehead, and his eyes moved quickly over the details. The tension in the room shifted as Paddy's expression transformed from anger to contemplation.

"Well, I'll be damned," he muttered, a mix of surprise and realisation in his voice. "Congratulations."

"Oh no – I haven't said yes yet. It's just an idea." I reassured him, noting the hurt behind his eyes.

He nodded, "What about Belles of Belfast? You're just going to give up on it?"

I paused, confused. "I don't have a choice. I can't host the show anymore. It's not an option."

"Hmm… I just didn't think you'd give up so easy." He pursed his lips, contemplating, "Maybe you find a new host. Pass the baton?"

He was right. The idea of finding a new host for "Belles of Belfast" ignited an immediate spark within me. I felt a surge of energy, realising that *even if* my path led to New York, the show that had been such an integral part of my life could endure.

"You might be onto something." I said, enthusiasm building within me.

Amir, observing the exchange, chimed in, "It's not about abandoning what you've built here; it's about evolving and starting something new. 'Belles of Belfast' can thrive with a fresh perspective, and you can embark on a new adventure with 'Belle in the Big Apple.'"

Paddy nodded, a hint of pride in his eyes. "Fuck we're geniuses. Book your flight – to fuck."

The prospect of two exciting opportunities lay before me, and with Paddy's encouragement, I could navigate the transition without abandoning the show that had meant so much to me.

However, a knot of anxiety tightened in my stomach as I contemplated the conversation I needed to have with my mum and dad.

CHAPTER THIRTY-FOUR
Keep 'er lit

Definition: keep it going

"Absolutely not," Dad's refusal echoed through the room, his eyes fixed on the TV as he sank into the sofa. "I'm not entertaining this conversation with you, and neither will your mother. She's out in the garden."

My heart raced, the weight of the decision pressing on my shoulders. His immediate disapproval joined the growing list of reasons against seizing the opportunity in New York.

Venturing outside, I discovered my mum knee-deep in soil, meticulously planting new flowers in a patch by a large tree in the garden.

"Hi, darling," she greeted me with a warm smile as I approached.

"Any spare gloves?" I asked.

Her brow raised, and she pointed to the garden shed. Returning a minute later, I wore pink gardening gloves on my hands.

"Bit late to be gardening…" I chuckled. It was almost 7 pm, but the lingering light allowed for the task.

"Sure, I don't believe in time," she laughed. "I've just finished a week of night shifts and won't be able to sleep until 6 or 7 am probably." She ironically yawned as she spoke. "I feel like I haven't seen you in forever."

I nodded in agreement and began weeding part of the garden.

"Are you alright?" She sighed.

I turned, perplexed at how she could discern my emotions so accurately.

"Is it that obvious?" I chuckled to myself.

"Anna… you've never once gardened with me, and anytime I asked you to as a child, you ran away." She sprinkled some seeds onto the soil, a knowing look gracing her face. "So… what is it that you need to talk about? What's happening with your show? I'm sure the station is livid about the articles."

I bit my lip, "Yeah, it's been rough. The show's been cancelled."

She gasped, taken aback. "You're having a laugh! No way…"

Concern etched across her face.

I nodded, "Yeah, it's just a whole lot more complicated now, so they won't take the risk."

She sighed, sadness weighing heavy.

"But the reason I came to talk to you is because of something else…" I spoke, anxiety building in my throat.

"What is it?"

I took a deep breath, the weight of the words hanging in the air. "I've been offered a job opportunity in New York with Apex."

Her eyes widened with surprise, and I could feel the tension building.

"It's a significant career move, and I wanted to talk to you about it before making any decisions," I explained, the gravity of the situation sinking in.

She looked thoughtful, processing the unexpected information. "Tell me more about it. What kind of job is it?"

As I began to share the details of the opportunity, her expression shifted from surprise to curiosity, and we delved into a conversation about the potential changes and challenges this move might bring. The sun began to set, air growing cold as I explained my thoughts.

She took a moment, still processing the news. "New York is a world away, Anna. It's such a drastic change."

I nodded, acknowledging the monumental decision I was considering. "I know… but I'm taking a step back in Belfast with my career. If I took the chance and went to America, I'd be taking a huge step forward."

"You'll be a small fish in a big pond," she cautioned. "It's much easier to be a success in Belfast than it is in New York City."

"I just want to be happy," I admitted, the raw honesty of my feelings hanging in the air.

"And Belfast can't make you happy?" she asked, a hint of curiosity in her voice.

I could sense her concern, and I took a deep breath before revealing another layer of my decision. "There's also… a man."

I filled her in on every detail she needed to know about Amir.

"So, you're just going to follow him to the other side of the world?"

"No, I'm not doing this for him. But risk! You always tell me to take risks… seek discomfort… I don't want to let this chance go and wonder what if?" I spoke, the passion in my voice growing.

As I continued to express my thoughts, I began to realise that I genuinely wanted to take this chance, and I'd made my decision.

She silently continued digging soil and plotting new flowers, deep in thought. "Go then." Tears began to well in her eyes.

I lost my breath, "What?"

"Go. If that's how you feel, don't let anything or anyone stop you. I don't want you to stay back and have regrets."

My heart swelled, appreciating her beyond words, "Thank you." Tears rolled down my cheeks.

Reaching across soil and seeds, we hugged understanding that what came next was unpredictable and huge.

"There's one last thing though…" I mumbled into her sweater.

"Oh christ… what?" She laughed. "I'm not sure I can take anything more."

I chuckled back, wiping the tears that continued to fall, "Can you speak to dad for me?"

"Your dad can't say much. He was going to London to work and instead, stayed in Belfast to be with me." She admitted, "And I know… I know you said you aren't doing this for a man – but let's be honest, you are a little bit."

I sighed, contemplating her words. "He gives me hope. And it might not work out… but also, it could? Also, I've never even considered the opportunity to move abroad and work. Belfast is such an amazing comfortable place to live that it never entered my head to… leave." My heart felt heavy, "But… I don't know. Something within me is niggling. The timings of everything that's happened in my life lately… it all feels aligned. Amir was there from my first episode to my last, and even though I've dated other men, the thought of him wouldn't leave my mind. We've just started things and I don't want it to end. I think I want to take the risk."

"Well…" Mum paused, thinking heavy before she spoke, "Love is worth it. Sometimes the biggest… toughest challenges pave the way for the greatest rewards."

I hugged her tightly.

"I do need to meet him though." She added.

***

The countdown started. I pulled the mic closer to my face and nervously adjusted my headphones.

"This marks the final episode of Belles of Belfast. But let's not dwell on sadness. Instead, let's make this episode a celebration. And I'm not alone today; I'm joined by some remarkable women... or 'Belles,' as we call them on this show.

In reflecting on this journey, I've come to understand that love is multifaceted. Throughout this series, we've explored various forms of love, each carrying its own unique beauty and significance.

Firstly, there's self-love—the cornerstone upon which all other forms of love are constructed. Learning to love and accept ourselves unconditionally is a journey that demands patience, compassion, and courage.

It involves embracing our imperfections, celebrating our strengths, and prioritising our well-being. Personally, I've grappled with self-love, and I'm still navigating this path of self-discovery.

However, every step forward, no matter how small, is significant and worthy of acknowledgment.

Then, there's the love of friendship—a bond forged through shared experiences, trust, and mutual support. True friendships enrich our lives, offering companionship, understanding, and a sense of belonging. They're the ones who stand by us through life's ups and downs, cheering us on and lifting us up when we falter. I have a friend here today, Miss Sensibility, as you know her by. So, I'm going to pass the mic to her."

I released an overwhelming breath, as Grace nervously began to speak. "Finding your tribe is incredibly tough, maybe even tougher than people let on. It's not just about having people around you; it's about finding those friends who really get you, who support you through thick and thin, and who love you unconditionally.

You know, they say you become like the people you spend the most time with, and it's true. That's why it's crucial to take a good, hard look at your circle and make sure you're surrounding yourself with the best. And let me tell you, there's something truly special about female friendships. The bond you share, the laughs you have, the late-night heart-to-hearts—it's irreplaceable.

I mean, think about it: there's nothing quite like getting dolled up together before a night out, or diving into deep conversations about life, love, and everything in between. And those moments of quiet companionship, like chilling on the sofa together, binge-watching your favourite show… Or helping each other prep for a big date or when you read the same book and discuss it passionately —those are the moments that make it all worthwhile.

But friendship has its tough moments too. It's about being there for each other when times get rough, offering a shoulder to lean on, or a listening ear when they need to vent. It's about showing up, even when it's not convenient, and reminding your friend just how much they mean to you.

So yeah, friendship isn't always smooth sailing, but it's so worth it. Because when you find those people who truly have your back, who lift you up when you're down, and who celebrate your victories like they're their own—that's when you know you've won at life."

Tears streamed down my face, my voice quivering as I took hold of the microphone once more. "I'm incredibly grateful for my best friend," I began, my emotions threatening to overwhelm me. "I truly believe that after hearing her story, you'll all love her just as much as I do." Pausing to gather myself, I continued, "Now, family love… it's something truly profound. It goes beyond blood ties, embracing chosen family members who stand by us through every twist and turn of life. It's a love that knows no bounds, offering unwavering support, comfort, and a sense of belonging. And for me, I'm blessed to have two families. One of them is Spotlight." Turning to Mia, I saw that she too was wiping away tears, her emotions mirroring my own.

"Wow," she began, her voice filled with awe. "This show has been an absolute necessity, far beyond what I initially anticipated. Week after week, I've seen the online community grow and witnessed the courageous truths shared on this platform. In an industry like ours, it's imperative that we empower more women to step into the Spotlight, excuse the pun, to become hosts, and to share their own unique stories. It's time to banish any lingering doubts about our worthiness and to silence the inner critic that whispers 'imposter.' My hope is that this podcast has ignited something within you, a spark of realisation that you are capable of anything. Countless women, some of whom you've never even met, are standing on the side-lines, cheering you on towards success." She crumpled, hands shaking holding the piece of paper in front of her. Her writing was now stained with tears.

Surveying the room, I felt a rush of gratitude as I stepped back up to the microphone. "Romantic love," I began, my voice carrying across the room, "it's undeniably significant in our lives. It's a journey filled with passion, intimacy, and shared aspirations. And let's be real, it hasn't been an easy road for me, as many of you can attest. But you know what they say—sometimes the toughest challenges pave the way for the greatest rewards."

My mum took a shaky breath and began to speak. "But you know what, despite all these fears and doubts, love is this incredible force. It has the power to heal, to bring joy, and to create these connections that are just, like, magical. But... Love starts with you. I know, it sounds cheesy, maybe even cliché, but you've got to love yourself first. And it's not always easy, so it's not. Sure, we might have our reservations, those moments of hesitation, but when you find that person who gets you, who accepts you with all your flaws and imperfections, it's like this beautiful symphony playing in the background. Love is complicated and imperfect, so it is, but it's so worth it. It's in those vulnerable moments, those shared dreams, and the warmth that you realise maybe all those fears were just stepping stones to something truly amazing. Because, let's face it, love is a wild roller-coaster ride that we all secretly crave. So, embrace the adventure, face your fears, seek discomfort and don't be afraid to open your heart. Love is not something that has to be earned.

It's just something you have to be open to accepting. And trust me, when you do, the magic happens."

Tears streamed down my face, my emotions raw and unfiltered. "Lastly, there's the love for humanity—a universal bond that connects us all on this shared journey called life," I managed to say amidst my sobs. "It's a love that drives us to show compassion, empathy, and kindness to one another."

An epic soundtrack kicked in, and I pictured all the women out there, whether alone at home, driving in their cars, or hanging out at a friend's place, tuning in.

"As I say goodbye to Belles of Belfast, I urge us all to continue to nurture and embrace love in all its manifestations, recognising that it's love that truly brightens up our world and gives life meaning. I'm Anna Mulholland, and I am profoundly grateful to have been your host on this journey. And now, it's time for me to pass the torch to someone new, someone who I trust will carry this show forward and make it even more extraordinary."

I locked eyes with Grace, who nodded in acknowledgment, ready to embrace the adventure that lay ahead.

The end.

Or is it?

Dedications

Imagine this: it's 4:30 in the morning... or maybe 5:30. Honestly, I never kept track. Once I sat down at the kitchen table in my mum's house, put on my headphones, and began to write, time ceased to exist. Inevitably, my mum would walk in—often scaring the shite out of me—and offer to make me a cup of tea or coffee to keep me going.

This book is dedicated to you, Mum.

You are my best friend, my biggest supporter, and the one who has always believed in me.

Thank you for waking up in the middle of the night to check on me. Thank you for reading my work, even when it wasn't great, and encouraging me to keep going.

I'm endlessly grateful for your presence, whether it's listening to my endless dialogue revisions or embarking on trips to Galway, Portrush, and Belfast to ensure the authenticity of my writing.

Thank you for teaching me about manifestation.

Thank you for telling me that no dream is too big.

Thank you for always encouraging me to 'go for it' and 'ask for it' because the worst someone can say is no.

Thank you for your unwavering support.

Thank you for being my rock.

You have always inspired me to reach for more, do the impossible, and live a life beyond my wildest imagination.

This is just the beginning. I am who I am because of you.

***

To my family, thank you for your endless support and belief.

To Janet, Ali, Angie, Aileen, Roberta, Margaret, Jodie, and Evie, I am so grateful to have such empowering, encouraging, and wonderful women around me.

To Dad, thank you for reading every single Disney storybook to me as I grew up and for your excitement for Belles, alongside Janet and Jack.

To Granny, thank you for creating wonderful tales like "Little Lost Ann." Maybe that will be my next book.

To Drew Beckett, even though you are no longer with us, your legacy lives on. You changed everything.

To Karen, my publisher: Thank you for your patience and unwavering belief in me. You've been instrumental in bringing this idea to life since 2020, and I'm immensely grateful for your encouragement and support throughout this journey. I'm beyond excited for what comes next.

Lucy x

About the Author

Lucy McMullan bursts onto the literary scene with her debut novel, Belles of Belfast, a sizzling and empowering tale. With a flair for writing that blends steamy excitement with profound feminist themes, Lucy's stories are a breath of fresh air, inspiring women to embrace their true selves. A proud Belfast girl, Lucy infuses her vibrant hometown into her narratives, painting the city in a modern, dynamic light. Lucy's love affair with storytelling began at a tender age. From crafting her first tales as a 12-year-old content creator to captivating audiences on Wattpad, her journey is marked by a relentless passion for narrative in all its forms. Influenced by the rich worlds of film, books, and TV, Lucy's ability to weave compelling and relatable stories garnered her connections and excited readers, eagerly awaiting the release of Belles of Belfast. Her passion for storytelling isn't just a hobby—it's a lifeline. Every word Lucy writes is imbued with the fervor of someone who lives and breathes her craft. She doesn't just write stories; she creates worlds where readers can find empowerment and inspiration, reflecting her own journey of self-love and discovery. Join Lucy's exciting world of storytelling on social media, where she shares her creative passions as 'onlyjustlucy'. Dive in and you'll find not just a story, but a movement.

Milton Keynes UK
Ingram Content Group UK Ltd.
UKHW010646080724
445166UK00004B/137